CULTURE SHOCK

Book One: The Empire's Corps
Book Two: No Worse Enemy
Book Three: When The Bough Breaks
Book Four: Semper Fi
Book Five: The Outcast
Book Six: To The Shores
Book Seven: Reality Check
Book Eight: Retreat Hell
Book Nine: The Thin Blue Line
Book Ten: Never Surrender
Book Eleven: First To Fight
Book Twelve: They Shall Not Pass
Book Thirteen: Culture Shock

CULTURE SHOCK

CHRISTOPHER G. NUTTALL

The characters and events portrayed in this book are fictitious. Any similarity to real persons, living or dead, is coincidental and not intended by the author.

Text copyright © 2018 Christopher G. Nuttall
All rights reserved.
No part of this book may be reproduced, or stored in a retrieval system, or transmitted in any form or by any means, electronic, mechanical, photocopying, recording, or otherwise, without express written permission of the publisher.

ISBN-13: 9781983509964
ISBN-10: 1983509965

http://www.chrishanger.net
http://chrishanger.wordpress.com/
http://www.facebook.com/ChristopherGNuttall

Cover by Alexander Chau
(www.alexanderchau.co.uk)

All Comments Welcome!

AUTHOR'S NOTE

"I am, of course, not a lover of upheavals. I merely want to make sure people do not forget that there are upheavals."

-General Aritomo Yamagata, Imperial Japanese Army, 1881.

Like the other odd-numbered books in the series, *Culture Shock* is completely stand-alone. You do not have to be familiar with the other books to read and (I hope) enjoy it. However, historically, it takes place roughly six months after *When The Bough Breaks*, at roughly the same time as *No Worse Enemy*. You can download samples and suchlike from my website.

If you enjoy the book, please leave a review.

PROLOGUE

The tension in the air as darkness fell over the estate was so thick, Steward Joel thought as he paced the lines, that one could cut it with a knife.

Earth was gone. And so was the government that had protected the Forsakers against their enemies. Tarsus was still reeling after the news had finally arrived from Earth, its government trapped in endless debates over what should be done, but some of its population had already taken matters into their own hands. The attacks had begun almost at once, targeting isolated Forsakers on the streets and killing them. And the government had done nothing.

Of course they did nothing, Joel thought, bitterly. *There are no votes in protecting us.*

He gritted his teeth as a cold wind blew over the estate. The Forsakers had never been *popular*, not on Tarsus. They'd been moved from world to world by the Empire, seeking out a home that had never materialised. Joel had no doubt his people *could* have made a go of it, if they'd been given land and support, but no one had been interested in actually *helping* them. Instead, they'd been shoved into an estate and told to stay there.

It was no place for a Forsaker community, he thought, as he turned to walk back towards the warehouse. The estate was grey and soulless, despite their best efforts. No amount of work could hide the fact that it wasn't designed to hold people, not for long. The facilities were poor, privacy was very limited and opportunities for employment were non-existent. Some of the young men had tried to work, in hopes of earning enough money to buy land, but they'd been cheated and robbed by their employers. It was technically illegal, yet the government hadn't given a damn even *before* the economy had collapsed. They might have been forced to take the Forsakers, but the government felt no obligation to make them *welcome*.

He stepped into the guardhouse, his eyes flickering over the five young men on watch. They were armed, but only with baseball bats and other improvised weapons. Tarsus had strict laws forbidding the private possession of firearms and the Elders had forbidden the Stewards from seeking out illicit weapons. They'd warned of the dangers of provoking the government, but Joel found it hard to care. The government had made its feelings on the matter quite clear. They wanted the Forsakers *gone*.

"My brother hasn't returned," Steward Joshua said. He sounded grim. "He and his wife never came back."

Joel winced. Joshua's brother hadn't *quite* been Fallen - the Forsaker term for men who left their community - but he'd loudly argued that they'd reached the end of the line. He'd been beaten for his heresy, of course, yet no one knew just how many other Forsakers quietly agreed with him. And now he was gone. He might have been caught by a mob and killed...

...Or he might have decided to vanish into the planet's population, forsaking his heritage in exchange for a safe place to live.

And his wife probably encouraged him, he thought, sourly. *She never quite fit in either.*

"I'm sure he will be back," he lied, smoothly. Joshua's brother had taken his wife and left the community. It suggested he had no intention of returning. "And you can rebuke him then, if you wish."

He kept his real thoughts to himself. The Forsakers didn't *look* any different from the rest of the planet's population, not really. Their clothes might have marked them as outsiders, but it wasn't as if changing one's outfit was *difficult*. And Tarsus was cosmopolitan enough to accept a newcomer if that worthy made a definite attempt to blend in. He closed his eyes in pain as he turned back to the door. Joshua's brother was merely the latest Forsaker to forsake his heritage.

Traitor, he thought.

The attack began at midnight.

Joel had been sitting in the guardhouse when he heard the sound of several people moving outside. The patrol had only just gone out to sweep the edge of the estate. They shouldn't have been back so soon. And yet... he grabbed for his baseball bat as the door burst open, a trio of black-clad men smashing into the room. He barely had a moment to recognise the stunners in their hands before there was a flare of blue-white light and his entire body jerked violently. His legs buckled beneath him and he hit the ground face-down, utterly unable to move.

"Clear," a voice said. "Only one guard."

Joel tried to struggle as he felt strong arms rolling him over, but his body felt as limp and powerless as a sack of potatoes. A man, his face hidden behind a mask, patted him down, then rolled him back over and cuffed his hands behind his back. Joel fought a wave of bitter helplessness as the men walked out of the room, leaving him there. No matter how desperately he struggled, he couldn't move a muscle. His body was completely useless.

He heard shouts and screams, male and female, as the policemen worked their way through the estate. Rage flared through his mind at the violation of their most sacred spaces, but there was nothing he could do. His body was starting to twitch uncomfortably, a pins-and-needles sensation almost driving him insane...the stun blast was wearing off, he realised numbly. But his hands were still cuffed. It was hopeless.

A man strode into the room, caught hold of Joel by the scruff of the neck and hauled him to his feet. Joel stumbled, his legs still feeble, but somehow he managed to force himself to stagger though the door. Outside, he saw a nightmare. Hundreds of men and women were sitting on the ground, their hands cuffed; dozens of armed policemen were watching them, weapons at the ready. And, right at the edge of the estate, a mob of angry locals, shouting and jeering as the police completed their task. Joel had no doubt of what would happen, if he somehow managed to get away. The mob would beat him to death, then dump his body in the gutter.

His cheeks burned with humiliation, for himself and his community, as he sat there, forced to watch as the estate was searched and their possessions confiscated. God alone knew what would happen to the tools, the motley collection of hand-powered devices they'd preserved ever since they'd been forced to leave their last home. They *needed* them, damn it! But the policemen didn't seem to care...

It felt like hours before they were ordered to their feet and marched towards the lorries. The crowd's jeering grew louder as they were pushed into the lorries, the doors slamming shut as soon as each vehicle was crammed. Joel heard the engine roar into life as he struggled to find a comfortable position, the lorry shaking as it turned and headed out of the estate. He wished he could see outside, but there were no windows. All he could do was wait.

"They're going to kill us," Joshua said. He sounded as though he was on the verge of outright panic. "They're going to *kill* us!"

Joel found his voice. "They're not," he said, although he wasn't sure of it himself. "They can't kill us."

But he wasn't sure of that either. The Empire was gone. All the old certainties were falling everywhere. The Imperial Navy was fragmenting, planetary governments were bidding for independence…and Tarsus, which had resented the Forsakers from the moment they'd been ordered to take them, might have decided to rid themselves of a nuisance.

We should have fought, he thought, savagely. *We could have learned to defend ourselves.*

The lorry lurched to a halt. Moments later, the doors banged open and the Forsakers were pushed and prodded outside. Joel had half-expected a detention camp or a firing squad, but instead…it took him several moments to realise that he was looking at a spaceport. A dozen shuttles sat on landing pads, surrounded by heavily-armed guards. Behind them, there were more lorries and more guards…had the police rounded up every last Forsaker on Tarsus? It was starting to look like it…

He glanced at the nearest policeman. Experience had taught him that it was dangerous to talk to policemen, but there was no one else to ask. "What's happening to us?"

The policeman's face was hidden behind the mask, but there was a hint of heavy satisfaction in his voice. "You are being deported."

Joel stared. "Deported? To where?"

But the policeman said nothing, merely nodded towards the shuttles.

Joel swallowed, hard. Tarsus hadn't been a friendly place, but…but where would they wind up *next*? The entire community had just been uprooted without a fight, men, women and children yanked out of their beds and transported to the spaceport. And then…? Who knew where they were going next? Cold bitter rage throbbed in his breast as he watched the shuttle hatches opening. They looked like the gateways to hell.

Never again, he promised himself silently. He should never have listened to the Elders when they'd forbidden him to buy weapons. They could have fought. *Whatever happens, never again.*

CHAPTER ONE

> In theory, unlike pre-space Earth, the Empire should have had no problems with ethnic, racial and cultural conflict. As a noted philosopher of the times pointed out, what cultures needed to learn to get along was distance and space - enough space for everyone. Naturally, it didn't work out like that.
> - Professor Leo Caesius. *Ethnic Streaming and the End of Empire.*

"Premier?"

Premier William Randolph Huntsman cursed under his breath as he opened his eyes. He wasn't sure how long he'd slept, but it felt as though he had barely closed his eyes when his butler stepped into the bedroom. It had been yet another late-night Cabinet meeting, debating precisely what - if anything - Arthur's Seat could do about the news from Earth and the economic crisis it had brought in its wake. And, as always, nothing had been decided. They knew too little to make any long-term decisions.

Sitting upright, he rubbed his eyes. The clock on the wall insisted that it was 0445, local time; 1445, Galactic Standard Time. Sykes, the butler, looked coolly professional, wearing a suit even though it was the middle of the night. William didn't know how he did it, although he had a theory. Sykes, damn him, didn't have to worry about anything, beyond serving the Premier. He'd serve William's successor as well as he'd served William himself.

"Yeah," he said, finally. "What is it?"

Sykes held out a mug of steaming coffee. "We have received an alert signal from the Orbital Guard, sir," he said. "An Imperial Navy cruiser

- ISS *Harley* - has dropped out of Phase Space and transmitted a text-only FTL message. Her commander wishes to speak with you as soon as his ship reaches communications range."

William blinked in surprise, torn between relief and shock. Arthur's Seat had no real defences, save for a pair of destroyers so old he sometimes thought they predated the Empire itself. They certainly predated his homeworld! The ships were enough to deter pirates, but he had no illusions about their ability to stand off a *real* attack. If one of their neighbours decided to launch an invasion - and they might, now the Empire was gone - Arthur's Seat's ability to resist was almost non-existent. Commodore Charles Van Houlton had made the point very clear during the planning sessions, when he'd asked for more money for the Orbital Guard.

But we can't build warships for ourselves, William thought. *And no one is likely to sell them to us.*

He pushed the thought aside, savagely. "Did *Harley* say why she's here?"

"No, sir," Sykes said. "Merely that it's urgent."

William contemplated the problem as he sipped his coffee. It was excellent, as always...and yet, it was growing increasingly rare. The Jamaica Blue blend came from Earth...and Earth was gone. Arthur's Seat grew its own coffee beans, of course, yet it didn't quite seem to live up to Jamaica Blue. But William suspected he would have to get used to drinking it soon, whatever happened. The price of *anything* from outside the star system had already skyrocketed. It wouldn't be long before there wasn't a single can of Jamaica Blue available for love or money.

"How long until she enters communications range?"

"Two hours, as of the last communication," Sykes informed him. "She's red-lining her drive."

William gritted his teeth. He was no spacer, but even *he* knew that trained engineers and spare parts were in short supply. *Harley's* commanding officer was taking a considerable risk in pushing his ship so hard. Whatever was going on - and his imagination provided too many possibilities - it had to be urgent. There was no way Arthur's Seat could repair an Imperial Navy cruiser.

"Inform the Cabinet that I want an emergency meeting in three hours," he said, finally. "And then prepare a breakfast for when they arrive."

"Yes, sir," Sykes said.

William finished his coffee, then swung his legs over the side of the bed and stood. His head swam for a long moment, reminding him that he hadn't had anything like enough sleep. He glanced at the bedside cabinet, where he kept a small collection of painkillers and stimulants, then dismissed the thought. He had a feeling he'd need to keep his wits about him for the coming discussion and stimulants could be dangerous. Sykes fussed about him, wiping his face with a hot towel before producing a neatly-pressed suit and shirt. William shook his head in tired amusement as his butler helped him to dress, then peered into the mirror. As always, Sykes had ensured that there wasn't a single hair out of place.

But I still look old, he thought. *Too old.*

He studied his reflection for a long moment, feeling a twinge of dismay. He'd been Premier for two years, elected just in time to face the decline and fall of the Empire…and it had changed him. His brown hair was now grey, his face was lined…he looked more like a bureaucrat or an accountant than a planetary leader. He honestly wasn't sure he *wanted* to stand for re-election, even though he was midway through his first term. The job was taking a toll.

And if it does this to me, he thought, *what does it do to other Heads of State?*

It was a bitter thought. Arthur's Seat was not an important world and never would be. She lacked the economic and military base necessary to reach for greatness. And really, she didn't *want* greatness. William had never dreamed of building an empire of his own, even though he knew that at least two of the neighbouring worlds were planning their own conquests. Arthur's Seat was a quiet sleepy backwater…

…And yet, serving as her leader had drained him more than he cared to admit.

He pushed the thought aside as he walked through the door to his office and sat down at the desk, keying the terminal to bring up the latest briefing notes. His staff had done their usual efficient job, yet they had very little information to draw on. ISS *Harley* had been attached to the sector fleet, they'd noted, but there was little else about her in the files. Even her commander's name was a mystery. William shook his head slowly, then started to write a quick letter to his ex-wife. If trouble *was* coming, he wanted her to be aware of it.

It was nearly two hours before the communications link came online, the terminal blinking up alerts and warnings that William had honestly never seen before, outside drills. The communications link was completely secure, isolated so completely that no one else could *hope* to intercept and eavesdrop. It struck William as needless paranoia, but if something was dangerously wrong…

And if this level of paranoia is justified, he thought grimly, *just what is happening out there?*

He straightened as a face appeared in the display. The officer - an Imperial Navy Commodore, if William was reading the rank badge correctly - could have stepped off a recruiting poster, save for the tiredness etched into every line of his face. William felt a shiver running down his spine as he studied the newcomer. This was a man, he realised slowly, who no longer cared.

"Premier," the officer said. "I am Rear Admiral Carlow."

"Premier Huntsman," William said, automatically. He'd never heard of a Rear Admiral Carlow, but that proved nothing. There were more crewmen and officers in the Imperial Navy than there were people on some planets. He keyed his terminal, ordering his staff to check for the Admiral's file, then leaned forward. "Welcome to Arthur's Seat."

"I'm afraid I can't stay," Carlow said. "I must inform you, Premier, that Arthur's Seat is about to receive a number of refugees."

William blinked in surprise. "What?"

"Tarsus has kicked a vast number of Forsakers into space," Carlow said. "I'm in the position of having to find a new home for them. Their transports will be arriving within the next two days."

"Impossible," William said. Forsakers? Arthur's Seat had a long history with the Forsakers, but that was all in the past. "Admiral, we cannot…"

"Under the terms of the Imperial Charter, you are obliged to take them," Carlow said, cutting him off. "My legal staff will be quite happy to forward you a copy of their briefs, if you wish."

"Please," William said, stunned. "Admiral...why can't they stay on Tarsus?"

"They are no longer welcome," Carlow said. "But then, they never were."

William cursed under his breath. Tarsus wasn't anything like as powerful as Terra Nova or Kennedy, but her system defence force *was* powerful enough to give the Imperial Navy pause. A confrontation could only have one outcome - or would have done, before Earth had fallen - yet it would have cost the Imperial Navy dearly. And now, with Earth gone and the Empire steadily collapsing, Tarsus was powerful enough to bend the sector fleet to her will.

And us too, he thought, numbly.

"They need a home," Carlow said. His voice was curiously flat. "And they *do* have a claim on Arthur's Seat."

"A claim that was dismissed by the Supreme Court," William said, automatically. It hadn't taken long. The planet's original settlers had been conned by the man who'd sold them the settlement rights. "Admiral, are you planning to merely dump them here?"

"Yes," Carlow said.

William stared at him in absolute disbelief, realising that protest would be futile. He'd met polite officers and officers who enjoyed lording it over the weaker worlds, but he'd never met an officer who was just too tired to proceed. Carlow no longer believed in the Imperial Navy, let alone the Empire. He was trying to rid himself of one problem before a nastier one reared its ugly head.

"Once the convoy arrives, they will be transported down to the surface," Carlow informed him. "And then they will be in your hands."

"I see," William hedged. "And how many people are we talking about, Admiral?"

"Around fifty thousand," Carlow said. He hesitated, noticeably. It was clear he didn't quite believe his own words. "Perhaps more. Tarsus is not the only world to consider forced relocations."

I suppose we should be grateful they didn't just kill the poor bastards, William thought. *It would have been easy - and no one would have cared, not after eighty billion people died on Earth.*

He kept his face as impassive as possible. "I will have to discuss the matter with my Cabinet," he said. Fifty thousand? Were they coming in one convoy or several? He had no idea where they could be held, let alone how they could be integrated into the wider community. Arthur's Seat had never attracted many immigrants. "I trust you can wait that long?"

"I can wait until the convoy actually arrives," Carlow informed him. "But after that I need to empty the ships as quickly as possible."

William nodded in understanding. Transport ships had been in short supply ever since the Grand Senate's taxes and regulations had driven independent spacers out of business or sent them fleeing to the Rim. Carlow would need those freighters back as quickly as possible...and besides, the life support would be red-lined too. A small systems failure, harmless under normal circumstances, might be absolutely catastrophic. He didn't want to imagine just how many people could die if the life support failed.

"Accordingly, I must demand that you put your shuttles at my disposal," Carlow added, grimly. "Their crews will be required to serve under my authority. I can cite Imperial Law if necessary..."

"We don't *have* many shuttles," William said. He cursed under his breath. What were they going to do? "But those we have will be placed under your command."

"Then I will contact you again, when the convoy arrives," Carlow said. "Thank you for your time, Premier."

His image vanished. William stared at the terminal for a long moment, then tapped the message that had just appeared in his inbox. Admiral Carlow's file - which listed him as a commodore - was surprisingly detailed. Carlow's family had close ties to the Grand Senate, which probably explained the promotion. But they were listed as living on Earth... they might be dead, if they hadn't managed to get off the planet before the end. Carlow wouldn't know, any more than William himself. Doubt and fear were no doubt already gnawing at his mind.

Maybe he got promoted as an emergency measure, William thought, as he finished reading the file. *Or maybe he promoted himself.*

He shook his head, mentally. Carlow hadn't struck him as the type of vainglorious fool who would promote himself, let alone invent a whole new title just for himself. But it hardly mattered. All that mattered was that Carlow's solution to his problem had created a whole new problem for William. Arthur's Seat had enough problems without adding one more.

"And this will give the Opposition all the excuse they need to push for a vote of no-confidence, if they want it," he muttered as he rose. He raised his voice. "Sykes?"

The door opened. "Yes, sir?"

"Inform the cabinet that the meeting is now being held immediately," William ordered, grimly. None of them would be pleased at being dragged out of bed, not even his political allies, but there was no choice. Carlow had seen to that, damn him. "And ask the kitchen staff to hold breakfast until after the meeting."

Sykes looked doubtful. "They will need to eat, sir."

"I know," William said. Sykes had always insisted that politicians - and everyone else - should take the time to eat before making any final decisions. A good meal made people feel better. "Have biscuits sent in with the coffee, but nothing else."

"Yes, sir," Sykes said. He didn't sound approving, but William knew Sykes would do as he was told. "I'll see to it at once."

William nodded, then walked through the door into the conference room and strode towards the window. Lothian - the capital city - seemed to glow in the darkness, streetlights marking out roads that seemed to twist and turn at random. Visitors to Arthur's Seat had often commented on the randomness, William recalled, but there was something about the twisting streets that looked more *natural* than the straight lines and planned communities so common on many other worlds. Arthur's Seat had never planned its own growth, beyond the bare minimum. The government had allowed the planet to evolve naturally.

For better or worse, he thought, morbidly.

He shook his head, slowly, as he picked out patches of darkness. Arthur's Seat wasn't heavily dependent on interstellar trade, unlike some of their neighbours, but his homeworld hadn't been able to escape *some* dependence. A number of businesses had already failed, as economic shockwaves rolled over the planet; others, too, would fail as the full impact finally became clear. The cabinet had been debating ways to relieve the pressure on surviving businesses, but hours of argument hadn't led to any conclusion. Arthur's Seat simply wasn't rich enough to buy what it needed, even if anyone was selling.

And no one is selling now, he thought. *Not now they have a pressing need for such supplies themselves.*

His eyes sought out the Parliament building, positioned on the other side of the city from Government House. The Empire Loyalists had ended up with egg on their face after the Empire collapsed, but so far the Opposition hadn't made a big issue of it. William rather suspected they didn't want to take responsibility for solving the problems themselves. If they managed to get a vote of no-confidence through Parliament, they might just *win* the General Election. And if that happened, they'd find themselves caught in the same bind facing William and his allies.

And if they could do a better job, William told himself, *they'd have tried to remove me from office by now.*

He saw a faint glimmer on the horizon and shivered. Dawn was breaking, the sun rising over a planet that no longer quite knew what was going on. Thousands of people had already lost their jobs; thousands more knew their own jobs were on the line. And, no matter what the Freeholders said, not everyone was qualified to run a farm or work in the planet's very limited industrial base. Arthur's Seat couldn't just batten down the hatches and avoid the interstellar turmoil washing through the galaxy. But his homeworld couldn't play a major role on the galactic stage either.

Sykes entered the room, his measured tread echoing in the quiet air. "Sir," he said. "The Cabinet members are on their way. The staff are already deflecting calls from their aides, asking for background briefings and suchlike."

He hesitated. "The media has already caught wind of *something*."

William nodded, never taking his eyes off the city below. *Someone* in the Orbital Guard would have talked, of course. It wasn't as if they had a *professional* military. An Imperial Navy starship racing towards Arthur's Seat like a bat out of hell? Of *course* someone would have talked! And the Cabinet being summoned so early in the morning? The media on Arthur's Seat wasn't anything like as intrusive as the media of a dozen other worlds, but they *did* keep an eye on the government. They knew *something* was up.

Centuries of galactic peace coming to an end, he thought. It still stunned - and terrified - him. The Empire had been omnipresent for over a thousand years. *Dominoes falling everywhere. And everyone wondering just when the next blow is going to fall.*

"It doesn't matter," he said, quietly. There was no point in making a fuss about it, not now. "Have the Cabinet shown into the conference room, then serve the coffee. The rest of the world will know soon enough."

"Yes, sir," Sykes said.

CHAPTER TWO

This may seem perplexing. As of Year Fifteen of the Post-Empire era, over four thousand life-bearing worlds were charted and colonised by humanity, not to mention the eleven thousand worlds that could be terraformed with a certain amount of investment. How could there not be enough room for everyone?
- Professor Leo Caesius. *Ethnic Streaming and the End of Empire.*

The starship felt profoundly...unnatural.

John, Son of John, made his way down the long corridor, trying desperately to keep from flinching at every random sound as he looked for his sister. The entire hull was quivering slightly, an omnipresent background hum echoing through the air. He'd spent his entire life on Tarsus, waiting desperately for the promised farm. The starship felt utterly unreal, utterly dangerous beyond words. A single mistake could kill him.

They told us that high technology could solve all our woes, he thought, remembering the founding words. *But it only made them worse.*

He shivered as he heard a clunking sound, then turned and inched through the hatch into the observation blister. Very few Forsakers had dared to make their way out of the holds, let alone explore the remainder of the giant ship. It was the perfect hiding place for someone who didn't want to be found, someone who knew her own people wouldn't dare to come looking for her. And, as the eerie lights of phase space flickered outside the blister, John found himself in perfect agreement. The primal urge to run back to his bedroom and hide under his bed was so overwhelming that it was all he could do to keep walking forward.

"John," his sister said. She didn't sound pleased to see him. "Why are you here?"

"Looking for you," John said. He forced himself to close the hatch. "Why are *you* here?"

Hannah said nothing for a long moment, then turned her head so she was staring out of the blister again. "I wanted to be alone."

John nodded as he forced himself to walk up to the bench and sit down next to her. It was hard to believe, sometimes, that they were twins. He was tall, but slightly pudgy; Hannah was shorter, but so thin that it was easy to believe she was actually taller. They shared their mother's dark hair, yet hers was so long it touched the small of her back while his was cropped close to his skull. And while she *should* have been wearing the white cap of an unmarried girl, she was bareheaded. It took him a moment to realise that she was holding it in her right hand.

"You shouldn't be here," he said, softly.

Hannah glanced at him. "Neither should you."

"I came here after you," John said, ignoring her tone. "Hannah, this isn't a safe place…"

His sister snorted. "As opposed to spending my time in the hold?"

"You'll get a whipping for sure if someone else catches you here," John warned, frantically. There were times when he thought Hannah *liked* provoking the Elders. He couldn't name another girl who had *quite* so many remonstrances to her name. "You could be contaminated…"

Hannah shrugged. "I've had worse."

"I'm serious," John said.

"So am I," Hannah said. She sobered. "I should have stayed on Tarsus."

John winced. He'd heard that all of the young women - particularly the unmarried ones - had been offered the chance to stay, if they chose to abandon the Forsaker lifestyle. Hannah…Hannah had been dissatisfied for years, dissatisfied enough that John thought she *would* have left, if she'd been given the opportunity. He'd assumed the whole story was a rumour, one spread by the starship's crew. There was little love between them and their unwanted passengers.

"I'm glad you didn't," he said, truthfully. Hannah could be a handful at times, but he loved her.

"Mother needed me, I thought," Hannah mused. The bitter regret in her voice shocked him. "I told myself I couldn't leave her."

She shook her head. "And now Joel is bringing me flowers."

John stared at her. "Joel?"

"Joel," Hannah confirmed. "And do you really think Konrad is going to turn him down?"

John bit off a nasty word that would earn *him* a whipping, if their mother had heard it pass his lips. Konrad, their stepfather, never denied Joel anything. If Joel wanted Hannah's hand in marriage, Konrad was unlikely to raise any *real* objections. It wasn't as if Joel and Hannah were *actually* related, after all. And people had been muttering for years that Hannah should be married. There was something profoundly unnatural about a nineteen-year-old girl without a husband.

"You could refuse him," he pointed out.

Hannah snorted. "And you expect Joel to *accept* it? Or mother?"

John shook his head, slowly. Joel was a Steward, with every prospect of becoming an Elder when his father died. No one doubted he had the well-being of the community at heart, even though his zeal worried - if not terrified - quite a few people. And Hannah's reputation didn't help, either. Very few fathers would approve their sons playing court to her. Their mother was worried, desperately worried, that Hannah would *never* get married. She'd do everything in her power to make sure that Hannah and Joel were married without delay.

"You should have told me," he said, finally.

Hannah snorted, again. "And what would you have *done* about it?"

John flushed angrily, but he had to admit she had a point. He'd never had the nerve to stand up to anyone, not even his sister. He hadn't even fought when the police had arrived to round up the entire community and march them onto shuttles. It had just seemed…*pointless*.

"Mother will nag me senseless if I go back," Hannah said. She rose and paced over to the blister. "And Konrad will push Joel's suit."

"She sent me to find you," John said. "Hannah…"

His sister turned to face him. "I should have stayed," she said, again. "I could have blended in…"

John couldn't disagree with her. The Forsakers had been forced to send their children to local schools, back on Tarsus. It hadn't been an enjoyable experience for John, but he knew Hannah had enjoyed it. She'd been free, if only for a short time, from the demands that came with being a young girl in the community. And she'd fitted in far better than himself. John knew he should have reported her for wearing Outsider clothes, listening to Outsider music and watching Outsider flicks, but he hadn't. In truth, he wasn't sure *why* he hadn't. Everyone knew that learning about the Outsiders was the first step to Falling...

And if she had left, he thought, *I would be alone with Konrad.*

He shook his head, slowly. Everyone said that Elder Konrad had done their family a favour by marrying their mother, after her husband had died. And perhaps he had, John admitted, reluctantly. He'd been too young to succeed his father as head of the household. But Konrad was too stiff, too unbending, to make a good stepfather. John had been able to talk about anything with his father, even matters that would get him in trouble if he spoke about them to anyone else. He'd never been *scared* of his father. But he didn't dare talk openly to Konrad.

"You would have Fallen," he said, finally. "Hannah..."

Hannah laughed, bitterly. "Would it have mattered?"

"It would have mattered to *me*," John said. "Hannah..."

His sister cut him off. "What sort of life *was* it? Being trapped on a stinky estate, endless promises of farms and lands that were never kept... John, do you think the promises *would* have been kept?"

John shook his head, morbidly. The Forsakers had been promised farms and land of their own for years. But the farms had never materialised. His entire generation had grown up without ever seeing anything outside the city. Hell, many of the younger children had never left the estate.

"Exactly," Hannah said. "And really...why stay?"

John shook his head. He had no answer.

The first Forsakers *had* had land, he knew. There was no doubt about that, although schisms in the community had sometimes obscured precisely what the founders had and hadn't believed. They'd moved away from modern technology, founding communities that had been almost completely self-sufficient. John had heard enough stories about their world to know it sounded like paradise. But times had changed, the community had scattered…

…And they'd become unwelcome guests on a dozen worlds.

They could have rebuilt the first communities, John was sure, if they'd been given land and space. The tools they needed had been carefully preserved, ever since they'd been moved from Haven to Tarsus. But it was clear that Hannah was right. Tarsus had never intended to give the Forsakers anything, certainly nothing more than the bare minimum. And the Empire, which had guaranteed their safety, was now gone. It hadn't taken long for Tarsus to rid itself of its unwanted guests.

And they would have kept me, he thought, *if I'd left the community.*

He shuddered at the thought. There was nothing stopping him from leaving, but he wouldn't have been able to return. The Fallen were permanently excluded from the Forsakers, stricken from their families…his mother would have disowned him, his stepfather would have pretended he'd never existed. And anyone who stayed in touch with him would have been shunned by the remainder of the community. He couldn't have severed all ties to his family and friends.

"I should have stayed," Hannah said. It would have been easier for her, John was sure. She had few friends in the community. Most girls her age were already married. "No one would have missed me."

"*I* would have missed you," John said, honestly.

"And now we're going to some other hellhole where we will be trapped too," Hannah added, ignoring him. "They should have just dumped us on a penal world. It would be more *honest*."

She met his eyes. "Does Konrad talk about arranging a match for you?"

John shook his head. It bothered him, more than he cared to admit. Men weren't encouraged to marry until they were at least twenty-one and believed mature enough to raise a family, but it was common for betrothal talks to start earlier. His father would have started them already, John was sure; Konrad, a man who was technically in a better position to arrange a good match, had done nothing of the sort.

"I think he's too interested in arranging a match for his natural son," he said, sourly. "I…"

He broke off. "I'm sorry…"

Hannah sighed. "If I had left," she said, "it would have been easier for you to marry."

"It doesn't matter," John said.

"Oh, *goody*," Hannah said. She didn't believe him. "Are you sure?"

John shrugged. He'd never had a real conversation with any young woman, save for his sister. Young men weren't encouraged to talk to young women. He couldn't say he knew *any* of the unmarried girls very well. When the time came to marry, the two sets of parents would chat and come to a final decision before allowing the youngsters to meet under careful supervision. A young man and woman who talked without supervision would be in deep trouble, forced to either marry or leave the community. John…didn't think he was *ready* to marry, not yet.

"It isn't as if you're older than me," he said, lightly. "My marriage isn't dependent on yours."

"True," Hannah agreed. "But how long will that last?"

John shook his head. He didn't want to think about it, not yet. He'd told himself that he would get established before he started asking Konrad to find him a bride, but as the years passed getting established had started to seem more and more like a pointless dream. He wasn't going to be one of the men who did nothing, apart from keeping his wife pregnant, yet he didn't know what *else* he was going to do.

"I have to go back to the hold," he said, instead. Talking to Hannah had helped him to forget that he was on a starship, but he still wasn't comfortable. "You should come with me."

Hannah smirked. "Aren't you going to try to drag me?"

"No," John said. He wouldn't have dared. Their mother would never have forgiven him if they'd made a scene. Konrad and Joel wouldn't have been happy either. "Hannah…"

"I'll be along in a minute," his sister promised. She turned until she was staring into the eerie lights of phase space. "You can tell them you never saw me, if you like."

John sighed. "Mother won't be pleased if I lie to her," he said. "I'll stay out of her way until you get back. She'll be too mad at you to ask questions."

He turned and strode out of the compartment, hurrying back down the corridor towards the lower decks. A couple of crew passed, their eyes narrowing disdainfully at him. Both of them were women, wearing clothes so tight that it was hard not to stare. Their bodies might have been covered, but it was easy to see the swell of their breasts and the shape of their thighs. He had to fight the urge to look behind him as they passed, reminding himself that it would only get him in trouble. The security detachment on the ship hadn't hesitated to use neural whips whenever the passengers got uppity.

A faint smell wafted through the air as he walked down the stairs. The women were cooking in their compartment, trying desperately to turn their rations into something edible. John wasn't sure if the passengers were being given unpleasant-tasting rations deliberately or not, but nothing the women had done had succeeded in improving the taste. The best of the ration bars tasted like cardboard, no matter how many sauces were smeared onto the muck.

He frowned as he saw an opened hatch and peered inside. Joel was standing there, his back to the hatch, talking quietly to one of the starship's crew. John blinked in surprise - the Elders had insisted that none of the passengers talk to the crew, save when absolutely necessary - and stared. It looked, very much, like a friendly conversation. A set of boxes lay on a table, all unmarked. And Joel was passing something to the crewman...

John inched backwards, trying not to be seen or heard. Seven Forsakers - four boys, three girls - had been harshly punished for ignoring the Elders. They'd chosen to talk to the crew, to ask them questions about their ship and life in space...even though no *true* Forsaker would want anything beyond a farm. John had no idea what they'd asked, or even what they'd been told, but it didn't matter. He didn't want to be punished himself.

"Thank you," Joel said, loudly enough to be heard outside. "And if you have any others..."

The rest of his words were lost as John slipped down the corridor and turned the corner. A pair of Elders were standing outside one of the female cabins, making sure the unmarried girls weren't disturbed by the crew. They didn't know Joel was talking to a crewman, John guessed. Joel might have Konrad for a father, but Konrad wasn't the *only* Elder. The others wouldn't be amused if they caught Joel defying his father.

I never defied my father, John thought, as he reached the hold. He wondered, suddenly, just how different his life would have been if his father had survived. *But Hannah would have defied him too.*

"John," a stern voice said. John turned to see Elder Peter, an old bearded man given to long-winded sermons on the sins of the modern world and the rightness of the Forsaker path. "Your father is looking for you."

Stepfather, John thought. He didn't dare say it out loud. Correcting an Elder would get him in real trouble. It would be taken for cheek, even if he happened to be right. Perhaps especially if he happened to be right. *He's my stepfather, you...*

He stopped that thought before it showed on his face. "Thank you, Elder," he said, as politely as he could. The Elders might choose to maintain the polite fiction that John was Konrad's son, but John knew better. "I'll go find him at once."

"He's in his section," Peter informed him. "And I expect to see you for prayers tonight."

John nodded. There was no point in trying to get out of it. Someone would notice his absence and report him to his stepfather, who would throw a fit. John's behaviour would reflect badly on Konrad, after all. Perhaps that was why he was trying to get Joel to marry Hannah. Hannah's behaviour was *already* reflecting badly on him.

And if I had half the courage Hannah has, John thought, *I would have told him off by now.*

He shook his head, feeling - not for the first time - utterly trapped. Even if he *did* tell Konrad where to go, the remainder of the community would turn on him. Hannah, he acknowledged, probably felt the same way too. They were bound by invisible chains, held in place by silent disapproval and the threat of punishment. And there was no way to resist.

"John," a new voice said. John felt a sinking feeling in his chest as he turned to see Joel, slipping into the compartment as if he had just been at bible study, rather than an illicit meeting. "You will be coming to the sermon tonight, won't you?"

John kept his expression blank. Joel had been known to react badly to any hint of disagreement. He was young, barely four years older than John, but he already had a fearsome reputation. If Konrad hadn't been his father...

"Of course, Steward," John said. He knew there was no getting out of it. "I'll be sure to attend."

CHAPTER THREE

The answer, alas, lies in the twin demons of human nature and the response of political and corporate elites to perverse incentives.
— Professor Leo Caesius. *Ethnic Streaming and the End of Empire.*

"Out of the question," Steven Troutman snapped. The Leader of the Opposition thumped the table to make his point clearer. "We can barely support ourselves! We cannot take umpteen million new immigrants on a day's notice!"

"Fifty thousand," William said, quietly.

"And how do you know," Troutman demanded, "that it will *stay* at fifty thousand?"

He went on before William could say a word. "There are Forsaker settlements all over the sector," he added, sharply. "How many other worlds don't want them? How many other worlds will dump them on us, if we give them half a chance?"

"There are Forsakers on our world," Vice Premier Sondra Mackey pointed out. Her red curls shivered angrily as she spoke. "Many of us are *descended* from Forsakers."

"And when was the *last* time you worked on a farm?" Troutman asked. He looked Sondra up and down. "And when was the last time you stepped aside to let the men make the hard decisions?"

Sondra coloured. "My family hasn't followed those traditions for three hundred years!"

"Quite," Troutman agreed. "And what makes you any different from the *rest* of us?"

He thumped the table, again. "Your family dates all the way back to the first settlements on our homeworld," he said. "But if you don't look or act any different from the rest of the population…is there any difference at all?"

William hated to admit it, but Troutman had a point. Sondra was an effective political operator, a woman who had climbed through the ranks until he'd had to offer her a place in his government. There was no way she could be mistaken for a traditional Forsaker woman, a woman who cooked, cleaned and otherwise stayed out of sight while her menfolk ran the farm. Wearing traditional clothes on Remembrance Day didn't make her a Forsaker. But, at the same time, Sondra *did* have ties running all the way back to the first settlement. It wasn't something she could easily deny.

"Right now, we are in the midst of an economic crisis," Troutman continued. "We are having problems keeping basic services going, for crying out loud! And you want to add fifty thousand newcomers?"

"We can't just turn them away," Sondra said.

"Of course we can," Troutman snapped. "This is *our* world. We settled it…"

"My ancestors got here first," Sondra snapped back.

"Yeah," Troutman said. "And just how relieved were they when *we* arrived?"

William sighed. It wasn't uncommon for settlers to arrive at their new home, only to discover that someone else had got there first. Even in the days of the Empire, claim-jumping had been a major problem. The Forsakers who had settled Arthur's Seat had been sold the settlement rights by a con artist, who'd correctly reasoned that the Forsakers were so desperate for a homeworld that they wouldn't check his credentials before making the purchase. And then they'd discovered that Arthur's Seat was nowhere near as habitable as they'd been told. By the time the *real* settlers arrived, the Forsakers had been on the verge of extinction.

And they realised the folly of living without technology, he thought. *They practically abandoned their culture overnight.*

"That isn't the point," Sondra said. She jabbed a finger at the map. "We have plenty of land to share!"

"That's *our* land," Troutman said.

"You're always saying we need more farmers," Sondra said. "And here are fifty thousand men and women who *want* to farm!"

"Fifty thousand people who won't fit into our culture," Troutman said. "And who will probably need help to tame and settle the land, help we cannot afford to provide."

He looked around the table. "We should tell them to leave."

"We can't," Commodore Charles Van Houlton said, quietly.

"We should," Troutman snapped.

Van Houlton cleared his throat, loudly. "The Forsakers are being shipped here by the Imperial Navy," he said. "There is no way we can keep them from dumping the poor bastards on the surface. The Orbital Guard doesn't even *begin* to have the firepower to stand off a naval squadron. If we tell them to leave - and they refuse to go - we have no way to enforce it. They have already demanded the use of our shuttles and spaceports."

"Which I have granted," William added.

"They have no *right* to dump unwanted guests on our world," Troutman snarled.

"Might makes right," Van Houlton countered. "Earth no longer exists, sir. There's no higher authority to appeal to, not now. That squadron can do whatever the hell it likes."

Troutman glared. "I *told* you that trying to build ties to the galactic economy was a mistake!"

"I don't think it would make a difference, if we'd tried to remain self-sufficient," William pointed out. "We would still seem a convenient dumping ground."

"Then let the bastards dump them on Minoa," Troutman said. "There's plenty of room there."

"They'll die without help," Sondra snapped. "You'd be condemning fifty thousand people to death!"

"And our duty is to the ten *million* people on our homeworld," Troutman snapped back. "I am not unsympathetic, but there is no way we can absorb so many people without serious problems. And what the hell are they *expecting* from us? Land and farms?"

"You're the one who wanted to encourage more people to move out to the farms," Sondra sneered. "Or are you reluctant to take on new farmers after all?"

"My *plan* was to have new farmers spend five or so years learning the ropes beforehand," Troutman said. "I don't think we could accommodate fifty thousand new farmers."

"Not all of them will be farmers," Chief Constable Jacob Montgomery said. "A number will be women and children."

"Maybe only ten thousand of them are farmers," Troutman said. "That's still more people than we can accommodate in a hurry."

He paused. "The Freeholders will not tolerate it."

"The Freeholders are not in government," Sondra said, nastily.

Troutman gazed back at her. "And how long do you think that will last?"

William kept his face impassive, although he had to admit it was a direct hit. Arthur's Seat had four political parties: Empire Loyalists, Freeholders, Unionists and Isolationists. The Empire Loyalists had been in power for the last six years, but the economic shockwave had weakened their grip at the worst possible time. And while the Freeholders and the Isolationists didn't *normally* have enough support to unseat the government, it was just possible that a combination of economic disaster and unwanted immigrants could give them a boost. Hell, the Unionists might not be so keen to remain allied with the Empire Loyalists if the economic crisis got worse.

There are two years until the next election, he reminded himself. *Unless they push for a vote of no-confidence.*

He cleared his throat. "This is no time for petty bickering," he said, sternly. Two years…a lot could happen in two years. "I believe the facts are simple. Fifty thousand refugees are going to be dumped on us. And there is nothing we can do about it."

"We could say no," Troutman said.

"Which we have no way to enforce," William reminded him. In hindsight, maybe it had been a mistake to refuse to strengthen the Orbital Guard. But the only realistic concern for over three hundred years had been pirates. "They'll dump them on us anyway and to hell with our quibbles."

He paused, trying to gauge his support. "We cannot simply let them die," he added, after a moment. "It would be utterly inhuman. There is no *way* I will give orders designed to indirectly slaughter fifty thousand men, women and children because I find their presence inconvenient. And I do not believe that the vast majority of our population would *condone* mass slaughter."

"Now, perhaps," Troutman said. "But that is likely to change."

"These are *Forsakers*," Sondra snapped. "We're not talking about Nihilists or Reformed Vagabonds or some group that may actually pose a danger!"

William slapped the table before the argument could restart. "We always intended to expand our settlements," he added. "Let us welcome the newcomers and blend them into our society."

"And what will you do," Troutman asked, "when they refuse to blend into our society?"

Sondra blinked. "My ancestors did."

"Your ancestors were starving because they were stupid enough to believe their own lies," Troutman sneered. "They had no choice. It was join or die. And even *then* there were problems. Now…fifty thousand people, born and raised in a very different culture, *without* the incentive to just give up…it isn't going to end well."

He met William's eyes. "And why *were* they expelled from Tarsus in the first place?"

"They weren't wanted there," William said, flatly.

"Yes," Troutman said. "They're not wanted here, either."

"We are going in circles," William said. "They are going to be landing soon. We have to be ready for them."

Troutman shook his head. "I want it clearly noted, on the record, that I was against allowing them to land," he said. "There is no way we can provide everything they need, at once. I don't know if we can even provide food and drink…we didn't bother to stockpile vast quantities of ration bars, did we? With the best will in the world, sir, we cannot provide for them. And even if we do, the cost will be immense."

"These people are not criminals," Sondra snapped. "It isn't fair to blame them for…"

"No?" Troutman smiled, rather coldly. "And if they were such paragons of decency, why did they get kicked off Tarsus in the first place?"

He shrugged. "In any case, it doesn't matter," he added. "There is no way we can absorb so many people in a hurry. Their culture will not be diluted by contact with ours."

William nodded slowly. "Commodore," he said. "How quickly could you empty the freighters?"

"It would depend on a number of factors," Van Houlton said. "Assuming we red-lined the shuttles, which would be grossly unwise, we could evacuate the ships within two weeks. If we followed a more practical course, we could have everyone down within a month. Frankly, though, a great deal depends on how many shuttles the Imperial Navy sent along. I don't know if they were counting on us to assist or not."

"And let us not forget," Troutman added, "that we cannot replace a lost shuttle."

William nodded, curtly. Troutman was right - Arthur's Seat *couldn't* build a shuttle from scratch, let alone a starship - but there was no point in making an issue out of it.

The Chief Constable cleared his throat. "The problem of accommodation will not be solved easily," he admitted. "We dismantled the old transit barracks over a hundred years ago. If we started now, we could probably assemble a whole set of replacements within the next four weeks, but until then we might have a problem. We certainly don't have a stockpile of tents or other forms of portable accommodation. We might have to resort to using schools and requisitioning other buildings until we can build barracks."

"Or we could put out an appeal for families to take in refugees," Sondra said. "I'm sure there are many people who would be happy to take guests, at least for a few weeks."

"I'm not," Troutman said.

Sondra scowled. "The Forsaker families will be delighted…"

Troutman laughed, unkindly. "How many families like yours practice strict segregation of the sexes?"

He looked as if he wanted to say something else, but held his tongue. Instead, he looked at William.

"I think I speak for most of the rural dwellers when I say that we will *not* accept having refugees quartered on us, unless they can work," he added. "And that means they actually have to be able to do *useful* work. I don't want untrained monkeys wandering around a farm."

"People can learn," Sondra said.

"Yes," Troutman agreed. "But providing training would be a nightmare."

"There will be other problems," the Chief Constable added. "And some of them will only become apparent after we get started."

He paused. "With your permission, Premier, I would like to put the police on alert," he added. "And summon the medical staff we'll need to vet the newcomers."

William nodded. "Can they handle it?"

"I'm not sure," the Chief Constable admitted. He looked doubtful. "Our contingency planning was always very limited, sir. About the only practical experience we have comes from evacuating city districts during a fire and…well, this is on a much greater scale."

"And with newcomers," Troutman added. "People will be much less willing to provide emergency accommodation."

"There are going to be a lot of problems along the way," the Chief Constable agreed. "I don't say we can't handle it, sir. I just say it isn't going to be easy."

"Vetting immigrants is going to be impossible," Troutman said. "And scaling up the process, such as it is, to cope with over fifty thousand newcomers…."

William nodded, reluctantly. Arthur's Seat had never been a magnet for immigration, not when there were other worlds with more land or larger industrial bases. The handful of immigrants who *did* arrive were easily absorbed into the population. Hell, it was rare for the planet to get more than a few hundred immigrants a year. But fifty thousand…no matter how he looked at it, absorbing them was going to be hard.

We cannot refuse to take them, he reminded himself. *And we cannot leave them to die.*

"We can handle it," he said, firmly. "And if we all pull together, we can make it happen."

"This is a fool's game," Troutman said. "And I will take no part in it."

"You have a seat on the Cabinet," Sondra reminded him.

"I don't get a vote," Troutman countered. "And I doubt Parliament will accept this so calmly."

He rose. "Enjoy your small triumph," he added, as he strode towards the door. "It won't last."

"It will have to," William said, as the door closed behind Troutman. "Commodore, have the Orbital Guard coordinate with the Imperial Navy, but don't put too much strain on the shuttles. Chief Constable, make the preparations for receiving the newcomers...get the spaceport ready and empty out some of the disused factories. They'll do for the moment. Schools too, if necessary..."

"That'll get you the schoolchild vote," Sondra commented.

"Thanks," William said. He had to smile. "But I'll have to wait for a decade before they can vote for me."

He dismissed the rest of the cabinet to breakfast and turned to her. "Do you think Parliament will approve an emergency spending bill?"

"If we can get enough MPs to support us," Sondra said. She considered the issue for a long moment. "Steven is going to be rustling up the Opposition...we might have to do some horse-trading with the Unionists. The Isolationists aren't likely to side with us."

"Not over this," William agreed. "I don't think they've realised that everything's changed."

He scowled. The Isolationists wanted to isolate Arthur's Seat from the rest of the universe, something he considered to be a dangerous and futile goal. They'd oppose mass immigration on principle, pointing out the danger of a large ethnic minority population - and the troubles it could cause - that could be used as an excuse for intervention. Hell, the Empire *had* done just that several times in the last decade alone. But now the Empire was gone. There was no one willing and able to do the intervention.

Unless our neighbours start getting frisky, he thought. Arthur's Seat didn't have *much* to attract an invader, but imperialists had never been interested in practicalities. *And if they do, we're screwed.*

"See what the Unionists want, in exchange for their support," he said, finally. "And then arrange a press conference for later this morning. I'll need to tell the people what's coming before it leaks."

"It will leak," Sondra said. "Steven will see to that."

"I know," William said. There were some advantages to living on a world without a first-rate datanet or a thoroughly disrespectful media culture. "But hopefully it won't spread very far before I get my version out there."

"Hah," Sondra said. She shook her head. "Did you speak to your wife?"

"I've asked Molly to come back to Lothian today," William said. "There'll be opportunities for her to talk to the newcomers. If there are minor problems…we can smooth them out before they become major problems."

"I would like to speak with them too," Sondra said. "I feel a certain responsibility towards them."

William smiled. "Don't let Steven hear you say that," he warned. "He'll see it as outright treason."

Sondra shuddered. "Does he have to object to *everything*?"

"He's the Leader of the Opposition," William said. "It's his job."

He sighed. "And besides, the Freeholders love him for it," he added. "That's why they keep returning him to Parliament."

"Yes," Sondra agreed. She met his eyes. "And if we did manage to integrate fifty thousand newcomers, William, what would that do to voting demographics?"

William frowned, totting up the numbers in his head. "It would give us a boost, at least at first," he said. "Enough, perhaps, to keep power for the next decade."

"Exactly," Sondra said. "The Freeholders will be outvoted, constantly. And *that* would keep them firmly out of power."

"True," William agreed. He wasn't sure if he would benefit, but *Sondra* certainly would. She was well-placed to take his position when his term expired. "And yet, it all depends on managing the situation perfectly. We must *not* mess up."

He watched her leave, shaking his head in amusement. Trust Sondra to find a way to profit from the situation. And, perhaps, to ensure that the entire *party* profited. But a single mistake would be disastrous. Troutman wasn't wrong. Absorbing so many people would be difficult.

But we can do it, he told himself, as he followed her out the door. *We've done it before.*

CHAPTER FOUR

> Humanity's expansion into space can be said to fall into four phases. First, there was the expansion into the Sol System itself. Second, there was the launch of multiple 'slowboat' (STL) starships aimed at prospective colony worlds relatively near to Earth. Third, there was the early phase drive expansion into the Sol Sector and beyond. Fourth, and last, there was the Empire's determination to transport as many people from Earth as possible.
> - Professor Leo Caesius. *Ethnic Streaming and the End of Empire.*

Joel wrinkled his nose in distaste as John entered the compartment, looking around nervously at the other young men. Joel found it difficult to understand how a young man with such a heritage could be so *weak* - John's father had been a stern man, one of the few who had even cowed Joel - but he supposed it had its advantages. A strong man in John's position might have objected to Joel's father assuming the role of family head and control of Hannah's ultimate disposition. He might even have brought his sister to heel.

"Close the hatch," he ordered, curtly.

Ben, one of his closest allies, scrambled to obey, slamming the hatch shut with a disconcerting *thud*. A number of young men winced, their reactions clearly visible no matter how hard they tried to hide it. The starship felt claustrophobic at the best of times. Joel kept his own face carefully expressionless as he motioned for his friends to sit down, silently assessing their suitability for their roles. They were all young, they all burned with rage and humiliation...

"When we were moved to Tarsus, we were promised lands and farms," Joel said, as soon as everyone else was sitting down. "Instead, we were herded into estates and fed promises. We will be given land next year! No, *next* year! No, the year after *that*! And while we waited, desperately praying that those promises would be kept, our children were fed lies that seduced them from the path. How many of our people chose to Fall rather than stay with us?

"And then we were dragged from our homes, as pitiful as they were, and thrown bodily onto shuttles. Our homes were smashed, our women were abused, our children were threatened with dogs...we were uprooted, as casually as one uproots a plant! We were wrenched from our lives and dumped on this ship! And wherever we are going now, is there any reason to think it will be any better?"

He paused, assessing their response. He'd always been good at reading his audience - it was why he'd become a Steward so young - but this was different. This was no ordinary sermon, not really. None of the Elders, not even his father, knew why he'd gathered forty-one young men in a single compartment. And while he hoped they would understand, when they found out the truth, he knew it wasn't certain.

The Elders have been in charge for too long, he thought. He'd been raised to respect and obey his father, but the old man was sometimes painfully wrong. *And it is time we chose a different path.*

"Why?"

He let the word hang in the air for a long second, then continued. "Why did this happen to us?"

Ben watched him with shining eyes. Joshua seemed grimly determined - his sister had been one of the harassed women, although she'd chosen to stay with the community rather than move away. And John...John's face was weak as always, his doubts clearly visible to anyone who knew to look. Joel felt his lips twist, once again. John was truly contemptible.

"We were weak," Joel said.

"We were not allowed to gather weapons until it was far too late. Even when we *were* allowed to purchase weapons, the Elders forbade us from obtaining anything lethal or training in its use. They obeyed the planetary government, never realising that the government hated us, that the government would do nothing to help us. And when the police came for us, what good were we? We were overwhelmed in moments, forced to watch as our lives were destroyed."

Humiliation burned through him. He swore, once again, that he would put the emotion to good use.

"We should have made a stand for our rights," he hissed. "We should have prepared ourselves to fight. We should have armed ourselves and stood tall, making it clear that we were prepared to fight! And yet, the Elders wouldn't *let* us prepare for war. We had to just sit there and endure the hostility, endure the threats, endure the knowledge that one day we would be wiped from the planet. And it happened! We were lucky they didn't decide to merely kill us all.

"Never again.

"I say to you, never again.

"We will soon be dumped on a whole new world," he warned. "And when that happens, we have to be ready to make it clear that we are going to *fight* for our rights."

He paused, once again. Officially, they hadn't been told their destination, but it hadn't been hard to find a spacer willing to take a bribe. Arthur's Seat...a world embedded in Forsaker hearts. And a world with a population that might - just - remember its roots. *And*, perhaps most importantly of all, a peaceful world. Fighting on Tarsus might have been suicidal, giving the government all the excuse it needed to exterminate the Forsakers, but fighting on Arthur's Seat...

And his friends were ready to fight. They *had* been humiliated; worse, their *families* had been humiliated. Wives and mothers had been molested, unmarried girls had been urged to abandon their families and stay on Tarsus. Oh, it had been easy to keep the pot boiling, to keep reminding his brethren of the humiliation they'd suffered. The only problem had been in keeping the pot from boiling over before it was time.

"I have obtained weapons," he said, into the silence. "We will spend the next two days learning to use them. And we will be ready when the time comes to fight."

He turned and picked up one of the boxes he'd placed on the table, opening it up to reveal the assault weapon within. A low hum of admiration and fear echoed through the room for a long chilling moment. It was rare, almost unknown, for civilians on Tarsus to own weapons, certainly not assault rifles. Joel had planned to find contacts amongst the criminal underworld, hoping to purchase weapons, but his father had scorched that plan. It would give the government all the excuse they needed to take decisive steps, he'd argued. He hadn't realised that the government didn't *need* an excuse.

"This is power," Joel said, bluntly. "And this" - he opened up another box to reveal the ammunition - "is the key to making it work."

He removed the weapon from the box, holding it in the air. "This is the last resort," he said, grimly. "But, when the time comes, we will use them."

There was a long chilling pause. "Any questions?"

John looked as if he wanted to say something, but held his tongue. Joel was tempted to call him out, to find out what he'd wanted to ask, yet it would have been pointless. John wasn't the most popular man in the compartment, even if he *was* Joel's stepbrother. And John being beaten halfway to death would have been hard to explain. God alone knew what would happen if the Elders reacted badly.

It was a gamble, Joel admitted. They wouldn't use the rifles, not at first. They'd use baseball bats and other improvised weapons, devices that could be used to fight without posing a serious threat. Arthur's Seat could not be goaded into taking strong action until it was too late. And yet…he had no illusions. A war against the entire planet would end badly. But at least they'd go out fighting.

We cannot give up what we are, he thought, as he opened the hatch. The Outsider was unpleasant - Joel had caught him eying some of the girls, even in their shapeless dresses - but useful. *And if we have to make use of Outsider technology to preserve ourselves, then that is what we shall do.*

"This is a friend," he said, simply. "He's here to help."

The Outsider - damn him - had promised him that the weapons were easy to use. And he was right, going through the motions time and time again until Joel and his loyalists could use the weapons without hesitation. They hadn't actually fired a shot, unfortunately - there was no way to hide the noise - but he thought he could handle a weapon if he had to fight. And, by the time the meeting finally came to an end, so could his allies.

"We'll be meeting again tomorrow," he said, after a final speech. "You know what you have to do."

The Elders would not be amused, he thought, as his loyalists slipped back into the corridors and vanished. Some of them would be horrified, either at Joel's preparations to fight or his embrace of the demon technology; others, more perceptively, would see it as a challenge to their power. And they would be right. He bore them no ill will, but they were old and feeble and utterly unprepared for the changes buffeting the Empire. Some of the old geezers were even still talking about appealing to Earth!

"John," he said, when the room was clear. He didn't know why his unwanted stepbrother had stayed, but it hardly mattered. "Where is Hannah?"

John's face flickered. "I think she's with mother," he said, flatly. Joel was almost sure it was a lie. "They were sewing."

"Oh," Joel said. "And where was she *before*, seeing she *wasn't* with her mother?"

A wave of emotions washed over John's face, coming and going too quickly for Joel to identify them. Not, he supposed, that it mattered. John was weak, ineffectual...really, what could one *make* of a brother who allowed his sister to walk all over him? Part of him was tempted to admit that Hannah certainly had more life about her than two or three other girls her age put together, but it wasn't *right*. A young woman her age should be married - she *would* be married, once the date was set. And her brother had given up the right to object.

"Answer the question," he said, coolly. He might not be married yet, but he still had certain rights. "Where was she?"

John blinked, then made the visible decision to lie. "In the female quarters."

Joel lunged forward, allowing his anger to show. "No, she wasn't," he said, as John scuttled backwards. "Where *was* she?"

It was a bluff - even Joel wouldn't have dared enter the female quarters, not when trying would have gotten him shunned by the entire community - but it worked.

"Exploring the ship," John said, reluctantly.

"You should make sure she doesn't leave the hold," Joel said. "She's your sister. Who *knows* what could happen to her."

John flushed. "She's safe."

"No, she isn't," Joel said. A starship wasn't safe and both of them knew it. "You have to keep her safe."

John looked as though he wanted to say something, but didn't quite have the nerve. Joel wondered, absently, why John hadn't simply left, back when he'd had the chance. He wasn't quite as aggressive as some of the other Forsakers. He'd even done his best to actually *earn* money, even if it had meant working in an Outsider office. Joel wasn't sure what John had done to earn money, but he had. And yet, he'd come back to the estate every night and been rounded up with the rest of his family.

He probably just didn't want to leave his sister, he thought, amused. There was no doubt that John loved his sister, even though he wasn't doing right by her. *And his mother*.

"When I marry her, she will be taught the error of her ways," Joel added. His stepmother had insisted that Konrad find Hannah a husband, nagging Joel's father until he'd agreed. "A young woman should not be so defiant."

"She isn't defiant," John protested, weakly.

"She shouldn't have left her mother's side," Joel pointed out, sweetly. It was easy to make John aware of his own failings, failings he didn't seem interested in addressing. "Who *knows* what could happen to a young girl like that?"

He shrugged. Tormenting John was fun, but it grew old fast. John didn't seem capable of resisting, not even in defence of his sister. It was pathetic. Joel would have gone through hell to protect his sister, if he'd *had* a sister. His mother had died in childbirth, her infant son stillborn. Perhaps she would have survived, if she'd had proper medical care. But no one on Tarsus wanted to help a Forsaker...

"Go back to father," he ordered. His father would have lectured Hannah until her ears were bleeding - perhaps literally - but he hadn't had a go at John yet. Joel would keep his opinions to himself, at least until they were actually married. Hannah would learn to behave herself after that, or else. "I'm sure he's waiting to speak to you."

"I'm sure," John said. He paused. "Why did they sell you the weapons?" He paused, again. "And how did you pay for them?"

"Outsiders are always interested in profit," Joel reminded him. They'd been told that right from birth. Outsiders put profit ahead of everything else, from common sense to long-term thinking. An Outsider would sell his son, his daughter…or his coat, even if the weather was growing cold. "It was easy enough to make a friend."

He shrugged. He didn't care why someone would choose to sell fifty assault rifles and several thousand rounds of ammunition. It wasn't as if they could take the freighter and sail off into the sunset. He would be the first to admit he didn't know *how* to fly the giant starship, even if they could. All that mattered was that they had the weapons they needed to make a stand, if their rights were disrespected again. Who *cared*? There was little to be gained from looking a gift horse in the mouth.

"But you had money," John pressed. "How did you…?"

Joel moved forward with stunning speed, shoving John back against the bulkhead. "Don't ask such questions," he snarled. John's face paled. "It's none of your business!"

He stepped back, letting go of his stepbrother. "Go back to father," he hissed. John would obey. He was too much of a coward to do anything else. "And keep your damn mouth shut!"

John turned and practically fled the compartment. Joel watched him go, snorting in disgust at such craven cowardice. Hannah was braver than her brother, even though she was a young woman. Maybe she'd inherited their father's masculinity even as she'd inherited their mother's body. Joel pitied John's future wife and children. Without a strong hand to guide them and keep them in line, they'd Fall for sure.

I might wind up having to take them in, he thought. *If John is unable to do it…*

He returned the rifles to their boxes, then sealed and locked the crates. No one should touch them, but he knew better than to take chances. There was very little private property amongst the Forsakers. Almost everything, save for a handful of small possessions, was communal property. He took one final sweep around the compartment, just to be sure, and then hurried through the hatch. The Elders would probably notice if he wasn't on duty with the other Stewards as the day drew to a close.

Although no one would notice that the day is over, he thought, sourly. There was *nothing* natural about the giant starship. The lights burned constantly, day or night. Joel had a feeling the crew refused to dim them just to be unpleasant. *We don't even know what time it is on our new world.*

He stopped as he turned the corner and saw a young couple kissing. Mary - a distant relative of his - was kissing a starship crewman. She broke off as she saw him, her face flushing bright red. Joel stepped forward, bunching his fists and caught her arm. The crewman had no time to object before Joel had dragged her into the hold and sealed the hatch behind him.

"You utter idiot," he snapped, as he marched her over to her parents. "Do you know what could have happened to you?"

He pushed Mary into her father's arms, then gave a brief explanation before turning to find the other Stewards. Mary would probably be shunned for the next few days, once word got round. Kissing an Outsider... it was dangerous, very dangerous. Mary couldn't have married him without leaving the community, cutting herself away from her entire life. And if the Outsider had refused to marry her...

Behind him, Mary's mother started screaming her outrage. A slap echoed on the air. He didn't look back.

She could have fallen pregnant, he thought, morbidly. It had happened before. Young girls were taught almost nothing about their bodies until it was far too late. Hell, Joel himself was still a little fuzzy on the details. *Or worse.*

He shook his head as he stepped into the outer compartment. Tarsus had been dangerous as well as unwelcoming. There had been too many temptations for men and women, threatening to seduce them from the path. Things would be different, he promised himself, on Arthur's Seat. He'd *make* them different. Lands of their own, farms...a place where they could grow, away from the demon technology. The Forsakers would become what they were meant to be, rather than parasites on Outsiders...

...And if a few Outsiders got hurt...well, he didn't care. But then, they hadn't cared either.

CHAPTER FIVE

The first expansion phase gave birth to a number of cultures that considered themselves to be space-based, first and foremost. Like the modern-day RockRats, they tended to distance themselves from the 'groundhogs' and move further away as launch systems improved and governments extended their control over outer space.
- Professor Leo Caesius. *Ethnic Streaming and the End of Empire.*

Constable Mike Whitehead was in the shower when the telephone rang.

"I'll get it," his wife called, as he stuck his head out of the bathroom. "It's probably Suzie."

Mike rolled his eyes as he stepped back into the shower. Suzie and Jane, his wife, had been plotting *something* over the last few weeks, probably something to do with his birthday. He wasn't too worried about it. His wife had a mischievous sense of humour, which led to the occasional practical joke, but she wasn't particularly cruel. He'd fallen in love with her sense of humour, years ago. She still made him laugh.

Which is something you need on the job, he thought. *Something to keep you from losing your humanity.*

He scowled at the thought as he turned off the water and reached for the towel. Police officers on Arthur's Seat had an easier time of it than officers on Earth, if the entertainment flicks were to be believed, but it was still a taxing job. He'd seen more accidents and crimes than he cared to think about - and, even if they were small fry compared to problems on Earth, they still took a toll on innocent civilians caught in the middle. He wouldn't have worked on Earth for anything, even enough money to buy his own planet. The horror stories he'd heard, filtering through the police grapevine, made him wonder why *anyone* would want to live and work on Earth. Humanity's homeworld seemed trapped in a permanent nightmare.

Was trapped, he reminded himself. Earth was gone. The news had shocked Arthur's Seat, although very few people had ever set foot on Earth. *Earth has been destroyed.*

There was a tap on the door. "Mike, that was the office," Jane said, sharply. She sounded alarmed. "They want you there now."

Mike glanced at the clock, alarmed. Was he late? No, he still had two hours before his shift was due to start. An emergency? He hadn't heard anything, but emergencies rarely announced themselves in advance. Cursing under his breath, he finished drying himself and hurried out of the bathroom. His blue uniform was lying on the chair, waiting for him. He donned it quickly, taking the opportunity to study himself in the mirror. There was no way he'd win any beauty prizes, but he looked honest, friendly and trustworthy. Police on Earth might go around looking and sounding like soldiers in a war zone - an apt description of Earth's CityBlocks - but Arthur's Seat preferred a softer vision of policing.

"You spend more time in front of that mirror than I do," Jane teased. "Would you like to borrow some of my make-up?"

Mike glanced at her. She was shorter than him, her dark hair falling nearly to her shoulders and spilling around a white blouse and skirt. Her pregnancy was only just starting to show, a faint bump he would have missed if he hadn't known to look for it. It wouldn't be long before they had to talk to her bosses and make arrangements for her to take maternity leave, even though there was a good chance she'd lose her job. The economy was too weak for someone to be allowed to take long-term leave.

But she's a nurse, he thought. *She shouldn't have any trouble finding a new job.*

"I think I look handsome enough already," he said, striking a dramatic pose. His muscles failed to ripple, much to his disappointment. Fictional cops were either strikingly handsome, if they were the good guys, or ugly as sin, if they were the bad guys. Flicks rarely portrayed decent cops as ugly or vice versa. But then, the flicks were about as realistic as the old novels about a girl who went to magic school. "And make-up wouldn't improve my looks."

"Probably not," Jane agreed. She glanced at her watch. "I'll be heading out in an hour. Text me if you're coming back late."

Mike nodded, feeling a flicker of nervousness. It wasn't *common* for him to be called into the station ahead of time. If he was in trouble...but he wasn't in trouble. He *knew* he hadn't done anything to earn the ire of his superiors. And there was no drill scheduled, no football game on... something must have happened. But what?

He kissed his wife and walked out the door, collecting his bike from its shelter beside the garden path and wheeling it onto the road. A handful of people were already going to work, but the streets still seemed largely deserted. Rush hour didn't start for at least another hour as people hurried to their workplaces. Even then...he mounted the bike and peddled down the street, glancing from left to right. If there *had* been a disaster of some kind, there was no hint of it on the streets. In hindsight, he should have checked the datanet before he left the house.

Kicking himself, he kept pedalling until he finally reached the police station, a small building on the edge of the city centre. He dumped his bike into the rack - no one would dare to steal from a police station - and hurried into the building. It was surprisingly quiet, only two prisoners sitting on the benches waiting to be processed. They both looked like teens who'd had a little too much to drink the previous night, their eyes flickering nervously from side to side as if they expected the death penalty. Mike rather suspected their parents would be called to take them away, but nothing else. Arthur's Seat wasn't the kind of planet that locked up teens - still children, really - for drinking. If no one had been hurt, there was no need to take it further.

He smiled at the two prisoners, then walked through the security gate and into the briefing room. It was crammed. The room hadn't been designed to hold more than twenty men, but now there were nearly seventy packed into the compartment. Sergeant Steve Cox stood at the front of the room, glaring at the constables, while Captain Duncan Stewart was reading a datapad, his face growing darker and darker. Mike had never seen Stewart quite so upset before. Something must have gone *really* badly wrong.

"Take a seat," Cox ordered.

Mike nodded. Some helpful soul had brought in chairs and coffee from the cafeteria. Mike snagged a plastic cup of foul coffee and found a seat. It was so cramped that there would be complaints from the jails, if prisoners were forced into such close confines. His eyes swept the room, silently matching names to faces. There were just over a hundred constables assigned to the station - one of five in Lothian - and it looked like nearly all of them had been called in. He couldn't remember seeing so many officers in one place before, not even before football matches, when tempers ran high and fist-fights were the norm.

"Hey, Mike," Steve said. He'd entered training at the same time as Mike himself and they'd become fast friends. "You have any idea what's up?"

"Nothing," Mike said. "You?"

"Apparently, there was an emergency Cabinet meeting this morning," Steve said. "But I don't know what they were talking about..."

Mike frowned. Was the planet about to be attacked? Arthur's Seat had little to interest any *rational* conqueror, but he'd been a policeman long enough to know that some people - most people - weren't rational. And the Orbital Guard was puny. If Tarsus or Night's Dawn or Haven had decided to invade the system, there was very little standing in their way. And then...what? Were the police about to be told that they would have to serve an invading force? Or go into POW camps because they might lead resistance?

Not that it would make any difference, he thought, numbly. He was no military expert, but he'd read a lot of books set in the glory days of the Empire. *As long as the enemy controls the high orbitals, they can hammer us into submission.*

"Quiet," Cox said. The babble died away to nothingness. "Captain?"

Captain Stewart took the stand. "An emergency situation has developed," he said, his voice icy cold. "You - we - are being charged with dealing with it. I shouldn't have to say this, but I will. The matter we will be discussing today is *classified*. I will *break* any man who shares this information before a formal announcement is made."

Mike glanced at Steve, who looked equally puzzled - and concerned. Captain Stewart wasn't normally *that* much of a hard-ass. His men respected him as well as liked him. He didn't *need* to stamp around like a fictional police chief to get the point across. And that meant...

Someone must have been leaning on him, Mike thought. A chill ran down his spine. *And if there was a Cabinet meeting earlier today...it can't be a coincidence.*

"Within the next couple of days," Stewart continued, "a substantial number of refugees will be landed at the spaceport. These refugees were kicked off Tarsus shortly after the local government heard that Earth no longer existed. The Imperial Navy - or what's left of it - is shipping those refugees here."

Damn, Mike thought.

"The Cabinet has decided to accept the refugees," Stewart continued, darkly. He lowered his voice. "Reading between the lines, I suspect they weren't given a choice. This will put immense pressure on our emergency services, but we will rise to the challenge."

He paused. "You have all been assigned to relief services," he added. "You'll be moving out to the spaceport after we finish this briefing, with orders to start preparing emergency supplies, control lines and everything we need to ensure that the refugees are registered as quickly as possible. We'll be taking over the entire spaceport complex, working hand in hand with the other emergency workers. This will not be an easy task."

Mike swallowed. He couldn't help noticing that Captain Stewart had *not* mentioned any numbers. Stewart was too smart to miss that accidentally, which meant...what? Did he know? Or did he feel that his men didn't need to know? How *many* refugees were they talking about? And what *were* they?

Constable Mathews stuck up a hand. "Captain, can we rely on the civilian emergency workers?"

"We're about to find out," Stewart said. He didn't sound pleased. "They were called up shortly after yourselves."

Mike winced. The civilian emergency workers hadn't been mobilised for years. Hell, if he recalled correctly, the last full-scale drill had been three *years* ago. The civilians might have seen signing up as nothing more than a way to get an extra note on their résumé. It wasn't as if they were *needed*. The entire set of contingency plans had come close to being junked, several times. Disasters just didn't *happen* on Arthur's Seat.

"The estimated ETA for the refugees keeps changing," Stewart added, when no one else tried to interrupt. "The least-time estimate is thirty-six hours from now. I want to have the bare bones of a reception service ready before then. This will not be easy, but we can do it."

"Hah," Steve muttered.

Mike was inclined to agree. The police *did* have stockpiles of emergency supplies, but how long would they last? God knew they'd never been allowed to increase the stockpiles - the damned beancounters had insisted they were nothing more than a useless drain on resources - and they were scattered all over the continent. It would take a great deal longer than thirty-six hours to assemble them all in one place. And then? Who knew?

We might have to collect supplies from the farms, he thought. *That won't go down well.*

"These people have been through hell," Stewart warned. "They've just been kicked off one world and transported to another. Expect them to be distrusting, at first. Be calm, be reasonable, be understanding. They are not bad people merely because they've been dropped on us with only a few hours warning."

Sure, Mike agreed. *But there might have been a reason they were kicked off Tarsus.*

"The briefing notes are in the office processor," Stewart concluded. "Get yourselves some more coffee - and breakfast, if you need it - and then assemble at 1000 in the vehicle bay. We'll be moving the portable command post to the spaceport."

Mike rose with the rest of the officers. It was 0934. Just enough time to grab a bacon sandwich and another cup of foul coffee. He'd eaten breakfast, of course, but he had a feeling he was going to need more. There wasn't much at the spaceport, not when interstellar travel had been on the decline for years. And the emergency planning was so disorganised that it was quite possible that someone would forget to send food.

"Refugees," Steve said, as they hurried down the corridor. "What *sort* of refugees?"

Mike shrugged. "Good question."

"You do realise we're late for class?"

Judith Parkston shrugged. An evening dancing at the club, a night spent making love and a morning filled with gentle cuddles...she found it hard to care if she missed a class or two. Besides, she'd heard rumours that the entire course was going to be cancelled in the next month or two. The Arthurian University had never been a very big institution and it didn't have the political clout to keep claiming funds from the planetary government. And then...who knew?

She smiled at her girlfriend as Gayle rose and straddled Judith. They were different, strikingly different. Gayle was dark-haired, her narrow face suggesting descent from one of the Forsaker lines; Judith was blonde and bubbly, her muscles testament to her childhood on a farm. And yet, they'd found enough in common to share an apartment - and a bed - for the last six months. God alone knew where it would end - she doubted Gayle would be happy on a farm, if Judith had to go back home - but for the moment they were happy.

The phone bleeped just as Gayle's fingers were stroking the space between Judith's legs, sending shudders of ecstasy down her body. She cursed bitterly, then reached for the phone on the dressing table. She would have ignored her professor - as if the old goat would have bothered to call and find out where she was - but it was an emergency call. She'd been told, years ago, that failing to answer would result in a fine, perhaps even jail time. Judith wasn't sure how seriously to take the threat, but she knew her parents would be disappointed in her if she didn't answer. They were already annoyed with her for going to university.

She tapped her lips, warning Gayle to be quiet, then keyed the phone. "Parkston."

"Miss Parkston," a man's voice said. He sounded oddly familiar, but she couldn't place him. "This is an emergency situation. The designated assembly point in your area is the University Hall, 1100 hours. Your presence is requested. I say again, your presence is requested."

The call cut off before she could say a word, leaving her staring down at the phone in shock and disbelief. Her parents had urged her to sign up for emergency work, pointing out that she could use the stipend - and her skills might be useful, if there *was* an emergency. But she'd never really believed there *would* be an emergency. She'd certainly passed up several chances to withdraw her name from the roster before it was too late.

Gayle's hand reached down again. Judith pushed it away, gently.

"I need to go," she said. Gayle rolled off her, looking hurt. "That was an emergency call."

She swung her legs over the side of the bed and rose. The bedsit was standard student accommodation; she hurried into the kitchen to switch on the coffee maker, then ran into the bathroom. She *should* have enough time to take a shower and dress…what was she supposed to *wear*? She'd never given it any thought. She cursed herself under her breath as she washed away the evidence of their lovemaking, then dried herself and hurried back into the bedroom. Most of her student outfits would be grossly unprofessional, but she *did* have a tunic and shirt that would probably be suitable. Hell, if nothing else, she could sit through the briefing and then find something different to wear if necessary.

Gayle was sitting on the bed, her legs drawn up to cover herself. It was odd, Judith had thought, how her modesty came and went at the oddest of times. Gayle might have come from a Forsaker family, but none of them could be said to follow the old ways. Her distant ancestors were probably turning in their grave at the thought of Gayle's relationship with Judith.

"Do you have to go?"

"Yeah," Judith said. She pulled on her panties and bra, then found her trousers. "I get paid to go."

Gayle nodded. "Do you want me to come with you?"

"Not yet," Judith said. She'd never encouraged Gayle to sign up too. That might have been a mistake. "If they want additional manpower, do you want me to recommend you?"

"If you like," Gayle said. She paused. "It isn't going to be dangerous, is it?"

"It's probably just a drill," Judith said. The last drill had been chaotic. She'd only just signed up and she hadn't had the slightest idea what she was doing. "I'll be back tonight, ready and raring to go."

"Good," Gayle said. "And be careful."

Judith looked at her. "Why…?"

Gayle flushed. "It might not be a drill."

CHAPTER SIX

These people were often the pioneers of the slowboat era. Choosing to break all contact with Earth, they fitted fusion drives to their starships - in reality, hollowed-out asteroids - and boosted themselves into interstellar space. In the absence of a workable FTL drive system, they believed that interstellar traffic would be very limited - indeed, that it would never become practical to build and maintain an interstellar empire.

- Professor Leo Caesius. *Ethnic Streaming and the End of Empire.*

"Well, come on," the spacer snapped. "We don't have all day."

John braced himself and inched through the airlock into the shuttle. The air smelt faintly unpleasant, the scent of high technology blending with the stench of too many people in too close proximity for too long. It wasn't the first shuttle he'd ridden in, but last time he'd been too distracted to take note of his surroundings. This time, he couldn't help noticing that there was something oddly fragile about the shuttlecraft. The chairs looked…flimsy, as if they were made of plastic.

He made his way slowly down to the front of the craft and sat down by the porthole. There was nothing outside, but darkness. Surely there should be stars? It took him longer than it should, he realised numbly, to deduce that the porthole was pressed against the freighter's hull. The darkness was nothing more than hullmetal. Hannah sat next to him, her face pale and wan. A nasty bruise on her cheek showed where their mother had slapped her, several times, after she'd finally returned to the hold. She'd practically spent the next day as a prisoner in the female quarters.

John winced, cursing - once again - his own weakness. Their father had forbidden their mother to beat her daughter, but now their father was gone. And John himself was too weak to forbid their mother - or Konrad - from disciplining Hannah as they saw fit. He hoped, desperately, that they could find a way to save Hannah from marrying Joel, but nothing had come to mind. Joel was popular and powerful even without his network of fighters.

I'm sorry, he thought, bitterly. *Why am I so weak?*

He turned his head as a stream of passengers slowly filed onto the shuttles. Five of the nine Elders, led by Konrad…the remainder would stay on the freighter, at least until they knew it was safe to land. Not that it would matter, John thought. Joel had made it pretty clear that the Forsakers were going to be dumped on their new homeworld, whatever they had to say about the matter. And while John wouldn't normally have trusted anything Joel said, he doubted Joel would see any point in lying. The truth would come out very quickly.

"Buckle your straps, then remain in your seats until you are ordered to move," a voice said, firmly. "Anyone who attempts to get up and walk around will be stunned without warning."

John looked up and saw a spacer, standing by the hatch to the cockpit. A female spacer stood next to him, wearing yet another form-fitting outfit. He forced himself to look away, knowing that his mother might see him staring and report it to Konrad. God alone knew what Konrad would say, but John doubted it would be anything pleasant. He rubbed his forehead as the outer hatch slammed closed, a loud clang echoing through the shuttle. It was a relief to be *finally* off the big ship, but the shuttle was terrifyingly claustrophobic. He wouldn't feel safe until he was down on the surface, once again.

And what, he asked himself, *if we're being dumped on a penal colony?*

He'd heard the stories, back when he'd been forced to attend school on Tarsus. He hadn't believed them. Worlds where hardly anything grew, worlds where survival was a constant battle against the elements, worlds ruled by the strong…Surely, no place so unpleasant could exist. But if his entire community could be rounded up and kicked off Tarsus, maybe penal worlds *did* exist. And if they were being dumped on one…?

At least we'll be a community, he thought. *And there's a lot of us.*

He pushed the thought aside as the shuttle shook once, the gravity field seeming to grow stronger for a long second before slowly returning to normal. Hannah let out a quiet gasp as the shuttle shook again, then leaned forward so she could peer out the porthole. John followed her gaze, feeling a cold shiver running down his spine. The view had changed. The freighter hung in the midst of an endless darkness, cold pinpricks of light glaring down at them…below it, a green-blue orb dominated the scene. It looked terrifyingly small against the vastness of space…John felt his head spin as he tried to make sense of what he was seeing. The starship…

Man is not meant to walk amongst the stars, he thought. He'd been told that, again and again. And yet, the Forsakers had left their original homeworld over three hundred years ago, settling dozens of other worlds. *What does that make us?*

He gritted his teeth as the shuttle picked up speed, turning away from the freighter and heading down towards the planet below. John felt… *something*…running through the craft, a faint sensation that felt vaguely unpleasant. Behind him, he heard someone start to pray, calling on God to preserve them from the demon technology. The spacer, sitting on the other side of the row, looked annoyed, but did nothing as the prayers grew in volume. John wasn't sure if he should be relieved…or annoyed himself.

The shuttle rocked, suddenly. Outside, the darkness of space was blurring into blue-white wisps…the shuttle rocked, again and again. The sound of panic grew louder as the hull started to creak ominously, suggesting the entire craft was on the verge of falling apart. Had they been sent to their deaths? Cold logic suggested the freighter could have been depressurised - easily - if the crew had wanted them dead, but it was so hard to cling to logic as the shaking grew worse. A loud *BANG* echoed through the compartment, as if God had reached down and slapped the shuttle. John cringed, reaching out for Hannah's hand as another *BANG* shook the craft. What was going on?

"Remain in your seats," a voice said, calmly. "We are currently experiencing some mild turbulence."

Mild? John thought. The shaking was growing worse. *This is mild?*

He heard someone being noisily sick behind him. The stench was appalling, but there was nothing he could do. He closed his eyes, muttering prayers under his breath, hoping desperately that the shaking would end soon. If it was the end...he thought he might accept death, if it saved him from life. But instead...

The shaking slowly faded away, but he refused to open his eyes as faint tremors continued to run through the shuttlecraft. He was dimly aware of Hannah pressing against him as she peered out the porthole, yet he found it hard to care. No doubt Konrad would give him a hard time over letting her peer outside, but what was he meant to do about it? Cover her eyes and tie her hands? If she could bear to stare out of the shuttlecraft, more power to her.

Hannah elbowed him, none-too-gently. "Konrad's thrown up," she whispered. "Serves him right."

John swallowed, hard. "Keep your voice down," he hissed back. "He's right behind you."

He opened his eyes, somehow. Bright light was streaming through the porthole. He braced himself, then peered outside. They were flying over - or through - a vast blue expanse. A sea? He'd heard about the sea, yet he'd never seen it. Children at his old school had been offered trips to the seaside, but Konrad had refused to pay the fee. *He* had no interest in allowing his adopted children to play by the seaside. Hannah had been furious about it, afterwards. *She* could have gone with her friends.

The shuttle shuddered again, lightly. John tried to ignore it as he peered down towards the blueness below. Were those water-*ships* down there? He'd seen plenty of ships in picture books, but he'd never seen one in person. Did the children on their new home play on the water? It had seemed so much fun, according to the videos...yet he'd never had the chance to do that either. When he hadn't been at school, he'd been studying the holy books and learning to recite prayers. He certainly hadn't been taught anything useful.

"That must be the land," Hannah breathed. "We're going to be landing soon."

John sighed as the shuttle dropped towards the green land ahead. It looked pleasant from their height, but he was sure it wouldn't be any different from Tarsus. The people would be unwelcoming, there would be nothing for him to do…and, in the end, he'd be trapped with Joel and Konrad and the rest of the Forsakers, denied even the room they needed to breathe freely. There would be no farms or land, nothing but another grey estate. And it would be far worse for Hannah. Joel's wife wouldn't have any freedom whatsoever.

Unless Joel manages to get us all killed, he thought, morbidly. *Or if we get shipped back off-world in the next few weeks.*

"If I could have your attention, please," a voice said. It wasn't the spacer, not this time. The voice came from overhead. "We will be landing in twenty minutes, once ground control clears us a space. When you are told to rise, unbuckle your belts, get to your feet and walk to the hatch. You will have to pass through immigration processing before being allowed to proceed further. Obey all orders from personnel on the ground, whatever they are."

There was a long pause. "Oh," the voice added. "And welcome to Arthur's Seat."

Arthur's Seat? The name meant nothing to John. He'd known a kid called Arthur in class, years ago, but he doubted the planet was named after the kid he'd known. He tried to recall any starcharts he might have seen, yet nothing came to mind. He'd never taken any interest in space and space technology, knowing that it would merely get him in trouble. But…

Hannah gripped his arm. "This is where the lost colony went," she whispered. "They landed here, hundreds of years ago."

John blinked. Trust Hannah to remember something the Elders would probably prefer she forgot. He remembered hearing about the lost colony, but he didn't recall any actual details, save for Elder Chisholm using it to remind his flock that Outsiders couldn't be trusted. The settlers had been cheated, if he recalled correctly. And something else had gone wrong.

He looked back at his sister. "Do you think they'll welcome us?"

"I don't know," Hannah said. "The colony failed."

The shuttle seemed to come to a halt, then dropped. John clutched his stomach, all thoughts of the lost colony vanishing as the craft plummeted like a stone. He was *sure*, just for a second, that they were all about to die, a moment before the craft steadied itself. Outside, grey buildings were coming into view. They looked no more or less soulless than the buildings he remembered on Tarsus. A handful of people were standing by the nearest building, watching the shuttle as it came in to land. It was hard to make out details, but none of them *looked* like Forsakers. One of them was definitely a woman; the others *probably* male, although he wasn't sure.

Outsiders don't care what they wear, he thought.

He smiled, even though his stomach felt as if he'd left part of it behind. The tunic he wore - and the dress Hannah wore - told people everything they needed to know about him. He was male, old enough to marry and yet unmarried…they didn't need to know anything else. But Outsiders… women wore trousers and men wore skirts…it made no sense. How could you tell the difference?

You look, he told himself. *And you try not to look too closely.*

The hatch opened. "You may rise," the voice said. "And walk, one by one, out of the shuttle."

John looked at Hannah. "We're here," he said.

"Yeah," Hannah agreed. She sounded distracted. "We are."

Getting everything ready had been a nightmare, Constable Mike Whitehead thought, as he watched the first shuttle come in to land. Fifty *thousand* refugees? An estimated ten thousand landing every day? His experience told him that the estimate was wildly optimistic, but even so…how the hell were they going to process fifty *thousand* refugees in a reasonable space of time? He hadn't anticipated more than a couple of thousand during the desperate struggle to prepare the spaceport for guests.

He shook his head, slowly. The old transit barracks were long since gone, as were the prefabricated buildings that could have been assembled in short order. They'd had to commandeer the nearby warehouses under emergency powers, which had meant assisting the owners in clearing out the goods and finding somewhere else to store them. Mike suspected, from what he'd overheard, that the goods couldn't be sold any longer, not with the economic downturn in full swing. Hell, the owners were probably losing money all the time.

At least we got the warehouses cleared, he thought. *And stockpiles of food, drink and bedding are on their way.*

"Hey," he heard a female voice say. Mike turned to see a blonde girl walking towards him, wearing overalls that marked her as a civilian emergency worker. Her overall really was quite distractingly tight…he reminded himself, sternly, that he was married. "Sergeant?"

"Constable," Mike corrected. He'd occasionally thought about trying for promotion, but the qualification examinations were more murderous than the last five murderers arrested on Arthur's Seat. Besides, he didn't spend enough time with Jane as it was. "What can I do for you?"

The girl looked pained. "Is it *necessary* to seal off the entire spaceport?"

Mike hesitated. She wasn't the first civilian to question the need for wire. Hell, Mike wasn't sure himself why they had the wire in stock. None of the emergencies they'd *planned* for had any reasonable call for it. But they'd used it to seal off the entire spaceport and warehouse complex, leaving only two entrances. No one would be entering or leaving without checking with the guards.

"Yes," he said, finally. "We have to keep control of the situation."

The girl gave him a sharp look. "Are we going to be able to fit fifty thousand people into the complex?"

"They'll need tents," Mike said, grimly. The warehouses were huge, but fitting even a thousand people into the complex would be an absolute nightmare. Lothian spaceport hadn't been designed to handle thousands of passengers, let alone thousands of long-term guests. "It will not be comfortable."

He sighed. Winter was coming. He'd been in rough places before, during his training, but he had to admit he didn't like the idea of living in a tent during winter. Snow alone would make the tents largely unliveable. And who knew what would happen then? It would be hard to blame the refugees for rioting and demanding better accommodation.

Except there isn't that much better accommodation, he thought. *It's too soon to see how many people will open their homes to refugees.*

"Of course it won't be comfortable," the girl said. Mike dragged his attention back to her with an effort. "Something must be done."

"I suggest you speak to the captain," Mike said, after considering and rejecting several possible answers. When did a young girl from a farming background - she didn't *sound* like someone who had been raised in the city - get so demanding? It must be something in the university's water. "I'm just a constable. I do what I'm told."

He turned his attention back to the shuttle. Three men were disembarking and advancing towards the welcoming committee, two looking like Forsakers from the historical documentaries that detailed life during the early settlement period. Long beards, handmade clothes…there was something oddly primitive about them, something that bothered him more than he cared to admit. And yet, he couldn't put his finger on it.

"They're *real*," the girl said.

Mike glanced at her, sharply. "Did you think this was all a drill?"

The girl flushed. "That's not what I meant," she said. "I meant…they wear those clothes as if they *mean* something. You know…like you wear your uniform."

Mike stroked his chin. Any fool could dress up as a policeman - although it was technically illegal - but no impostor would be able to fool a real policeman for long. And fooling a member of the public would be difficult too. Wearing the uniform alone didn't make someone a policeman. They'd need everything from stance and posture to a comprehensive knowledge of the law. *He* had training and experience no imposter could hope to have.

And the girl had a point. The two Forsakers weren't actors, they weren't some of the older families wearing traditional clothes for the Harvest Festival or Winter Night; those *were* their clothes. They had nothing else. Hell, who knew *what* had happened to their communal possessions? The manifests Mike had seen hadn't been too clear.

"They *are* Forsakers," he breathed. He couldn't help wondering what some of the older families would make of their cousins. Good news…or bad? "And they're here?"

He turned away from the girl, studying the newcomers. The older man looked resigned, the younger man…looked like a fighter. Mike had seen people like that before, men - usually men - spoiling for a fight. They could be dangerous…

I must bring it to the captain's attention, he thought. *And let him decide what to do.*

CHAPTER SEVEN

> The various governments on Earth rarely sponsored these programs, seeing the asteroid ships as giant wastes of resources at best. Accordingly, those who did set sail on the interstellar sea tended to be self-selected groups, people who tended to be strikingly monocultural. Whatever their culture, they could not tolerate the prospect of dissent within an enclosed ecosystem.
> - Professor Leo Caesius. *Ethnic Streaming and the End of Empire.*

Joel couldn't help feeling a flicker of concern as his father stumbled towards the shuttle hatch and out onto the landing field. Konrad hadn't enjoyed the flight at all, throwing up several times into a bag the spacers had generously provided. Even now, with his feet on a planetary surface once again, Konrad looked weak and feeble. Joel was quite prepared to believe - and spread the word - that the Elders were weak and feeble, but he was worried about his ancient father. The old man couldn't be allowed to die just yet.

Because that would complicate matters, Joel reminded himself, as he took his first breath on Arthur's Seat. *And because I would miss him.*

The air tasted…strange. It was better than the canned and recycled air on the freighter, yet bore unfamiliar hints of something *alien*. Arthur's Seat had had a surprisingly strong native biosphere, according to the files he'd read. It was part of the reason the original colony had run into trouble before the *second* group of settlers had arrived. The spaceport itself was a gray monstrosity: a giant control tower, a network of hangars and terminals and buildings with no obvious function. He glanced up, sharply, as he heard another shuttlecraft high overhead. But he saw nothing. The skies appeared clear.

He put out a steadying hand - as a good and dutiful son should do - and supported Konrad as they walked towards the welcoming committee. One of them was clearly a woman, with curly red hair and a narrow face that reminded Joel of his mother. A Forsaker? Or, perhaps, someone who had a Fallen somewhere in their family tree. Would that make her a Fallen herself or an Outsider? He didn't particularly care to know. The others were all men, he thought. None of them looked particularly threatening.

Good, Joel thought. *That will make matters easier.*

The spacer glanced at them, then stopped. "Go on," he said. "I'll speak to them afterwards."

Joel frowned, but kept walking forward. The woman greeted them with a blinding smile, an expression so wide and open that Joel distrusted it on sight. What was she *doing* amongst the group? If she was a Forsaker, she should know better than to put herself forward. And her outfit...Joel had seen worse, on Tarsus, but still...he wouldn't have allowed any wife, sister or daughter of his to wear anything of the sort. It didn't show much bare flesh, yet he could still make out the shape of her body.

"Greetings," the woman said. She didn't have a Forsaker accent, he noted absently. But then, that proved nothing. "Welcome to Arthur's Seat."

Konrad stiffened, clearly unsure how to proceed. Joel didn't blame him. One simply did *not* talk to an unrelated female, at least not without a very good excuse. It was considered polite to simply ignore the woman's presence, rather than call attention to her. But who should Konrad address?

"I am Vice Premier Sondra Mackey," the woman continued. If she was aware of Konrad's bemusement, she showed no sign of it. Her title made her sound fairly senior, although Joel had no idea how Arthur's Seat was governed or where a Vice Premier fitted into the structure. "We are truly sorry that you were evicted from Tarsus. We intend to do everything in our power to make sure you fit into our society as quickly as possible."

"I...thank you," Konrad managed. He stood as though he was addressing everyone, not just Sondra. It was, Joel considered, an admirable compromise. "It has been a very long journey."

A flicker of...*something*...crossed Sondra's face. "You and your people should vacate the shuttle as quickly as possible," she said, indicating one of the giant buildings behind her. A massive door led into darkness. There didn't seem to be any light inside. "Once the shuttle is empty, it can return to orbit for the next load."

Joel nodded in approval. The more people on the ground, the harder it would be for the locals to push them around. And more of his allies would be coming down on the next two shuttles. They'd have to explore their new environment as quickly as possible, learn how to sneak around without being detected...and then start pressing demands.

Konrad seemed to have other ideas. "We were promised lands," he said, flatly. "When will we be able to take them?"

"A final decision will be made once you have passed through immigration," Sondra said, carefully. Joel suspected that meant that *no* lands would be forthcoming. He would have felt betrayed, if he hadn't already anticipated it. "We had no time to make preparations for you."

"Understandable," Konrad said.

He glanced at Joel. "Call the others out of the shuttle."

"Yes, father," Joel said.

He blinked in surprise as Sondra held out a hand to his father. Did she expect him to *shake* her hand? Perhaps she did...Outsiders had no understanding of the importance of keeping a barrier between male and female. Konrad was an Elder. He couldn't speak to an unrelated woman, particularly an Outsider, without having his position questioned by his fellows. And if Konrad happened to be stripped of his title, Joel doubted it would come to him.

Sondra withdrew her hand, her face expressionless. She was a practiced politician, but Joel thought she was irked. It hardly mattered. Her embarrassment was irritating, yet his father losing his position would be far worse. And besides, it would make it clear that the Forsakers would not be changing their ways. He turned, shouted for the rest of the shuttle's passengers and then allowed a young man to lead them into the giant warehouse. It was immense, larger than the warehouses on Tarsus, yet far too small for the freighter's passengers...

And then there are the other freighters, he thought. *And there might be others still.*

He smiled at the thought as he collected a blanket, a bedroll and a small packet of rations from the immense pile. The spacer had warned him that other planets might follow Tarsus's lead and start deporting their Forsakers too. And if that happened...

We might grow to be the majority very quickly, he thought. *And won't that be interesting?*

Judith barely noticed when the cop excused himself and headed off to do some police work on the other side of the spaceport. She was too busy watching the Forsakers as they disembarked from the shuttle, many of them staggering around like students who'd just drunk themselves silly for the first time since leaving home. Forsakers didn't drink, according to the briefing notes. They'd probably reacted badly to the flight through the upper atmosphere and down to the ground. Judith was no expert in space technology, but she wouldn't have willingly boarded the shuttle they'd used. It looked as though it was steadily falling apart.

It probably is, she thought, as she studied the next set of immigrants. She'd seen a bulletin on the datanet from a Rear Admiral Carlow, practically offering the sun and the moon to any space-certified engineers willing to sign on with the Imperial Navy. *If they're that desperate for manpower, what does it say about their ships?*

She dismissed the thought as the immigrants slowly gathered themselves and marched towards the hangar. They looked odd, although it was hard for her to put her finger on *why* they looked odd. They moved with a sullen resignation mixed with defiance, their eyes flickering around as if they were unsure if they should be cowering back from a blow or getting ready to deliver one. The older men and women just kept their heads down, the younger ones seemed more alert. She found herself staring at a handsome young man, his face covered with flecks of stubble, wondering just what was going through his mind. Men had rarely interested her, but there was an oddness about him that called to her.

Gritting her teeth, she moved her attention to a pair of young girls. It was impossible to be *sure*, if only because their dresses were utterly shapeless, but she placed them at being no older than seventeen. Their eyes were constantly looking down, as if they were reluctant to look up and make eye contact with anyone. An older woman was following them, watching them like a hawk. Judith couldn't help noticing that they shied away from men, even their fellow Forsakers. Were they *that* reluctant to be near them?

She'd been right, she told herself. These weren't men and women wearing traditional clothes for a day, either to celebrate or to remember what they'd left behind. These *were* their clothes and…and that was their life. She'd never really considered the Forsakers to be different from their fellows, but none of the Forsakers she knew - like Gayle - were *true* Forsakers. How could they be? Their ancestors had been so desperate, when the rightful settlers arrived, that they'd abandoned their traditions with terrifying speed.

But these people are different, she thought, grimly. *They never had that experience to shape their lives.*

She felt a stab of pity as a dozen children, boys and girls wearing archaic clothing, were escorted across the tarmac and into the hangar. They looked…beaten down, their faces shadowed by their experiences. Judith had no idea what it was like to be disliked, if not hated, by everyone, just for being different, but she could imagine it. Her life would have been unliveable if everyone had hated her family. The children were thin, terrifyingly thin…had they been fed? Or had the spacers not bothered to provide food for the children?

The ground crew hurried over to the shuttle and started to work, helping a handful of older men and women out of the craft. Judith felt another flicker of sympathy, mixed with a strange kind of contempt. The older folk looked ill, their skins pockmarked with the remains of diseases… diseases that could be beaten, easily, with the right kind of medicines and vaccines. But the Forsakers had never been keen on any form of modern medicine, if she recalled correctly. *Their* women still suffered through monthly bleeding a simple implant could halt.

Poor bitches, she thought. Judging by the way the ground crew was working, some - perhaps most - of the passengers had thrown up. There were treatments for that too. *It's no life for anyone.*

She sighed as she turned back to the workplace. More shuttles appeared overhead, dropping down towards the spaceport. She'd been on a break, but there would be more work for everyone in the next few hours. The newcomers would have to be processed before they were moved into the warehouses, where they would be held until…until what? No one she'd met had had any idea of what would happen in the future. Fifty thousand…Judith's father had often ranted about the need to get more farmers into the countryside, but fifty thousand untrained newcomers? She hadn't forgotten the handful of students who'd volunteered to live and work in the country without the slightest idea of what they were getting into. Only five out of twenty had lasted the entire month…

…And only two of them had chosen to stay, afterwards.

We'll have to see what happens when it happens, she told herself, firmly. Making a mental note to call Gayle - her friend might have some insight - she headed back to the control room to receive her next assignment. *Until then, all we can do is take care of them.*

John and Hannah hung back as the shuttle emptied, allowing the others to go first before they reluctantly left the craft. The air smelt funny, but it was better than the stench of vomit from the craft's interior. Konrad hadn't been the only one to be sick, apparently. John knew it was cruel, but he savoured the memory anyway. It was nice to know that Konrad was weaker than he acted.

And perhaps he wasn't the only one, John thought. *Did Joel throw up?*

He barely noticed the giant warehouse - or whatever it was - as he stared around the spaceport. It was immense, huge beyond words…it seemed large enough to take the entire community and have room left over. And yet, as more shuttles dropped from the sky, he couldn't help thinking that he wouldn't be happy there. The spaceport practically *stunk* of technology.

"Move along," a voice called. "This isn't a safe place."

John looked up. A man was standing there, wearing a blue uniform that made him look like a spacer. His face was pleasant, although there was a hint of paternal firmness that reminded John of his father. A man who was on his side, a man who would fight for him…but also a man who wouldn't hesitate to correct him when he was wrong. John felt a stab of bitter regret, which he swiftly suppressed. His father was in a better place, leaving him and his family alone. If only he'd been older when he died…

"Nowhere is safe," Hannah said, bitterly.

John glanced around, automatically, as she spoke. Speaking to a strange man…their mother would be furious. Konrad would be upset too. And Joel…

"No one is going to hurt you here," the man said. He pointed to the giant warehouse as another flight of shuttles screamed overhead. "Go get something to eat and drink, then wait."

John met his eyes. "For what?"

"For processing," the man said, simply.

"Thank you," Hannah said. "Who are you?"

"Constable Mike Whitehead," the man said. He smiled at her. "But I suggest you move, now."

John stared at him. "You're a policeman?"

"Of course," the policeman said. He sounded amused, rather than upset. "I've been a policeman for nearly seven years."

Despite himself, John nearly accused the older man of lying. The policemen on Tarsus had never struck him as trustworthy. They'd walked around in groups, wearing armour, carrying weapons and generally looking more fearsome than soldiers. And they'd done nothing, nothing at all, when gangs had hurled insults, threats and rocks at Forsakers. They'd made their opinions quite clear. And there were plenty of horror stories about what happened to their prisoners…

But this man was a policeman?

"Move now," the policeman advised. His voice was gentle, but firm. "There'll be more people passing through in a moment."

John caught Hannah's arm and led her towards the warehouse, his mind spinning. A nice policeman? It was unthinkable. And yet, he was *sure* the policeman was a good guy. He hadn't looked at them with scorn or hatred, his eyes hadn't undressed Hannah - or John either, for that matter - he'd treated them like real people. What, he asked himself, did that mean?

And if the policemen are nice, he thought as they stepped into the giant building, *what does that say about the rest of the world?*

It wasn't as dark as he'd feared inside the building. The fifty-odd shuttle passengers were clumped up at the far end, some lying on bedrolls while others were eating from small ration packs. Joel and a couple of others were trying to rig up a shelter for the women, hiding them from the couple of locals near the main doors. John rolled his eyes, then took a ration pack and a bedroll for himself. Hannah took one too, then winked at him as they made their way down to the far end.

"Hold this," Joel directed, holding out one end of a blanket. "And keep facing outwards."

John nodded, unwilling to speak. The policeman had upended everything he'd feared about their new world. And he'd done it just by being a nice guy. And that meant…what?

"Anyone who looks back will get a beating," Joel added, raising his voice so everyone could hear. There was no disagreement. "The women are to have their privacy!"

Konrad coughed in agreement. He didn't look any better, John noted. His stepfather looked as if he were on the verge of outright collapse, as if the only thing keeping him upright was his cane. John knew he should feel guilty for thinking that, but it was hard to care. Konrad might have tried to do his duty by them, yet he put his own son first. John might have been less offended by that if Konrad hadn't been planning to marry Joel to Hannah.

But we're not settled yet, he thought, as he shifted position. The next set of refugees were already spilling into the warehouse, led by a pair of Stewards. Joel hurried forward to talk to them, leaving the human shields alone. *And they can't get married until they're settled.*

He yawned, suddenly. He wanted to sleep, but he knew that wasn't possible. Joel probably hadn't thought to ask if the women could have a separate compartment all to themselves. Or perhaps he hadn't had time to make his wishes known…no, that wasn't possible. Joel was *very* good at making his wishes known. Konrad practically gave him everything he wanted, without question. John's father hadn't been quite so accommodating.

And if anyone gets a farm, John thought bitterly, *it will be him.*

He shook his head. The policeman had given him hope, but all he could do now was wait…

…And see what happened next.

CHAPTER EIGHT

And then the Phase Drive was discovered. All of a sudden, high-speed interstellar traffic became possible. The result was an immediate land grab, resulting in the establishment of settlements all across the Sol Sector. These colonists either landed on worlds settled by the slowboats or established colonies before the slowboats arrived.
- Professor Leo Caesius. *Ethnic Streaming and the End of Empire.*

"You are to take their fingerprints and check them against the records," Director Melbourne said. Judith listened as the older woman spoke, her voice tired. "If they don't raise red flags, screen their blood, give them the vaccination injection and send them on to the next chamber."

Judith nodded. She wasn't a qualified medic - although she did have a first aid badge - but any fool could handle an injector tab. Sitting down at the table, she ran her eye down the checklist, silently reminding herself of the potential dangers. Most people didn't have any bad reactions to broad-spectrum vaccines, but it was well to be careful. A bad reaction could be very dangerous.

But so could allowing them to set foot outside the spaceport without it, she thought, as she lifted her eyes and surveyed the room. *Even bringing them down to the planet without a blood test could be dangerous.*

The room itself was clean and sterile, mind-numbingly bland. Director Melbourne and her team had set up a row of six tables, crewed by her personnel. It would take hours, Judith knew, to get the refugees - or at least the ones who had already landed - through the screening process. And weeks, perhaps, to screen all fifty thousand Forsakers. The refugees had been landing for barely two hours and the hangars were already crammed with warm bodies.

At least they're not on the ships any longer, Judith thought. She checked her terminal, then the alarm button as the main doors opened. *That has to count for something, doesn't it?*

"Form into lines," Director Melbourne ordered. Her voice echoed in the air. "Once you have been screened, proceed immediately into the next chamber."

The refugees started streaming into the room. Some looked dazed, glancing around as though they didn't quite know where they were; others looked tired or angry or just plain wary. Judith felt a stab of sympathy as the lines started to form up. The sooner they were through the screening process, the better. And yet, the refugees seemed to be milling about, rather than advancing forward. Why were they reluctant to move?

She looked up as a middle-aged woman limped towards her. Judith frowned - modern medicine would have fixed that in an hour, perhaps less - and then keyed her terminal as she motioned for the woman to sit down. She wore yet another shapeless dress, so baggy that Judith honestly wasn't sure if she was desperate to hide her body's curves or really just incredibly fat. Her face looked disapproving, her eyes crossing Judith's body in a manner that made Judith want to cover herself. She'd known jerk jocks who were more subtle about ogling her.

"Please, be seated," she said. It crossed her mind, suddenly, that the woman might not speak Imperial Standard. Legally, *everyone* had to speak the same language, but a Forsaker community might have evaded the requirement. "I need to ask you a few questions."

The woman eyed her, balefully. "Why?"

"We need to know who we are dealing with," Judith said. She'd expected the refugees to be a little more *grateful*. "Do you have a birth certificate?"

"No," the woman said.

Judith blinked. *Everyone* had a birth certificate, without exception. Imperial Law mandated it. She couldn't imagine any world, certainly not one as cosmopolitan as Tarsus, neglecting to issue birth certificates. Its population couldn't travel off-world without one. Hell, the fines alone would have been disastrous.

"You never had a birth certificate?"

"It was stolen when we were deported," the woman said. Her voice twisted, bitterly. "It isn't important."

Judith swallowed the urge to correct her, sharply. Birth certificates *were* important. How *else* would anyone know the woman's history? But there was no point in demanding a certificate the woman didn't have. She shook her head, then leaned forward.

"Name?"

"Alicia, Daughter of Bridget," the woman said. "Mother of Sven and Elsa."

Judith frowned. "Is your mother in the refugee party?"

"My mother died months ago," Bridget said. "She was killed by a mob."

"I'm sorry to hear that," Judith said. The system wasn't set up to track Forsakers. The more traditional families didn't even have *surnames*. "And your children?"

"With their father," Bridget said. She nodded to the rear, then turned and motioned them forward. "They're sweet kids."

Judith kept her face impassive as Sven, Elsa and a middle-aged man she assumed was their father appeared behind Bridget. Both children looked to be in their early teens, although their clothes were so baggy it was hard to be sure. Sven took one look at her, then looked away; Elsa eyed her expressionlessly, her eyes flickering over Judith's face. Judith looked back at her for a long moment, wondering what was going through the girl's mind. Her brother, blushing furiously, was easy to read. And their father…Judith couldn't help feeling that he was looking at her as if she was something particularly nasty he'd scraped off his shoe.

She entered their details into the database, then held out the scanner. "I need to check your blood, just to make sure you're not carrying anything dangerous," she said. "Bare your upper arms, please."

Bridget recoiled in shock. "You're going to take blood?"

"Yes," Judith said. She felt her patience start to crack. The older man was still staring at her with deep hostility. "And when your blood has been tested, you will be given a vaccination to make sure you can live on our planet safely..."

"Out of the question," the older man snapped. He pulled his children back. "We do *not* allow our children to be vaccinated."

Judith - barely - managed to refrain from asking how they'd survived on Tarsus. A cosmopolitan planet - and city - would have visitors from all over the galaxy. The prospect of catching something nasty, perhaps one of the innumerable variants of the common cold, couldn't be dismissed. Children normally received vaccinations at birth and booster shots throughout their lives, just to prevent diseases from spreading. Maybe they'd just been very lucky.

"It's a requirement," she said, glancing towards Director Melbourne. The older woman seemed to be in the middle of an agitated discussion with two of the other refugees. "If you don't have your blood tested and your children screened, you can't leave the spaceport."

She looked up at him. He seemed torn between glaring at her and looking away, his face twitching as if he wasn't quite sure what to do. His son seemed torn too; his wife and daughter studiously looking away, allowing him to deal with the situation. Judith wondered, suddenly, just what sort of life the womenfolk endured. If they weren't allowed to have vaccinations, what else weren't they allowed to do?

"We are not going to be staying here," the man thundered. "We were promised land!"

Judith flinched back as he waved his fist under her nose, her finger hitting the panic button as the crowd pushed forward, shouting in several different languages. She couldn't understand most of them, but it was clear that half the crowd didn't understand. They thought she intended to take *all* of their blood, then poison them. And Director Melbourne seemed entirely incapable of taking control.

She half-rose, then stopped herself as the shouting grew louder. The police would be on their way, wouldn't they? And then...and then what? More and more refugees were being landed, every hour on the hour. If they all refused to be vaccinated, the spaceport population would keep growing until the wire burst. And then...

Someone pushing at her table brought her back to reality. The crowd was pushing her back, pushing them all back. A terminal fell off a table, smashing to the ground; an aid worker, one of the youngest in the group, turned and fled. The sign of weakness seemed to embolden the crowd, just as the rear doors opened and a stream of policemen flowed into the room. It crossed Judith's mind, just for a second, that the police weren't carrying any weapons...

Riots, Mike knew, were rare on Arthur's Seat. The occasional football match might end badly, a few dozen people might have too much to drink and end up starting a fight...but outright riots were rare. He'd never seen anything more dangerous than a drunken brawl in a pub after nightfall. Dealing with them wasn't too difficult...

...But the scene before him was different. Hundreds of Forsakers were pressing forward, smashing their way through the tables and chairs by sheer weight of numbers. He couldn't understand half their words, but it was clear, just from what he *did* understand, that they were angry about something. Director Melbourne was doing her level best to calm the crowd, yet it was clear - even to her - that they weren't listening. There was a *lot* of pent-up frustration being released...

"Form up, truncheons out," Sergeant Cox snapped. "Get the workers out first!"

Mike winced. *And then what?*

He cursed under his breath. The makeshift registration centre was no place for a fight, not when they didn't have any stunners or anything else that could be used to control a riot. Two constables hurried over to the fire hose mounted on the wall and started to get it ready for use, but he doubted it would be enough to do more than drench the rioters. Perhaps it would bring them back to sanity, perhaps it would just make them mad. But they were already mad.

"We keep them in here," Cox added. He'd put in a call for reinforcements as soon as the alert had sounded. "And we don't let them out!"

Mike gritted his teeth as he took a firmer grip on his truncheon. He'd rarely needed to use it, not outside combat training. It was designed more for intimidation than anything else - and even *that* was considered a last resort. But now, with a mob advancing on him, he wanted something more solid. A gun…the police didn't use guns, not on Arthur's Seat, but perhaps it was time they changed. They didn't normally face rioters bent on tearing them apart either.

They'll be summoning a posse, he told himself. There just weren't many other policemen within easy reach of the spaceport. *But will they get here in time?*

The mob surged forward, shouting and screaming; the constables turned the hose on them, playing the water over their bodies. Mike watched in relief as the crowd came apart, their bodies drenched in cold water. They didn't seem inclined to keep going, thankfully. But he knew that wouldn't last. Standard procedure was to break up a riot into smaller, more manageable groups, but there were too many people confined within too small a place. The Forsakers outside the compartment would just keep pushing into the room…

"Enough," a voice said.

Mike stared. An older man - probably in his fifties, although it was impossible to be sure - had clambered onto one of the tables. He looked formidable as he harangued the crowd in a language Mike couldn't understand, although the tone was clear. The crowd was being stupid and needed to stop. Mike wasn't sure if he should admire the man's nerve - it took courage to berate an angry crowd - or suspect trouble. Was the man their leader? Or was he trying to take advantage of the near-riot?

Fuck, he thought, morbidly.

The crowd, looking surprisingly shamefaced, started to inch out of the room. Mike watched them go, unsure if he should be relieved or worried. Training or no training, a fight in close quarters would probably have gotten a lot of police and refugees killed. They hadn't practiced riot suppression in months. It had just never seemed important.

Director Melbourne looked badly shaken. "Thank you for coming."

"You're welcome," Cox said. "What now?"

Mike ignored the brief discussion as he glanced around the room. Tables had been tipped over, computer terminals lay on the floor...they were designed to be tough, he knew, but would they survive the combination of the impact and water damage? The aid workers looked shocked, two almost looked catatonic. None of them had expected the refugees to turn nasty, all of a sudden. A handful had already started to put the tables back upright and test the computers. Mike wasn't sure if he should applaud their resilience or be concerned about their refusal to grasp what had just happened.

"We let too many people in at once," Director Melbourne said. She sounded stunned - and frustrated. "And others followed them in."

"You'll need to be more careful," Cox said. His voice was grim. "What set them off?"

An aid worker - the girl Mike had met earlier - leaned forward. "They objected to blood tests and vaccinations, sir," she said. She sounded shaken, although she looked unharmed. Her shirt was wet, clinging to her body in a manner that made Mike look away hastily. "That's what set them off."

Mike frowned. The original Forsakers had forbidden genetic enhancements, if he recalled correctly. He couldn't remember if they banned vaccinations or not, but the vast majority of modern-day vaccinations *were* designed to splice improvements into a person's genome. Or so he thought. It hadn't been covered at school and he'd been more concerned with first aid than long-term medical treatments during his training.

"They need them," Director Melbourne said. "We can't let them pass through the gates unless we're sure they're safe."

She closed her eyes for a long moment. "It will have to be referred to higher authority."

Mike wasn't surprised. Director Melbourne hadn't struck him as the type of person who would pass the buck, but the whole situation had already spun out of control. Either she insisted on the refugees taking the vaccinations anyway - probably restarting the riot - or she waived the requirement, which would run the risk of triggering a health crisis. And he honestly wasn't sure if they could stop another riot so quickly.

They've discovered that they can intimidate us, he thought, sourly. It was a chilling realisation. Most people he dealt with respected the uniform, even if they didn't respect him personally. None of the newcomers would have that experience. *And we're not allowed to intimidate them.*

"See to it," Cox urged. He reached for his radio. "I'll get the reinforcements briefed."

"Can you station some men here?" Director Melbourne asked. "It might keep the situation from getting out of control."

It's already out of control, Mike thought. *And that isn't going to change.*

He glanced at her. "Can you stop the inflow of refugees?"

"I can try," Director Melbourne said. She didn't sound optimistic. "But the Imperial Navy is trying to get them down as quickly as possible."

Mike nodded, running through the math in his head. There were fifty thousand refugees in total, give or take a few hundred souls who'd been overlooked. Assuming that two thousand were landed every hour, there were at least four thousand refugees on the ground now and another two thousand incoming. By the time the government made its decision, there might be upwards of *ten* thousand refugees on the ground…by which point the spaceport would be bursting at the seams. It just hadn't been designed to hold so many people.

They can't keep dumping so many people into a confined space, he thought. There were definite limits, surely. Even converting the entire spaceport into a refugee camp wouldn't provide enough space. *But will they just start dumping them outside the spaceport?*

"Mike, Joe, Roger, stay here and look intimidating until the captain gets here," Cox ordered, briskly. If he resented being left in the hot seat, he showed no sign of it. "I'm going to talk to the leader."

"Just ask them to take you to their leader, Sarge," Constable Johan said.

Cox gave him a stern look, then allowed Director Melbourne to lead him towards the rear doors. Mike took a moment to admire his nerve - walking into an angry crowd might easily get him killed - then cursed under his breath. They'd need to get more weapons - and training - before it was too late. And he honestly wasn't sure if the weapons they needed were anywhere on the planet.

Perhaps we should ask the Imperial Navy to lend us some spacesuits, he thought. He made a mental note of the idea, intending to pass it on to his superiors as soon as possible. *They'd serve as makeshift armour if we couldn't get anything better.*

He cursed under his breath as the reinforcements arrived, led by Captain Stewart. Stewart had been at the other side of the spaceport when the riot began, Mike knew, but that didn't stop him feeling a flicker of resentment. It was unfair - he *knew* it was unfair - yet he felt it anyway. Stewart should have been with his men, facing the danger…a danger they weren't trained to face. Hell, it wasn't as if Arthur's Seat had a real army. The Orbital Guard wasn't a military in anything more than name.

Of course not, he thought. *We never saw the need to build starships and raise an army.*

He shuddered at the thought. The police were the closest thing to a professional military on Arthur's Seat and, really, very few of them had any experience with firearms or military tactics. But he had a nasty feeling that was about to change.

CHAPTER NINE

Unsurprisingly, this led to conflict. The settlers might not be willing or able to integrate the newcomers. Worse, the side with FTL could and did bring in help from Earth. The slowboaters tended to get the worst of these conflicts because they hadn't thought to prepare for a war when they reached their destination.
- Professor Leo Caesius. *Ethnic Streaming and the End of Empire.*

Joel had to fight to keep the glee off his face.

It had worked perfectly. Hell, it had worked better than he'd expected. And he hadn't really had to do anything, beyond making sure his friends and allies were ready to take advantage of the chaos. *Something* had been bound to happen, *someone* had been bound to protest, when the community was told they needed to be vaccinated. And someone had. The only real surprise had been his father standing up and quieting the crowd before matters got even further out of hand...

He still has influence, Joel thought. *But does he have enough influence to make a difference?*

The waiting room was surprisingly quiet. Being drenched had shocked the Forsakers, even before Konrad had opened his mouth. A number of girls were trying, desperately, to hide themselves, their fathers and brothers forming protective circles around them. Their humiliation wouldn't be forgotten in a hurry. Indeed, a deep anger was burning through the room, threatening further trouble in the future. Konrad had calmed them, for the moment, but that wouldn't last. It wouldn't be long before the issue of vaccinations reared its ugly head again.

Konrad rose from his squatting position as the door opened, revealing a man and a woman stepping into the room. The woman looked shaken - Joel felt a flicker of cold satisfaction - while the man looked grim. His uniform marked him out as a person of authority, even though Joel found it hard to believe he was really a policeman. What sort of policeman didn't carry a gun? Or a stunner? Or a neural whip? The blue uniform made him look like an actor, not a very dangerous man.

He followed his father as he walked to greet the newcomers, trying not to stare *too* openly at the woman as he basked in her discomfiture. A woman should not try to assert authority over men, over the outside world. Nothing but embarrassment and humiliation would result. Joel would no more take orders from a woman than he would invade the female quarters and start cooking for himself. Women had their place, just as men did. People who tried to live in both worlds were doomed to disappointment.

"Greetings," the woman said. Even her *voice* sounded shaky, as if she had no true authority of her own. Clearly, she'd been allowed to *think* she had authority. "Who are you?"

"I am Konrad, Elder and First Speaker," Konrad said. He addressed the policeman, rather than the woman. "Our people will not be vaccinated."

The woman's face twisted. "You need to be vaccinated, if only to make sure you do not catch any diseases," she said, bluntly. "Your people will be vulnerable to diseases on our world."

She paused. "And you will not be allowed to leave the spaceports without registering, having your blood tested and being vaccinated," she added. "You'll be spending the rest of your lives in the spaceport complex."

Joel rather doubted it. He hadn't seen *much* of the spaceport, but he doubted it could hold over ten thousand people at once. Tarsus had uprooted and deported dozens of Forsaker communities. Cramming them *all* into the spaceport would be utterly disastrous. He had no doubt sheer numbers alone would allow them to break out and escape.

"I will not force my people to inject themselves with the demon technology," Konrad said, firmly. "It would be wrong."

The policeman leaned forward. "How did you escape vaccinations on Tarsus?"

"The government chose not to vaccinate us," Konrad said.

It was true enough, Joel knew. He had a private suspicion that the government had quietly hoped that something particularly nasty would reduce the Forsaker population to a more manageable level. He'd certainly used the suggestion to convince his allies that fighting was the only option, particularly when the government might eventually use more direct methods to rid itself of a problem. But they had escaped infection, proving that the Forsakers had been right all along. The demon technology brought misery in its wake.

"Our government is less equipped to deal with health problems," the woman said. She paused. "At the very least, we need to be sure you're not carrying diseases."

Joel felt a flicker of triumph. A sign of weakness, already! If they were prepared to compromise on vaccinations, what *else* were they prepared to compromise on? Blood tests weren't as bad as vaccinations, as far as the Forsakers were concerned…they took something out, rather than putting something in.

"We are clean," Konrad insisted, firmly. "None of us are diseased."

"We didn't mean to say that you were," the woman told him. "But we have to be sure before we let you leave the spaceport."

"We also need to register your population," the policeman added. "Why don't you have birth certificates?"

"Tarsus wasn't interested in issuing them either," Konrad said.

And the ones they did issue were stolen or destroyed, Joel thought. He allowed himself a cold smile. Passive resistance hadn't gotten them very far, but it was *something. And I sold a number of official birth certificates to raise money.*

"We will address the problem," the policeman said. "Until then, you will have to wait."

Joel smiled as Konrad nodded in agreement. Unless he was very wrong, the Outsiders would come back with an agreement to skip the vaccinations, if the Forsakers agreed to have their blood tested. And *that* was a concession, no matter how they chose to dress it up. They'd negotiated with the Forsakers, rather than forcing them to take the vaccinations.

And they have tacitly conceded some control, he thought. He smiled as the two Outsiders retreated. *A hole in their defences we can exploit.*

He allowed his smile to widen, even though his father was looking irked. The Elders would not be pleased. But it didn't matter. He turned back to the crowd, his eyes picking out John standing protectively in front of Hannah. It was nice to see the weakling protecting his sister, even though Joel doubted he would stay there for long. But at least Hannah's dignity would be preserved.

She must remain above suspicion, he thought, although he knew it was probably already too late. If Hannah hadn't had an Elder for a stepfather, she would have been shunned completely by now. *And when I marry her, she'll learn to behave herself.*

Her entire body was shaking.

Judith had undressed as soon as she'd reached the changing room, dumping her wet clothes in her bag and taking a warm shower before dressing in her spare outfit. She felt warm again, after feeling so cold her bones were shivering. And yet, she couldn't keep herself from shaking. She'd had accidents in the past, near-disasters that could have crippled or killed her if she'd been a little less quick, but this was different. The mob would have torn her limb from limb if the crowd had caught her.

She tried to calm herself, but the shaking refused to fade. She'd never been so scared in her life, not even when she'd accidentally driven her father's tractor into the ditch. The impact had been jarring, but she'd managed to climb out and summon help. She'd certainly never felt her father was going to *kill* her. But the crowd…who would have thought, really, that the mere suggestion they needed to be vaccinated would set them off so badly? Their rage had grown so rapidly that she'd been in trouble before she *realised* it was already too late.

Damn them, she thought. *Why don't they listen?*

She wrapped her arms around her legs, trying to control the shaking. Part of her was tempted to just walk out of the spaceport and head home. She would be fined, of course, for deserting her post, but she thought she could afford it. And even if she couldn't...being a debtor, working to pay off the fine, would still be better than putting her life on the line for ungrateful bastards.

And yet...

She remembered Elsa and shivered, again. The girl - and the other girls - were trapped, dominated by their parents in a manner Judith found hard to accept. *Her* father had been strict, when he'd been teaching her how to farm, but he'd never attempted to dominate her life. He'd pointed out all the problems with going to university, when Judith had announced that she intended to apply, yet he'd never tried to stop her. And if he had... well, Judith had been eighteen, a legal adult. She could have moved out if he'd tried to control her life.

But Elsa had been different.

Judith sighed, slowly releasing her legs and standing up. She was scared. She was honest enough with herself to *admit* she was scared. And yet, the refugees *did* need help.

But if they threaten us, she thought, *why should we help them?*

It was an odd thought. Her father had taken in guests before - children from other farms, students trying out the farming life - but they'd all been expected to work. Judith still smiled at the memory of how some of them had been unable to cope with rising before cockcrow, their bodies aching after a few hours of easy labour in the fields. But none of them had acted as though the farmers *owed* them anything.

There was a rap on the door. "Judith! Are you decent?"

"More or less," Judith said. The door opened, revealing Henry. "What's up?"

"The Director wants to see us in the conference room," Henry said. He'd made a cheerful pass at her last night, only to be turned down. "As in, right now."

"Oh," Judith said.

She put her bag in the locker, then followed him through the maze of corridors and into the conference room. It hadn't been *designed* as a meeting room, she was sure - the tables and chairs looked as though they had been kept in storage for years before being brought out and dumped in the room - but it would have to suffice. There was something oddly *unfinished* about the spaceport, even though it was over three hundred years old. But then, Arthur's Seat had never really invested in space travel.

Director Melbourne was standing at the front of the room, looking grim. She'd changed her jacket, Judith noted as the remainder of the room started to fill up, but her outfit still looked ruffled. None of the others looked much better, particularly the city-folk. They all looked as though they'd been in the wars. Judith couldn't help noticing that several faces were missing.

Were they hurt, she asked herself, *or did they simply go home?*

"Please, sit down," Director Melbourne said. "Take a cup of tea or coffee if you want it."

Judith winced, inwardly, as she poured herself a cup of coffee. She hadn't met Director Melbourne before the refugees had arrived, but she'd seen nothing to suggest the director was a particularly nice person. Judith rather suspected that Director Melbourne, like Judith herself, had added her name to the emergency roster in a fit of absentmindedness, never really believing that she'd have to do the job. She *did* have some role in government, but Judith had no idea what it actually *was*.

Bureaucrat, probably, she thought, darkly. Her father hated bureaucrats so much that he would have disowned her if she'd even *considered* joining the civil service. And to think that the civil service on Arthur's Seat was almost *reasonable*. The horror stories from other worlds about bureaucracy were truly terrifying. *She's certainly got the right attitude.*

She sat back down and sipped her coffee, waiting.

"I did not anticipate," Director Melbourne said, "that the refugees would react so badly to a suggestion they needed vaccinations. The decision of how to handle the issue has been forwarded to the Cabinet, who will make the final call."

"They won't be the ones issuing the vaccinations," someone said, from the back.

"No, they won't," Director Melbourne said. She paused. "And while I understand that most of you have been shocked, I have to remind you of your duty. Emergency powers are currently in effect. If any of you decide to desert your post, you can and you will be jailed."

There was an immediate roar of outrage. "I didn't sign up to be attacked," someone shouted, loudly. "None of us did!"

Judith nodded in agreement. They hadn't signed up for a posse, after all. They *certainly* hadn't expected to be threatened, let alone have to fight for their lives. God alone knew what would have happened, if the police hadn't taken quick action. And yet, the water hadn't done more than shock the refugees. Next time, it might take more to stop them from rioting in the spaceport.

"This isn't easy for any of us," Director Melbourne said, holding her hands in the air in the hopes of calming them down. "But we have a duty…"

"They're not being reasonable," someone else snapped. "They're the ones at fault!"

"That is not up for debate," Director Melbourne snapped back. "You have your duties. And you *will* carry them out!"

Judith gritted her teeth. If they *all* went on strike, if they *all* dared Director Melbourne to put them in jail…she had no idea what would happen. Technically, a jury would have to stand in judgement, but under emergency powers…they could be held indefinitely without trial, even though it *would* embarrass the government. She was tempted to dare Director Melbourne to arrest her anyway, yet…it would cast a baleful shadow over her life, even if she was released shortly afterwards.

Sharon stood up. "What sort of protection are you offering?"

Director Melbourne stared back at her. "What do you mean?"

"Those…*creeps*…were staring at my breasts," Sharon said. Her tunic jacket had been at least two sizes too small, making her breasts disturbingly prominent. Judith couldn't help noticing that Sharon had changed into a loose-fitting jacket. "What are they going to do next?"

"The police will be stationing additional guards in the registry room," Director Melbourne said, grimly. "And they will only be let through one at a time."

Which isn't going to make them feel any better about us, Judith thought. *We'll be treating them like prisoners.*

And how, her own thoughts answered, *are they treating us?*

"I don't feel safe," Sharon said. There was another murmur of agreement. "What if they *do* try something?"

"Then maybe you shouldn't have worn such provocative clothing," Director Melbourne snapped, loudly. "These people have been through *hell*. They're not going to relax in a hurry, are they? Give them some space!"

Judith felt a hot flash of anger. Her father had always taught her that she was responsible for what she did, regardless of the provocation. He'd certainly told her off for punching Jimmy Fisher in the face after he'd insisted a boy could do more work on the farm than a girl, although she had a feeling he wasn't as angry as he'd pretended. Sharon couldn't be blamed if someone tried to molest or rape her, no matter what she was wearing. How *could* she be?

But they may feel differently, she thought, remembering Elsa's baggy clothes. *They dress their women to hide their sexuality.*

She shuddered at the thought.

"You will report back to your desks in an hour, once I hear from the cabinet," Director Melbourne insisted. Her voice was so loud that Judith was sure she was using a megaphone to drown out everyone else. "And if you refuse to report for duty, you will be jailed. Do you understand me?"

Judith fought to keep her anger under control as Director Melbourne turned and swept out the room. She was a volunteer, damn it! She'd put her name forward because…because part of her had believed she'd never be called upon. But she'd come to help…she hadn't signed up to be threatened, or molested, or abused. And now Director Melbourne was snapping at her workers, instead of the refugees. She was just as shaken as Judith herself.

She glanced at Sharon. Judith had been honestly surprised when she'd seen Sharon at the first meeting. She'd met the older girl a couple of times, at university, but Judith had never thought much of her. Sharon had basked in male attention, rather than concentrating on her studies. She'd never struck Judith as the kind of person who'd risk her life for others. She too might have assumed that they would never have to actually do the job they'd signed up to do.

Careless of us, she thought, grimly.

She considered, briefly, just walking out of the gates and going home. Her ID card would get her past the police checkpoint, she was sure. Gayle would be pleased to see her, if no one else. But afterwards...she'd be jailed, if Director Melbourne had her way. And even if she didn't, Judith would definitely be expelled from university. Her father wouldn't be impressed either. One should not make commitments, she heard his deep voice rumbling, without intending to keep them. He'd never trust her again.

I never signed up to be threatened, she thought. Her people were sensible. Any genuine evacuation would be easy. Hundreds of people would volunteer to help. Hell, they'd recognise the limits, instead of making impossible demands. *None of us signed up for it.*

She sighed. They were trapped. And there was nothing she could do to escape it.

CHAPTER TEN

> These problems only grew worse as more and more groups settled planets, which were then eyed by more powerful and covetous powers. There was no single power capable of controlling the conflicts, so the question of who owned the newly-discovered systems tended to be settled by 'might makes right.'
> - Professor Leo Caesius. *Ethnic Streaming and the End of Empire.*

"Two hours," Steven Troutman said, as soon as the doors were sealed. "Two hours after landing and all hell breaks loose."

William resisted, barely, the urge to tell him to shut up. He'd been seriously tempted to refrain from sending Troutman an invitation to the meeting, even though it would have been technically unconstitutional. The Leader of the Opposition *had* to be kept informed, just in case he had to assume the premiership in a hurry. But now…if word hadn't already started to leak out, William would have been seriously concerned about Troutman organising a leak himself.

"Two hours," Troutman repeated.

"There was a minor cultural issue," Sondra said. She ran her hand through her red curls. "It can and it will be handled."

"A minor cultural issue," Troutman sneered. "They're refusing to allow themselves to be vaccinated. Or have I misheard?"

William wondered, sourly, just who'd spilled the beans. He couldn't see die-hard Freeholders joining the spaceport staff, although he had to admit it was possible. A near-riot at the spaceport might just have twisted a few attitudes. And there probably *were* Freeholders amidst the emergency workers. Someone with a portable terminal could have gotten the word to Troutman - and the media - before it had reached William himself.

"Forsakers do not believe in vaccinations," Sondra said.

"Your ancestors came to believe in vaccinations," Troutman pointed out. "*That* is why we have the pleasure of your company."

Sondra flushed. "*These* Forsakers did not have their experiences."

"No," Troutman agreed. "I…"

William slapped the table, half-hoping that Troutman would take offense and storm out again. He couldn't complain if he left the room of his own free will. And his supporters would be annoyed if Troutman didn't take part in the proceedings. But instead, the Leader of the Opposition fell silent. William hid his annoyance as he turned to Sondra. The Vice Premier looked irked.

He took a moment to gather his thoughts, then spoke. "What - precisely - happened?"

"The emergency workers set out to register the refugees," Sondra said. "This rapidly proved to be a difficult task. Tarsus was apparently not in the habit of issuing ID of any sort to Forsakers…"

"A likely story," Troutman injected.

"But true, it would seem," Sondra said. "I reviewed the files the Imperial Navy sent us. It seems that Tarsus was reluctant to do anything that could be construed as them taking responsibility for the Forsakers. They came up with a whole string of excuses for denying the Forsakers any form of ID, without *quite* crossing the line. No one on Earth seemed particularly inclined to force them to actually issue ID."

Troutman shook his head. "But they were at school, weren't they? And collecting benefits?"

"You don't need Imperial-grade ID for school," Sondra said. She shrugged. "Whatever the reasoning, the blunt truth is that most of the refugees don't have any ID."

She sighed. "But that wasn't the worst of it," she admitted. "It was the blood tests and vaccinations they objected to, rather strongly. Matters could have gotten out of hand if the police hadn't acted quickly."

"I should add a point here," Chief Constable Jacob Montgomery said. "There were no more than fifteen constables in the room, ninety covering the whole spaceport. None of them were trained or armed to cope with a violent protest. If my officers hadn't reacted with speed, there would have been a slaughter."

"They'd have to be mad to kill policemen," William said.

"Or desperate," Sondra said.

Troutman cleared his throat, loudly. "They want to live on our world," he said, sharply. "If they want to live on our world, they can live by our rules. And our rules say, very clearly, that anyone who passes through immigration has to be identified, tested and given a broad-spectrum vaccination. If these…*refugees* are unwilling to agree to our rules, then I fail to see why we have any obligation towards them at all."

"Common humanity," Sondra said, stiffly.

"Common humanity doesn't put money in the bank," Troutman countered. He held up a hand before she could say a word. "Our first priority is to take care of our citizens. The refugees come *second*. And if they're willing to balk at something as basic as a vaccination, who knows what they'll balk at next?"

"Vaccinations are against their principles," Sondra reminded him.

"And allowing people to enter *without* vaccinations is against ours," Troutman said. "Why should *we* be the ones to compromise *our* principles?"

He met William's eyes. "These people have had next to no proper health care," he said, sharply. "We don't know what they're carrying, because they won't even let us do a blood test. Just letting them out of the spaceport could cause a disaster."

"Our people have been vaccinated," Sondra said. "The only likely victims are themselves."

"The point remains that they are defying us," Troutman said. "We should not be compromising our principles for *them*."

"Director Melbourne believes they will tolerate blood tests," Sondra said. "That will let us know if they *are* carrying anything dangerous."

"They will *tolerate*," Troutman repeated. "What they are prepared to *tolerate* is not the issue, Sondra. The issue is just how willing we are to let them defy us!"

"Blood tests would at least let us know if they *are* diseased," William said. "It would be a suitable compromise…"

"This is not a business negotiation," Troutman snapped. "Nor is it a good-natured argument over who gets what seats on which parliamentary committees. This is…this is deciding to alter our system, purely for the sake of a bunch of idiots too stupid to realise the advantages of vaccinating their goddamned children! What next? Will we ban women from voting because traditionalist Forsakers believe women should remain in the homes and leave politics to the men?"

"No one has proposed anything of the sort," William said.

"It's only a matter of time," Troutman said. "We are being asked to bend rules that *cannot* be bent without calling everything else into question."

He shook his head. "Call the Imperial Navy and tell them to hold the rest of the refugees in orbit, then tell the ones on the ground that they can take the vaccinations or get shipped back to orbit," he said. "Their final disposition is *not* our concern."

"The Imperial Navy has flatly refused to do anything of the sort," William said. "Admiral Carlow is adamant that his ships and crew are required elsewhere."

"Probably finding more refugees to dump on us," Troutman said.

"We cannot force them to stop," Commodore Charles Van Houlton said, flatly. "If we refuse to let them land at the spaceport, they'll land somewhere in the hinterlands."

"Let them land on Minoa," Troutman snapped.

William took a long breath. "We'll give them the blood tests," he said. "And if there are reasons to be concerned, afterwards, we'll revisit the issue."

"This is not a compromise," Troutman said. "This is a surrender."

William ignored him. "Chief Constable," he said. "What is your impression of the situation?"

"Bloody worrying, sir," the Chief Constable said. "Bluntly, if it *does* turn into a full-scale riot, the officers on the ground will be overwhelmed. I've dispatched reinforcements from Lothian, at the cost of stripping police presence on the ground to the bare minimum, but we are short on riot foam and everything else we might need if matters *do* get out of hand."

"Call up a posse," Troutman suggested.

"A posse wouldn't have any training for riot control either," the Chief Constable pointed out, dryly. "And there would likely be a bloody slaughter."

He paused. "I've got men digging some of the older weapons and equipment out of storage, but we might have to build some items from scratch," he added. "That will not make our life any easier."

William nodded, ruefully. Arthur's Seat was a law-abiding planet, lacking the incivility or colossal overpopulation of Earth and the other Core Worlds. There were only five thousand police officers on the entire planet, perhaps seven thousand including the reserves. Getting five or six hundred constables in one place would be difficult. And training new police officers simply couldn't be done in a hurry.

"See what you can do," he ordered.

Troutman snorted. "And what happens if you lose control of the spaceport?"

He jabbed a finger towards the map. "The spaceport is only five miles from Lothian," he reminded them. "What happens when the howling mob descends on the capital city?"

"There isn't a howling mob," William said, sharply.

"Yet," Troutman snapped back. "How many people in the city are actually *armed*?"

William winced. The rural dwellers were armed, mainly with shotguns and hunting rifles, but it was rare for the urban population to carry weapons. It wasn't technically forbidden, it just didn't happen. But that might change, he thought, as rumours spread out of control. His staff informed him that the datanet was already buzzing with stories, each one more exaggerated than the last.

"These people think they can make demands on us," Troutman continued, when William said nothing. "Right now, they are demanding we change our immigration rules for them. Soon enough, they'll demand food that has been ritually prepared and separate quarters and schooling for men and women. They will *keep* going until they find something we physically cannot give them…and then they will riot. And by that point, organising resistance will be much harder."

He paused. "If they are prepared to integrate, if they are prepared to become like us, then they could be welcomed," he said. "But I think it's fairly clear that merely being on this rock isn't going to make them like us."

"You're being paranoid," Sondra said. "It's been less than a day since they landed."

"Yes," Troutman agreed. "Two hours. And in two hours, we've had a near-riot over a matter so minor it never occurred to any of us that it would be a problem. What next?"

He shrugged. "We need to confine them to the spaceport and start preparing for war," he added, grimly. "If we can't stop the Imperial Navy from dumping them on us, we have to be ready to make sure they don't cause trouble."

William sighed. "We can boost our police forces," he said. "And start issuing weapons…"

He sighed, again. There had been an…*innocence* about Arthur's Seat. Crime was rare, seldom anything more than theft or drunken brawling. The police didn't go armed because the police didn't *need* to be armed. But that might be about to change.

"Yes," Troutman said. "And what *else* are we going to do?"

"There will be teething problems," Sondra said, flatly. "I do not deny that there will be problems. Both we and they will have to adapt…"

"That's where you're wrong," Troutman said. "*We* don't have to adapt. This is our world."

Sondra ignored him. "I believe, in a year or two from now, we will be laughing over how wrong we were," she continued. "This planet has a long history with the Forsakers, a history that shows how two cultures can merge and become one. We can and we will integrate the newcomers."

"But that is a lie," Troutman pointed out. "There are people who wear traditional clothing for harvest festivals and suchlike. But do they actually do anything else? Do they pray? Do they farm? Do they send their sons to do manual labour and keep their daughters in the kitchen? Do they shun or expel those who talk to Outsiders…?

"Of course not. And realistically, they can't. The original colonists might have had an influence on our shared culture, but it was a very *mild* influence. There were too many of us and too much incentive to abandon the Forsaker path. Their descendants aren't even Forsakers in *name*! How much use did *you* make of your heritage before now? Did it even mean *something* to you?"

"I believe we have gone over this already," William said, sharply.

"And it has not lost its essential truth," Troutman said. "Has it?"

He shrugged. "The Imperial Navy has screwed us," he added. "Either we keep bending over to accommodate the refugees, ruining our civilisation in the process, or we take whatever steps are necessary to preserve it. And that too will damage our civilisation."

William took a long breath. "They can do the blood tests," he said. "And then we will revisit the issue."

He scowled down at the table. "Meeting adjourned."

Troutman nodded, then departed with a final sneer. William watched him go, followed by the Chief Constable and the Commodore. Neither man had a vote, technically, but they *did* have influence. The rest of his cabinet had remained silent, which was worrying. Did they agree with him? Or were they more inclined to back Troutman?

Because this issue could destroy us, he thought, morbidly. *And there would be no guarantee of winning a vote of no-confidence.*

"That man is an asshole," Sondra said, when they were alone. "I don't know how the Freeholders put up with him."

"He fights for them," William said. Whatever else could be said about Troutman - and William had a lot of words for his opponent that couldn't be said in public - he couldn't deny that the man was a fighter. "And while he's in the wrong, he's still fighting."

He glanced up as Sally, his secretary, peered into the room. "Premier?"

"Sally," William said. His secretary was in her late twenties, with long brown hair and an efficient manner he found more than a little intimidating. He'd been offered a civil servant, but he'd been careful to pick and hire his own secretary, rather than work with someone who might have divided loyalties. "Do you have the latest updates?"

Sally nodded, glancing down at the datapad in her hand. "The first set of reports were picked up and rapidly distributed around the datanet, sir," she said. "By now, I'd estimate a good fifty percent of the population has seen them. Various other reports, mostly exaggerated, have been spreading too, although not everyone appears to believe them."

Sondra snorted. "How many people *do* believe them?"

"It's impossible to say, Vice Premier," Sally said. "There simply isn't enough data to even hazard a wild guess. But from what we're seeing, quite a number of political commenters and bloggers have picked up the issue. The news media will not be far behind. I think most of the more extreme commentary comes from Freeholder sites, but it's hard to be sure."

"Of course," Sondra said, darkly.

Sally shrugged. "There were a great many doubts about the issue between the official announcement and the actual landings," she continued, "but public support for the government remained relatively steady. However, that may change in a hurry. I don't have solid figures yet, but the datanet reports may cause people to lose faith in the government."

William made a face. Troutman could call for a vote of no-confidence at any time, although the unspoken part of the constitution insisted that anyone who made the call and lost the vote had to step down himself. Part of him hoped that Troutman would try, even though there was no guarantee his successor would be any more reasonable. But that wasn't the real problem, not really. If the public turned against the government, his MPs would start to defect, suddenly making a vote of no-confidence all the more dangerous.

And they might try to unseat me even without one, he thought, sourly. *If they thought I was a certified vote loser...*

"I'll be addressing Parliament tomorrow," he said. "Do you think it will change radically?"

"I think a public statement from you would probably help to calm things down," Sally said, bluntly. "The datanet is all sound and fury, signifying nothing. However, the more worrying attitudes will not fade in a hurry. You need to apply corrective measures."

"Spin," William said.

"The public can be fickle," Sondra agreed. "And very prone to changing its mind at a moment's notice."

William nodded slowly. Perhaps, just perhaps, there was something to be said for the Forsaker path. The modern world was too fast, too changeable…these days, with the Empire crumbling into ruins, it was impossible to say what things would be like tomorrow. But living on a farm, growing crops and raising children…

He sighed. It wasn't something he would want, not when he'd devoted half of his life to politics. But he could see the attraction. There was something pure about living on a primitive farm, something lacking from the modern world. He knew so little about how things functioned, at base, that he knew he wouldn't survive if society collapsed. And yet, that wasn't true of a Forsaker on a farm. A decent farmer could plough his fields, repair his own tools and raise his children.

Troutman would probably agree, he thought, snidely. *But perhaps not about banning all technology.*

"I'll make a statement this afternoon," he said. He couldn't speak too early or it would look like he was panicking. "Hopefully, it will hit the datanet by the time most people get home from work."

"And hope that Parliament doesn't get cold feet," Sondra added. Her lips twisted in disapproval. "You don't want them to change sides. I could name a couple of MPs who would if the price was right."

"Just so long as Troutman *can't* name them," William said. He scowled. Troutman was far from incompetent. "But he'll be watching the datanet too."

CHAPTER
ELEVEN

> This naturally resulted in whole populations of dispossessed citizens who were deprived of their lands, but had nowhere to go. Some of them were lucky enough to be able to integrate or obtain passage elsewhere; others, less fortunate, formed an underclass that rapidly became bitter, resentful and utterly unwilling to either integrate or leave.
> - Professor Leo Caesius. *Ethnic Streaming and the End of Empire.*

Joel, John noted as they passed through the doors and into the reception chamber, was looking far too pleased with himself. A faint smile was clearly visible on his lips, even though his father had ruled that the Forsakers were to accept the blood tests. He thought he'd won, John thought, even though he wasn't sure *what* Joel had won. Maybe it was just the satisfaction of watching Outsiders give the Forsakers what they wanted for once.

Bastard, John thought. The policeman might have looked nice, but John doubted the planetary government would put up with Joel's antics for long. They hadn't invited the Forsakers, any more than the *last* planetary government had. *He'll get us all killed.*

The room had been hastily cleaned and dried, he noted. A single desk sat in the middle of the room, manned by a girl who couldn't be any older than Hannah or John himself. Her hair was strikingly blonde, a rarity amongst the Forsakers. John caught himself looking at her chest and hastily looked away, hoping desperately that his mother or stepfather hadn't noticed. They wouldn't be pleased if they thought he was interested in an Outsider girl.

His eyes swept the room. A trio of policemen were standing against one wall, eying him expressionlessly. It wasn't the hatred and contempt he recalled from Tarsus, where the police had never missed a chance to harass the Forsakers. It was something else, a caution, that bothered him more than he cared to admit. Something had broken in the last two hours and it would be a long time, if ever, before it came back. Behind the policemen, someone had moved extra fire hoses into the room. John wasn't sure if it was a warning or a desperate attempt to avoid lethal force.

"Please, be seated," the girl said. Her Imperial Standard was oddly accented, but John could have listened to her voice all day. She sounded strikingly exotic, unlike the girls he remembered from Tarsus. But then, *those* girls had believed all sorts of lies about the Forsakers. "We'll make this as quick as possible."

John sat on a plastic chair, feeling it shift uncomfortably under his weight. Joel sat next to him, looking like a king on a throne; Konrad remained standing, motioning for the women to stay behind the men. He'd already warned his wife and stepdaughter not to talk to the Outsider, even though she was a girl. Who knew *what* ideas they'd pick up from simple conversation?

"My name is Judith," the girl said. There was no patronymic or metronymic. John wondered idly if that meant anything on Arthur's Seat. Lacking either would have implied an illegitimate birth, amongst the Forsakers. "I understand that you are a family?"

"This is my son," Konrad said, nodding to Joel. He glanced past him, at John. "These are my stepchildren."

"So you're not their blood relative," Judith mused. Her hand danced over her console. "Can I have your name?"

Konrad snorted. "Konrad, Son of Elijah," he said. "Elder and First Speaker of the Commune."

Judith nodded, then looked at Joel. "And you?"

"Joel, Son of Konrad," Joel said, in a mocking tone that put John's teeth on edge. It *was* obvious, if one happened to be a Forsaker, but Outsiders had trouble following their relationships. "Steward of the Commune."

The Outsider's face darkened for a second, but she made no overt response. "And you?"

It took John a moment to realise that she was looking at him. "John, Son of John," he said, when Joel elbowed him. It was suddenly hard to speak. "And I'm just a member of the commune."

Judith smiled at him, then frowned as she tapped commands into her terminal. "The system isn't set up to track your naming system," she said. "But we'll see."

She looked up at Hannah. "And you?"

"Hannah, Daughter of John," Konrad said, before Hannah could say a word. He nodded to his wife. "And Mary, Wife of Konrad, Widow of John."

Judith's face went completely expressionless. "And are all of these part of your name?"

"*Her* name," Konrad corrected.

John gritted his teeth. He *missed* his father. He'd never spoken about his wife so dismissively. But then, they'd never had to go through a checkpoint either. No one had bothered to register the Forsakers on Tarsus. In hindsight, being kicked off the planet had been easy to see coming.

"Very good," Judith said. She glanced at Hannah for a long moment, then turned her attention back to her terminal. "I will be taking a blood sample from each of you, then you will be shown to your temporary quarters. If the blood test reveals nothing of great concern, you will hopefully be moved to your final destination. If there *is* a reason to be concerned, there will be further discussions…"

"We are clean," Konrad said, proudly.

"I certainly hope so," Judith agreed.

John cringed, hoping desperately that it didn't show on his face. He had heard all sorts of horror stories about life outside the commune, about how easy it could be to pick up something that would blight the rest of his life. And yet, he'd gone to school on Tarsus and never caught anything beyond the common cold. He'd certainly never socialised with the other children outside school.

If an Outsider breathes on you, his mother had said years ago, *you might become unclean.*

Judith reached into a drawer and removed a handful of tiny devices. John had expected needles, like some of the school medics had used, but the devices seemed to be nothing more than unmarked cylinders, the same size and shape as pencils. There were no needles, as far as he could tell. He wasn't sure if that was good or bad. He'd hated needles, back when he was a child, but at least he'd understood them.

"Who first?"

John hesitated, then waved. Judith smiled at him, so warmly he almost melted, then motioned for him to sit on the chair next to her. John rolled up his sleeve, bracing himself as she pushed the device against his bare arm. He didn't dare look at her as she pushed...there was a sudden sensation, as if she'd just poked him, then nothing. She pulled the cylinder away from his skin and placed it into the terminal.

"Well done," she said. John wondered, absurdly, if he'd just been tricked. The needles he recalled had *hurt*. "Do you want a lollypop?"

John shook his head. Joel was staring at the cylinders, his face pale. John hesitated, then rubbed his forearm hastily, trying to pretend that it was sore. Maybe, just maybe, Joel would believe it had hurt. He wouldn't be the first strong man to be afraid of a needle.

Konrad stepped up and allowed Judith to test him, then nodded for Joel to go next. Joel looked reluctant, his face even paler. John smirked, even though he knew Joel would make him pay for it later. Seeing him humbled was worth a beating. Joel sat down, his entire body shaking. John turned away to conceal his smile as Joel realised it didn't actually hurt. He would savour the memory for a long time.

Hannah cleared her throat. "What happens to the blood?"

John started. He wasn't the only one. Konrad looked torn between the immediate urge to tell her to be quiet and an understandable reluctance to discipline her in front of Outsiders.

"The blood gets tested for anything potentially dangerous," Judith said. She didn't seem reluctant to answer. "Everything from infections - active or passive - to long-term genetic dangers. We need to know if you are carrying anything dangerous. Or, for that matter, if we are dangerous to *you*."

Hannah paled. "Is that likely?"

"Not really," Judith said. "Our population has enhanced immune systems. But we do have to be careful."

She gave Hannah a brilliant smile. "Have you thought about becoming a doctor?"

John winced. There *were* doctors in the commune, but very few young men - and no women - were allowed to study with them. Women were allowed to be midwives - no husband wanted a male doctor attending his wife in childbirth - yet their role was very limited. John himself had once considered attempting to become a doctor, but none of the doctors were interested in taking him as an apprentice. Konrad had flatly refused to convince them to change their minds.

"I might," Hannah said. She'd pay for that later, John was sure. "Is it allowed?"

Judith shrugged. "I have a first aid badge," she said. "You'd need about three years of training, assuming you met the minimal requirements. But it's a good career, very respected."

John couldn't help himself. "Women are allowed to train as doctors?"

"Of course," Judith said. She smiled. "I considered it myself, for a while."

Konrad cleared his throat. "I trust the blood tests are satisfactory?"

Judith turned her attention back to the terminal. "There's no obvious red flags," she said, after a moment. "Certainly no reason to deny you entry. I advise you to get a full genetic analysis performed before you consider getting married, but that's something you'll have to arrange for yourselves."

John rather doubted anyone would bother. He didn't know what a full genetic analysis was, let alone how to get one performed. Was there anyone in the Commune who did?

"Your records have been entered into the datanet," Judith added, after a moment. "The blood will probably be tested further, over the next few days. If there are any problems, we will alert you."

Konrad scowled. "And what will happen to it then?"

"It will be disposed of," Judith said, briskly. She produced a set of plastic cards, swept them through the terminal and handed them out. "These are your ID cards. Keep them with you at all times and present them on demand. There's a steep fine for losing them, so don't. If you are caught without a card, the consequences will not be pleasant."

She nodded towards the doors at the rear of the room. "If you walk through those doors, you'll be shown to your accommodation."

John blinked. The card was semi-transparent plastic. No photo, no words…he thought he could see a golden web under the plastic, but his eyes might be playing tricks on him. He peered closer, turning the card under the light. There was still nothing, apart from golden glints of light.

He shook his head. "That was it?"

"That was it," Judith agreed. "Good luck."

Konrad nodded stiffly, then led the way towards the rear doors. John couldn't help noticing how Hannah hung back, as if she wanted to have a private word with Judith, before their mother caught her arm and pulled her forward. A flicker of…*distaste*…appeared on Judith's face before vanishing, again. John felt a stab of bitter sympathy for Hannah, mingled with an emotion he didn't care to identify. His sister had never really fitted into the commune.

Father would know what to do, he thought, as he passed through the doors. *He'd have said something…talked her out of being an idiot.*

A young man wearing a black uniform was waiting for them. John couldn't help thinking that he looked like a soldier, although he wasn't carrying any visible weapons. He greeted them shortly, then led them down a long series of corridors and through a set of giant chambers, all seemingly deserted. It looked, very much, as though the entire complex had been cleaned out before the Forsakers arrived. The only decorations were a set of paintings along one wall, all showing middle-aged men. One of them was very clearly a Forsaker.

Joel coughed. "Who was he?"

"Elder Simmons," the young man said, curtly. He looked annoyed as he stopped under the painting. "Simmons was the sole surviving Elder of the original colonists by the time the *second* group of colonists arrived. Most history books agree that Simmons was the one to convince his people to abandon their ways and join the newcomers."

John hesitated, then leaned forward. "*Most* history books?"

"There's some dispute over just what actually happened," the young man said. He turned and strode back down the corridor, forcing them to hurry after him. "There are history books that insist Simmons was actually *forced* into surrender by his own people and others that suggest that he was given a flat choice between surrender or certain death. And then there are the books that say Simmons actually *murdered* the other Elders, although *why* is a source of some dispute."

"An Elder would not murder other Elders," Konrad said, insistently.

The young man glanced back at him. "People can do bad things when they're under pressure," he said. "The colony was doomed. Everyone *knew* the colony was doomed."

He led them through a large pair of doors and out onto a concrete path. There was a cluster of houses and warehouses and a large green field, the latter covered in huge tents. A cold wind blew across the field, making John shiver. His shirt and trousers had been designed for warmer weather. He wondered, suddenly, what had happened to their supplies. Had the police on Tarsus even *bothered* to pack up their clothing and send it after them?

"You've been assigned one of the apartment suites, as befits your status," the young man said, as they reached the nearest building. A large sign read SPACER HOTEL. Inside, it looked as dark and silent as the grave. "I'm afraid the room service isn't operational."

He smiled as he opened the glass door. The lights flickered on a second later, making John jump. There was something oddly unnerving about it. The lobby looked neat, but utterly bland and soulless. He couldn't help feeling a chill running down his spine as he followed their guide down another corridor and into a set of rooms.

"Food and drink will be served outside," the young man added. He showed them how to work the lights, shower and entertainment complex, then headed back to the door. "You can explore the complex, if you like, but don't try to go past the fence."

Joel looked up. "Why?"

"Because we don't want you to," the young man said. He nodded, politely. "Bye."

John watched him go, feeling cold. The apartment was nice enough, he had to admit, even though it did feel a little cramped and soulless. He had the feeling that Konrad, Joel and himself would be sleeping in the living room while the women had the bedroom. But at least, he admitted to himself, they weren't going to be in a tent.

Konrad growled, just loudly enough to catch John's attention. He was staring at Hannah, who was looking back at him defiantly. "Why did you talk to her?"

"She's a girl," Hannah said. John winced, trying desperately to meet her eyes. She wasn't making any attempt to hide her defiance. "I was *not* talking to a man."

"You are not allowed to talk to Outsiders," Konrad snapped. "None of you are allowed to talk to Outsiders."

Hannah glared at him. "You are *not* my father..."

Their mother lunged forward and slapped her, right across the cheek. John started forward, unsure what - if anything - he meant to do, but Joel caught his arm and held him as his mother slapped her daughter again.

"He *is* your father," she said, sharply. A thin trickle of blood was running down Hannah's cheek, but she was still standing, still staring at them defiantly. "And you *will* listen to him."

"Get into the corner," Konrad ordered. "You will remain there until bedtime. You will *not* have any food and drink until morning."

John gritted his teeth as Hannah turned and stamped towards the corner. Normally, he would have tried to sneak her some food, but he had no doubt that their mother or stepfather would be in the room, keeping a sharp eye on her. Hannah was defiant enough to walk away the moment their back was turned, even if she had nowhere to go. He wanted to say something in her defence, but he knew it would be futile. Konrad was their stepfather. His word was law.

He could marry her off to Joel right now if he wanted, John thought. He felt cold. Hannah was his sister, yet he could do nothing to defend her. *And she wouldn't be able to say no.*

Joel tugged him back. "Let's go explore the complex," he said, brightly. John wasn't fooled for a second. "Who knows what we will find?"

"Fine," John said. He checked the wardrobes, half-hoping someone had thought to leave a coat or an extra sweater behind. But there was nothing. "There's nothing else to do."

"Not until evening prayers," Konrad said. "I shall expect to see you both there."

John nodded. Perhaps, just perhaps, he would have a chance to slip back to the room and give Hannah something to eat. Putting her in the corner was one thing, but depriving her of food - when she hadn't eaten for hours - was quite another. He glanced at their mother, wondering how she could condone it. But how could he blame his mother for not standing up to their stepfather when *he* didn't have the nerve either?

"As you wish," he said, shortly.

Konrad gave him a nasty look, but said nothing. John sighed, then allowed Joel to lead him out of the room. Perhaps they could find something to eat…

It wasn't much, but it was all he had.

CHAPTER TWELVE

> An alternate problem, which plagued the Empire until its fall, was the simple fact that corporations had a nasty habit of shipping in workers (miners and their supporters, for example) to worlds where they were needed, then abandoning them there. The newcomers rarely integrated well with the locals.
> - Professor Leo Caesius. *Ethnic Streaming and the End of Empire.*

The Houses of Parliament sat on the other side of Lothian from Government House, something William had been assured would help separate the different branches of government and prevent the rise of a political caste. Looking at the MPs as they took their places on the benches, wearing ties to denote their political afflictions, he couldn't help thinking it had failed. Far too many MPs voted in line with their party rather than thinking for themselves.

At least we avoided some of the bigger pitfalls, he thought. *Our MPs only serve for two-terms each.*

Sondra stepped up beside him. "The polling is still close," she muttered, keeping her voice low despite the constant buzz of chatter. "It could go either way."

William nodded. There were five hundred MPs in the chamber, two hundred and forty of them Empire Loyalists. It was a solid block, in theory, but he knew that at least two dozen of his MPs were wavering. The Unionists *might* back the government on this issue - he'd gone to some trouble to urge them to do just that - yet they'd have to remain solid if all the wavering MPs deserted. And who knew what would happen if the Freeholders remained united.

I can kick a wavering MP out of the party, he thought, sourly. The system had been intended to produce a whole series of checks and balances. *But his constituents might return him in a by-election.*

His gaze swept the chamber. Steven Troutman, Leader of the Opposition, was sitting in the forefront of the opposition benches. Tad Cleaves, Leader of the Isolationists, was sitting next to him. The Freeholders and the Isolationists disagreed on a lot of things, but it was evident that Troutman and Cleaves were considering making common cause. If their MPs voted together - and the Unionists refused to back the Empire Loyalists - the bill would not pass. It was as simple as that. William sought out Pamela Davis, Leader of the Unionists, but she was sitting towards the rear of the chamber, chatting with an Independent MP. He couldn't help thinking that was an ill omen.

"Honourable Members of Parliament," the Speaker said. He rose from his chair, his long wig masking his features. "Please take your places."

William sat down, resting his hands in his lap. The bill had been written and sent, in draft form, to the MPs. There was little else he could do now, but make the case for it as best as he could.

"The Honourable Members of Parliament for Dunny-On-The Wold and Haltemprice have sent their apologies," the Speaker continued. "As they are not present within the chamber, their votes will not be taken into consideration."

And they haven't tried to twin their votes either, William thought, making a mental note to have a word with the Party Whip. Two MPs choosing to remain absent rather than toe the party line or make a stand against it? It was cowardly as hell. *They just gave the Opposition two free votes.*

He kept his face impassive, despite his irritation and the rustle of conversation running through the chamber as the MPs hastily recalculated the odds. On the other side of the chamber, Troutman looked pleased. William wondered, idly, just what sort of under-the-table deal had been done, if any. The voting population wouldn't forgive outright treachery, but the Leader of the Opposition could offer all sorts of incentives to an MP who switched sides. And yet, it *was* possible that the cowards had simply been reluctant to commit themselves...

The Speaker tapped his staff against the ground for silence. "The issue before us is the Refugee and Resettlement Bill, proposed in Year 302," he continued. "I call upon the Premier to speak in favour of the bill."

William rose, taking a moment to gather his thoughts. He'd written and rewritten his speech several times over the last few days, as the polls and political discussions veered backwards and forwards. Sondra and her spin doctors had urged him to go in one direction; his personal advisors had urged him to go in the other. William had done his best to strike a middle ground, but he knew it wouldn't be easy. There had been too much fear-mongering over the last couple of days.

At least we managed to start getting the refugees through the blood screenings, he thought, as he surveyed the room. *The spaceport isn't about to explode.*

"Mr. Speaker, Honourable Members of Parliament," he said. "I shall be brief. And I shall be blunt.

"These refugees did not *ask* to be dumped on us, any more than we asked to take them. They were uprooted from their homes on Tarsus and shipped across the interstellar void to us. We cannot blame them for their arrival. And there is *nothing* we can do to keep the Imperial Navy from landing the remaining refugees at the spaceport."

He kept his face impassive, even though he knew that would be used against him. No one liked admitting to helplessness. Hell, his government could be blamed for not investing in more starships and orbital defences worthy of the name. But Arthur's Seat wasn't wealthy enough to build a real defence force. Successive governments had never seen the need.

"This crisis is not of our making," he continued. "But there is no way to avoid coming to grips with it. The bill, which I trust you have all read, allocates emergency funding to feed, clothe and shelter the refugees until they find their footing and integrate into our society. It does not drain resources earmarked for elsewhere."

There was a long pause. "I do not pretend that this will be easy. Until now, our society has only received a relative handful of immigrants. Indeed, over the last decade, we received no more than five *thousand* immigrants, a drop in the bucket. The challenges of absorbing so many newcomers at the same time are immense. But I believe we can turn the situation to our advantage.

"We have ample land that can be turned into farms," he concluded. "We have an entire continent that is largely empty. There is space enough for all of the refugees and more besides, allowing us to expand our settlements. Let us view this, not as a disaster, but as an opportunity."

He sat down. The speech had been received in silence, something that bothered him. MPs were supposed to be polite, but the absence of cheers or boos was odd. It suggested that most of them had already made up their minds, after reading the bill.

The Speaker cleared his throat. "I call upon the Leader of the Opposition," he said. "Mr. Troutman, the floor is yours."

Troutman rose. He looked surprisingly insolent for a middle-aged man, but that - William rather suspected - was part of his charm. Freeholders loved to consider themselves independent, defiant loners standing against the forces of nature and human government. It was an affectation, just as much as the suit and tie William wore, but it played well to his supporters. Troutman wasn't stupid enough to try to blend in at the price of abandoning his links to the voters.

"Thank you," Troutman said. He nodded to William. "Like my honourable friend, I shall be brief and blunt.

"This crisis is not of our making. The endless series of disasters washing over the galaxy, of which this is just one, are also not of our making. And I simply refuse to recognise that we have any moral obligation to put our lives and positions at risk to help solve this…this refugee crisis."

He paused, dramatically. "I was born on a farm. I was raised in a community where assisting others was considered the highest good. But it was never expected that I - that any of us - would be called upon to risk our families, our properties, everything we had to help our neighbours. And it was *certainly* never expected that we would be obliged to risk everything to help people who managed to get themselves into a mess.

"I can and I do choose to risk my life. But I do not choose to risk my wife, my children or my neighbours. And I do not concede that anyone has the right to say otherwise.

"My honourable friend has understated the true scale of the problem. We are looking at fifty *thousand* unwanted immigrants, all being dumped on our soil. The five thousand immigrants he mentioned earlier did not arrive as a group. No - they arrived in dribs and dabs and were easily integrated. Fifty thousand immigrants, perhaps more, is a solid mass that will take years to integrate, if they can be integrated at all.

"It has been two days since the first shuttles landed. In that time, we have seen everything from refusals to be vaccinated to episodes of sexual harassment and assault. I am sorry for whatever the refugees have undergone, but I do not view it as an excuse for bad behaviour *here*. And I certainly do not believe we have any obligation to help people who behave badly towards us."

He nodded towards William. "Our government does not agree," he stated. "Our government is prepared to compromise our principles rather than stand up for them. Tell me - when does it end? Which principles remain untouchable when the government has already wavered? A deadly precedent has already been set!

"I am sorry for men, women and children who have been torn from their homes, dumped on freighters and shipped into the interstellar void," he concluded. "But I am not prepared to tolerate bad behaviour, nor am I prepared to put the entire planet at risk to support a plague of human locusts too stupid or entitled to realise that they *need* us. Honourable members, I ask you to vote against the bill."

There was a loud buzz of chatter. William tuned it out as he tried to gauge the odds. The speech had scored a few good points, but he doubted it would change many minds. Troutman would know it too, which meant… what? An attempt to come to terms with the government, an attempt to rewrite the bill or an outright challenge to William's position? Maybe they'd have to have a private chat during recess…

The speaker tapped for silence, again. "Honourable Members, Honourable Members," he said. "Please! If you wish to speak, please signal for notice!"

Sondra keyed her button. The speaker nodded to her, inviting her to rise.

"Mr. Speaker, Honourable Friends," she said. "May I ask my honourable friend" - she nodded to Troutman - "precisely what he *meant* by calling the refugees human *locusts*?"

She went on before Troutman had a chance to respond. "These are not *numbers*," she continued, her voice shaking with rage. "These are living people! They have lives and families, loves and hates…they do not *deserve* to be demeaned by dehumanising insults and threats from - forgive me - a man who has enjoyed a safe and secure childhood. No one, including the refugees, asked for this nightmare. But we should attempt to deal with it without dehumanising them."

Troutman signalled for attention as Sondra sat down. "In an ideal universe, I would agree with you," he said. "But an ideal universe would be a post-scarcity society where there was infinite supplies of food, drink and…and *everything*. We do not *live* in an ideal universe and I flatly refuse to put my people at risk to feed outsiders."

He paused, then went on. "Are we supposed to put the interests of refugees ahead of the interests of our whole population?"

William sighed, inwardly, as the debate raged on. Constitutionally, *every* MP was entitled to have his say, either making speeches to the chamber at large or demanding clarification from the senior members. He wondered, as he rose to defend the bill for the umpteenth time, just how many people were still watching the debate through the datanet. It probably wouldn't have changed their minds.

And even if it did, he thought morbidly, *it would be too late.*

"Order, order," the Speaker thundered. "Are there any *new* questions?"

A Unionist MP bleeped for attention. "On a point of order, Mr. Speaker," he said. "Should the Leader of the Opposition not be censured for his earlier remarks about locusts?"

William resisted the urge to bury his head in his hands as the chamber dissolved into shouts and catcalls from all sides. Trying to censure an MP was asking for trouble. Indeed, it had only happened twice in three hundred years. Half the Empire Loyalists would vote against the motion, regardless of how they felt about the issue. No MP could tolerate an attempt to shut them up. William hadn't liked the locust comment any more than Sondra herself, but trying to penalise Troutman for it was - at best - a waste of time.

And at worst it will provoke a political crisis at the worst possible time, he thought. *It could lead straight to a vote of no-confidence.*

The Speaker clearly agreed. "That is not a relevant point of order," he said, firmly. A low *clunk* echoed through the air as the voting doors were thrown open. "I call upon the MPs to rise and vote."

William stood, leading his MPs towards the *aye* door. He'd often thought the whole procedure needed to be modified - it wouldn't be hard to give the MPs the ability to vote without leaving their seats - but he had to admit it had a certain grandeur that would be lacking in a modern system. And besides, it made it harder to cheat. Arthur's Seat didn't have as many problems with computer hackers as some other worlds, but that would change if there was something worth hacking. What would happen, he asked himself, if someone fiddled with the system to make sure it returned the *right* result.

He passed through the door, nodding to the Whips on either side. They'd be silently counting up the votes too, making sure there were no mistakes. A dispute could lead to a recount, causing all sorts of problems. The MPs wouldn't be pleased if they had to go through the whole procedure again.

If only because their party bosses will know which way they intended to vote, he thought, as he spotted a pair of Freeholders stepping through the door. Troutman would give them hell for defying him, afterwards. William would have been amused, if he hadn't noticed a number of Empire Loyalists passing through the *other* door. *Perhaps the defections will balance out.*

There was a long pause as the whips compared notes, then spoke quickly to the Speaker. "In favour, two hundred and nineteen," the speaker announced. "Against, two hundred and twelve. Abstain, sixty-nine."

Which includes the two treacherous cowards, William thought. The government had won, barely. Two hundred and nineteen was enough MPs to pass the bill, but nowhere enough to keep the Opposition from challenging it. A mere six MPs choosing to change their minds would turn everything upside down. *I'll have to refight the entire battle from the start.*

"The bill is passed," the Speaker said. He thumped his staff on the ground, again. "This session of Parliament is hereby dismissed."

He rose, signalling the end of the session. The doors were flung open a moment later, a number of MPs hurrying to get to the toilets before it was too late. William didn't move, thinking dark thoughts about traitors and backroom deals. Unless he missed his guess - and he doubted he was that lucky - the bill had only passed because of the Unionists. And Pamela Davis would want something in exchange for her support.

Unless her supporters turn on her, William thought. *But they're more likely to back the Opposition than us.*

Sondra leaned over to speak to him. "Someone's been talking."

William looked up. "I beg your pardon?"

"Troutman knew things that weren't put in the official reports," Sondra said. Her voice was very grim. "And the vast majority of the aid workers weren't allowed to leave the spaceport after the shuttles began to land. Someone deliberately blabbed to the Opposition."

"It happens," William said. He spotted Pamela Davis on the other side of the room, clearly waiting for him. By long tradition, the parliamentary chamber itself was not used for backroom deals. "I imagine some of them wrote emails to their friends. Or called them."

"That will have to stop," Sondra said. "Troutman's going to use these... these exaggerated rumours against us."

"Then counter with the facts," William said. He couldn't help thinking that she sounded personally offended. "And remember not to let him get to you."

"He doesn't make that easy," Sondra said.

"Politics," William said. He reminded himself, sternly, that Sondra hadn't faced a direct challenge. She'd been in politics for most of her life, but she'd never faced a contested election. "He wants to make you look bad. Or emotional. Or otherwise untrustworthy. Your family history gives him plenty to beat you with, if you let him. If he succeeds in calling your judgement into question, he'll win."

Sondra scowled. "Is it wrong of me to care?"

"He cares too," William said. The *locusts* remark had been out of line, but Troutman had a point. "You just care about different things."

He rose. "The bill passed," he added. It was time to find out what Pamela Davis wanted - and pray the price wasn't too high. "Let's count our blessings, shall we?"

CHAPTER THIRTEEN

> For example, the planet of New Jerusalem was settled by a deeply-religious sect who refused to use anything more advanced than steam technology (save, one assumes, for the starships they used to reach their promised land.) This sect abstained from alcohol, drugs and any other form of vice.
> - Professor Leo Caesius. *Ethnic Streaming and the End of Empire.*

"Definitely not," Judith said.

There was a low rumble of agreement. Director Melbourne looked shocked. She hadn't made herself particularly popular when she'd insisted that the aid workers had to stay or be jailed, something she didn't seem to have realised. And demanding that the aid workers turn over their portable coms…it just wasn't done. She might just have gone a step too far.

"It is a legal requirement," the director began, "that…"

"No it fucking isn't," a male voice shouted. "If that was true, you would have collected the coms back when we arrived."

There was another rumble of agreement. Tempers had been fraying over the last two days, with rumours spreading out of control. Judith didn't know *just* how many of them were true, how many were exaggerated and how many were outright lies, but neither the policemen nor the director seemed to know either. It wasn't the most reassuring thing she'd heard. A flat denial would have been preferable.

"I need my com to talk to my parents," a female voice added. "They'll be worried about me."

"They'll be told what they need to know," Director Melbourne insisted. "You'll be fine."

Judith snorted. She wasn't the only one. They were volunteers, damn it. They weren't soldiers - or slaves. None of them had signed up to be held in the spaceport, let alone deal with paranoid refugees from some world no one had ever heard of. And they were fast reaching their limits.

Director Melbourne tried to take control. "Deactivate your coms, then put them in the box," she ordered. "And then…"

"No," the male voice said.

He turned and strode out of the room. There was a pause, then nearly everyone else rose too and headed for the door. Judith ignored Director Melbourne's increasingly worried comments, ranging from threats to pleas, as she followed the rest of the group out the door and down the corridor. Half of them were already tapping on their coms, calling their parents or the media or *someone* before the police could confiscate the coms…if, indeed, the police *tried* to confiscate the coms. God alone knew what would happen if they tried.

Judith glanced at her watch as she hurried down the stairwell. Gayle would be in class, unless classes had been cancelled for some inscrutable reason. Her father never answered unless she called in the evening. There was no one she *could* call. She brought up a chat room, posted a brief message about the demand, then closed down the com and peered out the window. She wasn't due on duty, back in the registry room, for another two hours. By then, Director Melbourne would either have given up or called the police.

I should never have signed up, she told herself.

She shook her head, bitterly. Her father had often helped his neighbours and vice versa - and they'd been properly grateful. Some of her best memories centred around raising barns, building walls or other tasks that needed more hands than a single family could provide. But here…she'd been stared at by men and women, told to mind her own business and generally treated like a slave. It was strange, almost unbelievable, to think that Gayle - her loving Gayle - came from the same roots. God alone knew what *these* Forsakers would say if they ever met her.

Nothing good, she thought.

CULTURE SHOCK

The field outside the spaceport had almost completely disappeared under hundreds of tents, ranging from small two-person tents - Judith had shared one with her older brother back when she'd been a little girl - to a big top someone had borrowed from the local circus. She couldn't help feeling that it wasn't jolly any longer, now there were a pair of tough-looking young men standing guard outside. Dozens of men were in view, milling around as if they were desperate for something to do; there were no women, save for a handful who were following obediently behind their men. Judith wasn't one to question another person's choice of lifestyle - her people didn't care what others did in the privacy of their own homes - but there was something almost sickening about it.

She shook her head as she walked down the stairs, glancing from side to side as she wandered the grey corridors. The Forsakers rarely chose to return to the spaceport, even though it was technically open to them. They didn't like the interior, Judith had heard. She didn't really blame them. Arthur's Seat had never attracted enough interstellar shipping to make expanding and modifying the spaceport worthwhile. There was certainly no need for an extensive network of hotels, shops and red light districts…she'd heard that Earth's spaceports had been surrounded by wretched hives of scum and villainy, although the entire planet probably counted as a wretched hive. And now it was gone…

A banging sound caught her attention. She tensed, one hand going to the panic button in her pocket. Director Melbourne had issued them reluctantly, warning her workers not to use them unless truly necessary. Judith rather suspected the director would be furious with anyone who did, even if they were in *real* danger. Director Melbourne seemed more interested in keeping things quiet rather than anything else.

She inched forward. The sound was coming from a side room, one that had probably served as an office before the spaceport had been converted into a refugee centre. Keeping one hand on the button, she peered through the door and saw a dark-haired girl sitting on the floor, holding one hand against her cheek. The girl looked up as Judith entered, her eyes going wide with shock before relaxing, slightly. There were ugly red marks on both of her cheeks.

Judith stared. She *recognised* the girl. She was the sole girl who'd asked questions during registration. The others had kept their eyes on the floor, either sneaking glances at Judith or just keeping their heads bowed. But this one had asked questions…

She found her voice. "What happened to you?"

"My mother was not pleased with me," the girl said. She had an accent that suggested Imperial Standard wasn't her first language, although Judith could name a dozen entertainment stars who sounded vaguely funny to her ears. Imperial Standard was spoken right across the galaxy, but each planet put its own twist on the words. "She didn't like me asking questions."

Judith hesitated, then closed the door and knelt down next to the girl. "Why? Are you not *supposed* to ask questions?"

The girl looked up at her. "We're not supposed to be interested in *your* affairs."

Judith swallowed. "What…what's your name?"

"Hannah," the girl said. She didn't seem surprised or offended that Judith had forgotten her name, merely…accepting. Perhaps she'd wanted to be forgotten. "Hannah, Daughter of John."

"And Daughter of Mary," Judith said. She remembered now. "And Stepdaughter of Konrad."

"That's not part of my name," Hannah said. "I never chose to assume it."

Judith sighed. "What *happened* to you?"

Hannah laughed, bitterly. "I was slapped, then dumped in the corner, then kept busy until now…I just slipped off."

"They can't just *slap* you," Judith said, appalled. Her father had been strict, but he'd never slapped her face. A blow to the head could cause permanent damage. "They can't…"

Hannah rose, moving stiffly. "They can," she said. She shook her head as she leant against the wall. "As long as I am under their roof, I am under their rules."

It had the air of something repeated by rote. Judith looked down, utterly unsure what to say or do. Hannah…looked resigned, almost accepting. And yet, there was a spike of defiance in her.

"You're old enough to leave," Judith said, finally. "When they open the wire, run off and don't look back."

Hannah laughed, humourlessly. "I'd be leaving my mother and brother behind," she said, sardonically. "They'd never see me again."

Judith was tempted to point out that might not be a bad thing. Her mother had died when she was very young and her father had never remarried, but *she* wouldn't have stayed with a woman who slapped her for asking questions. And a brother who did nothing...if he didn't take part in the tormenting. Her elder brother had been a pain at times - it seemed to be a universal rule - but she'd never doubted he loved her. Perhaps it was different amongst the Forsakers.

It struck her, suddenly, that Hannah was hungry. The way she leaned against the wall...technically, she should tell her to get some food. But if Hannah wanted to stay away from her family...Judith sighed, then reached into her pocket and removed a ration bar. The refugees had been complaining, loudly, about being forced to eat them, but Hannah took it, unwrapped it and ate it with every evidence of gusto. She *had* to be hungry. No one who *wasn't* on the verge of starvation would cram a cardboard-flavoured ration bar into their mouth so eagerly.

"Thank you," Hannah said, finally.

Judith looked at her. "Do you *want* to stay?"

"No," Hannah admitted. "But I don't want to abandon my family either. If I leave them here...they'll never see me again."

"You could go back," Judith pointed out.

"I couldn't," Hannah insisted. "Anyone who leaves, anyone who walks away, is automatically shunned. I couldn't return to the commune."

Judith felt a sudden surge of sympathy as she saw the problem confronting Hannah. Unlike Gayle, unlike anyone else she knew, Hannah and the others who thought like her were caught in a trap. If they left, they could never return; if they stayed, they were trapped. And while *she* would have walked away from parents like that, Hannah seemed to feel differently. The Forsakers seemed to consider families to be of great importance.

So do we, she thought. *But we just express it differently.*

"I see," she said. "I'm sorry."

Hannah sighed, still leaning against the wall. "What's it like? Living here, I mean?"

Judith hesitated. "You get to make your own choices," she said, finally. "But you also have to deal with the consequences."

"Consequences?"

"I..." Judith scowled. It wasn't a happy memory. "One of my friends turned sixteen a few years ago - his father was a moonshiner, so his birthday party included vast amounts of bathtub gin. I drank and drank and drank...and spent the next few days feeling utterly wretched. My father was completely unsympathetic."

"My parents would have disowned me," Hannah said, quietly. "Why was your friend allowed the alcohol?"

"He was old enough to make his own choices," Judith told her. "Growing up on a farm...you get given a lot of responsibility. Dad...dad said some lessons had to be learnt the hard way. Drinking so much taught *me* a lesson."

Hannah smiled. "Don't drink?"

"Something like that," Judith admitted. "Why aren't you supposed to ask questions?"

There was a long pause. "We are told that technology weakens the soul," Hannah said, finally. "That technology weakens us. That..."

She shook her head. "Life is different for us, I think," she added. "Really."

"You're still human," Judith said.

Hannah shrugged. "There were girls my age, on Tarsus, who were wrecked," she said. "I knew girls who thought nothing of having a whole string of boyfriends. They weren't courting, they were...they were doing it. And they would *brag* about doing it. And there were boys who didn't care about the risks of...doing stuff with the girls. I knew girls who were mothers at *my* age, *unmarried* mothers. And there were...*things*...on the datanet that were utterly unspeakable."

She shook her head. "No one gave their parents any respect," she added. "And no one really cared about their lives."

"They had no responsibility," Judith said.

"Yeah," Hannah agreed. "There were pupils at my school who could threaten the teachers and get away with it. And teachers who would... who would *sleep* with their pupils. And governors who..."

She sighed. "But our society has its problems too," she added. "I don't *want* to fit in."

"I don't blame you," Judith said.

"Technology can be used for good or ill," she added, after a moment. Her father had taught her how to shoot hunting rifles as soon as she was old enough, warning her that a gun was a tool. How she used it was up to her. "For all the evil it does, it can also do great good."

Hannah frowned. "How?"

"Your people have a weak immune system," Judith said, after a moment. She'd heard whispers through the grapevine. "There are diseases, relatively minor diseases, that will cripple you, if you got infected. Or worse. *My* immune system is much stronger, thanks to genetic manipulation. Those diseases wouldn't get a grip on me."

She leaned forward. "And, because our immune systems are much better, there's no risk of you catching anything from us," she added. "Our technology protects you even though you don't have those genetic tweaks."

"Oh," Hannah said.

Judith reached into her pocket and pulled out the portable com. "I can call anyone on the planet with this," she added. "If your mother was on the other side of the world...you could call her. You wouldn't *need* to be right next to her to talk to her."

"I know those," Hannah said. She looked uneasy. "There were girls who used to exchange pictures of themselves with the boys."

"It happens," Judith said. "No one told them the dangers, I think."

Hannah met her eyes. "Did they tell you?"

"My father sat me down and had a long talk with me about it before he bought my first personal com," Judith said. Her father had been blunt enough to make her cringe. And he'd made it absolutely clear that he *would* be monitoring her behaviour online until she turned sixteen. "He said that I had to remember that he would be watching."

"And that you shouldn't do anything you knew he would disapprove of," Hannah said. "But you could meet a boy, you could talk to him behind your father's back."

"I talk to my girlfriend with it," Judith said.

Hannah didn't seem to hear her. "There were girls who used to have a dozen online boyfriends," she said, her voice weak. "They weren't *real*."

"People tend to grow out of it," Judith said. She had a few online friends, but she preferred people she actually met in real life. "It's funny how serious things seem when you don't *feel* like an adult."

Hannah looked at her. "Do you want to get married?"

"Not yet," Judith said. She had no idea if Gayle would be interested in marriage. "Why?"

"Mother wants me to get married," Hannah said. "And I will be married, as soon as we are settled. That's a given."

Judith recoiled. "They can't *force* you to marry someone."

Hannah gave her a look that suggested she'd said something very silly. "Of course they can," she said. "Either I marry Joel or I leave. They'll make my life hell if I refuse."

"...Shit," Judith said.

She stared at Hannah, torn between pity and horror. Gayle had never told her, never even *hinted*, that she might have to marry someone else one day. But she *wouldn't* have to marry someone. The Forsakers on Arthur's Seat didn't keep the old traditions. And if they did, society would crucify them. But everything was different now.

"You can't be a child of two worlds," she breathed. "You either stay with your family or cut all ties to them."

"Yes," Hannah said. "There's nowhere else to go."

She sighed, bitterly. "And I don't even know where I *can* go."

Judith closed her eyes in pain. Hannah was right. She had no birth certificate, no educational qualifications, nothing to imply she was suitable for a job...any job. Hannah was pretty enough, in a pinched sort of way, but she was ignorant as hell. The Forsakers might talk about farms - she'd lost count of the number of men who'd asked her when they'd get their farms - yet they didn't know how to work one. Hannah...

She could apply for university or vocational training, Judith thought. She'd have to spend some time working in menial jobs, if only to keep herself afloat, but *that* wouldn't be difficult. There were no shortage of jobs waiting tables. *And that would get her on the right track.*

"Wait until you get out of the wire," she said, finally. "There will be other options."

"I should have stayed on Tarsus," Hannah said. "There were jobs there, if I chose to walk away…"

The door crashed open. Judith turned, just in time to see three young men storm into the room. Their expressions…her hand dived into her pocket and triggered the panic alarm before her mind quite caught up with her actions. They were *furious*.

"On your feet," the leader growled. Hannah's brother? No, her stepbrother. He caught Judith's arm and yanked her up. "Now!"

Hannah let out a yelp. "Joel…"

"Now," Joel growled. He shoved Judith against the wall, then caught Hannah. Judith had no time to do anything before one of the other men caught her, gripping her upper arm so tight she knew she didn't have a hope of breaking the hold. "Move it!"

CHAPTER
FOURTEEN

> But when a greedy corporation set eyes on their territory and discovered that the inhabitants were unwilling to sell, the corporation went to the government, convinced the government to authorise a repossession (a land grab, in all but name) and then shipped in thousands of workers to mine the land.
> - Professor Leo Caesius. *Ethnic Streaming and the End of Empire.*

Joel was *beyond* furious.

Hannah sneaking out of the apartment when her mother's back was turned was quite bad enough, but sneaking into the spaceport? She'd been told - they'd all been told - not to go back into the spaceport, whatever happened. Joel wouldn't even have thought to look for her if he hadn't known there was nowhere else to hide. A young girl would draw attention anywhere in the giant campsite.

And talking to an Outsider?

He yanked Hannah forward, barely resisting the temptation to slap some sense into her pretty head. Didn't she *know* the danger of talking to Outsiders? Didn't she understand the risk she was running? Didn't she realise that she could lose what remained of her reputation? Or that the entire community might reject her if she persisted? Joel's friends wouldn't talk - he'd make sure of that - but someone else might easily have spotted her. And that person would blab before Joel even knew who to browbeat into silence.

Hannah resisted, just for a second. She wasn't as strong as him, but she tried to resist even though it was futile. It would have been admirable, in a man. In a woman, it was merely annoying. He shoved her out the door, barely aware of Adam clutching the Outsider bitch by the upper arm. How *dare* she speak to Hannah? Didn't she know Forsakers would defend the honour of their women? Joel remembered threatening a couple of boys, back on Tarsus, for showing interest in Forsaker girls. It had been easy to convince them to stay well away from the girls. Outsiders didn't have the courage to stand up for themselves.

He opened his mouth to berate her, then closed it sharply. It wasn't his job, not yet. Her mother - and her stepfather - would have to pronounce her punishment. She would be under their authority until she married him, whereupon…he silently promised himself that he wouldn't put up with bad behaviour. They were only getting married as a favour to his stepmother. He was doing her a favour! Couldn't she *see* that?

They slammed the door open and dragged the two girls out into the maze of tents. Joel gritted his teeth as dozens of eyes turned to look at them, some clearly amused. It wasn't the first time someone had been dragged back to face their parents, but it was always amusing to onlookers. Joel's cheeks burned with embarrassment and humiliation. The mere presence of the Outsider girl meant that Hannah's reputation was going to suffer, no matter what happened afterwards. *He* was going to be married to a loose woman…

The Outsider girl resisted, stubbornly. Joel turned, just in time to see her aim a nasty-looking kick at Adam's groin. Adam twisted, barely avoiding a blow that would have unmanned him, then pushed the Outsider to the ground. Joel stared, unsure what to do. He honestly hadn't expected Hannah to have company, certainly not Outsider company. A Forsaker could have been dragged back for public punishment, but an Outsider…?

"Get her on her feet," he ordered, sharply. He could hear the sound of running footsteps from the terminal building. "Now."

"Let go of me," the Outsider girl snapped. "You…"

Adam slapped her, hard. She twisted, then tried to kick him again. Adam caught her arms, yanking her forward as Olaf caught hold of her legs, carrying her between them like a lumpy bedroll. The girl screamed and swore at them in a manner that would have been shocking, if she'd been a Forsaker. Joel's father would have washed his mouth out with soap if he'd let even one of her words cross his lips.

Weak, he thought, as he pushed Hannah into the maze of tents. *A very weak world.*

Mike and his squad had been sitting in the break room, drinking coffee, when the panic alarm sounded. They grabbed their equipment, checked the location of the emergency beacon and ran out of the compartment, pounding down the empty corridors. There was no one to be seen in the office, but he could hear someone shouting and screaming in the distance. He hastily updated the captain, back in the control tower, then led the way down towards the doors. The tents were pressing against the building wall, but it was easy to see the small group of men carrying a young woman. They'd be out of sight in a moment...

He blew his whistle automatically, then ran forward. Most people would stop, if they heard a police whistle, but the Forsakers only picked up speed. Mike cursed - there were too many potential hostiles in a very small space - and hurried after them, drawing his truncheon as he moved. There was no time to summon reinforcements or seal off the area, not when a young girl was at risk. Mike had no idea why a group of Forsakers would carry her into their midst, but it couldn't be anything good.

"Let go of her," he barked, as the group slowed. There was another woman, he saw; a Forsaker girl, being pushed along by a man. She, at least, was on her feet. "Let go of her now!"

A Forsaker turned to face him, bringing up his fists. Mike cursed again - there seemed to be no way to avoid a fight - and rapped the truncheon straight into the man's arms. He gasped in pain, but kept coming. Mike gritted his teeth, then cracked the truncheon into the man's jaw, sending him tumbling to the ground. The blow shouldn't have caused permanent damage, he told himself, but it would put the man out of commission for a while. And he'd need proper medical attention soon.

The man holding the girl's legs let go of them, his face purpling with rage. Mike didn't hesitate, not any longer. He knocked the man down, just in time to see the other kidnapper letting go of the girl completely. Mike took a swing at him with the truncheon - he jumped back, avoiding the blow - and then scooped the girl up in a fireman's carry. She seemed utterly terrified, her eyes wide with fear. He didn't know if she could walk or not...

He sucked in his breath as he saw dozens of young men emerging from the tents, their faces twisted with rage. Someone was shouting in a language he didn't recognise, the chant hastily being picked up by the newcomers as they closed in. Mike glanced at the rest of his squad, then nodded back towards the doors. It was time to take off the gloves. They would be trapped and beaten to death if they stayed where they were.

"Move," he snapped.

It wasn't easy to use his truncheon while carrying the girl, but there was no choice. His squad fell in around him as they made their way back towards the door, lashing out at anyone who came too close. A shower of rocks and pieces of rubbish pelted down around them, but the aim wasn't very good. Or perhaps they wanted to scare him, rather than actually *hit* him. He had to admit, as he ducked a blow from a young man, that it was working. The sheer *murder* in the air was terrifying. He knew they'd be in trouble if they stopped.

The reinforcements should have gotten here by now, he thought, as he knocked a young man out of the way. He was vaguely aware of something hitting his leg, but he was too het up to care. *Where the hell are they?*

He gritted his teeth as the squad forced open the doors, then hurried into the building. The Forsakers seemed torn, unsure if they wanted to follow the squad or not. Mike took a moment to catch his breath, keying his radio and calling a medic as well as additional reinforcements. Where *were* they? The sound outside was growing louder, male voices rising into a hellish crescendo. He'd never seen or heard anything like it, not even in some of the more extreme training simulations. Even the riots after football matches weren't so...so primal.

The girl gasped, jerking against him. Mike carefully lowered her to the ground, hastily checking her body for injuries. There was a nasty red mark on her cheek and her clothes were rumpled, but she seemed otherwise unharmed. Her eyes were flickering from side to side in horror, as if her experiences had taken her sanity. Mike had been told that some people went catatonic, their minds shutting down when they could no longer endure their suffering, but he'd never seen it before. It just didn't happen on Arthur's Seat.

And where *were* those goddamned reinforcements?

His radio buzzed. "Mike, you are to make your way to the main entrance and link up with us there," Sergeant Cox said. "Can you reach it without assistance?"

Mike exchanged a look with Constable Paul Smith. Sure, they *could* make it to the main entrance - the spaceport terminal seemed deserted - but what was going on? The reinforcements should have come after them by now. He glanced from face to face, assessing his squad's situation, then nodded reluctantly. He'd just have to hope Cox knew what he was doing.

"Sure," he said, reluctantly. "We're on our way."

The howling from outside was growing louder as he helped the girl to her feet, then swung her back over his shoulder. She let out a yelp of protest - she wasn't catatonic, part of his mind noted - but he ignored her as the squad started to jog down the empty corridor. He kept a firm grip on his truncheon, wishing - again - that they had some proper stunners. The dangers in using them too freely were more than matched by the risk of being overwhelmed and beaten to death.

They could have killed us, he thought. It took an effort of will to keep his body from shaking helplessly. He'd been in danger before, but nothing like *that*. The Forsakers would have torn the policemen apart if they'd had a chance. *They could have...*

He pushed the thought aside as they jogged through a large terminal, passing a series of portraits hanging from the wall. One of them was missing, part of his mind noted. The paint behind where the missing portrait had been was brighter, somehow, than the remainder of the wall. He puzzled over it for a moment, his policeman's instincts telling him that it was important. But it seemed utterly unimportant compared to the risk of a violent death.

The faint noise of yet another shuttle, landing on the nearest pad, echoed through the building. He wondered, suddenly, just what was going to happen to the latest set of newcomers. They'd have to stay in the warehouses until the whole mess was sorted out...hell, he wasn't entirely sure just how many Forsakers were on the ground. Upwards of twenty thousand were supposed to have passed through the reception zone and been registered...

The tent city is going to have to be expanded, again, he thought, numbly. *Digging ditches for their shit is going to be quite hard enough.*

He let out a sigh of relief as they reached the main entrance. Sergeant Cox was standing there, a grim-faced medic right next to him. Dozens of policemen were clearly visible outside, some of them wearing protective armour. Mike had to suppress a flicker of envy at the sight. The armour wasn't mil-spec. It wasn't even close. But it was better than his uniform. He carefully lowered the girl to the ground - she refused to allow him to lay her down - and turned to the Sergeant.

"Sarge," he said. It was a struggle to keep his tone respectful. "Where the hell were our reinforcements?"

"Held back," Cox said. "The director felt they couldn't be sent into the chaos."

Mike stared at him, unable to quite comprehend what he was hearing. He'd been told time and time again, in basic training and on the streets, that policemen supported one another. A cop in trouble *had* to be able to rely on his fellows. And his squad had been left on their own, in the midst of a howling mob...

He found his voice. "We could have died!"

"I know, Constable," Cox said. He sounded bitter. "It was a political decision."

Mike felt his mouth drop open. Politicians made the laws, but they didn't interfere with actual policing. It had been the rule, ever since Arthur's Seat had been settled. The police were meant to be free of political interference. Hell, he couldn't think of any police officer who *was* a member of a political party. Policemen had the vote, of course, but actively campaigning on behalf of a party...it wasn't done.

"I'm sorry, but the orders were to hold back," Cox told him. "Captain Stewart is sealing off the spaceport now."

It wasn't his fault, Mike told himself, grimly. *He didn't have a choice.*

He swallowed, hard. "Sarge, there was another girl," he added. "They were dragging her into the tents."

Cox sighed. "Put it on your report," he said. "Right now, we have other concerns."

Mike blinked. "Sarge..."

"Report to the outer fence," Cox ordered, shortly. "And save the rest of the grumbling for later."

Not his fault, Mike thought, again.

He glanced at the girl they'd rescued, feeling a hot flush of...shame. They'd saved one of the girls, but the other was lost. He had no idea what was in store for her...he suspected, deep inside, that it wouldn't be pleasant. The police were sworn to protect everyone on the planet and they'd failed. Their political masters had prevented them from carrying out their duty.

Resisting the urge to tell Cox precisely what he thought of the whole affair, he turned and strode towards the gates. He *did* have his orders, after all. But afterwards...he looked down at the silver badge on his uniform, the badge he'd been given when his first mentor had cleared him for street service. He'd thought the badge meant something, at the time. But now...

He closed his eyes in pain. They'd failed. And he couldn't help thinking that there was worse to come.

Joel kept a firm grip on Hannah as the sounds of the riot faded away behind them, unwilling to take the risk of her breaking free and running. The police had been a surprise, even though they'd made no attempt to snatch Hannah as well as the Outsider girl. But then, they probably didn't give a damn about her. The police on Tarsus hadn't cared about Forsakers either. They'd certainly dismissed any reports of Forsaker girls being molested - or worse - by the locals.

"You shouldn't have been talking to Outsiders," he lectured, as they reached the hotel and marched inside. He'd already rebuked the men on the doors for allowing Hannah to leave, although they'd all sworn blind they hadn't seen her pass. "Do you know what they could do to you?"

Hannah gave him an angry look, but said nothing. Joel reflected, not for the first time, that she'd inherited all her father's determination and bloody-minded stubbornness. Those traits would have been considered admirable, if they'd surfaced in John, but instead...he shook his head in grim amusement. A young man could be stubborn. But a young woman...

He swung her around to face him as soon as they were alone. She met his eyes defiantly, instead of lowering them as a properly brought up young girl would do. Merely being alone with him was bad for her reputation, even if they *were* engaged. But that wouldn't be a problem, after they were married. He'd make sure of it.

A thought struck him and he smiled. If John had half his sister's nerve, Hannah would have had a far more agreeable life.

Hannah's face darkened. "Let go of me."

"Not yet," Joel said. He pushed her against the wall, firmly enough to make it clear that she was in his power. "How did you leave the building?"

She sneered at him. "Your guards let me go."

"Lying is bad for the soul," Joel said. He *knew* the guards. He'd chosen them personally, making sure they knew that Hannah was not to leave. And she'd somehow sneaked past them. "How did you leave the building?"

"I walked," Hannah said, mockingly.

Joel allowed his anger to show on his face. They weren't married. He had no right to touch her. But if she thought he would...she stared back at him, utterly unwilling to bend. The sudden surge of anger shocked him, more than he cared to admit. He lifted his hand, then lowered it again. Was she deliberately *trying* to provoke him?

He pulled her forward and marched her down the corridor. "Your mother will deal with you," he said, sharply. "And I suggest you listen to her."

Hannah snorted. "The way you listen to your father?"

"I have always loved and honoured my father," Joel said, stiffly. "And he is your stepfather too."

He shoved her into the room, then turned and hurried back to the campsite. The near-riot had faded, but he needed to make preparations. If the police were weak - and it certainly looked as though they were weak - it opened up all sorts of possibilities. Perhaps he could move forward faster than he had planned.

And he had to be ready.

CHAPTER FIFTEEN

> The result was utter catastrophe. The locals were unwilling to help the miners; the miners wanted booze, women and supplies the locals couldn't or wouldn't provide. A string of nasty incidents led to outright civil war, then the deployment of corporate police forces to protect the mines.
> - Professor Leo Caesius. *Ethnic Streaming and the End of Empire.*

Judith couldn't stop herself from shaking.

She sat in the makeshift office, her entire body shaking helplessly. The police medic had confirmed that she was uninjured, save for the nasty bruise on her face, but she just couldn't keep herself from shaking. She'd been taught how to defend herself, how to use a knife and a gun, yet she had been yanked out of the office and dragged into the campsite as easily as if she'd been a rag doll. No matter how hard she rubbed her skin, she couldn't get rid of the sensation of hands touching her.

It was strange. They hadn't groped her. They hadn't touched her breasts or buttocks or tried to slip their hands between her legs. There hadn't been anything remotely sexual in their touch. And yet, she still felt dirty. She felt helpless. They could have done anything to her and she couldn't have stopped them.

She rested her head in her hands as she remembered Hannah. The police hadn't grabbed her, had they? They'd been too focused on Judith herself…she thought. All of her memories from the moment she'd been dragged out of the office were jumbled, everything blurring together into a distorted mess. She thought Hannah's stepbrother had been among the men who'd grabbed her, but she couldn't swear to it. And she couldn't identify the one who'd slapped her either.

Her cheek hurt. She touched it lightly, remembering the nasty bruise she'd seen on Hannah's face. Hannah...what were they *doing* to her? They wouldn't kill her, would they? But what *would* they do? Judith's father had never treated her like a child, once she'd proved she could handle the responsibility of being an adult. Hannah...Hannah seemed to be constantly treated like a child, even though she was a mature adult. Who knew *what* they'd do to her?

Judith shook her head, sourly. She *liked* Hannah. It wasn't easy to form a connection with someone she'd just met, but Hannah had been strikingly forward for a Forsaker. She had nerve, Judith had to admit. The mere act of asking questions was strikingly brave, when one ran the risk of being punished. And *Hannah* had no one willing or able to help her.

The door rattled. Judith looked up, just in time to see Director Melbourne stepping into the office. The older woman looked irked, her eyes passing over Judith as if she was staring at something small and slimy. Judith felt a hot flash of anger, twisting her body to check that her personal com was still in place. She didn't give a damn about the director's threats, not any longer. Being in jail was starting to seem preferable to remaining in the spaceport.

"Miss Parkston," Director Melbourne said, shortly. "What were you doing with that girl?"

Judith felt a hot flash of anger. "She's in trouble," she said, standing. "We have to help her."

"She is not the issue right now," Director Melbourne said. "What were you doing with her?"

Judith stared at her for a long moment. "Hannah was hiding from her family," she said, finally. "They were abusing her..."

She paused, then went through the whole story from the beginning. "They dragged us both out," she concluded. "They...they were going to hurt me."

"You don't know that," Director Melbourne said.

Judith pointed a finger at her cheek. "Yes, I do," she said. "And they're *definitely* going to hurt Hannah!"

Director Melbourne didn't seem to care. "You had orders not to speak to any of the refugees," she said, firmly. "Why did you disobey orders?"

Judith stared at her. "Are you serious?"

"The orders were issued to *prevent* problems," Director Melbourne said, sharply. "Young lady, you talking to a refugee has sparked off a crisis."

"No, it didn't," Judith said. "I..."

She allowed her voice to trail off. Director Melbourne was mad. She *had* to be mad. Judith had been raised to recognise when she was responsible for a problem and this was *not* one of those times. The refugees were responsible for their own actions. She hadn't done anything to them. No reasonable person could possibly object to Judith and Hannah having a quiet chat.

But the Forsakers have a different view of the universe, she thought, numbly. She touched her chin, feeling the dull ache pulsing under the bruised skin. *Hannah admitted as much.*

"You will remain in this office until I can deal with you properly," Director Melbourne added, firmly. "Give me your com."

"No," Judith said.

"This isn't a game any longer," Director Melbourne snapped. "Give me your com!"

Judith hesitated. Director Melbourne wasn't kidding. If she refused... she found it hard to imagine the older woman trying to *take* the com, but Director Melbourne could easily call the police and have Judith arrested. If she was more interested in humouring the Forsakers than protecting her people, she might try to have Judith held in a cell for several days before letting her make a phone call. Judith didn't *think* the government could hold her for more than a day without charging her - it had been several years since civics class - but Director Melbourne might just be able to do it.

"Fine," she said. She reached into her pocket and produced the com, using her fingerprint to lock it shut. Director Melbourne *probably* couldn't break the encryption, but there was no point in taking chances. "And I want a receipt."

Director Melbourne took the com, then turned and strode out of the office, closing the door behind her. Judith rolled her eyes as she heard the sound of a key turning in the lock, then rose and paced over to the door. She listened for any sign there was someone outside before twisting the doorknob, testing the lock. Unfortunately, the door refused to budge.

This can't be legal, Judith thought, as she turned back to survey the office. There were two windows, but both of them were too small to accommodate anyone larger than a two-year-old toddler. And even if she had managed to open the window and crawl out, the office was at least five metres above the ground. *How long can they hold me here?*

Shaking her head, she started to search the office more thoroughly. If she was lucky, there would be a computer terminal, an unlocked personal com or something else she could use to get the word out. And if not, she might find something that would keep her from going insane worrying about Hannah...

And there's nothing else to do, she told herself. *I can't do anything trapped in here.*

"We got the aid workers out of the spaceport, sir," Cox said. He was speaking to Captain Stewart, but his voice was loud enough for everyone to hear. "The officers on duty have orders to send all of the incoming refugees into the warehouses to wait."

Which won't last forever, Mike thought. *The warehouses were already crammed before the riot.*

He cursed under his breath as another shuttle appeared overhead, dropping down towards the spaceport. There might have been a riot on the ground, but the Imperial Navy was *still* dumping refugees onto the planet. He'd sensed a slight slackening in their efforts over the last few hours, yet it wasn't anything like enough to make a difference. The backlog of unregistered refugees was growing all the time.

"Very good," Stewart said.

Mike rolled his eyes as he scanned the perimeter fence, silently relieved that neither of his superiors were looking at him. Captain Stewart was an experienced officer, but even a political boot-licker couldn't have made that sound convincing. And Stewart was no boot-licker. He knew the risks. Twenty constables were in the middle of the spaceport, too far from help if all hell broke loose...again. Mike doubted the police outside the spaceport could get to them before it was too late.

He scowled. The police had evacuated the aid workers and then withdrawn themselves, leaving the refugees with almost no supervision. God alone knew what was happening in the tent city. Mike couldn't help thinking about the girl they'd failed to save, the Forsaker girl...God alone knew what was happening to her, too. It was time, he told himself firmly, to put all of their preconceptions aside. The newcomers had nothing in common with the citizens of Arthur's Seat, not even the ones descended from Forsakers. And integrating them into the community would be one hell of a challenge.

Another shuttle - and another, and another - flew over his head as the hours ticked by. The police patrolled the fence, waiting for orders from their superiors. But it was clear that there *were* no orders. Mike scanned the fence, wondering precisely what they were supposed to do if every last Forsaker tried to break it down and burst out into the countryside. The fence was tough, but it wasn't unbreakable. And the police had no serious weapons.

They could reach Lothian in less than an hour, he thought, grimly. If only he had time to call his wife and tell her to bug out of town. But Captain Stewart would be furious if he made a personal call. *And after that...*

He shook his head. The media had been going wild about Steven Troutman calling the refugees *locusts*, but Mike couldn't help thinking that the bastard had a point. Mike had been an Empire Loyalist from the moment he'd reached voting age, yet the Empire Loyalists hadn't even *tried* to come to grips with the situation. And Director Melbourne had ordered the police to pull back, implicitly ceding the spaceport to the refugees. Mike knew enough about bargaining to know it was a bad idea to make concessions of any sort. It was hard, often near-impossible, to walk them back later.

Maybe I'll change my vote, he thought, as a group of young men appeared on the far side of the fence. It wasn't much, but it was all he had. *The Freeholders seem to know what's actually going on.*

Joel admitted, privately, that neither Adam nor Olaf would win prizes for intelligence. Both young men were too stupid to add two plus two and get four without a pocket calculator, a tool that was strictly forbidden in the commune. Joel wouldn't have trusted them to handle anything without supervision. They certainly couldn't be left alone with young women. But they were tough, loyal and utterly unquestioning. Their meaty fists had silenced quite a few people who would otherwise seek to challenge Joel's position.

"He broke my jaw," Olaf mumbled. His jaw looked bruised and swollen, although Joel rather doubted it *was* broken. He'd seen worse injuries caused by fistfights and they had healed without medical intervention. "The Outsider broke my jaw!"

"Yes," Joel agreed. Adam wasn't looking much better, with a nasty bruise on his throat and another on his upper arm. "Adam?"

"The bitch tried to hurt me," Adam rasped. His voice sounded odd. "And the policeman *hit* me."

Joel nodded. The policemen had been weak. He knew, all too well, what would have happened on Tarsus. The police would have stormed the commune in force, using stunners and real guns against unarmed opponents. Adam didn't realise it, but he'd been lucky. The whole affair had ended quickly *and* they'd learned something new about their unwilling hosts.

"Hurt her," Olaf said. "Really."

How lucky for Hannah, Joel thought, *that she isn't marrying either of them.*

He scowled at the thought, turning away to check on the other injured. There would come a time, he suspected, when he would *need* to find Adam and Olaf wives. And that wasn't going to be easy, not when their reputations were worse than Hannah's. They were too dumb to understand the role of a husband, let alone how they should treat their wives. Joel doubted that any father would be happy allowing them to marry his daughters. Luckily, it hadn't occurred to either of them - yet - that they could demand it of him in exchange for their service.

The policemen had been surprisingly mild, compared to some of the others he'd met, but that hadn't stopped them doing a great deal of damage. Twelve men had bumps and bruises; five had broken bones, injuries that would require modern medical treatment. And a young boy had a broken nose, although he refused to talk about how he'd actually been injured. Joel considered it, then dismissed the thought. It was something else that could be used to smear the police.

He strode out of the tent and peered down towards the fence. The police were clearly visible on the far side; a handful of men, a couple of vehicles and a bunch of equipment he didn't recognise. There didn't seem to be *many* policemen, certainly not as many as *he* would set to guard such a vast complex. But that proved nothing. He gazed westwards as the skies started to darken. There was a city in that direction, if he was any judge. He'd seen the lights at night.

They didn't move to crush us at once, he thought, as he turned to walk back to the hotel. Joel knew - anyone with half a brain knew - that a challenge had to be answered at once. But the police hadn't *tried* to answer the challenge. *And that proves that they are weak.*

Konrad would have to be briefed, of course. Joel was an old hand at manipulating his father, but this time he'd have to be careful. Konrad might just do something unpredictable. And yet, he'd been just as outraged by the company Hannah kept as everyone else. He wasn't likely to take *that* lightly. Joel smirked, shaking his head in amusement. Hannah didn't know it - and probably never would - but she'd done him a favour.

And all he had to do, now, was capitalise on it.

―――

John sat against the wall, rubbing his eye and trying not to hear the sounds from the next room.

He'd pretended to have no idea where Hannah had gone, when their mother had discovered her absence. Indeed, he had no idea *how* she'd gotten out of the hotel. But it hadn't been hard to guess where she'd go, if she wanted to be alone. And really, how could he *blame* her for wanting to be alone. *He'd* been allowed to explore the complex, although there wasn't much to see; *she'd* been trapped in the hotel, cleaning the room time and time again until it was utterly spotless.

Konrad had punched him, hard, when he'd tried to defend her. John had stumbled backwards and tumbled to the floor, his eye hurting so badly that he'd been unable to think for a few seconds. It had been long enough, more than long enough, for his mother and stepfather to drag Hannah into the next room and slam the door closed. John wanted desperately to charge in and save his sister, but he knew it would be futile. Even if he bested Konrad, the entire community would turn against him. It was far too late to claim to be the family patriarch.

Damn you, he thought.

He wasn't sure who he was cursing. Konrad, Joel…or himself? Or Hannah? Why couldn't she be a normal girl? But would he have liked her so much, he asked himself, if she *had* been a quiet little mouse? Whatever else could be said about her, Hannah wasn't boring. But he couldn't protect her from the world. He couldn't even protect her from the rest of their family.

Father would have understood, he thought, as the shouting died away. That wasn't a good sign. The two adults had practically screamed themselves hoarse. *He would have known what to do.*

But John didn't. He rose, pacing over to the window and peering outside. Darkness was falling over the camp, broken only by the glow of a dozen campfires. They'd been told not to set fires of their own, but - unsurprisingly - the rules had been ignored. No one seemed interested in actually *doing* something about it. Joel was down there somewhere, he was sure. Perhaps he'd already unpacked the weapons…

He winced as he heard the sound of a slap, followed by a gasp of pain. He'd hoped…but he'd known there was no way Hannah was escaping punishment. She'd been told to stay in the suite, she'd been told not to talk to Outsiders…she'd disobeyed her parents and everyone knew it. Another slap echoed through the closed door, followed by another. John closed his eyes, cursing his own weakness. There was no escape for either of them. She didn't have the strength and he didn't have the nerve.

You have to look after your sister, his father had said, years ago. *When I'm gone, you'll be the family head.*

But he'd let the chance slip through his fingers, John knew. And now they were both trapped.

I'm sorry, he thought. He wasn't sure who he was apologising to, either. Hannah, his father or…himself, for being weak. *I'm sorry.*

The door opened. Konrad stepped through, his face grim. "She's to stay in there until I say otherwise," he growled. "You are not to speak to her. Do you understand me?"

John felt a surge of hatred. Konrad might be his stepfather, but he was damned if he was treating the man as a *father*. And yet, there was nothing he could do.

"Yes," he said, finally. Maybe he could sneak in…given a chance, he could sneak into the room. "I understand."

CHAPTER SIXTEEN

And then the corporation lost interest and withdrew, abandoning the planet and the miners to their fate. The civil war spluttered on for years before finally burning itself out.
- Professor Leo Caesius. *Ethnic Streaming and the End of Empire.*

"So there was a riot," Troutman said. His gaze swept the table. "And the police did…what?"

He paused for effect. William cursed him mentally, keeping his face utterly impassive by sheer force of will. If there had been a way to deny Troutman entry to the meeting…but there hadn't been, not without forcing a constitutional crisis. The mere *hint* of improper behaviour would have caused outrage right across the continent.

And someone is definitely slipping information to him, William thought. *But who? And why?*

"The police decided it would be better to fall back and regroup, rather than push the issue," Sondra said. Her voice was very cold. "Under the circumstances, I feel they made the right choice."

"They showed weakness," Troutman said.

William cleared his throat. "They rescued the girl…"

"Yes, and they let her kidnappers go," Troutman said. "That is not acceptable!"

Sondra snorted. "Would you prefer a bloody battle that left dozens dead on both sides?"

"I would *prefer* never to have had this crisis at all," Troutman snapped. "But since we're stuck with it, we cannot afford to show weakness."

He scowled at her. "We have lost control of the spaceport," he said. "There is no way we can hold the fence, if the bastards decide they want out. And then...what? They could reach the city within hours! This is not a time to show weakness."

William held up his hand. "What do you propose?"

"First, we demand that the kidnappers be handed over for punishment," Troutman said. "And second, that the damned bastards *behave* themselves. Throwing a world-class fit because one of their people dares to talk to one of ours...it's not acceptable."

"Culturally," Sondra said. "A Forsaker..."

"*Fuck* their culture," Troutman snapped. He took a long breath. "Why are you so interested in making excuses for them?"

He tapped the datapad on the table. "I don't give a damn what consenting adults do in private," he added, making a visible attempt to calm down. "But no one has the right to do anything that puts non-consenting adults - or children - at risk. If one of their people wishes to talk to one of us...I don't think anyone has the right to object. Or are we intent on leaving them as a completely separate group?"

William hesitated, then looked at Sondra. "What did the blood tests show?"

Sondra looked surprised at the sudden change of subject, but answered the question.

"There's no potential threat to our population," she said. "A number of refugees tested positive for various mild diseases - you can download the full report if you like - but none of them are likely to spread into our population. Nor is it likely we have anything that can pose a threat to them. Our immune systems ensure that we cannot carry a disease that cannot actually infect us."

"That's a relief," William said.

"The more detailed analysis *did* turn up a number of problems," Sondra added. She hesitated, as if she were unwilling to continue. "There are a number of genetic problems, probably caused by having too small a gene pool. The medical staff think they're pushing the limits on relationships - a number of married couples were actually first cousins, for example."

"Sick," Troutman commented. "And illegal."

"They didn't get married here," William reminded him. It *was* sick, but there was no way they could charge someone for committing a crime on Tarsus. "As long as it doesn't happen here, we can't take action."

"And what will you do," Troutman asked, "when it *does*? And when they say that marrying cousins is part of their culture?"

William scowled. He'd never even considered the possibility. There had never been any suggestion that he would marry his first cousins, let alone someone even vaguely related to him. And Troutman, who had grown up in the countryside, would be even more revolted by the whole concept. Entire extended families would grow up together, playing together.

"We'll cross that bridge when we come to it," he said, finally.

Sondra looked annoyed. "The more pronounced cases will probably require gene therapy if they want to live normal lives," she said. "It will be costly, but doable. A number…it may be already too late for the ones who have grown into adulthood."

"Ouch," Troutman said.

"They're not *quite* baseline humans," Sondra admitted. "There are definite traces of long-term hackwork in their DNA. The medics believe that the original Forsakers probably had it somewhere in their family history, but made no attempt to remove it after…after removing themselves from normal society. Some of the more recent converts had more up-to-date improvements. However, they don't seem to have spread through the commune as much as I would have expected."

"Of course not," Troutman said. "They don't get the chance to spread their genes."

Sondra ignored him. "Overall, there's no great health risk," she concluded. "And the genetic problems can be overcome, given time."

"If they accept treatment," Troutman said.

He smiled, rather humourlessly. "Do you realise just how much that will *cost*?"

William met his eyes. "Enlighten me?"

"A basic genetic improvements package costs nearly three hundred pounds," Troutman said, dryly. "A package modified for a specific person's genetic heritage can cost over a thousand pounds. And you're talking about preparing such procedures for fifty thousand people. If they all have the cheapest package, Premier, it would cost fifteen *million* pounds. And if they all need a more advanced package...well, that figure will rise rather steeply."

He paused. "I don't think I need to remind you, by the by, that Parliament did *not* vote fifteen *million* pounds to support the refugees," he added. "And I am pretty sure that a renewed vote would not go in your favour."

Of course not, William thought. The datanet didn't have a *full* account of what had happened at the spaceport, not yet. But some of the rumours were horrific. And he'd been too busy to do the sensible thing and put a statement online. *You've had a golden opportunity to extract revenge and you're going to take it.*

"Money isn't the only problem," Damian Simpson said. The Minister of Health had been fiddling with a datapad. "I don't think my department *could* produce fifty thousand genetic improvement packages, not in a hurry. We never felt that expanding our productive capability was a worthwhile investment."

Sondra coughed. "Can't you borrow civilian equipment?"

"There's very little such equipment on the planet," Simpson said, bluntly. "My office has been looking at the matter since we realised there might be a problem. Frankly, our emergency plans are strikingly out of date. Several of the facilities we counted on have been closed down in the last five years."

He grimaced. "I don't think we could produce more than a couple of thousand packages over the next year, assuming we gave it full priority," he warned. "And...well, building up our production capability will be a nightmare."

"A *costly* nightmare," Troutman put in.

"Yes," Simpson agreed. "Premier, we would have to purchase supplies, equipment and know-how from off-world. Right now, that wouldn't come cheap."

"If at all," Troutman said.

"Right now, my very strong advice would be to warn the Forsakers to be a great deal more careful in their choice of marriage partners," Simpson said. "We can do genetic work-ups for prospective parents, telling them who is a good partner, but…"

"They won't like it," Troutman said. "Having large families is important to them."

Sondra snorted. "And it isn't to you?"

William silenced her with a look. "What do you mean?"

"You will be telling young men, who have learned from the cradle that they will marry and have children, that they can do nothing of the sort," Troutman said. "In some cases, you will be insisting on genetic tweaks; in others, you will be saying that they *can't* have children, based on something so small that it is invisible to the naked eye. And you expect them to *accept* it?"

"It's good medical advice," Simpson said.

"They won't believe you," Troutman said. "Why *should* they?"

"My staff are doctors," Simpson said.

"And they're not particularly trusting of doctors," Troutman said.

"We will cross that bridge when we come to it," William said, again.

"You need a plan now," Troutman insisted. "And you *also* need a plan for handling the current situation. Are you going to just let them sit in the spaceport indefinitely? Or eventually lose track of just *who* has been dumped on our world?"

"They cannot be blamed for what happened to them," Sondra snapped.

"Really?" Troutman asked. "An entire *community* got picked up and deported from a class-one world. What does that tell you about them?"

Sondra reddened. "That they were blamed for matters beyond their control?"

"Just because someone gets the short end of the stick," Troutman countered, "doesn't necessarily mean they're the good guys."

He turned to look at Charles Van Houlton. "Is there any point in asking Admiral Caraway if he has marines we could borrow?"

"Admiral Carlow," Van Houlton corrected, shortly. He didn't sound annoyed, merely frustrated. "And I don't believe he is willing to do anything beyond expediting the landings. His every communication with the Orbital Guard reeks of impatience. I don't think he will react well to any suggestion that we delay the landings any further."

"Great," Troutman said. "Just *brilliant*! Three fucking days, more or less, since the goddamned fuckers got dumped on our world. And we're on the verge of total disaster!"

"You exaggerate," Sondra said, coldly.

"I do not," Troutman said. He ticked off points on his fingers as he spoke. "We cannot house them. We cannot feed them. We cannot find *jobs* for them. We cannot even provide the medical care they need to survive their own stupidity. And, apparently, we cannot hold them to account for their crimes either. They try to kidnap a girl and…and what? We let them get away with it!"

He let out a faint, bitter laugh. "Perhaps we should just drop KEWs on the spaceport," he said, tiredly. "End the problem in one fell swoop."

"You are suggesting genocide," Sondra snapped.

"It's them or us," Troutman snapped back. "You know what? I think *us* comes first. And I am willing to bet that the voters would agree with me!"

"Not yet," William said.

"It has only been three days," Sondra said. She shrugged. "Weren't there problems back when this world was first settled?"

"Yes, there were," Troutman said. "But the situation was different. The Forsakers - your ancestors - no longer wanted to forsake anything. Here… they do. They think they can do what they like, on our world. And you don't want to stop them."

"It will get better," William said.

Troutman shook his head. "I've met fanatics before," he said. "They tend to have bullying personalities. If you give in to them on something, no matter how minor, they see it as a sign of weakness and double their demands. A single concession will simply lead to more demands. And every further concession makes it harder to resist the next one."

He leaned back in his chair. "So tell me," he added. "How do *you* propose to resolve the crisis?"

Sondra exchanged glances with William, then leaned forward. "We make it clear that we will not tolerate assaults on our personnel," she said, firmly. "Whatever happens within their community is not our concern..."

Troutman blew a raspberry. "You're *already* making concessions," he said. "They are on our homeworld. Either they are subject to our laws or they are not."

"I believe the Freeholders were strongly against any expansion of government power to regulate farming and settlement," Sondra said, sweetly.

"And yet we would *also* be against a father who molested his children," Troutman pointed out. "Or does that not count as a crime, because it takes place in the home?"

"It does," William said.

"Then why aren't we applying the same principle to them?" Troutman asked. He tapped the datapad. "As of the last update, there were over a hundred potential cases of physical abuse noted by the aid workers. Or don't you think Forsaker women are worthy of our protection?"

"And if we start prying into Forsaker homes," Sondra asked, "how long will it be before we start prying into Freeholder homes?"

William rubbed his forehead as the argument started to rage. It was an old argument, one that predated both of them. The Freeholders bitterly opposed any expansion of government authority, pointing out that each new authority would inevitably be abused. A Freeholder's freehold was his castle, as far as the law was concerned. But giving people complete independence inevitably produced its own problems. Who would step in to enforce the law if a freeholder *was* breaking it?

He'd be lucky to survive, William thought. *If the mob caught him, they'd lynch him.*

He shook his head. "Enough," he said. "We have to cope with *this* crisis."

"We also have to prepare for the next," Troutman snapped, sharply. "Arm the police; raise a posse. And whatever else we have to do to give ourselves *teeth*."

He turned the datapad over so they could see the spaceport. "There are around twenty thousand people crammed into that tiny space," he said. "The fence is going to burst, sooner or later. Or we'll run out of tents. And what happens then?"

William scowled. The spaceport was large, easily the largest installation on Arthur's Seat, but it had its limits. Director Melbourne had made it clear that the Forsakers were already overcrowding the tents. The weather was too cold for them, she'd said, and it would grow colder as winter approached. A more permanent solution was needed, urgently.

"We'll think of something," he said, finally.

"You better had," Troutman said. He rose. "Because there are people on this planet who will *not* accept this…this invasion without a fight."

William resisted the urge to make a childish gesture at Troutman's back as he stalked out of the room. The bastard had a point. As much as William hated to admit it, he had a point.

"We'll discuss the remainder of the problem tomorrow," he said, addressing the table as a whole. "For the moment, we need to sleep on it."

He watched the rest of the cabinet depart, leaving him alone with Sondra. None of them had tried to argue, he noted as Sally stepped into the room. He couldn't help wondering if that was a bad sign. The parliamentary vote had been alarmingly close. If a handful of MPs switched sides, William would be out of a job and his cabinet would have to look to their own political futures. They'd probably drop him the moment he turned into a liability.

"The news isn't good," Sally said, bluntly. "There are seven different stories currently trending on the datanet, all hugely exaggerated. But the absence of an official press release doesn't help."

William rubbed his forehead. He'd never *had* to worry about staying ahead of the news cycle before. Arthur's Seat wasn't a world where everything changed overnight. Getting a press release out within an hour of *something* happening wasn't desperately important. Or at least it hadn't been…

He looked up at her. "How bad is it?"

"It's never easy to be sure," Sally said. "But I'd say that a goodly percentage of the population is having second thoughts about the refugees. I don't know - of course - how it will translate into votes."

Troutman will push for a vote of no-confidence as soon as he thinks he can win it, William thought, grimly. The datanet wasn't always a reliable predictor of how things would go, not when only a third or so of the population used it regularly. But still...a slide towards rejecting the refugees was troublesome. *And even if he loses, my position will be undermined.*

He frowned. "Do you have any predictions?"

"It depends," Sally said. "We need to put out a truthful version of the story before it's too late."

"We also need to solve the problem," Sondra said. "And *quietly*."

"The datanet is insisting that the government is already covering up horror stories from the spaceport," Sally warned, tiredly. She pulled a terminal out of her pocket and passed it to William. "Anything you do to keep this quiet may rebound badly on you."

"Quite," William agreed.

He looked at Sondra. If he could make her carry the can for anything that went wrong with the refugees...it wasn't very charitable, but he wasn't *feeling* charitable. She was an ally, yet any half-decent politician knew there were times when one's allies had to be thrown under the oncoming shuttle. And besides, she *was* their loudest advocate on the cabinet.

"Deal with it quietly," he ordered. "And make sure it *stays* quiet."

"Understood," Sondra said, curtly. She closed her eyes for a long moment, then looked back at him. "I'll speak to Valetta personally."

William nodded. Director Valetta Melbourne had been Sondra's hatchet-woman for years, long before Sondra had risen to her current post. She'd understand what she was being told, without anything explicit needing to be said. And Sondra would understand, too, that her career rested on a quick end to the whole affair. If she got too hot to handle, William would have to dump her before it was too late.

Because this could bring down the government, William thought. If enough MPs switched sides - or were recalled by their constituents - Troutman wouldn't need a vote of no-confidence to take control of the planet. *And then the bastard will find a final solution to the problem.*

CHAPTER
SEVENTEEN

> This pattern repeated itself time and time again. Indeed, it only got worse under the Empire. Earth had millions of unwanted citizens, people who refused to abandon their customs even as the land was covered in giant megacities.
> - Professor Leo Caesius. *Ethnic Streaming and the End of Empire.*

The meeting room was larger than Joel had expected, he noted, as he followed Konrad into the chamber. A table - it looked wooden, but there was something about it that suggested it wasn't made of wood - stood in the exact centre of the room, surrounded by a handful of comfy chairs. The whole arrangement spoke of a meeting between equals, rather than supplicants and superiors. It wasn't quite what he wanted - he would have preferred something that made it clear that *he* was the superior - but it would do.

Weak, he thought.

Konrad took his seat at the table as the two Outsiders entered from the other side of the room and strode towards them. Joel allowed himself a flicker of amusement, mingled with contempt. They'd sent Director Melbourne, her face strikingly unreadable, and a policeman, his face taut with anger. *Weak*. No one sent a woman to lay down the law. No, they wanted to *negotiate*. And, in doing so, they'd tacitly conceded far too much. He wondered, absently, if any of them knew it.

Director Melbourne sat, resting her hands on the table. The policeman stood behind her, his stance suggested irritation and reluctance. Joel rather suspected, although there was no way to be sure, that the policeman hadn't been in favour of the meeting. But he'd clearly been overruled by his superiors. He still couldn't understand how any man could bring himself to take orders from a woman, particularly one outside the female sphere, but he had no qualms in taking advantage of it. A male opponent would be considerably more challenging.

"I must lodge an official protest," Konrad said, before Director Melbourne could open the conversation. "Seventeen of our people, including two children, were injured by your policemen."

Director Melbourne's face tightened. "That is unfortunate," she said, stiffly. Joel resisted the urge to cheer. *He* wouldn't have given a damn about people injured in the midst of a small riot, particularly if they'd *been* rioting. "Your people were attempting to kidnap one of *our* people."

"An unfortunate mistake," Joel said, blandly. In truth, he wasn't sure what he *would* have done, if they'd kept the Outsider bitch with them. The police might have been pushed into doing something violent. "Your policemen *did* manage to injure the would-be kidnappers."

Director Melbourne relaxed, slightly. She was good at hiding her expressions, Joel noted, but he was better at reading them. He'd offered her a fig-leaf to calm the entire situation down, rather than make things worse by demanding their immediate surrender. Joel had no idea *why* she was so keen to end matters - she'd arranged the meeting at midnight, rather than waiting for a more civilised hour - but he was just as determined to quit while he was ahead.

"That is good," she said, slowly. "But I must warn you that any further kidnapping attempts will not be tolerated."

Konrad nodded. "I have already spoken quite sharply to my people," he assured her. It was true enough, Joel knew, although Konrad hadn't understood what was *really* going on. "The whole affair started because of a misunderstanding. I hope it will not repeat itself in future."

"So do we," Director Melbourne said.

The policeman stiffened, just for a moment. Joel rather suspected he understood. No self-respecting policeman could accept an unspoken truce, not on his territory. Either the police were in control or they weren't. There was no middle ground.

"The Stewards will continue to police our community," Konrad added. "And all further contacts between our people and yours will be discouraged."

"Good," Director Melbourne said. "Hopefully, it will calm matters down before it is too late."

She paused, implicitly dismissing the whole affair. "However, there are a number of other issues," she added. "Your people require medical assistance. You have a number of long-term problems."

Konrad leaned forward. "We also need to move out of the spaceport," he said. "The crush is growing unbearable."

Joel made a face. Konrad was right. They were cramming more and more people into tents and hotel rooms, while the washing facilities were poor and the toilets unspeakable. The spaceport simply hadn't been designed to host so many unwanted guests, certainly not for very long. Problems were appearing all over the complex. And the aid workers, who *had* been striving to cope with the problems, had been withdrawn.

"Your people will be allowed to leave for short periods," Director Melbourne assured him, "once they have passed the second set of blood-screenings. But…"

Konrad coughed, loudly. "The *second* set?"

"Yes," Director Melbourne said. "As I noted, many of you have significant long-term health problems. They will have to be countered."

Joel thought fast. Konrad looked bemused. They'd considered a number of scenarios, but none of them had included medical issues. It hadn't been a problem on Tarsus. The government might have forced the children into schools, yet it hadn't bothered to provide any kind of medical attention. And besides, the Forsakers had their own doctors.

"It is something that will have to be considered at a later date," Konrad said, finally. "And I will have to discuss it with my fellow Elders."

"As you wish," Director Melbourne said. She didn't seem pleased or displeased. "But no one will be allowed out of the spaceport - or wherever you end up - without passing the blood screenings and, if necessary, agreeing to a course of treatment."

Joel frowned, thoughtfully. What *sort* of treatment? Mending a broken bone was one thing, splicing genetic modifications into the human genome was quite another. The different Forsaker sects had never been too clear on where the line was drawn between permissible treatments and forbidden medical procedures. The Elders would probably spend days debating the issue *before* they requested clarification. And then? Who knew?

"We understand," Konrad said.

"Very good," Director Melbourne said.

"We require the immediate return of the aid workers," Joel stated. "The campsite will eventually collapse into squalor without their work."

"You could do it yourselves," the policeman said. It was the first thing he'd said. "Our people will not be cleaning your toilets indefinitely."

Joel shrugged, keeping his expression under tight control as Director Melbourne shot the policeman a sharp look. She'd *definitely* wanted to end the crisis as quickly as possible. Joel had prepared a long explanation about how men wouldn't clean toilets and women couldn't - there were too many strangers about - but it didn't seem to be necessary.

"They will be returning tomorrow morning," Director Melbourne said, finally. "It is our hope that we can start moving you out soon."

Konrad nodded. "But to where?"

"That has not yet been decided," Director Melbourne said.

"Our people are getting impatient," Joel warned. "Even on Tarsus we were allowed to walk around."

"We understand," Director Melbourne said.

She rose. "And thank you for coming."

"No," Joel said. "Thank you."

Judith sat in the chair, staring up at the blank ceiling.

In all honesty, she was starting to wonder if she'd been forgotten. No one had brought her food or drink, no one had come to check on her… she'd lost her personal com, but the steadily darkening sky outside proved that hours had passed since the door had been locked, trapping her. She'd never really understood why prisoners normally preferred to serve on work gangs rather than enter the sole prison on Arthur's Seat, yet she thought she understood it now. She was trapped, unable to leave or entertain herself. Her world had shrunk to four walls, a desk and a comfortable chair.

Perhaps she hopes I'll starve to death, Judith thought, sourly. Did the police know where she was? Did anyone? Director Melbourne could easily have told them some cock-and-bull story about sending Judith back to town. *And then she'd just have to dispose of the body.*

She was half-asleep, her body craving water, when she heard the key turning in the lock. Her eyes felt heavy, but she managed to force herself to sit upright as the door opened and Director Melbourne stepped into the room. The older woman looked tired, dark marks clearly visible under her eyes. Judith would have been more concerned if she hadn't spent the last few hours trapped in a confined space.

"Director," she said, stiffly.

Director Melbourne studied her for a long moment. Judith looked back, silently weighing up her chances. If she lunged…but she was in no state for a fight. She was weak, utterly dehydrated…even if she broke past the older woman, where would she go? The police were probably downstairs, patrolling the building. God alone knew what Director Melbourne had told them.

"Miss Parkston," Director Melbourne said. "Do you have any idea just how much trouble you caused?"

Judith blinked in surprise. "*I* caused?"

"This is a very delicate situation," Director Melbourne said. "You shouldn't have talked to that girl. Or anyone…"

"Oh," Judith said. She was too tired and thirsty to argue. "I need something to drink."

"You are *not* to talk to any Forsakers, outside the bare necessities," Director Melbourne added. Her voice was very cold. "And you are *not* to talk about your experiences."

Judith forced herself to stand. "They beat that poor girl," she said, despite her dry mouth. It was harder to speak than she'd realised. "They grabbed me and attempted to kidnap me…who knows what they would have done to me? And you're saying *I'm* the bad girl?"

"This is a very delicate situation," Director Melbourne said, again. "Cultural misunderstandings could have the most unpleasant effects."

"Cultural misunderstandings," Judith repeated.

"Correct," Director Melbourne said. "Young girls are not expected to talk to Outsiders."

Judith stared at her, unsure she'd heard correctly. "Director?"

"I am aware that many people will find it hard to accept," Director Melbourne continued, smoothly. "But right now, we cannot afford an explosion."

She met Judith's eyes. "You are *not* to repeat your mistake. Do you understand me?"

"I understand," Judith said. She might understand, but she wasn't going to agree. "Can I get something to drink now?"

"You may," Director Melbourne said, grandly.

She paused. "I've taken the liberty of approving you for two days leave," she added. "I advise you to relax, forget everything and then return to duty."

Judith swallowed, hard. Two days leave? Was that all her life was worth?

She doesn't want me near the others, Judith thought, numbly. She had no doubt that rumours were already spreading. But the truth would be far worse. *She wants to give them a chance to forget about it before I return.*

"A taxi is already waiting for you," Director Melbourne added. "You'll be back in the city in thirty minutes."

"I need to get something to drink," Judith said. "And eat..."

"There's a vending machine downstairs," Director Melbourne told her. "And one other thing?"

Judith lifted her eyebrows, suddenly feeling very unsteady. "What?"

"This is a very delicate situation," Director Melbourne warned. It was the *third* time she'd said that, Judith was sure. Or was it the fourth? It wasn't easy to think straight. "It would be strongly advisable for you to do nothing that might throw fuel on the fire."

It was a threat, Judith thought, as Director Melbourne escorted her down the stairs. But it was a curiously weak threat. Her father had never spoken to her like that. Nor had any of her teachers. They'd always told her what not to do, rather than dancing around the issue. There was something weak about Director Melbourne's words, as if she wanted to threaten Judith, but didn't quite dare.

Sort it out later, Judith told herself, as she purchased a bottle of water and a ration bar from the vending machine. *When you're in a better frame of mind.*

"I'll see you in two days," Director Melbourne said, once they were outside the building. A taxi was already there, as the director had promised. "Have a nice rest."

Judith bit her tongue to keep from saying something sharp, something that would probably get her in real trouble. Director Melbourne *had* claimed emergency powers, after all. And yet...she *hadn't* threatened Judith openly, leaving no room for interpretation. It suggested...what?

"Thank you," she said, instead. "I'll try."

She climbed into the taxi, gave the driver her address and leaned back in the chair as the vehicle rumbled to life. She'd get back to her apartment, meet Gayle - her girlfriend hadn't seen her for a *week* - and then...

Take legal advice, she thought. A light flickered overhead as yet another shuttle came in to land. *And* then *decide what to do next.*

Mike was tired, utterly exhausted, by the time his shift finally came to an end. Saving the girl was one thing, but patrolling the outer edge of the spaceport as darkness fell was quite another. There were groups of young men roaming the other side of the wire, hooting and hollering every time they saw a policeman. Mike had a suspicion - and he knew most of the other officers shared it - that there would be a breakout as soon as the entire spaceport was cloaked in shadow. The police didn't have night-vision gear, let alone enough spotlights to make a difference. And cutting the wire wouldn't be hard at all.

They won't need tools to get through, he thought. He didn't know if the Forsakers *had* any tools, but it hardly mattered. *There's enough of them to push down the fence if they try.*

He briefed the reinforcements quickly, then hurried back towards the makeshift barracks. It was irritating to have to sleep in a barracks - he hadn't done that since basic training - but there was no choice. His superiors wanted to have extra manpower close by, just in case the shit hit the fan. Mike rather suspected that nothing short of the *entire* planetary police force would make a difference - if that - but there was no point in questioning the decision. It had probably been *political*...

A man - no, *two* men - were waiting outside the makeshift barracks. Mike recognised one of them as Lieutenant Owen Wilson, Captain Stewart's second; the other, wearing an unmarked uniform, was unfamiliar. He had the faint air of smugness that came from working behind a desk, although almost every officer in the police force was expected to spend at least two days per week on the streets. Mike couldn't help feeling that his presence didn't bode well.

"Constable," Wilson said. "If you'll please come with us...?"

It wasn't a request, Mike knew. Cursing under his breath - he was too tired to do anything, but sleep - he followed the two men around the barracks and into an office that had probably once belonged to a warehouse manager. It was utterly bland, the only sign of individuality a faded pornographic calendar from two years ago. Mike suspected, as Wilson nodded for him to sit down, that the office had been abandoned years ago. Someone had given it a good clean, but there was still plenty of dust in the air.

"Constable," Wilson said, grimly. He sounded deeply worried. Mike *knew* that was a bad sign. Wilson was generally respected throughout the police force. "This is Commander Edwin Coombs, Police Complaints Authority."

Mike blinked, feeling a chill running down his spine. Every decent officer feared the PCA, even though most of its investigators were former policemen. He couldn't recall ever meeting one of their officers, but he'd heard horror stories...the police were supposed to believe a man was innocent until proven guilty, yet all the rumours insisted that the PCA believed that suspects were guilty until proven innocent.

"Constable Whitehead," Coombs said. He had a smug, self-satisfied voice to match his appearance. "It is my duty to inform you that a number of complaints have been made, concerning your recent conduct. While you are not under arrest, I must inform you that you will be required to conduct yourself in a certain manner until the charges against you are either proven or dismissed. In particular…"

Mike barely heard the rest of the speech. His head was spinning. A PCA investigation would look *very* bad on his file, even if all charges were dismissed. The promotions board would wonder why the charges had been raised in the first place. He might be cleared, only to have the whole affair still casting a shadow over his life.

"You do *not* have the right to remain silent," Coombs concluded. "Failure to answer any of our questions will be held against you."

He paused. "Do you understand me?"

Mike hastily replayed the conversation in his head. "I understand," he said. What charges had been brought and why? He hadn't done anything that deserved investigation. Or had he missed something in the rush to prepare the spaceport? "May I call my wife?"

"You can call her when we're back in town," Coombs said. He rose. "Do *not* attempt to speak to anyone until we reach the station. It will be held against you."

He strode out the door. Mike glanced at Wilson - the older man looked ashamed - and then turned to follow Coombs. Mike hadn't looked up PCA procedures since basic training, but he thought he had a right to be informed of the charges against him. And yet, that might not be true when the PCA was involved. Policemen knew all the tricks for evading questions…

Damn it, he thought, numbly. He passed a pair of policemen, but he didn't even dare nod in response to their greetings. *What happened?*

CHAPTER EIGHTEEN

> Often, all too often, they were rounded up and transported to other worlds, then simply dumped there. No provisions were made for their care and feeding, let alone teaching them how to survive. If they weren't fed by the locals, they often starved.
> - Professor Leo Caesius. *Ethnic Streaming and the End of Empire.*

"*That* was a very good morning," Gayle said, as she stepped back into the room carrying a large tray. "I'm *very* glad you're back."

Judith smiled. Gayle - naked Gayle - was as far as it was possible to get from the horrors of the refugee camp. She couldn't help feeling as though she'd stepped into another world. And yet, her body refused to forget what had happened...had it really been only yesterday? Her mind refused to quite believe it.

"Me too," she said, softly. She sat upright, allowing the cover to fall down to expose her breasts. "Did you miss me?"

"It hasn't been the same," Gayle said. She passed Judith the tray, then sat on the bed and leaned forward for a kiss. "Why do you *think* I made you breakfast?"

She sobered as she took one of the plates for herself. "Prices are going up," she added, quietly. "I was lucky to get the eggs."

Judith frowned. Scrambled eggs with toast and fragments of charred bacon...it was a very simple breakfast. She'd eaten more, back when she'd been on the farm, but she'd also worked her ass off every day. And yet, prices were going up? The planet was practically *drowning* in eggs.

She took a bite, puzzled. "Why?"

"People are suddenly buying more food," Gayle said, grimly. "Half the shops in the district were cleaned out by the time I went shopping. Demand just skyrocketed."

She met Judith's eyes. "And your father called," she added. "He said... Judith? What's wrong?"

Judith could barely move. Just for a second, she'd thought she'd seen Hannah's features on top of Gayle's. The two girls didn't look *that* different, but Hannah was thin and drawn while Gayle was in very good health. Her creamy skin was unmarked. Judith remembered the bruise on Hannah's face and shuddered, helplessly. Her fingers shook so badly she almost dropped the tray.

"Judith," Gayle said. She sounded alarmed. "What's happening?"

"There was a girl," Judith said. It was so hard to think clearly all of a sudden. Gayle's voice sounded as though she was very far away. "She was...she was being abused."

Her hands shook, again. Gayle hastily removed the tray before Judith could tip the remains of breakfast onto the bed, then snuggled up next to her, wrapping one pale arm around Judith's shoulder. Judith leaned into the embrace, welcoming the feel of Gayle's breasts pressing against her arms, but she felt...bad. It was wrong, part of her insisted, to do *anything* with Gayle while Hannah - and countless other girls - were suffering.

"It's ok, it's ok," Gayle said. "You're with me. Everything is fine."

Judith shook her head. "It isn't fine," she managed. Tears prickled at the corner of her eyes, dripping down onto her cheeks. "I saw..."

She shook her head. "There was a girl," she said, finally. "She's trapped amidst the others."

Gayle frowned, turning until she was kneeling in front of Judith. "Start from the beginning," she said. "What happened?"

Judith swallowed, then ran through the whole story. Trying to register the newcomers, the blatant disrespect, meeting Hannah...and, finally, her near-kidnap. Halfway through, Gayle leaned forward and wrapped her arms around Judith, holding her tightly as she finished the story. Her breasts were brushing against Judith's, but she was too wound up to care.

"Shit," Gayle said, when Judith had finished. "Are you sure she was telling the truth?"

"I saw the mark on her cheek," Judith said. She rubbed her own cheek, grimly. The bruise had largely vanished, but she could still feel hints of pain. "They slapped her, right across the face."

She looked up at Gayle. "Did your mother ever slap you?"

"No," Gayle said, quickly. "She never touched me."

Judith looked down at her bare legs. "These people are monsters," she said, softly. She felt a pang of guilt as Gayle tensed against her. "That poor girl is trapped!"

"She could leave," Gayle said. "Anyone who wants to leave the Forsakers *can* leave."

"At the cost of abandoning her family," Judith pointed out. "And trying to fit into an unfamiliar world."

She shook her head. "And that *bitch* of a director tried to tell me to be quiet!"

"She might have a point," Gayle said. Judith looked up at her in astonishment. "There's a *lot* of nonsense on the datanet. You telling your story will make it worse."

"And if I don't tell my story," Judith said, "will that change the facts?"

She scowled as she drew back her legs, then stood. Her legs felt wobbly, but after a good night's sleep and breakfast she felt a great deal better. "What happened to me *happened*," she said, stiffly. "And what happened to Hannah happened, too."

Gayle followed her into the lounge. She'd piled books everywhere, Judith noted. Her course required her to read dozens of books, even though her professors had admitted - openly - that not all of them were strictly necessary. Judith removed a pile of books, then sat down in front of the computer terminal. It blinked to life, revealing a string of emails from various student groups. They all seemed to be welcoming the refugees.

"We're being urged to help them settle in," Gayle said, by way of explanation. "I think…"

Judith skimmed through the emails in a growing state of disbelief. The hacks who'd written them - she wondered if they were majoring in creative writing - seemed to have no understanding of the actual situation. There were puff pieces on student volunteers helping refugees, long articles on how much the Forsakers had contributed to Arthur's Seat and several opinion pieces decrying the Freeholder Party for daring to oppose the refugee program. She couldn't believe her eyes.

"Whoever wrote these," she said finally, "doesn't have the slightest idea of what is actually going on."

She flicked through the news sites, shaking her head in astonishment. There were wild stories - so many of them, she suspected, that the truth would be buried beneath a mountain of bullshit. And countless *more* opinion pieces, commenting on the refugees, on the response to the refugees and on everything else under the sun. Reasonable voices were being drowned out under a hail of accusations, counter-accusations and absurd comparisons that wouldn't have stood for one moment in a debate chamber.

"They're being optimistic," Gayle agreed. "But…"

"But nothing," Judith said. "You weren't there. You don't know what it's like!"

She took a breath. Gayle and Hannah might look alike, but they were so different that they might never come to understand one another. Gayle had no understanding of how her ancestors had truly thought, let alone what they'd gone through to change their minds. And *she* didn't have to worry about being shunned - or worse - simply because she put a foot out of line. Hannah, on the other hand, had to know that she was in danger all the time.

Judith felt her blood run cold. *What if they kill her?*

It wasn't a pleasant thought. There had been relatively little violence in the spaceport campsite, at least until the mini-riot, but all that *really* meant was that she didn't know about it. Anything could be happening inside the tents and the watching observers would never know. Wives and daughters - and sons, she added - could be being abused all the time. Or worse. If Hannah turned up dead, her body dumped somewhere in the spaceport, would the police bother with a proper investigation?

"I have to tell them the truth," she said. Director Melbourne hadn't *explicitly* told her to keep her mouth shut, had she? And even if she had, Judith wasn't sure it would stand up in front of a jury. "Gayle…"

"I've been appointed to the Refugee Friendship Committee," Gayle said, quickly. "As a Forsaker..."

"You're *not* a Forsaker," Judith snapped. "Don't you see? You have *nothing* in common with them!"

Gayle stared at her for a long moment, her mouth working soundlessly. Time seemed to slow as Judith looked back at her, wondering if she was about to be dumped. And then Gayle swung around and marched into the bedroom, slamming the door behind her. Judith half-rose, intending to go after her, then stopped herself. Gayle didn't understand, not yet...

She'll think I've betrayed her, she thought, as she turned to the terminal and started to type her story. *But she wasn't there...*

Mike was no stranger to interrogation rooms. He'd chatted to witnesses and suspects in the bland rooms, the latter often cuffed to the table while the police asked questions. But it felt different, somehow, when he was on the hot seat himself. There were no cuffs, there were no formalities... but that, somehow, made it worse. The PCA had very little regard for his rights.

Coombs sat at the front of the room, flanked by a male and female officer. They both had the same sense of smugness that pervaded Coombs. Neither of them had bothered to introduce themselves, let alone shake hands. Mike had spent plenty of time trying to build a rapport with potential suspects, but the PCA didn't seem interested in trying. They'd practically already judged him guilty...

...And they hadn't even bothered to tell him the charge!

"Constable Whitehead," Combs said. "Please, in your own words, explain for us *precisely* what happened before, during and after the riot."

Mike sucked in his breath. The riot? He'd never considered that they might be interested in the riot. They'd put the whole procedure together with astonishing speed, if that was the case. Unless this was the formal investigation procedure, carried out before the PCA recommended that charges be either filed or dropped...

"Yes, sir," he said, carefully. He knew he didn't have much time to think, yet a single mistake - no matter how minor - would be held against him. The PCA would watch for *any* inconsistencies in his words. Theoretically, it was meant to make it easier to catch him in a lie; in practice, any cop with half a brain knew it was dangerous. "I was assigned to the rapid reaction force in the spaceport."

He took a breath. "The seven of us were in the pilot lounge, as ordered, when the panic alarm sounded," he continued. "We checked the location, put in a call for reinforcements and hurried down the stairs. When we reached the location, we saw a number of Forsakers dragging a girl into the campsite. Naturally, we ran after her."

Coombs held up a hand. "Did you not think to wait and assess the situation?"

Mike kept his temper under sharp control. "Sir, there was no *time* to assess the situation," he said, flatly. "The girl was in serious danger."

He forced himself to go on. "I led the charge into the campsite to recover the girl," he said, carefully. "At that moment, I realised that there were actually two girls - the second one dressed in Forsaker clothes. The kidnappers were turning to face me, so I knocked my way through them and recovered the first girl. I scooped her up onto my shoulder, but the second girl was dragged further into the campsite before we could intervene."

Coombs leaned forward. "And you did nothing to help her?"

Mike gritted his teeth to keep his annoyance from showing. Coombs hadn't been there, not when the shit was hitting the fan. He'd shown up afterwards, like a vulture attracted to carrion, intent on making everyone's life miserable. Regulations or no regulations, Mike would have bet good money that Coombs had *never* been on the streets. Perhaps he'd spent all of his pre-PCA career in a little police station in a peaceful village.

"At that point, dozens of other young men began emerging from the tents," he said. "It was clear to me that there was no hope of escape unless we beat a quick retreat. Accordingly, I ordered the squad to lead the way back to the spaceport doors. I did not see any other choice."

He paused. "Despite our clear retreat, they continued to close - or throw things - until we were safely through the doors," he added. "I expected them to come after us, but nothing happened. The doors seemed to deter them, even though they would have broken if they'd been kicked a few times.

"Our reinforcements did not arrive. Instead, we were ordered to make our way back to the entrance hall. We handed the girl over to the medics, then joined the squads sealing off the spaceport."

"I see," Coombs said. "Do you know why they took the girl?"

"No, sir," Mike said. It was a very odd question. "With all due respect, sir, does it matter?"

"It might," Coombs said.

The woman leaned forward. "Constable," she said. She had a surprisingly smooth voice for a PCA investigator. "Do you feel you used excessive force when recovering the girl?"

"No, madam," Mike said. There was no point in trying to lie. "I believe we used rather *less* force than we *should* have used."

Coombs exchanged a look with the woman. "Elaborate."

"The situation was extremely dangerous," Mike said, flatly. "We were utterly outnumbered. None of us had any form of armour, beyond our uniforms. Our weapons were nothing more than truncheons. The risk of being swarmed and beaten to death was uncomfortably high, sir; an innocent victim was at risk of being raped and killed too. I believe we were extremely lucky that we made it out without serious injuries."

"But you injured at least seventeen people, some seriously," Coombs said. He produced a datapad and held it out. "Several broken and dislocated jaws, three broken arms and one child with a broken nose. The doctors insist that your squad caused these injuries."

Mike frowned. "A child?"

"An eight-year-old refugee child," Coombs said, flatly. "His nose was smashed. Not broken; smashed."

"These are serious charges," the other man said. "How do you wish to respond?"

Mike met his eyes, evenly. "I appreciate that...that civilians may have a different attitude to such matters," he said. "However, under the circumstances, when we were fighting to protect both an innocent civilian *and* our own lives, I feel that we had no choice. I do not believe that we could have resolved the situation through *negotiation*."

"You should have done," the woman said.

"And what would have happened," Mike asked, "to their victim while we were trying to *negotiate*? They could have raped and killed her before we even knew what had happened."

He took a breath. "Even *finding* her within the tent city would have been tricky!"

There was a long pause, followed by a breathtaking hail of questions from all three of his interrogators. Mike did his best not to let them get to him, even though they were clearly trying to trip him up. They went over the same areas time and time again, then switched tracks and invited him to offer his opinions on everything from refugee policy to police weapons and armour. Mike wished, desperately, that he'd been allowed to get a lawyer. He had the nasty feeling that he'd been set up for something.

Coombs finally called a halt. "Constable Whitehead," he said. "Under normal circumstances, you would be placed on administrative leave until a decision was made regarding your case. However, as we are short of manpower, you will merely be rotated back to your original police station until a decision is made. This will change, of course, if we proceed with the case."

Mike narrowed his eyes. Their decision made no sense. Did they think he was guilty? Of what? But if they thought they had enough evidence to charge him, why *not* charge him? He couldn't understand it. Unless they were trying to gather more evidence…they'd be interrogating the rest of the squad, of course. But they could probably convince a judge to order his detention if they had a case…

"You are hereby cautioned *not* to speak to any of your fellow officers, the media or anyone else about this case unless it has been cleared through this office," Coombs continued. "You are to make no attempt to contact anyone else involved in this affair. Be warned that any contact at all will be held against you."

And if I run into one of them at a police station, Mike thought, *I'm dead.*

"Thank you, sir," he said, aloud. "Can I ask for a written statement of the charges and evidence?"

The woman cleared her throat. "You have not yet been charged," she said. "You are merely the subject of an investigation."

Mike - somehow - managed to resist the urge to glare at her. She was technically correct. He *had* a legal right to know the charges, but only if he was formally *charged*. And yet, under the circumstances, the PCA was slipping dangerously close to mishandling the investigation, something he could use against them if the case ever came to court...

And that means...something, he thought. *But what?*

He rose. "If you don't mind, I would like to go home to my wife," he said. He also needed a shower and a change of clothes. Sleeping in the station had brought back old memories, none of them good. And he had the nasty feeling he smelt terrible. "When do you want me to report to duty?"

"Tomorrow," Coombs said. "But remember - not a word to anyone until the case is resolved."

Mike nodded. "Yes, sir."

CHAPTER NINETEEN

> This may seem odd. But remember, the average citizen of Earth knew nothing about how the world worked. The source of food was a complete mystery to them. Indeed, Earthers tended to react badly when they discovered 'real' meat. They were utterly unprepared to survive on a new and untamed colony world.
> - Professor Leo Caesius. *Ethnic Streaming and the End of Empire.*

"You look...different," John said.

"So do you," Hannah countered. She smiled, even though she looked to be in pain. "And no one is going to look *twice* at me."

John frowned. He had no idea *how* Hannah had walked out of the hotel - she'd refused to tell him - but he had to admit that it had worked. She'd changed her dress, adjusted the cap she wore and even tinted her face - somehow. She still looked feminine - she would be in real trouble if she was caught in male garb - but she didn't look like herself.

He met her eyes. "Are you sure you want to do this?"

"Yes," Hannah said, flatly. "I need to get out for a while."

John nodded. He'd managed to sneak her a couple of ration bars and a bottle of water, when his mother wasn't in the room, but she still looked starved. And he'd seen the nasty marks on her arm when she hadn't realised he'd been looking. Their mother had done more than slap her face, this time. John didn't know how Hannah could stand it.

He took her arm and led her back towards the spaceport. The tent city had grown over the last four days, so many people crowding into the complex that it was easy enough to hide, as long as one was careful. Konrad had been spending much of his time with the other Elders, arguing over just what was permissible on Arthur's Seat; Joel had been off, helping the Stewards to police the campsite. John was just relieved that he was staying out all day and only coming home to sleep.

They walked through the spaceport complex and down towards the main gate. A couple of doctors sat there; one male, one female. John hesitated, unsure if he really wanted to do it, then shook his head as Hannah strode forward and sat down next to the female doctor. He sighed, then looked at the other doctor. The doctor looked back, amused.

"This is a secondary blood screening," the doctor informed him. "If there are any problems, I'll inform you in a moment."

John nodded impatiently as the doctor performed the blood check, then studied his terminal as the results started to blink up. "You had an ancestor a couple of generations back who was a convert, I'm guessing," he said. "Does that sound right?"

"I don't know," John said. His father had never talked about *his* family. John's grandparents had both been dead by the time he'd grown old enough to ask about them. "What makes you say that?"

"You have traces of more modern genetic hackwork in your DNA," the doctor said. He paused. "No long-term genetic conditions, as far as I can tell, but I would advise you to marry someone outside your community. Too many of your people are too closely related."

John blinked. "Is that a bad thing?"

"Yes," the doctor said. There was a faintly amused tone to his voice. It took John a moment to realise that he'd probably not been the first person to ask that question. "How much do you know about DNA?"

He went on before John could answer. "Basically, DNA is your body's building blocks," he continued. "It's a little more complex than that, but you get the idea. Your DNA determines everything from your gender to your skin colour, height and suchlike. Being siblings, you and your sister share the same DNA, but put together slightly differently. That's why you're different genders.

"When a man and a woman conceive a child, their DNA is mixed together. Again, it's a little more complex, but that's the basic idea. When those two sets of DNA are too similar - as they are, if you're related - it causes problems for the child. If both parents have a tendency towards weak eyesight, for example, that will be doubled in their children."

"I see, I think," John said.

"Come back here before you get married and we'll run a comparative analysis," the doctor added, dryly. "You don't want to marry someone too close to you if you're unwilling to undergo gene therapy to avoid genetic problems."

He took John's ID card, ran it through his terminal and held it out to him. "You can pass through the police checkpoint," he said. "I suggest you check with the staff outside before getting on the buses."

John nodded, then followed Hannah through the doors and down towards the police checkpoint. The police eyed him carefully as they approached, but allowed them to pass through without comment. A couple of young women, their eyes concerned, were waiting beyond the checkpoint. One of them approached Hannah; the other watched John carefully, but said nothing.

"The cards will get us into town," Hannah said, as she strode back to John. "But we have to be back at the spaceport before six."

"I see," John said. They made their way over to the bus stop, where a large vehicle was waiting. "Do you have a watch?"

Hannah said nothing as they climbed onto the bus. The driver didn't look happy to see them, but he showed them how to scan the cards through the reader a moment before the vehicle roared to life. John sat down, hastily, as the bus started to move, heading away from the spaceport. He wasn't sure what he'd expected, outside the giant complex, but he had to admit that Arthur's Seat looked better than Tarsus. The handful of buildings by the side of the road looked friendlier.

Traffic grew heavier as the bus slowly made its way into the city. The street was suddenly lined with houses, each one small and neat rather than the giant apartment blocks he recalled from Tarsus. There were dozens of trees everywhere, some familiar and others oddly unpleasing to the eye. And the people…he couldn't help staring at them as the bus drove past. There was an…*ease* about them that he found himself envying, even though he didn't understand it. The women…

Hannah elbowed him. "Stop staring."

John flushed. "I wasn't staring," he protested. "Really."

"Yes, you were," Hannah said. She sounded happier, now they were out of the spaceport and well away from anyone who might see them. "You were practically licking the windows."

"I wasn't," John said.

"Last stop," the driver called. "Town Centre!"

They scrambled off the bus, looking around with interest. The air was fresh and clean, compared to the foul stench he remembered from Tarsus; the buildings looked special, rather than hastily put together to house an expanding population. There was a *charm* about them that made him wonder if they'd been specially designed…perhaps they had. Lothian - or so they'd been told the city was called - was tiny, compared to Tarsus City.

And the people…

They were different, very different. The men wore suits and ties; the women wore a dazzling variety of clothing, ranging from long dresses to short skirts and shorts that revealed the underside of their buttocks. John found himself blushing helplessly as he looked away, hoping that Hannah hadn't seen him staring. And the children…they ran around gaily, as if they didn't have a care in the world.

They stopped in front of a map and studied it, thoughtfully. There was a library, a school, a set of government buildings…and dozens of small shops. John glanced up and down the street, marvelling at just how many small shops there were. There were nothing, but big department stores on Tarsus, all owned by a small number of corporations. Here, they looked more like family businesses than anything else.

He saw a young man staring at him and frowned, worried. A chill ran down his spine, reminding him of the days on Tarsus when he'd known that attacks could come at any moment. He tensed, wishing for a weapon. The young man wasn't the only one looking at them, their expressions concerned or fearful. John wanted to run, but he knew he didn't dare show weakness.

We're wearing Forsaker clothes, he thought. *They can pick us out easily.*

"This way," Hannah said. "We need to go to the library."

John was tempted to insist that they returned to the bus and head back to the spaceport, but he knew Hannah wouldn't listen. Instead, he followed her as she led the way towards the library, shaking his head at the collection of strange buildings. The library itself was inside a giant stone dome, dotted with windows. There were more books in view, as they walked into the antechamber, than he'd seen anywhere else, even at school. *Printed* books, not electronic volumes. And behind them, newspapers. He couldn't help wondering just what Konrad and the other Elders would have made of so many *real* books. They'd always forbidden the youngsters from using e-readers or data terminals.

He looked at his sister. "What are we doing here?"

"Learning about the planet," Hannah said. She nodded towards a seating area, a rack of newspapers positioned neatly next to it. "Shall we begin?"

John nodded, opening a newspaper and recoiling in shock as he saw a photograph of a topless girl around the same age as Hannah. He hesitated, then hastily turned the page before Hannah saw what he was looking at, hastily reading a story about a debate in the local parliament. Apparently, a local MP - whatever an MP was - seemed to be at risk of losing his seat. John honestly had no idea what it all meant.

"This is a little more interesting," Hannah mused. She passed him a thicker newspaper, printed on better paper. "What do you make of this?"

John scanned the story as quickly as he could, parsing out the words he couldn't identify. A young girl had been abducted at the spaceport, then rescued by police. He didn't need Hannah to tell him that it had been Joel and his friends who had kidnapped the girl, even though the article made no mention of Hannah. Apparently, the girl was telling her story on the datanet…

"It's the girl you met," he mused. "Isn't it?"

"There's no photograph," Hannah said. "But who else would it be?"

John shrugged and rose, leaving Hannah to read her way through the newspapers as he explored the library. It was vast, bigger than he'd realised; five large halls, each one crammed with shelf after shelf of books. He picked up a book with a particularly gaudy cover and rolled his eyes when he realised it was a fictional novel. The Elders had always discouraged the youngsters from reading fiction, particularly Outsider fiction.

They preferred moralistic stories that told children that they should listen to their elders and refrain from thinking for themselves.

Half of these books are nonsense, he thought, as he studied a book featuring supernatural creatures. He had no idea what sort of creature had bright red eyes and magic powers, but he didn't want to know. *And the rest are utterly absurd.*

The next set of shelves held history books, all focused on Arthur's Seat. John picked a small volume - *A Short History of Arthur's Seat* - and read through the first four chapters, carefully sounding out the words he didn't understand. The author was clearly an Outsider - the contempt he'd felt for the Forsaker settlers was striking - and yet, there was a hint of warm compassion in his words that John found perplexing. On one hand, he treated the settlers as idiots; on the other, he seemed to understand their plight. But the basic gist of the story was all too clear. The Forsakers who'd settled the planet first hadn't had the slightest idea what to expect.

And so they came very close to dying out, John mused, as he reread the second chapter. *They would have died out, if help hadn't arrived.*

He returned the book to the shelf, then picked out another one. It told the same story, although in somewhat more compassionate terms. Indeed, there was a mournful tone to the writing that he found quite striking. He glanced at the back cover and realised, to his surprise, that the author was a Forsaker. He'd never even *heard* of a Forsaker writer.

And a woman, he thought. Seeing her picture was a *real* surprise. *A woman who wrote a book.*

A voice spoke from behind him. "Are you looking for anything in particular?"

John spun around. A young girl was standing there, wearing a bright pink tracksuit that matched her pink hair and revealed all of her curves. She was decently covered, yet he had no trouble making out the shape of her body. She wasn't even wearing a bra! Her face was stained, pockmarked with...*something*. And she had a dozen pieces of metal implanted in her cheeks. She was so striking he found it hard to look at her.

His throat was suddenly very dry. "Nothing," he said, somehow. "I'm just...I'm just looking for books."

The girl's eyes flickered over him. "You're a Forsaker?"

"Yes," John said.

"Cool," the girl said. She gave him a brilliant smile. John found himself suddenly torn between helpless lust and a striking revulsion. What had she *done* to her face? He'd seen girls with earrings before, but this girl had mutilated herself. "My father's a Forsaker."

John shook his head. It was impossible. He couldn't imagine *any* Forsaker father allowing his daughter - or his son - to wear such an outfit, let alone mutilate their face…And she was alone, without a male protector. No, she was no Forsaker. And her father was no Forsaker either.

"He is," the girl insisted. She sounded very sure of herself. "Come round for dinner if you wish."

"No, thank you," John managed. He'd never *ever* had a girl ask him for dinner. It was against every rule in the book. Courtship was done between two families, not between two lovers. "I…"

The girl shrugged, expressively. John tried not to stare as it did interesting things to her breasts. "See you around, sometime," she said. "My name's Casey, by the way."

She paused. "You do know you can take books out, right?"

John blinked. "I can…?"

"They gave you a card, right?" Casey leaned forward, as if she were imparting a secret that no one else was allowed to hear. Her perfume made his head swim. "You can use it to take out books, twelve at a time. Just make sure you bring them back when you're done."

She turned and walked away, swaying her hips in a seductive rhythm. John stared after Casey, only catching himself when she turned the corner. He'd never seen anything like it, not when every young woman in the commune wore shapeless dresses and stayed out of sight, when she wasn't escorted by her male relatives. And she claimed to have a Forsaker for a father…?

He put the book back on the shelf, then turned to find Hannah. She was nowhere to be seen until he glanced into the computer section and saw her sitting in front of a computer. A young man was standing next to her, talking in a very low voice. John felt a hot flash of anger, which he rapidly suppressed. He couldn't start a fight, not now.

The young man nodded politely to John as he approached. "Do you want an email account too?"

John blinked. "An email account?"

"Yes," Hannah said. "You do know what one is, don't you?"

"Yes," John said, crossly. He'd had a private email account at school, although he'd never used it. The Elders had flatly forbidden their use, without exception. He assumed Hannah had one too...had she been using it, despite the ban? "But I don't want one."

"You should," Hannah said. She was sending a message...to *who* was she sending a message? "They're quite useful."

"I can show you how to set one up," the young man offered. "It only takes a couple of minutes."

"Thank you, but no," John said, firmly. He made a show of glancing at the clock. "We really should be heading back now."

Hannah looked annoyed, but nodded in agreement. She blanked the screen, thanked the library assistant for his help and then followed him towards the door. John caught sight of Casey, bent over a book trolley and forced himself to look away. It was achingly clear that Casey wasn't wearing any panties either. He could make out the shape of her buttocks, the curve of her thighs...

"You're still staring," Hannah said.

John felt another surge of anger, mixed with embarrassment. "And you were talking to that man!"

"Yes," Hannah agreed, dryly. Her tone dared him to jump to the wrong conclusion. "He was helping me to set up an email account."

"Oh, really," John said. He caught himself before he said something she'd make him pay for, later. "Hannah...what do you want with an email account?"

"Oh, this and that," Hannah said. She sighed. "It's a shame we can't take books home with us."

"Konrad would hit the roof," John said. Their stepfather would rip the books to shreds, then...he didn't know, but he doubted it would be pleasant. "We'll just have to keep coming back here."

Hannah favoured him with a brilliant smile. "You'll come with me?"

"Of course," John said. They'd be caught sooner or later, he was sure, but it was better than hanging around the hotel room. "What are brothers for?"

CHAPTER TWENTY

> The Empire rarely bothered to ask for permission from the locals. It simply didn't care. The locals, on the other hand, found themselves asked to help unwanted and largely useless immigrants - and being told that refusing would result in punishment. Unsurprisingly, ethnic hatred and tension rose sharply right across the settled regions of space.
> - Professor Leo Caesius. *Ethnic Streaming and the End of Empire.*

The shower, all things considered, was pathetic.

Joel gritted his teeth as he scrubbed furiously at his body, cursing the low pressure under his breath. Water dribbled down so weakly that it would have been better, if he'd had the time, to heat up a bucket of water and splash it over his body. The soap was pathetic too, smelling faintly of flowers, but at least there was plenty of it. They'd been given enough for a small army.

He turned off the shower, still feeling dirty as he reached for his towel and dried himself thoroughly. Being *clean*, constantly clean, had been drummed into him from birth, yet there had been little water on Tarsus or the freighter that carried them to Arthur's Seat. He couldn't help wondering if the Outsiders had deliberately rationed the water, just to annoy the Forsakers. There was certainly no excuse for doing it on a planetary surface. He donned his robe hastily, glanced at himself in the mirror and then hurried out of the shower block. A long line of men were already waiting to take his place.

Not enough showers or toilets or anything, he thought, grimly. Twenty thousand people needed a *lot* of water, yet the spaceport didn't seem to have anything *like* enough. *And we're all grimy as hell.*

He walked down to the hotel, nodding to the guards as he stepped through the doors and into the building. He'd doubled the guards over the last two days, making sure that no one could enter or leave the building without his permission. The beating he'd given the two idiots on duty when Hannah slipped out had concentrated a few minds, ensuring that no nook and cranny was left unguarded. He wished, grimly, for weapons - most of their supplies had yet to be unloaded - but what they had would have to suffice. Shaking his head, he passed through the secondary doors and into a large room.

Olaf met him there, looking concerned. "Steward? Did you get back from town?"

Joel bit down a rather sarcastic response. Olaf was an idiot - Joel was right in front of him, damn it - but he was *useful*. And loyal. An intelligent man might start thinking about his own future, rather than mindlessly supporting Joel. And yet, it was frustrating at times.

"Yes, I did," Joel said. "And I still feel filthy."

He sat down and waited while the remainder of the group trickled into the room. He'd half-expected to be arrested, the moment he stepped into the guardpost, but the policemen had merely checked his ID before waving him onwards. There weren't *many* Forsakers heading to Lothian, it seemed. Joel had certainly done his best to discourage it. But even a handful of refugees visiting the town presented the police with a whole series of problems. How could they keep track of so many people without making it blatantly obvious?

And they weren't following me, he thought. *I kept an eye out and saw nothing.*

He smiled at the thought, then sobered. Lothian had been much less hostile than Tarsus City, where a person wearing Forsaker clothes could expect to be attacked at any moment, but in some ways that only made it more dangerous. His skin still crawled when he thought about everything he'd seen, the seductions that would inevitably draw hundreds of Forsakers out of the commune. The government didn't realise it - he thought - but their mere presence was a challenge to the commune. How could the commune maintain its integrity if half - or more - of its people left?

And we are short of women, he reminded himself. He'd seen too many women in the city, practically flaunting their availability. *Sex will lure too many of us away.*

He rose as soon as the doors were closed, his eyes scanning the room. Olaf and Adam were sitting in the front row, their eyes following him with interest. Behind them, the remainder of the group - including a tired-looking John - were sitting on the floor, waiting. John didn't look too happy to be there, but the invitation had been mandatory. Joel wasn't going to give up his hold on his stepbrother - and Hannah's brother - too easily. He might have other ideas concerning his sister.

"I went down to the city," he said, without preamble. "It is a disgusting nightmare, a place of sin and degradation."

He spoke from the heart, freely outlining everything he'd seen; the women, the shops, the freedom to sin...and the books, the books that lied about the past. It was impossible to believe that the original colonists had abandoned their ways so completely, not in a single generation. Joel and his commune had survived *decades* of oppression on Tarsus, maintaining their integrity no matter how many chose to leave. It was impossible to believe that their long-lost kin wouldn't do the same.

But they might have been broken down, he thought, grimly. *Who knows what actually happened?*

"We must defend our right to exist, to protect our culture," Joel continued, once he'd finished his story. Olaf and his fellows looked enthusiastic; others, perhaps more thoughtful, seemed doubtful. "These people are weak! We can carve out a place of our own and hold it!"

He had to smile. A *strong* government would have demanded that the Forsakers surrender or die. But the government on Arthur's Seat didn't seem *strong*. He'd read enough about the world - on the ship, before their landing - to know that their government wasn't *designed* to take strong action. It was a curious oversight, but one he intended to exploit. Every little concession would make it harder for the government to refuse the next. And then...?

Keep your eye on the prize, he told himself, firmly. *A place of our own.*

"But we must be prepared to fight," he added, sternly. "And we must remain strong."

The training session lasted for nearly an hour, running through everything they'd learned over the last few weeks. It wasn't much, Joel was sure, compared to police or military training, but the police on Arthur's Seat seemed reluctant to enforce their authority. He wouldn't have taken the risk on Tarsus. A set of armoured policemen could have effortlessly slaughtered the entire commune.

"Watch your families," he concluded. Sweat was trickling down his back. He'd need to take another shower. "Many will be tempted to walk away and leave the commune. They must not be allowed to go."

He expected a challenge, but none was forthcoming. He'd picked his men well. Forsakers might be allowed to leave - at the price of never returning, of never seeing their families again - but his men no longer cared. A person who left - now - was nothing more than a traitor to the entire commune. Joel knew he couldn't stop *everyone* from leaving the spaceport, but he could try to limit the outflow.

And the seductions, he thought. *Word must not be allowed to spread.*

"Your father wants to speak to you," John said, as soon as the rest of the group had left. "He asked me to let you know."

My father, Joel thought. Konrad was *John's* father too, in everything but blood. John had passed up the chance to declare himself patriarch. Joel rather suspected he regretted that now. At fourteen, he'd been a child; at nineteen, he was an adult. *He still isn't used to his position.*

"Very good," Joel said. John was his *brother*, too. "You didn't think to tell me earlier?"

John said nothing. Joel eyed him for a long moment, wondering what - if anything - he was hiding. John could have made a dangerous opponent, if he'd had the nerve. His father had been renowned for being brave. But Hannah - not John - had inherited *that* particular trait from their joint father. How strange it was, he thought, to have such nerve and determination trapped in the body of a woman.

"Then I will go see him," Joel said, finally. "And I trust your sister is well?"

"Mother is taking care of her," John said. He didn't seem to believe that Mary was *Joel's* mother too, at least in law. But then, Joel had been sixteen when Konrad had married the widow. "She has recovered."

"Good," Joel said, as he led the way out of the room. John didn't understand, sometimes, that punishment had to be meted out. Disciplining someone was never pleasant, but it had to be done. Hannah could not be allowed to get away with defying her family. Or her husband, when they were married. "You may inform her that I will speak to her afterwards."

John shook his head. "You cannot talk to her alone."

Joel concealed his amusement. What had brought on *this* burst of bravery? He'd spoken to Hannah before in private, although his father had always been close by. It wasn't as if anyone cared, not really. Hannah's reputation had been soiled long before Konrad had agreed to her betrothal to his eldest son.

And our relationship is a little more tangled than it seems, he thought, dryly.

"You may lurk in the next room," Joel said, pleasantly. "Until then..."

He strode off down the corridor, leaving John staring after him. John wouldn't do anything, Joel was sure. He lacked the *nerve* to do anything. If he'd claimed his father's title...but he hadn't and now it was too late. Joel couldn't help wondering if it had been *Hannah* who'd talked him out of it. *That* had been a mistake on her part, if she had. She'd exchanged a brother she could dominate for a stepfather she couldn't.

The thought made him smile as he entered the room the Elders had claimed for themselves, a day after they'd been allowed into the tent city. It was a mess. Bedrolls were piled up against the wall, the table was covered with books...five of the nine Elders were sitting in a circle, arguing frantically about *something*. Joel was silently relieved that the four remaining Elders hadn't disembarked yet, even though it was awkward. There had to be at least seven Elders for a quorum.

"Joel," Konrad said. He rose, leaving the other four Elders to their argument. "Did you enjoy your trip?"

"It was disgraceful, father," Joel said. "Lothian is a sinful city."

"And yet, we must work with its people," Konrad said, tiredly. It struck Joel, suddenly, that his father was *old*. He'd known, of course, that his father was in his early forties, but he'd never quite realised what it *meant*. The strong man who'd raised him was gone. "There's nowhere else to go."

Joel blinked. His father had been strict, watching everything he did with a gimlet eye. Joel had never been scared of his teachers or the other boys, but he'd always been fearful of his father's reaction. He'd never doubted that his father loved him, or that his father would *fight* for him… and yet, the thought of disappointing him was terrifying. But now…his father seemed frail and old, as if a gust of wind would blow him away.

"We can build our own community," Joel managed. He felt shaken. "Father…"

He looked at the other Elders, still arguing in their circle. He'd looked up to them as a child, seeing them as the font of all wisdom…but now… now they looked like doddering old men, unable to comprehend that the universe had changed. His head spun as he struggled to come to grips with what he was seeing. If they were old and weak, they wouldn't do what was necessary to save the commune. They wouldn't even *notice* as the entire structure came apart and melted into the local community.

"If we can," Konrad said.

Joel tried to speak, but no words came. Where was the man who could quell opposition with a single sharp glance? Where was the man whose slightest *hint* of displeasure could cow him effortlessly? Where was the man…

"We have already been uprooted from one community," Konrad said, gently. "What will happen if we are forced to leave again?"

Joel felt a hot flash of bitter anger. "Father, we have to stand up for ourselves!"

His father looked back at him. "With what?"

Weapons, Joel thought. *They're in the supply crates…*

He bit his tongue before he could tell his father about the weapons. There was no way his father would approve. It had taken weeks of arguing to convince the Elders that they could use baseball bats and makeshift swords as weapons, even though the entire community was under constant attack. Konrad would not agree to let him use weapons, certainly not modern weapons. The Forsakers were all about seeking out a simple way of life.

But that simple way of life isn't going to help us if we're threatened with extermination, he thought.

It had already happened on Arthur's Seat. An entire Forsaker community - perhaps not much larger than his - had been destroyed. Not physically, perhaps, but their way of life had been utterly crushed. Their descendants were not Forsakers. How could they be? They hadn't grown up in a Forsaker community. Nor had they chosen to leave the modern world behind and join a commune...

"We have to assert ourselves," he said, almost pleadingly. He'd known his father wouldn't accept *everything* he'd done, but he'd never imagined that his mighty father would be so...so *weak*. "Father..."

"We have to see to the future," Konrad said. He shook his head, slowly. "You and Hannah will have children. I want them to *have* a future."

Joel nodded, shaken. Of *course* he'd have children. It was his *duty* to have children. And motherhood would quieten Hannah, make her more dependable. She'd stop dreaming of...whatever...and take up the role of wife and mother. The children would ground her in the real world.

"But we may have to fight for that future, father," he said.

His father didn't seem to hear him. "Your mother was a remarkable woman," he said, his voice barely above a whisper. "I wouldn't have married again, you see, if I hadn't owed John a favour. His family *needed* to be protected. Their future needed to be assured."

Because John was a selfish bastard, Joel thought. He might not have needed a stepmother, but John and Hannah had definitely needed a father. *And because Hannah had compromised herself.*

"Your future has to be preserved," Konrad added. "And so does theirs."

"It will be, father," Joel said. "I promise."

"You're a good lad," Konrad said. "I'm proud of you."

Joel said nothing. He was a Steward. It was his job, amongst other things, to support the Elders and enforce their decisions. But now...he looked at the old men and felt nothing, nothing but contempt. They'd been pushed too far. The shock of being uprooted and transported light-years - literally - from their homes had been too much. And now...

He closed his eyes, unwilling to let his father see his internal struggle. He'd been raised to respect the Elders, to accept them as the leaders of his community. And he had served them faithfully, punishing or expelling those who defied the will of the community. He knew he'd been a good servant. He'd known he would inherit Konrad's place in the circle when his father died...

And yet, the Elders had proved themselves unworthy of the role. They hadn't even *begun* to face up to the challenges confronting them. And they didn't realise that they had to stand up for themselves. His fists clenched with bitter anger. Lives were at stake. The entire *community* was at stake. And the Elders were prepared to roll over and die!

"Thank you, father," he said, finally. It was hard, so hard, to keep his voice from shaking. "I hope I will always make you proud."

Konrad clapped him on the shoulder. "You will make Hannah a fine husband," he said, seriously. "And she will make you a decent wife."

Joel nodded, slowly. "Thank you, father," he said, again. "Once we are settled, I will marry her."

"It is a good thing to marry," Konrad agreed.

"Yes, father," Joel said.

He wondered, suddenly, just *what* his father had had in mind. A wife for his only son...or a husband for a girl of questionable virtue, the daughter of one of his oldest friends? It didn't matter, he told himself savagely. Hannah would make a good wife. Her wandering ways would come to an end as soon as they were married. He'd make sure of it.

But first, he had other concerns.

He hugged his father, feeling oddly unsure of himself for the first time in years. His father had been a towering presence in his life for so long that it felt odd to think of him as anything else. As a son, it was his duty to look after his elderly relatives...

...And yet, he also had responsibilities to the entire community.

Shaking his head, he turned and walked out of the room. The Elders would have to go, sooner rather than later. They'd turned into doddering old fools who would only get in the way. And then...after the community was established, he could make sure that only *sensible* men were raised to Eldership. They would never be allowed to grow weak again.

And that will preserve us, he told himself firmly. *From everyone.*

Chapter Twenty-One

> This should not have been surprising. A world - particularly a stage-one colony - might not have the surplus food to feed the newcomers, let alone the resources to train them to survive. Adding a few hundred thousand extra mouths might tip the colony over the edge, forcing them to deny the newcomers food.
> - Professor Leo Caesius. *Ethnic Streaming and the End of Empire.*

"You're still going out on the beat? After everything?"

Mike nodded, reluctantly. His wife - the only person he'd told about the PCA investigation - had loudly told him to resign, after she'd heard the full story. Jane had a point, he had to admit. Everything he'd read on the datanet and in the newspapers suggested that the government was searching desperately for scapegoats, rather than actually coming to grips with the problem. But he'd sworn an oath, the day he'd started his training. He was damned if he was putting it aside...

But they're betraying you, a nasty voice whispered at the back of his mind. He frowned as he checked his appearance in the mirror. *They're setting you up to take the fall.*

"There's no shortage of work outside the cities," Jane added, as Mike reached for his helmet and put it on. "We could leave altogether and..."

"I haven't been charged yet," Mike said. It had been a week since the interview...no, the *interrogation*. Mike was experienced enough to know that it could take weeks to put together a charge sheet, if it was a complex case, yet the lack of any demands for a second interrogation suggested that the PCA didn't *have* a case. "They might be hoping I'll quit so they can take it as a sign of guilt."

His wife snorted. "And to think I thought they were loyal," she said, resting one hand on her stomach. "What's going to happen if they *do* charge you?"

"A trial," Mike said. "But I don't think they will."

He kissed his wife, then hurried out the door and down the road before she could come up with anything else. He loved Jane dearly, yet he didn't want to hear her concerns. Part of him knew she had a point - the PCA probably *did* want someone to blame for the whole affair - but the rest of him refused to give in. He tapped his radio, calling into the station as he strode down the street, his legs falling into the policeman's stride. Technically, he wasn't on patrol until he'd reached the station and picked up his partner, but as long as he was wearing his uniform he had an obligation to be on alert for trouble.

The streets seemed surprisingly quiet for a weekday. Adults should have been heading into work while children headed into school, but there were only a handful of people on the streets. Mike couldn't help finding that ominous. He lived in a residential area - there were only a handful of small shops in the district - but it was usually more lively than this. His skin prickled as he turned the corner and walked towards the police station. Thankfully, it looked reassuringly normal.

"Hey, Mike," the Duty Sergeant called. He had a cheerful voice that made half the officers in the station want to hit him. So far, no one had, but there were no shortage of bets on who would be the first to snap. "You're going down Main Street today. Isn't that grand?"

"I suppose," Mike grunted. He picked up the briefing folder and blinked in surprise at the sheer number of reports. "How many reports have been submitted overnight?"

"Fifty-seven," the Duty Sergeant said. His voice was suddenly serious. "Mostly complaints about refugees."

Mike looked up. "Complaints?"

"Nothing too serious," the Duty Sergeant said. "People complaining about being stared at...nothing else. Apparently, harsh words were exchanged between a husband, a wife and a refugee. The report wasn't too clear."

"I see," Mike said. He glanced at the first couple of reports and wondered, nastily, if they'd been filed by the PCA. There were more weasel words on the first page than he recalled from his last datanet access contract. Policemen were meant to be precise - and stick to the facts - but the report was vague to the point of uselessness. "Anything from HQ?"

"Just a warning to be on the alert," the Duty Sergeant told him. "We've had about nine different reports of shoplifting. It might be nothing more than a random upswing, but it's still worrying."

"I see," Mike said. The door opened, revealing Constable Bobbie Parkhurst. "Bobbie?"

"I'm partnering you today," Bobbie said. She was blonde and bubbly. Few people would have taken her for a policewoman if she hadn't been wearing her uniform. "Excited?"

"It's just Main Street," the Duty Sergeant put in. "Bring me back an ice cream?"

Mike snorted. "We'd eat it on the way home," he said. He winked at Bobbie. "Shall we go?"

Main Street was normally the busiest street in Lothian, even though cars and trucks were permanently banned. It was lined with shops and stalls, ranging from farmer's markets to giant clothing stores headquartered hundreds of light-years away. The latter had never been particularly big on Arthur's Seat, but their garments were popular with a certain subset of the city's youth. Mike remembered his father angrily pointing out that *he* wasn't going to spend five hundred pounds on a pair of jeans from a million light-years away, even if they *were* in fashion. He'd been right, Mike thought, although his younger self had thought otherwise. He could have bought enough clothing for his entire family for the price of a single pair of imported jeans.

And my kid will do the same, he thought, as he caught sight of a young girl arguing with her mother. He couldn't hear their words, but he could guess. She wanted something fashionable and expensive; her mother had no intention of blowing a month's wages on something that would probably go out of fashion in a week. *I'll wind up having to tell him no, too.*

They strode on, glancing unobtrusively from side to side. Everything seemed normal, yet there was…*something*…in the air. A wariness, Mike thought. Main Street was normally safe - he wouldn't have walked through a CityBlock on Earth without powered armour and armed backup - but now…a couple of the farmers had weapons clearly visible, while others were moving with exaggerated care. Mike had no difficulty in telling they were armed.

They're uneasy, he thought. *And so are we.*

He saw the first couple of refugees as they reached the middle of the street. They were easy to spot, wearing clothes that wouldn't have been out of place in a historical novel or entertainment flick. The two young men eyed him warily, keeping their hands clearly visible at all times. Mike puzzled over it for a moment, then realised that someone who grew up on a more dangerous world would have developed ways to prove he was harmless. He glanced past them and saw three more boys, all peering into a bookshop window. There were no refugee women in sight.

Bobbie coughed. "Should we move them along?"

Mike shrugged. "They're not doing anything wrong," he said. Main Street was full of wandering citizens, browsing the stalls and chatting to vendors. "Just keep an eye on them."

A wolf-whistle split the air. Mike swung around, just in time to see one of the refugees waving cheerfully to the girl - and her mother - he'd seen earlier. The refugee glanced at him, then took to his heels and ran. Mike hesitated, honestly unsure if he should give chase or not. Wolf-whistling was normally harmless…

…But, in the current political climate, he had a feeling it meant trouble.

"It's quiet," Sondra said, as she stepped into his office. "Too quiet."

William rolled his eyes, but nodded in agreement. There had been a bunch of leaked reports from the tent city, starting with a witness account of an attempted kidnap that had turned into a riot. And those reports had been joined by a whole series of horror stories - theft, rape, murder - that had spread through the datanet faster than a starship could travel from world to world. And yet...

"Troutman's said nothing," he mused. "Why?"

Sondra made a face. "He's up to something."

William was inclined to agree. There were hundreds of Freeholders - including most of their MPs - arguing against both the refugees and the planned resettlement committee, which the Unionists had demanded as the price for their support. And yet Troutman himself had said nothing. William had wondered if Troutman was deliberately trying to keep his options open - the Freeholders weren't as hostile to outside contact as the Isolationists - but sooner or later he would start to lose support within his own party. His silence was mystifying.

"We'll just have to wait and see what happens," he mused. "Did the whips get back to you?"

"Yeah," Sondra said. "Apparently, both deserters had" - she held up her fingers to make quotation marks - "emergency medical appointments that could not be delayed. They didn't even have time to arrange a swap with opposition MPs. The whips would like to put their positions to a vote."

William weighed up their chances for a long moment. A political party could expel an MP who hadn't toed the party line, but that would only force a by-election. If the expelled MP hung on to his seat in the house, the party would have a new enemy. And there was no guarantee that the party's chosen candidate would win, even if the expelled MP lost. The election might throw another seat to the Freeholders.

He shook his head, slowly. "Remind them of the need for party unity," he said. "And inform them that repeated absences will result in discipline."

Sondra didn't look pleased. "Are you going to let them get away with it?"

"We might lose," William pointed out. The Empire Loyalist MPs wouldn't react well to any attempt to discipline their fellows, even if they *had* technically betrayed the party. They *certainly* wouldn't like having their support taken for granted. "And even if we win, it will set an awkward precedent."

"I suppose," Sondra said. "We can't afford a prolonged period of in-fighting."

William nodded. Troutman had the same problem, of course, but *he* didn't have to worry about commanding a majority in the house. His position was not at stake, nor was his party's grip on power. There was much more room for him to discipline his balky MPs without risking himself. Maybe *that* was why he was so quiet. He was getting his own house in order before resuming the attack.

He cleared his throat. "Did you get anywhere with the negotiations over the Kinsman Estate?"

"The owners are holding out for a sizable rent, but I think they'll change their minds in the next couple of days," Sondra said. "We'll probably wind up having to underwrite the property, just in case the galactic economy suddenly takes an upswing…"

She shrugged. "Right now, the whole estate is a costly drain on their resources," she added, dryly. "I think they'll be glad to have someone else paying for it."

"As long as we can pay for it out of the original funds Parliament voted us," William warned, sharply. "The Freeholders won't be the only ones opposed to paying for that…that white elephant."

He rose and paced over to the window, his eyes searching out the estate in the distance. The Kinsman Corporation had established a local franchise twenty years ago, building an industrial estate that - they'd promised - would bring off-world money flowing into Arthur's Seat. But none of the industrial equipment had ever materialised, let alone the investment that would defray the money the original investors had ploughed into the project. William had been a teenager at the time, but he still remembered how the collapse had nearly destroyed the Unionist Party. The Empire Loyalists had been lucky to escape most of the political fallout.

"It isn't as if they can do anything else with it," Sondra said. "The owners have been trying to find a buyer for fifteen *years*."

William snorted. He would have been more sympathetic if the original investors hadn't done a staggering amount of damage to the planet's economy. Millions of pounds had been tied up in the whole project, only to evaporate when the off-world investors had pulled out. The Freeholders believed - or claimed to believe - that the whole scheme had been intended to provide an excuse for outside intervention. There were times when William wondered if they had a point.

"At least they'll be getting *some* money out of the deal," he said, reluctantly. Technically, the government could just seize the property - and the owners might be glad to see it seized - but it would cause too many political headaches. He could name a dozen MPs who would switch sides instantly if the government started seizing private property. "And it will give us somewhere to put the refugees."

"For a while," Sondra said. "There's no way we can fit fifty thousand people into a single estate."

"And they'll certainly have an effect on the electoral roll," William added.

He considered it for a long moment. There were roughly five hundred thousand people in Lothian, assuming one counted the suburbs surrounding the capital city. The sudden infusion of fifty thousand - or even ten thousand - would definitely shake up the population. It would be better, he suspected, to have the refugees scattered over the continent, but the Forsakers had made it clear they wanted to stay together. Splitting them up might be impossible.

"It favours us," Sondra pointed out.

"Troutman will see that too," William countered. The Freeholders believed - with reason - that the cities were unduly represented in Parliament. Adding an extra fifty thousand voters to the electoral roll would give the Empire Loyalists a major boost. "We'll have to be careful."

"Of course," Sondra said. She smiled. "And we are already making progress in offering medical treatment. There will be some teething problems, I think, but the newcomers will integrate smoother than Troutman thinks."

"Let us hope so," William said.

Sondra cleared her throat. "There is, of course, a different question," she said. "We know who did at least *one* of the leaks from the spaceport."

William lifted his eyebrows. "So?"

"So we should do something about it," Sondra snapped. "She was told not to disclose anything…"

"I don't think that would stand up in court," William said, dryly. He'd read the original story when it had been posted to the datanet. It didn't look to be exaggerated, let alone untruthful, but it definitely came down hard against the refugees. "And unless she signed an agreement not to talk, it would be difficult to prove she was *forbidden* to talk."

"But she's throwing fuel on the fire," Sondra protested. "We cannot allow it to stand."

"But trying to stop her from speaking will make the problem worse," William countered, bluntly. "We *cannot* simply put her in jail without due cause, certainly not *now*. If we try, we will find ourselves under attack from both sides."

"Then she can be charged with threatening public order," Sondra said.

"And then people will wonder what we are trying to hide," William pointed out. "I understand that we need this to remain quiet, Sondra, but this is one of those times when doing nothing is the best option."

Sondra looked murderous. "She's slandering *my people*!"

"And anything you do to silence her will only cause more problems," William said. He rubbed his tired eyes. Sondra seemed to be taking the whole affair far too personally. She, far more than anyone else, had staked her political future on it. He'd been glad to let her do it, but if she went too far she'd bring him down too. "Just leave it, Sondra. If things get better, everything will be forgotten."

"She's caused too many problems," Sondra insisted. "The students alone…"

"Silencing her will not solve anything," William said. He allowed his voice to harden. "We have worse problems."

Sondra met his eyes for a long moment, then nodded once. "As you wish, Premier."

"Keep working on the estate," William said. "The spaceport is going to burst soon, whatever happens. The Imperial Navy is keen to drop the last of the refugees on us."

"We have shortages everywhere," Sondra said. "And conditions are growing increasingly unpleasant. We're just lucky we have plenty of ration bars and the ability to make more."

"Yes," William said. The equipment hadn't been touched since the planet had become self-sufficient. They were just lucky it was still in working order. "But they're going to become sick of ration bars soon enough."

"I know," Sondra said. "We really need to start establishing farms."

"Which will cause other problems," William pointed out.

"We can establish them on Minoa," Sondra said. "It will be costly, but it will solve all our woes."

"Costly," William repeated. "Parliament will not be pleased."

He dismissed her, then turned back to the window. Lothian looked unchanged, but opinion polls suggested that the citizens were growing uneasy. And, beyond the capital, other cities and settlements were growing concerned. There was already a resolution in New Glasgow's District Hall to ban the settlement of refugees within its territory. And there would be others…

He caught a glimpse of a shuttle heading towards the distant spaceport. More refugees, all trapped in a nightmare. And he was trapped in a nightmare too. The problem was growing bigger, yet there was little he could do to solve it.

And if I lose too much support, he reminded himself grimly, *Troutman will be the next man to take this office. And who knows what he will do to solve the problem?*

CHAPTER TWENTY-TWO

The behaviour of these unwanted immigrants was often unspeakable. People raised in the megacities, where bad behaviour was often rewarded, simply had no idea how to behave outside them. The concept of working for food - or money - was alien to them. Crime tended to rise sharply when the newcomers arrived.

- Professor Leo Caesius. *Ethnic Streaming and the End of Empire.*

Judith sat in the quiet cafe, slowly drinking a steaming mug of coffee and feeling sorry for herself.

It was the kind of cafe she would have enjoyed visiting with Gayle, a mere two weeks ago. A cafe lined with bookshelves, a barista who knew the difference between good coffee and recycled crap, a chance to just sit back and relax…it was definitely something she would have enjoyed. But now, after the article had been posted and shared so many times that it had spread around the world, Gayle was no longer talking to her. Nothing official had been said, but Judith suspected she'd been dumped. Their last kiss had been strictly formal.

She closed her eyes in pain, remembering happy hours spent together. They'd shared an apartment, they'd shared classes…they'd even shared a holiday to the jungle, where they'd made love under the trees. But now… part of her wanted to go back to Gayle, to beg for forgiveness, to plead to be taken back. The rest of her knew it would never happen.

I had to tell the world what nearly happened to me, she thought, grimly. *But I never knew the cost.*

Her personal com bleeped. Judith scowled, in no great hurry to read the message. She'd had to send several emails before Director Melbourne had deigned to return it, but there were times when Judith wished she hadn't bothered. Someone - she didn't want to think it might have been Gayle - had leaked her personal com code to the datanet, allowing hundreds of people to bombard her with messages accusing her of everything from being cruel and sadistic to being a flat-out liar. She'd blocked each and every one of the senders, but the messages still kept coming. And while there were a number of supportive messages, they seemed thinner on the ground...

She reached for the device and stared as a name blinked up. HANNAH JOHN-DAUGHTER.

Impossible, Judith thought.

She kicked herself a moment later. Using a personal com - or a datanet terminal - wasn't exactly *difficult*. The user interface had been designed for idiots, although that didn't stop the university's IT Department from having to sort out all sorts of problems. Hannah might have been raised among the Forsakers, but an intelligent girl would have had no difficulty using a terminal. If, of course, she'd been able to find one.

It could be a trap, she thought. It was a paranoid thought, but some of the messages she'd received had threatened death - or worse. If someone had learned Hannah's name, using it to request a meeting would be child's play. And yet, there was something odd about the way the message had been put together. *It sounds like her.*

She hesitated, then tapped a response into the portable com. She'd heard that dozens of refugees had been coming into the city and exploring. Maybe Hannah had found a way to get out without being noticed. Nothing she'd said about her family had suggested they would be interested in letting her go to the city. Indeed, most of the refugees she'd seen on the streets had been young men.

Giving your location out on the datanet can be dangerous, she reminded herself. But she was too depressed to care. *I won't be here for long.*

She sent the message, then waited. The coffee tasted better, but she was too concerned with plotting out possible lines of retreat to pay close attention to the flavour. Twenty minutes later, the door opened and Hannah stepped into the cafe, followed by a young man who looked strikingly like her. If she hadn't known they were brother and sister, she would have suspected it just by looking at them.

The barista coughed, loudly. "Do you have money?"

"They're with me," Judith called. The ID cards the refugees had been issued *did* have some cash, but they couldn't be used everywhere. Most civilians preferred to use paper money and coinage. "Can we get a menu?"

She beckoned Hannah and her brother over, nodding to a pair of chairs. Hannah looked…alive, although she moved with a curious stiffness that bothered Judith. Her brother took one look at Judith's chest - she'd worn a comfortable sweater, rather than her uniform - and then looked away, blushing furiously. Judith kept her amusement to herself. She'd never quite understood why city-boys found it so hard to speak to women - farm boys didn't seem to have that problem - but it could be sweet.

"Judith," Hannah said. She sat stiffly too, a faint wince flickering over her face. "This is my brother, John."

"Pleased to meet you, again," Judith said. She held out her hand automatically, curious to see what he would do. John hesitated, then shook her hand lightly. He didn't seem to savour the contact at all. "How are you coping with life?"

John flushed. "Badly," he said.

"My brother is not used to talking to girls," Hannah said. John's flush grew deeper. "The spaceport is steadily growing worse."

"I'm not surprised," Judith said. The barista appeared with a pair of menus, which he held out to the two refugees with deep suspicion. "It wasn't designed to take so many people."

"We've been lucky," Hannah admitted. "We got a room. Others have been rather less lucky."

"They're in tents," John said. "And sleeping ten to a tent, these days."

Judith winced. She'd never enjoyed sharing a room with her brother, even though it hadn't happened very often. Even sharing a room with Gayle - the thought caused her a nasty pang - had had its problems. The idea of sharing a cramped tent, one designed for three or four people, with nine others…it was horrific. She thought she'd go stir-crazy within the week.

Hannah's eyes flickered down the menu. "What can we order?"

"Drinks and snacks, basically," Judith said. She had enough money to get them both a drink and a sandwich, but little else. "Try the coffee?"

"We're not allowed to drink coffee," John said, morbidly. "Is there anything on this list we can eat?"

"Everything, as long as there's no alcohol," Hannah said, briskly. She paused. "Is the food natural or vat-grown?"

Judith concealed a smile. She'd heard horror stories about visitors from Earth who'd been sick when they'd discovered they were eating dead animals. Honestly! What had they *thought* they were eating? It made absolutely no sense at all. But then, she supposed they'd never eaten *real* meat. Earth's handful of remaining farms were solely for the wealthy.

And they're all gone now, she reminded herself. *The entire planet is a wasteland.*

Hannah coughed. "Judith?"

"The meat will have come in from the nearby farms," Judith assured her. She sniffed the air, tasting the scent of freshly-baked bread. "They'll make the bread here too."

"I'll have a chicken sandwich and tea," Hannah decided. "John?"

John looked hesitant. "We don't have any money."

"I'll pay," Judith said. She shrugged. "Unless you want to spend more than fifty pounds, in which case we have a problem."

She smiled at him. "A chicken sandwich? Or beef?"

"Beef," John said.

He looked almost cringingly embarrassed. Most boys would be a little embarrassed at having a girl buy their food - even though it wasn't a real date - but John seemed to take it to extremes. Perhaps it was different amongst the Forsakers. From what she'd heard - and from what she'd looked up - young Forsakers would rarely be allowed alone time with the opposite sex. Men and women had different spheres and they weren't supposed to mix. Just sitting facing her was pushing John to the limit.

Maybe I should have worn a dress, Judith thought, as she rose. John looked away, blushing furiously. Her shirt had tightened, just a little. *Or maybe I should be hiding behind a wall.*

She ordered the food, then returned to the table. Hannah looked a little embarrassed too, although Judith couldn't tell if it was because of her brother or simply sitting in a cafe with a friend. Her family would not be pleased, no matter what happened. Making friends outside the commune was forbidden.

"I'm sorry about what happened to you," Hannah said. "My stepbrother...he can be a pain at times."

"A pain," Judith repeated. She'd had nightmares over the last few days, nightmares where the police didn't get to her...or joined in the fun. "I would say he is more than just a *pain*."

"He has a lot to live up to," Hannah said.

"He's a bastard," John said, flatly. He didn't look up. "He's nothing more than a monster."

Judith swallowed. "What happened to you?"

"Nothing I couldn't handle," Hannah said, quietly. "I've endured worse."

"I'm sorry," Judith said. It seemed so...inadequate. "Why don't you just leave?"

"I can't leave my mother," Hannah said. She shook her head. "And where would I go?"

Judith winced. Hannah's dress covered everything below her chin, but it was clear, just from the way she'd been moving, that she'd been beaten. There *had* to be aches and pains all over her body. Judith couldn't imagine *her* father doing anything like that to anyone. It was horrific. It was utterly unspeakable.

And the government wanted to keep it quiet, she thought, sourly. *Would they even care if the story went public?*

"Your stepfather is a monster too," she said, finally.

Hannah laughed, bitterly. "He's supposed to be doing us a favour. His son is betrothed to me."

Judith stared at her. "Your stepfather's son is betrothed to you? Your stepbrother?"

"We're not actually related," Hannah said, sourly. "It's not forbidden."

"You allow first cousins to marry," Judith pointed out. Her head was spinning. Had Hannah's stepfather married her mother just to ensure his son a bride? What sort of monster could *think* like that? "And even if you're not *that* closely related, you practically grew up together."

"My fault," John said, miserably. "If I'd declared myself patriarch…"

"You were too young," Hannah said.

Judith shook her head. Hannah was making excuses…*why* was she making excuses? Her stepfather was a monster. And her stepbrother… technically, Hannah and her stepbrother weren't *actually* brother and sister, but they'd grown up together. Legally, she didn't think it was forbidden; morally, she could see all sorts of problems with it. And besides, there *was* the possibility that Hannah *was* related to her stepbrother. She'd have to check their genetic profile before marrying.

"Sick," she said, finally.

"My mother was desperate," Hannah said. "She thought she had no choice."

The food arrived. Judith watched in amusement as Hannah and John marvelled over the giant baguettes, the layers of meat, vegetables and sauces…if they'd been stuck eating ration bars, the sandwiches would have seemed wondrous to them. Judith rather doubted the aid workers had managed to get some proper food to the refugees. Prices had been rising sharply over the last week.

"This is very good," John said. He seemed to have forgotten his shyness. "And all this is from a farm?"

"I imagine so," Judith said, dryly. "Where *else* would it have come from?"

She leaned forward, nibbling on her own sandwich. "Who decides? I mean…how do marriages get organised?"

Hannah's face darkened. "The patriarch of the boy's family talks to the patriarch of the girl's family," she said. "Normally, that's the girl's father. It depends - sometimes it's the girl's uncle instead. The girl's patriarch decides if the marriage is acceptable, after consulting his other relatives and checking the boy's reputation. If everything looks good, the girl and boy meet under strict chaperonage."

She made a face. "If they get through *that*, the girl spends time with her prospective in-laws," she added. "And if she survives *that*, the wedding is conducted and she is a blushing bride."

Judith cursed as she saw the true scale of the problem facing Hannah. Her patriarch and her stepbrother's patriarch were the same person. The stepfather could merely approve the match without bothering to consult with anyone. And then...

She met Hannah's eyes. "What happens if you refuse the match?"

Hannah looked down at the table. "It depends," she admitted. "If the match isn't important, I might be allowed to make the decision for myself. But if the match *is* important, for the family..."

"Shit," Judith said, as Hannah's voice tailed off. "They'd force you to marry him."

"They will," John said, bitterly.

Judith stared. "But why?"

Hannah shrugged. "They forced us to go to school on Tarsus," she said. "The government, I mean. Normally, we would have been schooled at home. We were told to have nothing to do with the Outsider kids. Just sit in their classrooms, pretend to pay attention...head home immediately afterwards without looking back. Me...I liked talking to them. I was friendly with them. Some baboons started talking...before I knew it, my reputation was under threat."

Judith stared. "But you were a *child*!"

"They don't care," Hannah said. She made an odd motion with her hands, as if she couldn't quite keep them under control. "The mere thought of...*contamination*, of perhaps choosing to leave the commune...maybe if our father had lived it would have been different. But he didn't. And I drove my reputation into the mud. I wasn't interested in cooking or cleaning or sewing...I wasn't even interested in becoming a midwife. I wanted to do *something* with my life."

She shrugged. "Joel is really the only person who will marry me," she added. "My mother was desperate to find me a match. I'd be married by now if we had a proper place to live."

The bleak hopelessness in her voice chilled Judith to the bone. She'd never even *considered* rebelling against her father...but she'd never *had* to consider it. Her father had never ordered her to marry someone...he expected her to work on the farm, if she wanted to live there, yet that was different. She could choose her own path.

"You can be whatever you want to be," her father had said, years ago. "But you have to actually work at it."

"Leave," she said. She glanced at John. "Would you let your sister go?"

"I wouldn't want to lose her," John said.

"Leave *with* her," Judith urged. "Find a place to stay here."

"I don't think I could live here," John said. He shook his head. "It's too different."

He glanced around, looking embarrassed. It took Judith a moment to realise he was looking for the toilet. She pointed a finger at the sign, then hid her amusement as he rose and hurried towards the door. No doubt he'd been too embarrassed to ask her - or the staff - where the toilets were hidden.

"He's uncomfortable here," Hannah said, softly.

Judith frowned. "Why?"

Hannah waved a hand. "This place…it's too different, like he said," she admitted. "The people, the women…he's not used to seeing women dressed so…so revealingly. We were always taught to cover up, even when we were alone. We shouldn't attract attention…"

"That sounds like an excuse to blame women for being raped," Judith said, a little sharper than she meant. She'd received messages that said just that, accusing her of exciting the poor little refugees with her tight-fitting clothes and long blonde hair. "Do *you* believe it?"

"I think it doesn't matter," Hannah said, bitterly.

"Leave," Judith urged. "My…my roommate is probably about to go. Even if she isn't, there's plenty of room for us. You could move in with me…we could try and find you a place at university. Or…my father would probably be happy to have a willing worker, if you're actually willing to work."

Hannah stared at her. "Really?"

"Yes," Judith said. "And we could probably find a place for John too."

"My mother would be left behind," Hannah said.

Judith gritted her teeth. She barely recalled Hannah's mother, but she found it hard to feel any respect for a woman willing to force her daughter into a loveless marriage. Maybe, by her standards, she was doing the right thing…Judith still found it unforgivable. And there was something creepy about Hannah's stepfather. Marrying a woman just so her daughter could marry his son…

"I don't understand," she said, instead. "Why can't you go back to see her?"

"Because we're meant to be committed," Hannah said. "We - our ancestors - made a deliberate choice to turn our backs on the modern world. The demon technology…it made lives worse, or so they said. They chose a simple life. And if someone isn't committed to that life, better they leave instead of weakening the entire community."

"Then leave," Judith said. She supposed it made a certain kind of sense. Most of the would-be farmers who had worked for her father had gone home, instead of staying in the countryside. "You're *not* committed."

"I know," Hannah said.

Judith looked up. There was a sound coming from down the street. People were shouting and screaming…she could hear the sound of shattering glass. The barista took one look out the window, then started slamming his shutters into place.

She glanced at Hannah. "What's that?"

Hannah paled. "A riot," she said, jumping to her feet. "We have to get out of here."

She raised her voice. "John! We have to get out of here!"

CHAPTER TWENTY-THREE

> This led to a number of responses. Some worlds managed to build up enough of a defence force to convince the Empire to negotiate, rather than engage in a pointless and costly war. Others insisted on carefully screening and integrating the newcomers, offering to feed and clothe the immigrants in exchange for complete control. And still others took the immigrants and either dumped them on undeveloped parts of the planet or simply killed them.
> - Professor Leo Caesius. *Ethnic Streaming and the End of Empire.*

"So, what's your name?"

James turned…and saw a strikingly pretty young girl. He stared, unable to quite believe his eyes. Long flowing blonde hair, a perfect face, bright blue eyes…and a dress that revealed far too much of her breasts. He couldn't stop himself staring, his eyes trailing down to a shamefully-short skirt that was barely long enough to cover her thighs. His heart began to pound as he looked up again. He'd never seen anyone like her, not even on Tarsus.

"I'm Sue," the girl said. "Welcome to Arthur's Seat."

"James," James managed.

His throat was suddenly dry. He'd never imagined a girl like her, someone so shamelessly sexual. His sisters wore long dresses and hid themselves from unrelated men, as women should do. He knew he should turn and walk away before the slut captivated him - he'd heard all sorts of horror stories about shameless Outsider girls, luring decent Forsakers away from the commune - but his legs refused to budge. His body was intent on making its interest known.

Sue touched his arm. "This is Main Street," she said. "You can buy anything here, anything at all."

James barely heard her. He'd come with a group of friends, intending to explore the city and see if the rumours were actually true, but now...he was torn between the urge to stay and a desire to run. Sue's friends looked strange, a collection of boys and girls, all wearing outrageously skimpy outfits. A couple of the boys were staring at him approvingly, even though he was right next to Sue. One of them even gave him the thumbs up sign. No *Forsaker* would have allowed such contact, certainly not in public. It made no sense.

"You're just down from the spaceport," Sue continued. Her voice was sweet. "What's it really like?"

"Bad," James said, finally. He'd thought the estate on Tarsus was bad, but the starship had been worse and the spaceport was unspeakable. Privacy was a joke. His mother and two sisters had had to move to a different tent, just to make room for more unattached men. "I can't wait to move to a farm."

"I'm sure there will be a farm soon," one of the boys said. "They're always asking for more farmers to move out to the countryside."

Sue caught hold of his arm and led him down the street, chattering happily. James couldn't force his body to pull free, not when her touch was sending electric shocks up and down his spine. He didn't *want* to pull free. His body was aware, very aware, of her breasts bobbing in her dress, mocking him. He wanted to reach for them, to pull them free and run his fingers over them...

He shook his head, angrily. It was wrong. He shouldn't be staring at them, let alone thinking of *touching* them. It was wrong. He should pull free, then run all the way back to the spaceport and purify himself. There was a reason young men weren't allowed to be alone with young women. But his body refused to move. His heart was pounding so loudly that he was surprised she couldn't hear it. It was so hard to think straight...

"There's a party on tonight to raise funds for resettlement," Sue told him. "Are you interested in going?"

James hesitated. Joel had been clear, when they'd headed down to the city. They were to be back on the buses and on their way back to the spaceport before dark. James didn't want to annoy Joel or *any* of the Stewards, but his body insisted he needed to spend more time with Sue. He *wanted* her. God help him, he'd *never* felt so...so what? He didn't have the words for his own feelings. All the quiet banter he'd heard, when the Elders and Stewards had been nowhere to be seen, didn't seem to fit the situation. His body was *demanding* he promised her anything, as long as he got to touch her.

"Maybe later," he managed. Joel and the Stewards would be furious if he failed to return in time. The last thing he wanted was a public whipping. And besides, he didn't quite trust his own body. He'd never been at odds with it before. "We're not meant to be wandering the city after dark."

A young man snickered. "What are you? Children?"

James flushed, feeling his free hand clench into a fist. "I'm eighteen!"

"Not if you have a curfew," the young man said. James felt a surge of sudden hatred, so strong that it almost overpowered him. "Only *children* have curfews."

"They're new to this world," Sue reminded her friend. James wondered, suddenly, if they were lovers. It would be unthinkable in the commune... but then, friendships between men and women were also unthinkable in the commune. What sort of men and women stayed together when they weren't related? "Their rules are different."

She turned, standing in front of James. He couldn't help looking down at the swell of her breasts, rising and falling in tune with her breathing. A flush of hot excitement ran through him at the sight, making it impossible to think straight. And then she stepped backwards, sharply. Her face was bright red as she pulled her dress up, hiding her breasts.

"You shouldn't stare," she said, reprovingly.

James started forward, too angry to think clearly. She'd tempted him... and now she was taunting him? How *dare* she? The rage blinded him. He reached for her, unsure if he wanted to pull her dress away or hit her. His body demanded revenge, demanded that he hurt her for toying with him...how *dare* she? Sue's face crumpled, turning fearful...somehow, the fear made his blood boil. She'd lured him in and *now* she was fearful?

"Enough," the young man said. "Get away from her."

It would have been threatening if his voice hadn't been shaky. James's temper boiled over. He swung around and slammed a haymaker into the young man's chin. His victim tumbled backwards, just as two of his friends came forward. James ducked the blow one of them hurled at him, then slammed a punch into the nearest man's throat. His friends were fighting too - he saw Simon knocked to the ground by one of the locals - but there were more and more locals heading towards them. A young man slammed into him, shoving him backwards; he slapped him back, only realising that his target was actually a young woman when he saw her hit the ground. Her hair was cut so short that she could pass for a man.

Joel had been right, he thought, as he turned. Sue was on her knees, screaming helplessly; the sight made his anger boil over, once again. She'd lured him into her clutches, she'd seduced him...just like Joel and the Stewards had *warned* him would happen. What was *she* screaming about? He hadn't even *touched* her! But he would. He'd make her pay as soon as he fought his way free of her defenders...

The sense that trouble was brewing had been bothering Mike over the past few days, as he patrolled Main Street with a selection of partners. There were just too few police on the ground to cope with any problems, he'd heard; too many policemen had been drawn off to supervise the tent city and guard the spaceport. Not that it mattered, he thought, if several hundred refugees were allowed to visit the city every day. Rumour had it that a number had already vanished, lost without a trace.

It isn't like you need ID to live here, he thought, as he passed a pair of stalls. The newcomers didn't look *that* different from the locals. *Someone could hide out easily if they spoke the language and didn't mind doing shitty jobs.*

He glanced at Bobbie in alarm as he heard the commotion up ahead, then hit the panic button as he pelted up the street. Shutters, some of them newly installed, were already coming down, vendors hastily grabbing weapons - shotguns and baseball bats - as they prepared to defend their stores. Civilians were streaming in all directions, some heading towards the trouble while others were heading away from it. Mike felt his heart start to race as he heard the Duty Sergeant respond, promising that help was on the way. Every last copper in the district would already have been alerted.

But we don't have enough organisation yet, Mike thought, grimly. He'd been told that they'd be running through new training scenarios, but nothing had actually been done. *If this is a real riot, we're in trouble.*

He turned the corner and swore out loud at the sight before him. Five or six Forsakers, judging by their clothes, were fighting seven or eight locals. Several more were lying on the ground, some badly injured. A young girl wearing a very revealing yellow dress was screaming her head off, her arms jerking up and down as if she didn't quite know what to do with herself. Mike drew his truncheon as he saw a handful of bladed weapons being drawn, then blew his whistle loudly. He had a suspicion he should wait for backup, but he knew it wouldn't arrive in time to help.

"Get down on the ground," he shouted, as he started forward. "Now!"

The locals hesitated, some turning and running while others did as they were told. Mike cursed under his breath - it was unlikely the runners would be caught, unless their friends tattled on them - and braced himself. The Forsakers didn't look as though they were going to give up. From what he'd heard, they had no reason to trust the police - or the courts. Tarsus had blamed everything on its unwanted minority.

"Get down," he shouted. "Get down!"

A Forsaker lunged at him, dagger drawn. Mike swung his truncheon and rapped the young man's hand, sending the dagger spinning away. It was a poor decision, but he was damned if he was risking a stab wound in the middle of a wrecked street. The Forsaker yelped, then drew back his fist for a punch. Mike sighed, then slammed the truncheon into the young idiot's jaw. He staggered to one side and collapsed to the ground.

Another came forward, followed by two more. None of them seemed to be carrying knives, but one of them had picked up a baseball bat from somewhere. Mike knocked the first down, then ducked a wicked swing with the baseball bat. Bobbie cracked the swinger on the head a moment later, his companion throwing himself at her a moment later. Mike turned, just in time to see both of them tumbling down, the Forsaker on top. Bobbie's helmet protected her head, but she couldn't get her assailant off her...

Mike caught him by the scruff of his neck and practically threw him across the street. The Forsaker landed badly - clearly, no one had taught him how to land - but he rolled over and started to stand up at terrifying speed. Mike jumped forward and knocked him down again, slamming the idiot into the ground.

"Stay down," he growled, then spun around. "You! Stop!"

James was barely aware of what was going on behind him as he walked towards Sue, his fists itching to slam into her face and *hurt* her for what she'd done. She was screaming, pleading wordlessly for help.... help that would never come. A slut like her didn't deserve protection, didn't deserve a man putting himself in danger for her...she'd encouraged him, then pulled back when it was too late. He was going to hurt her and he'd enjoy it...

He reached for her, a moment before *something* slammed into his back and sent him falling face-first to the ground. It came up and struck him with terrifying force, stunning him for a long chilling moment. A weight was on his back...no, *someone* was on his back. James tried to move, only to discover that he was being expertly held down. Strong hands gripped his wrists and pulled them behind his back, pulling them so hard he could barely resist. A moment later, he felt cold metal snapping around his wrists.

"You are under arrest," a voice growled. James froze. A policeman? His rage turned into fear. Hundreds of Forsakers had gone into police cells on Tarsus, few had emerged. And those who *had* emerged had told all sorts of horror stories. "You have the right to remain silent, but I am obliged to inform you that anything you say will be taken down and used in evidence against you. You have the right to contact a lawyer, which you may do once you have been processed; you may also contact a person of your choice at the same time. Do you understand me?"

James said nothing. His entire body was shaking. He wasn't sure *what* to do. Play dumb, pretend he didn't speak Imperial Standard? It wouldn't work for long, if it worked at all. He hadn't had any trouble speaking to the policemen at the checkpoint, had he? Or perhaps just keep his mouth shut? How the hell had he managed to get into such a mess? Sue...had Sue set him up, right from the start? All the horror stories about Outsider bitches suddenly seemed very believable.

The policeman shook him. "Do you understand me?"

"Yes," James managed.

He couldn't keep his body from shaking. If he was lucky, he'd be spending the next few days in a cell with a monster. The stories...how many of the stories were actually true? Was he going to be someone's girlfriend by the end of the week? Or maybe the police would just take him behind the station and beat him up, just to teach him a lesson.

"Good," the policeman growled. "Stay there."

He rose. James turned his head, just in time to see a trio of *new* policemen arrive. The street suddenly seemed *full* of policemen, as well as a number of men in white coats. Doctors, he assumed. They were certainly helping with the wounded, moving them onto stretchers and carrying them off into the distance. Beyond them, he saw a handful of middle-aged men and women carrying notebooks. He had no idea who or what *they* were.

Sue walked past, her head downcast. A policeman - no, a *policewoman* - walked next to her, holding her arm gently. She didn't look at him as she passed. James stared after her, wishing that he knew exactly what had happened. She was still wearing the striking dress, but she no longer seemed attractive. Had she meant to seduce him? To get him into a fight? Or had it all been a horrific misunderstanding? How could it all have gone to hell so quickly...?

He was dead. The police would probably kill him. God knew a number of prisoners had vanished into the cells on Tarsus and never been seen again. Or maybe they'd kill him. And, if he actually *was* released, the Elders would pass judgement on him and the Stewards would punish him. Or maybe he would simply be shunned by everyone. He'd have to leave the commune if everyone decided to pretend he didn't exist. He couldn't bear it.

Gritting his teeth, he forced himself to relax. The ground was hard, the weather was cold and the cuffs were cutting off his circulation. But it was paradise compared to what he knew was coming. And then…how could everything have gone to hell so quickly? He didn't understand what had happened or why. All he knew was that his life was over…

…And that the worst was yet to come.

"Nine injured, sir," Bobbie said. "Three stabbed; they're already loaded into stasis pods and on their way to hospital. The remainder have a set of minor injuries, but they're on their way to hospital too. One of them is also under arrest."

Mike nodded. "And the witnesses?"

"Constable Nobbys got a list of names for later interviews," Bobbie said. She rubbed her sweaty forehead. She was even less used to violence than Mike himself. "I think we'll be collecting statements over the next few days."

Mike nodded, shortly. Six Forsakers were under arrest, one of them *en route* to hospital under police supervision. The remaining five were lying on the ground, their hands cuffed behind their backs. Twelve locals were also under arrest. They'd be held in custody until the statements were taken or their families bailed them out. Mike sighed as he looked around, silently toting up the damage. Windows had been smashed, produce had been stolen…and none of that took the wounded into consideration. They were damn lucky no one had ended up dead.

It could have been a great deal worse, he told himself, firmly. *A riot on Earth would have done far more damage.*

He sobered. *And the wounded may not survive.*

"We'll get them back to the station," he said. There weren't many locals in sight, save for the ones under arrest, but *none* of the ones who were visible looked friendly. "And then we can hand them over to the Duty Sergeant."

"Yes, sir," Bobbie said.

CHAPTER TWENTY-FOUR

> Does that sound harsh? Of course it does. And yet, the survival of the colony itself was at stake. They simply could not afford to feed additional mouths.
> - Professor Leo Caesius. *Ethnic Streaming and the End of Empire.*

John hadn't been sure what to make of *anything* that had happened, since he'd followed Hannah into the cafe. Merely *being* in such a building was bad enough, but he'd had to fight to keep his eyes off Judith *and* endure the indignity of having her pay for his tea and sandwich. It had tasted heavenly, of course, but that wasn't the point. The *man* was supposed to pay, the *man* was supposed to put food on the table and support his family...

He certainly wasn't sure what to make of *Judith*. Hannah's friend - and he had no idea how Hannah had even made contact with her - was odd. She wasn't as modest and composed as Hannah, nor was she as blatantly sexual as Casey the librarian. Indeed, there was something about the way she moved that bothered him, even though he couldn't put his finger on it. Part of him rather suspected she was considerably more *mature* than him, although it wasn't something he would have openly admitted. She wasn't coy because she didn't see him as a prospective husband.

And then they'd heard the riot.

John glanced out the door, then swore. Men and women were fleeing in all directions, some being knocked down as they fled. He'd seen riots before, on Tarsus. They invariably ended with the police using extreme force to stop them. And the Forsakers who'd been caught up in the madness got the blame.

"We have to move," he said. Hannah was already on her feet, one hand clutching at her dress. A dignified woman would never lift it up, but if Hannah had to run...John silently promised her he wouldn't tell her off, afterwards. "Judith...?"

"You could come back to my apartment," Judith said. "It's safe..."

"For the moment," John said. The only safe place near a riot was somewhere else. "We have to get back to the spaceport."

Hannah hesitated. "John..."

"If you vanish now, they'll think you're missing," John said, sharply. Joel would find out Hannah was missing and then...John didn't want to know. "You have to *tell* them you're leaving."

The sounds outside were growing louder. John saw a blue-clad man run past, followed rapidly by another one. The police...the police might be nice here, but he doubted they would be kind to any rioters. Or anyone caught too close to the riot. He caught Hannah's arm and dragged her out of the cafe, leading her down the street. They had to get away from the riot before circling round to get on the shuttle bus.

"I'll contact you," Hannah called. It took John a long moment to realise she was talking to Judith. "Take care."

John kept a tight grip on her arm as they hurried down the street. Storekeepers glared at them, some fondling guns as if they were intended to start firing at random. John was used to suspicion and hatred, but he'd never been threatened with a gun before. Tarsus had had very strict gun control laws, none of which had kept guns out of criminal hands. Joel had used to say that the local government was quite happy to let weapons flow to rogue groups that would take care of the Forsakers for them.

"John, we can't go back," Hannah said. "Joel..."

"Won't notice as long as you get back before he thinks to check," John said. He had no idea how Hannah had escaped their mother, but she clearly had. "Besides, he's going to have other problems."

Gritting his teeth, he kept running. They had to get to the bus before someone thought to cancel the bus service. And then...? He hoped - prayed - they could get back to the spaceport in time. Joel wouldn't be remotely pleased if he discovered that Hannah had gone down to the city, even with John's supervision. He'd complain to his father and Hannah would be punished. John too, probably.

But he's going to have to worry about the riot, John told himself, grimly. *That should keep him busy.*

And he hoped, desperately, that he was right.

Joel hadn't really expected trouble, not in Lothian. He'd given explicit orders to everyone he'd escorted down to the city to stay *out* of trouble. But now...

"They arrested five of us," Gavin said. He was breathing hard, gasping for breath. He'd run desperately until he'd found Joel. "They're taking them to the station! They were attacked and *they* were arrested!"

Joel cursed under his breath. He really *should* have expected it. The same had happened on Tarsus. Someone started trouble and the Forsakers were blamed. The police couldn't be allowed to take the prisoners into their cells or they'd never be seen again. He thought rapidly, barking out orders to the Stewards as he consulted his map. Technically, he should have called back to the spaceport for orders, but the Elders would hesitate until it was too late. The doddering old men could not be allowed to get in the way.

"The closest police station is here," he said, tapping a point on the paper map. Thankfully, he'd explored Lothian thoroughly enough to have a fair idea of how the map translated into reality. The map was actually accurate. "They'll have to take the prisoners there, won't they?"

Gavin nodded enthusiastically. Joel wasn't so sure. There were seven police stations in the city - Tarsus City had had over thirty, all much larger - and there was no *guarantee* that the prisoners would be taken to the one he'd picked. It *was* the closest, but the prisoners might be marked down for special attention. God knew some prisons on Tarsus had a worse reputation than others. No one in their right mind went anywhere near the secret police headquarters.

"They'll have to go down this road," he added, after a moment. "We'll catch them there."

He smiled to himself as he led the small crowd down the street. There were forty Forsakers with him - and they'd meet others, if they were lucky, along the way. It wasn't much, but he felt his heart singing at the thought of doing something - anything - to stem the collapse of his community. His father would disapprove, but it hardly mattered. Joel - not the Elders - was doing something to save their world.

This could go wrong, his thoughts reminded him.

But he refused to believe it. The local government was weak. Nothing he'd seen in the last few days had forced him to change his mind. They'd allowed the Forsakers to make demands - and they'd conceded those demands - instead of brutally crushing all resistance. And now...they couldn't be allowed to get the impression that the Forsakers would accept their people being turned into scapegoats, not any longer. They were no longer on Tarsus. And the local government wasn't *itching* for an excuse to wipe them out.

He snapped out orders as they turned the corner. "Grab our people, then turn and run," he ordered, sharply. "Do *not* kill any of the locals."

He hoped - prayed - that his men would obey orders. *No one* liked the police, not after everything they'd endured on Tarsus. But dead policemen could easily force the local government into an overreaction. Joel had every faith in his people, yet he knew the locals could do a great deal of damage. He refused to admit the possibility of being exterminated.

And then the police came into view. Joel took one moment to check that they *were* escorting prisoners, then gave the order. The mob surged forward...

Mike had never enjoyed escorting prisoners to the nearest police station. Sure, there were some utter scumbags who deserved to be filmed as they made their handcuffed way to jail, but others were arrested merely for being drunk and disorderly, or for merely being in the wrong place at the wrong time. And while there had never been a case of a prisoner being assassinated during his march to jail, at least on Arthur's Seat, he had a nasty feeling it was a possibility. There were too many angry people watching them as the Forsakers were marched away.

We should have brought the vans in, he told himself. *But that would have meant having to wait.*

A low rumble caught his attention. Mike looked up, just in time to see a mob of people running towards him, shouting and screaming. He grabbed his truncheon, letting go of the prisoner's arm; the prisoner slammed his shoulder into Mike, sending Mike staggering to the side as the mob crashed into the policemen. The truncheon went flying as Mike hit the ground, booted feet kicking at his body. Mike grunted in pain, then curled into a ball, covering his head as best as he could. He had no body armour, no other way to protect himself…it was the only way to keep himself safe.

The noise was deafening. The mob was chanting *something*; he braced himself, curling up again as more feet kicked at him. Someone - a woman, he thought - was screaming, the high-pitched noise so loud it echoed over the chant. A foot came down on his back, the pain so intense that he thought, just for a second, that he'd been fatally injured. And then…

Joel hung back, just a little, as the mob hit the police lines. The police fought desperately, laying about them with their truncheons, but there were just too many Forsakers for them to win. Joel watched, grimly, as the policemen were knocked down, then hurried past them to snatch the prisoners. They'd been cuffed, but he knew from experience that unlocking handcuffs was easy with the right set of tools.

"Get them out of here," he snapped, shoving the first prisoner to Olaf. He vaguely remembered the young man, one of many who'd attended his sermons. "Move, damn it!"

A scream split the air. Joel turned, just in time to see Adam clutching a policeman's arms while Jack struggled to pull down his pants. The scene was so disgraceful that Joel, just for a second, didn't comprehend what he was seeing. It wasn't until the pants - and a pair of shamefully thin undergarments - were pulled down that he realised he was looking at a policewoman. He couldn't help noticing that she'd shaved between her legs. It was one of the signs of a slutty woman...

He remembered himself as Jack started to undo his belt. "Get away from her," he snapped, sharply. Jack wasn't *much* smarter than Olaf - perhaps the Outsiders had a point about not allowing first cousins to marry - but he should know better than *that*! "Now!"

Jack looked up at him, stubbornly. Joel cursed under his breath. Jack was deep in the throes of lust, unable to think of anything but fucking the policewoman. Nothing mattered, but spending himself...Joel darted forward and slammed a punch into Jack's chest, doubling him over. Adam let go of the sobbing policewoman, as if she was suddenly red hot. Joel wouldn't have hesitated to hit him too if necessary.

"Grab Jack," Joel ordered. Jack - damn the bastard - might have ruined everything. Joel would whip him until his back was bleeding, once they got back to the spaceport. A public whipping might teach the idiot to obey orders. "Hurry!"

He glanced at the remainder of the prisoners, then turned and ordered his friends to start running. The local prisoners could run themselves, if they wished, or stay with the policemen. He didn't care. They weren't his concern, certainly not now. Let them live or die as they wished. *He* had to get back to the spaceport before it was too late.

And hope this doesn't come back to haunt us, he thought. Snatching his people back was a risk, but one that had to be borne. And Jack...Jack was going to *suffer*. He could have ruined everything just because he thought that Outsider women were sluts. *The government might decide to take more violent steps.*

Mike grunted in pain as he slowly uncurled himself, his entire body aching. He hadn't felt so bruised and battered since training, when he'd been put through hell by the instructors. And now...he groped for the panic button and pushed it, hoping that one of the other constables had had the presence of mind to hit the switch before being overwhelmed. *He should have done it...*

A sob caught his attention and he spun around. Bobbie was lying on the ground, her pants around her ankles and her legs splayed open...her eyes were staring up at nothing, as if she was bracing herself for an ordeal. Mike recoiled in utter horror, realising just what their attackers had meant to do. There was nothing sexual in the sight, merely...

He shrugged off his jacket, despite the pain, and draped it over her legs. The touch made Bobbie jerk, then sit upright. She buried her head in her hands a moment later and started to sob, great heaving sobs that chilled Mike to the bone. They'd broken her, he realised numbly. The mob might not have raped her - he hadn't seen any signs to suggest they'd actually raped her - but they'd crushed her soul. She might never be able to return to duty.

We're not used to this, Mike thought, as he heard the sound of reinforcements finally arriving. Five policemen, clad in riot gear that had been outdated years ago...they looked intimidating, but Mike knew they didn't have any experience with their equipment. *And they made fools of us.*

He stood, then helped Bobbie to her feet. After a moment, when she made no move to do it for herself, he knelt and pulled up her pants, trying not to look. She was swaying on her feet, her face so vague that he wasn't sure if she knew what had happened or not. Part of him hoped she'd zoned out completely, even though he knew it was a problem. Like him, she should have been pushed hard during training. But then, no one had expected riots on Arthur's Seat.

And it was a tiny little riot compared to the monsters on Earth, he thought, bitterly.

A medic arrived, looking reassuringly competent. Mike pushed Bobbie towards her, then looked around for the Incident Coordinator. *Someone* would have taken command by now, organising the first and second responders as they arrived. As shaken as he was, Mike knew he couldn't leave. His job came first, always.

And what will happen, his thoughts mocked him, *if things get worse?*

He sighed. He had no answer.

The sound of the riot faded quickly as Judith headed away from Main Street, keeping one hand on the knife in her pocket as she hurried back towards the university. There were fewer people on the streets, thankfully, but those that were looked nervous, watching grimly for signs of trouble. Judith kept her distance from the others, knowing that a single mistake could prove disastrous. She didn't feel safe until she reached the campus...

She sighed as she saw the large poster, proclaiming a welcoming rally for the refugees. A dozen students stood below it, handing out pamphlets encouraging students to befriend the newcomers. Judith wondered, as she hurried past them, just what they'd think of Hannah's story. A young girl had the choice between abandoning her family and being married to some asshole she didn't even *like*.

The apartment felt empty as she stepped inside. Gayle's possessions were still there - she couldn't help a faint smile as she saw the underwear hanging from the rail - yet there was no sign of Gayle herself. She glanced into the smaller bedroom, where Gayle had been sleeping for the last few days, but she wasn't there either. A dozen different leaflets littered the bed, some addressed to students and others aimed at Forsaker families. The latter encouraged them to open their homes to refugees.

And that will end well, Judith thought, sarcastically. *Gayle and Hannah are very different.*

It was an odd thought. Gayle and Hannah *looked* a little alike, but their personalities were very different. Gayle was delightfully sensual - Judith tingled at the memory of some of the things they'd done together - while Hannah was stiff and restrained. It was hard to imagine Hannah doing anything more than lying back and opening her legs, after marriage; she'd just lie still until the man was finished, then wash herself. She certainly wouldn't experiment with another *girl*. And her brother...

She sighed, putting the thought aside. Hannah would be safe, she told herself firmly. She wouldn't be killed for daring to go down to the town. Or would she? Her stepbrother - who was also betrothed to her, a truly disgusting thought - might throw a fit if he caught her sneaking out. And then...

But there was nothing Judith could do.

She cursed as she walked back into the living room and turned on the terminal. The local news stations were already talking about the riot, although *real* information seemed to be scarce and there were at least four different explanations in the first ten minutes. But the different commenters all agreed that refugees had started the riot and attacked the police. It didn't look good.

Oh, Gayle, she thought, feeling a bitter pang of grief. She missed her girlfriend, more than she cared to admit. *Where are you?*

And what, her thoughts added, *do you think of your cousins now?*

Chapter Twenty-Five

> The problem, as with so many other issues that eventually brought down the Empire, was that the majority of the Grand Senate simply did not care. They were more concerned with problems at home, such as milking the system to produce more patronage and graft.
> - Professor Leo Caesius. *Ethnic Streaming and the End of Empire.*

Troutman was looking particularly smug, William noted, as he walked into the conference room and took a seat at the table. And well he might, William had to admit, feeling a surge of hatred that almost blinded him. The riot hadn't just given the Freeholders a boost, it had upset and alienated Empire Loyalist and Unionist voters. Lothian might just switch sides completely during the next election, giving the Freeholders an unbeatable position...

This is not the time for calculating political advantages, he told himself, sharply. *We have to find a solution before all hell breaks loose.*

And if Troutman kicks you out of office, his own thoughts answered, *he'll be in charge of finding a solution instead.*

William sighed, then nodded to the usher. The doors were closed, firmly. There were no coffee or sweet biscuits, not this time. This was an emergency meeting. Perhaps, just perhaps, the absence of refreshments would help concentrate a few minds. But night was slowly falling over the city. They might *need* coffee after all.

"This meeting is hereby called to order," he said. "Jacob?"

CULTURE SHOCK

Chief Constable Jacob Montgomery looked grim. The preliminary reports suggested that a number of policemen had been injured, perhaps even killed. It would have been a disaster at any point, but now it was an utter nightmare. Recruiting more constables would be difficult if the job was suddenly more dangerous.

"The witness statements are a little vague," he said. "At one extreme, we have a fight that broke out between a refugee and a local boy; on the other, we have an attempted rape that was stopped by said local boy. Regardless, the fighting sucked in a number of other refugees and locals. By the time the police arrived, nine people were injured, three seriously. All of them are currently receiving treatment in hospital. Several dozen other people were badly traumatised by the whole affair."

He paused. "But that wasn't the worst of it," he added, after a moment. "The policemen escorting the prisoners to the station were attacked by another gang of refugees. They were knocked down - a policewoman was molested - and the prisoners were taken. The gang faded back into the streets and vanished."

"Vanished," Troutman repeated.

"We believe that most of them headed back to the spaceport," Montgomery said. "By the time anyone thought to cancel the bus service, it was too late."

His face darkened. "A couple of policemen were badly injured during the second fight," he admitted. "One had a broken jaw, perhaps in revenge for the spaceport riot; the other had a broken leg. And a policewoman was threatened with rape. She's currently off the active-duty roster and it is unclear if she will ever be able to return to duty."

There was a long silence. "You say the accounts differ," Sondra said, finally. "How do you mean?"

"Susan Pettigrew, the girl who was nearly raped, stated that her assailant practically drooled over her before trying to touch her," Montgomery said. "Hamish, Son of Henry - the sole Forsaker in custody - insists that Susan was trying to seduce her assailant in public. By *his* account, Susan was practically asking for it."

215

His lips twitched in distaste. "We do not, of course, accept that justification."

"I should hope not," Troutman snapped. "I don't care if she was walking down the street wearing her birthday suit! That doesn't give every Tom, Dick and Harry the right to fuck her."

William winced, inwardly. The whole episode was a political nightmare. Who *knew* where the female vote would go, as word spread? There were too many rumours on the datanet - already - for them to cover the whole affair up. No, that wasn't remotely possible. The riot had been rather noticeable, after all.

Sondra cleared her throat. "He might well have misunderstood what she was saying…"

"You're a woman," Troutman pointed out. "Do you *really* believe that that justifies anything?"

"I believe that the case needs to be considered carefully," Sondra answered. Two hot spots burned on her cheeks. This is not a simple open-and-shut case."

"Yes, it is," Troutman said. "He had no right whatsoever to touch her. It's as simple as that."

"But he might well have misunderstood what she was doing," Sondra said. "He was born and raised in a community where sexual contact between unmarried men and women is practically unknown…"

Troutman snorted. "So what?"

"So he may not have understood what was happening," Sondra said, patiently.

"Jesus Christ," Troutman said. "Are you *seriously* making excuses for a fucking rapist?"

"Language," William said.

Troutman ignored him. "And have you forgotten," he added, "that the prisoners were snatched out of our hands by *another* group of refugees? That a policewoman was fucking molested by them? That…"

He shook his head in disbelief. "This is a challenge to our authority," he snapped. "This is an *outright* challenge to our authority. We have to stamp down on it hard!"

Montgomery cleared his throat. "That may not be easy."

Troutman swung around to glare at him. "Explain."

"There are roughly thirty thousand refugees crammed into the spaceport," Montgomery said, slowly. "We've actually had to move the fence twice in the last couple of days, just to provide more living space. In the chaos, we're not quite sure how many refugees are in the spaceport, let alone how many are in Lothian. We have twenty-seven confirmed cases of refugees leaving the spaceport and not returning."

"Oh, that's just *great*," Troutman said.

"Right now, the police force is utterly overstretched," Montgomery added. "We never anticipated this crisis - or anything, really. Too much of our manpower is tied down at the spaceport. Wading into the spaceport to drag the...the wanted criminals out may be impossible."

"They have no weapons," Troutman snarled.

"Don't count on it," Commodore Charles Van Houlton warned. "Improvising weapons isn't *that* hard."

"Then drop a KEW on the spaceport, as soon as the last shuttle is down," Troutman insisted, loudly. "Smash them flat!"

William felt his temper surge, but kept it under iron control. "Are you prepared to kill fifty thousand people?"

"I grew up on a farm," Troutman said. His voice hardened. "Farmers don't have the luxury of being idealistic. I've shot wild boar and foxes and wolves because they threatened my animals. The numbskulls who whine about shooting harmless animals have never seen the damage those animals have done."

"We're talking about people, not animals," William said, quietly.

"And our people come *first*," Troutman answered. "How many times do we have to go over the same argument? Our people come first!"

He took a breath. "Push them into the sea. Ship them to Minoa. March them to detention camps and put them to work in chain gangs. But don't just let the problem grow worse and worse...

"Tell me. If they get away with this, with assaulting young women and attacking policemen, what will they do next?"

"We don't know their Elders *meant* to assault the policemen," Sondra said.

"Oh, yeah," Troutman sneered. "They just *happened* to see the policemen and they just *happened* to snatch the prisoners and they just *happened* to molest a policewoman…"

He sighed. "Do you have any idea just how bad this could get?"

"We should try to talk to them," Sondra said. "Perhaps we can convince them to return the prisoners - and the others - without further ado."

"And that will make it clear that we are *not* negotiating from a position of strength," Troutman said, sharply. He slammed a fist into his hand. "We have to convince them that they have a flat choice between knuckling under or getting crushed."

His voice hardened. "I don't think we have any obligation to help them if they refuse to behave themselves," he added. "*Our people come first!*"

And that will be their election slogan, William thought, grimly. Troutman *had* to be kept out of power. His first order would be to exterminate the refugees, even if it meant destroying the spaceport. The Empire mandated that every planet *had* to have at least one spaceport, but the Empire was gone. *I can't let this crisis get any worse.*

He glanced at Sondra. "We will find a solution soon," he promised. It wasn't going to be easy, not with Troutman breathing down their necks. "Until then…we will address the problem tomorrow."

Troutman snorted. "And do you plan to magically make them all go away?"

He rose. "I don't think I have to tell you that unease is already spreading," he added. "There isn't a single gunshop that hasn't run out of guns, ammunition and other weapons. I dare say it won't be long before people start taking pot-shots at refugees on sight. What happens, let me ask, when the people no longer trust the government to protect them?"

William watched him stride out of the room, cursing under his breath. The urban residents had never seen a riot, certainly nothing this serious. They looked to the police to protect them, but the police were already overstretched. A change in government wouldn't change that, not in a hurry. And once that sank in, who knew *what* would happen?

But the farmers are used to looking after themselves, he reminded himself grimly. *They'll be happy to fight, if necessary.*

He sighed. They needed a solution and fast. But what?

"I don't mind telling you," Doctor Jones said, "that you've looked better."

Mike looked at himself in the mirror. There was a nasty bruise on his face and several more running down his side. He twisted, ignoring the twinge of pain from his back. Sure enough, there was a mark that looked like a footprint on his rear. It wasn't the first time he'd been injured in the line of duty, but it was definitely one of the more extreme cases.

"Thank you," he said, sourly. "Can you clear me for duty?"

"I would advise a hot bath and a nap, but you wouldn't pay any attention," Doctor Jones said, dryly. She was a tall dark woman, the granddaughter of an immigrant couple. "Try to take it easy for the next couple of days, Mike."

"I don't think that's possible," Mike said. He had no doubt the PCA would want a few words with him about the riot. Maybe, just maybe, they'd try to blame it on him. Hell, merely losing the prisoners was awkward enough. Someone who hadn't been there could make a case for incompetence, if they tried. "But I'll do my best."

He turned and started to get dressed, tugging on his pants. "How is Bobbie?"

"Not good," Doctor Jones said. "Physically, she's largely unharmed; they knocked her down, but they didn't give her a beating. Mentally... she's not in a good state. Being rendered vulnerable like that is going to cast a long shadow over her life."

Mike frowned. Rape was rare on Arthur's Seat. A combination of DNA testing, lie detectors and a robust attitude to self-defence ensured that very few rapists remained uncaught long enough to strike again. It wasn't as if they were on Earth, where rape victims had helplessness hammered into them from a very early age and rapists went unpunished, unless they happened to pick on someone with very good connections.

Hell, he'd heard that defending yourself on Earth could win you a one-way ticket to a stage-one colony. And Bobbie hadn't *actually* been raped...

But she was rendered helpless, he thought, grimly. *And she would have been raped.*

He gritted his teeth as he finished dressing. Captain Scott hadn't allowed him to take part in any of the interrogations, but he'd listened as each of the prisoners outlined what had happened when the police had been attacked. It was clear, chillingly clear, that a *Forsaker* had saved Bobbie from being raped. And *that* suggested that the whole affair wasn't random violence, but something that had been planned in advance. And *that* suggested...

He'd taken his concerns to Captain Scott, during the debriefing. But Scott had been more interested in getting Mike and his fellows back on the streets as soon as possible. Mike rather suspected Scott had forgotten to mention Mike's thoughts to his superiors. And if that was the case, Mike would have to pass them up the chain himself.

"Thank you, Doctor," he said. "And I hope I won't see you soon."

The doctor laughed and waved him out the door. She'd had a busy night - and, Mike suspected, it was only the beginning. He smiled as he strode down the corridor, then sobered as he caught sight of Bobbie in an examination room. She was sitting on a medical bed, her eyes downcast. Mike knew she was at least twenty-five, but she looked younger. The gown someone had forced her to wear didn't help. He would have taken her for eighteen if he hadn't known better.

"Bobbie," he said, gently. He'd been warned not to loom over rape victims, not when they would almost certainly be on edge. Bobbie might not have been physically raped, but her mind had been...twisted. "How are you feeling?"

"Rotten," Bobbie said. She didn't look up. "Did you get cleared by the doctor?"

"Yeah," Mike said. He felt a hot flash of pure rage. The bastards who'd hurt her were going to pay! But even *that* was a sign that things had changed. He was treating her as someone who had to be protected, rather than an equal. "I can go back on duty."

"Good," Bobbie said. There was no enthusiasm in her tone at all. "Good luck."

Mike gritted his teeth. It was better, his instructors had said, when the victims of crime wanted to fight back. It proved they hadn't lost their nerve, that they hadn't allowed the criminal to steal their determination as well as their property. Some people never quite recovered from having their house burgled, or being mugged on the street...or being raped.

Because the crime struck them on a very intimate level, he recalled. *And they no longer feel safe in their homes...or anywhere.*

"We'll find the people responsible," he said, finally. They *did* have descriptions, although most of them were vague. There was no DNA evidence, not this time. "And put them in a work camp until they're fifty."

"No, you won't," Bobbie said. She still hadn't looked up from the floor. "If the government is prepared to treat you as a criminal, just for saving that poor girl, what are they going to do to me?"

"File a charge," Mike urged. He had no idea if Bobbie had filed one or not already, but a filed charge was harder to deny. "Don't *let* them get away with it."

Bobbie looked up at him, her eyes hopeless. "But they will," she said. "Who *cares*?"

Mike ground his teeth in silent - and helpless - fury. Bobbie had been broken. She'd been stripped of her uniform, stripped of her dignity, stripped of her sense of security...and she hadn't even saved herself. No, the reports had made that clear. She'd been saved from two criminals by *another* criminal. And she was right. The bastards would probably get away with it.

Unless we can identify them, he thought, grimly. *They may not know there isn't any solid evidence...*

He shuddered. He had a wife, a pregnant wife. He had sisters and cousins; he knew almost every girl on his street, from the newborn babies to a young lady who'd asked him about joining the police. Were they all at risk? Should they be urged to cover themselves, to cower in their homes as more and more refugees landed on the planet? Or would the government find its balls and *stamp* on the refugees?

Of course not, he thought. *That would mean admitting they were wrong.*

"I care," he said, finally. He reached out to touch her shoulder, then stopped himself. In her vulnerable state, touching her would probably be disastrous. He couldn't treat her like a fellow cop, not any longer. "And it will get better."

Bobbie snorted. "You think?"

"Yes," Mike said. He tried to push as much encouragement into his voice as he could, even though he didn't *feel* encouraging. "I think so."

He paused. "I'll talk to you later," he added. "And don't hesitate to call me if you need a friendly ear."

"Thank you," Bobbie said.

Mike gave her a long look, then nodded. He turned and headed down the corridor, keeping his thoughts to himself. Captain Scott would probably keep Bobbie off the duty roster permanently, ending her career, unless she got better before too long. And if he didn't, Doctor Jones probably would. She had never bowed to pleas, demands or threats when she'd felt someone was not suited to active duty.

And this may be what it's like from now on, he thought, grimly. *Or worse.*

He shuddered. He'd read a book several years ago, an autobiography written by a woman who'd left Earth in her early twenties. The woman had been blunt; she'd grown up in the middle-class regions of Earth, yet she'd still been raped several times. She'd taken it in her stride, Mike recalled. To him, it was horrific; to her, it was part and parcel of living on Earth, just one of many things that had to be endured. And the hell of it, as she'd made clear, was that *her* experiences were hardly the worst…

Dear God, he thought, as he stepped into the duty office. *Is that what we're going to become?*

CHAPTER
TWENTY-SIX

And those who did care were almost worse. Their ideas of how the universe worked were so out of touch that they might as well have been in different universes to their subjects. Their idealism - they were always idealists, simply because they never had to give up anything of importance - led them to take truly unwise steps.
- Professor Leo Caesius. *Ethnic Streaming and the End of Empire.*

The entire spaceport was buzzing with rumours as John followed Joel and a handful of other Stewards through the endless rows of tents. Joel hadn't even noticed Hannah's absence - it hadn't been until much later that John had realised that *Joel* had been in the city too - nor had he bothered to look for her, as night fell over the tent city. They'd endured a largely sleepless night, fearful that *something* would happen. And the rumours were growing darker and darker.

But nothing *had* happened.

John fretted helplessly as they reached a large square, the sole open space in the giant spaceport. A small frame had been erected in the exact centre, surrounded by a cluster of Stewards holding the crowd back. John gratefully stepped aside as Joel headed onwards, passing through his fellows and walking over to the frame. It looked like something stolen from a child's playground.

Joel turned and opened his mouth. "Bring forth the prisoners!"

John tensed, suddenly realising what was about to happen. Jack and Adam were marched forward, their hands tied in front of them. Neither of them looked to have had a wink of sleep, judging by the way they inched towards the frame. But then, neither of them *wanted* to be there. John was surprised that they were there at all. Joel had considered them allies, hadn't he? Adam had *definitely* been at the meeting where Joel had first started talking about fighting.

"These two fools decided they could assault a woman," Joel said. His voice echoed through the silence. "They have confessed their crimes. They now come to claim their repentance."

John shivered, unable to look away as the two men were tied to the frame, their shirts lifted to reveal their broad backs. Joel was making a point to everyone, he realised numbly. He was restoring discipline, such as it was, and also making it clear that *he* was in charge. John looked from side to side, but none of the Elders were visible. He hadn't seen Konrad since they'd returned to the spaceport. Had the Elders passed judgement on the two fools? Or had Joel usurped their responsibilities for himself?

"Adam and Jack," Joel said. He didn't mention their family names, a clear warning that they were on their own. "Do you accept this punishment?"

"Yes," Adam said.

Jack merely nodded. John gritted his teeth. He'd never liked Jack. The young man had always struck him as dangerous. It was possible that he'd turn on Joel, at some point, after being humiliated in public. But, if Joel had bothered to uphold tradition, Jack could also have left the commune instead of accepting his punishment. He was more than old enough to make his own decisions.

Unless his father pushed him into accepting punishment, John thought. There was no way to know. *He might not want his son kicked out of the commune.*

He tensed as Joel raised the whip, then brought it down on Adam's back. He'd wondered, morbidly, if Joel would go easy on his own men, but it was clear - as an evil red mark appeared on the young man's back - that the stroke had hurt. Adam gasped in pain, gripping the frame tightly as the second blow fell. John forced himself to look away, but there was no way he could hide from the sound. Adam was sobbing helplessly after ten strokes.

Joel moved on to Jack, lashing him with brutal force. John turned his head, just in time to see blood trickling down Jack's back. Joel had broken the skin, he realised. John was no doctor, but he couldn't help thinking that was a bad sign. Cuts could easily become infected. But Joel kept lashing the bigger man until Jack's back was covered in blood. John caught a glimpse of Joel's face and shuddered. He was *pissed*.

"They have paid for their crimes," Joel informed the crowd. He released Adam from the frame, then gave him a hug. "Let no one hold it against them from this day forth."

John watched, grimly, as Jack was freed too. The older man looked angry, blood staining his trousers and dripping to the ground. He declined Joel's hug. Instead, he turned and stormed off, heading back towards his tent. John felt a stab of sympathy for Jack's roommates, mixed with a desperate hope that Jack would attack Joel. A great many problems would be solved if Jack killed Joel, then was killed himself by the rest of the Stewards.

And I wonder, he thought. *Did Konrad and the others really authorise this?*

A young boy - one of the children who idolized Joel - hurried through the crowd towards Joel. John recoiled in shock. Whippings - public whippings - were no sights for young boys or women. Hell, they were so rare that he'd never attended one until now. Had Joel let the youngsters watch? Or was the boy bringing him a message?

Joel stepped forward to address the crowd. "Steward Roth will speak now," he said. "I have been called away."

He turned, following the young boy out of the crowd. John watched him go, wishing he dared follow. But *someone* would notice if he crept out and report him to Konrad…no one was allowed to skip a sermon, particularly not now. Shaking his head, he turned and listened as Roth began a lengthy sermon on the proper treatment of young women. It made him wonder, grimly, just what Jack and Adam had actually done. Joel wasn't normally concerned about Outsider women…

Maybe they defied orders, John thought. It was as good a guess as any. *And Joel decided to make an example of them.*

William had only visited the spaceport four times in his entire life, three of them after becoming Premier. There hadn't been any real *need* to visit, save for a handful of diplomatic functions that had been - thankfully - rare. The Sector Governor had never seen any need to pay more than a brief visit to Arthur's Seat when the world was neither rich enough to be worth courting nor vulnerable enough to be worth taking. Even then, the spaceport complex had struck him as a giant white elephant. It was easily three or four times the size it needed to be to handle the - very limited - traffic that passed through the system.

Not that we're complaining, not now, he thought. *We needed space for the refugees.*

He shuddered at the sight before him. The rows upon rows of tents stretched as far as the eye could see, their inhabitants staring at him as the car carried him towards the spaceport terminal. Despite everything, his heart went out to the refugees. Their clothes were tattered and torn, their faces pale and wan…it was clear, all too clear, that they didn't have anything like enough food to eat. They'd been stripped of everything, even human dignity. Who could blame them for chafing against their restraints? He saw a young boy kneeling outside the tent and shivered helplessly. There was something bleak and hopeless in the young boy's gaze.

We need to get more people to sign up to house them, William told himself. A number of names had been removed from the list, after the riot in Lothian. The remainder would probably want security guarantees before too long. *Even putting them in the estate isn't going to be enough.*

The car passed a police checkpoint and came to a halt in front of the terminal. William waited for his driver to open the door, then stepped out into the biting cold. The air stank of fear and faeces and sheer desperation. He could see faces pressed against the wire, staring at him with palpable resentment. And who could blame them? He was well-fed, wearing a tailored suit that had cost enough money to feed hundreds of refugees for a week…the policemen fell into formation around him as he walked into the terminal, his footsteps echoing oddly on the shiny floor. There was something *eerie* about the deserted building, something he didn't want to face. It looked as though it belonged to another world.

He glanced at the policemen and shuddered, again. They looked... grim, their hands never far from their truncheons. A couple were carrying other weapons, weapons that looked strikingly lethal. William was no weapons expert - he'd grown up in Lothian - but they looked terrifying. He wondered, absently, if the refugees were scared of the police.

We penned them up like animals, he thought. He couldn't help feeling guilty. His office was being bombarded by waves of angry messages, demanding that something be done about the refugees, but none of his constituents had visited the refugee camp. *And we weren't even the first to pen them up, either.*

The meeting room looked identical to a dozen others he'd visited over the years; a table, a set of comfortable chairs, a drinks machine that looked to be non-functional...he took a seat as the other doors opened, allowing two refugees to step into the room. William studied them both with interest, knowing they were studying him too. The elder of the two looked old enough to be his grandfather - William had to remind himself that Forsakers rarely used rejuvenation treatments - while the younger looked...*young*. It was vanishingly rare for anyone to become an MP on Arthur's Seat before they turned thirty-five, even though it wasn't illegal. A youngster would lack the maturity of his elders.

"Premier," the elder man said. His voice was firm, but raspy. William had the impression that Imperial Standard was very much his second language. "I am Elder Konrad. This is my son, Steward Joel. We are honoured to meet with you."

William nodded, rising to shake hands with both of them. Troutman was going to have a field day if - when - he heard about the meeting. The Premier of Arthur's Seat, deigning to meet with a bunch of refugees as equals? William knew, all too well, that he was gambling his position - and his entire government - on the meeting. A failure now would bring everything crashing down.

"Please, sit," he said. He sat himself, taking the opportunity to quietly study Joel. The young man burned with a deep-seated anger, an anger William understood. Anyone stuck in a refugee camp would be angry, all the more so after being rounded up and kicked off their previous homeworld. "We have to talk."

"Indeed we do," Joel stated. "The conditions here are unacceptable."

William nodded in hasty agreement. Which of them was actually in charge? William knew very little about their community, but he understood human dynamics. Konrad and his fellows would only remain in charge as long as they met the needs of their people. If they failed to do so - if they *clearly* failed to do so - their followers would turn to leaders who promised to actually come to grips with their problems. Hell, Troutman was quietly positioning himself to present himself as a leader who actually *understood*.

"I agree," he said, out loud. "But your behaviour has also been unacceptable."

He looked directly at Konrad. "Several of your people were arrested after attempting to assault a young lady," he said. "And then *more* of your people snatched them back, assaulting *another* young lady in the process. We want those people handed over to us for trial."

"Because you will *surely* give them a fair trial," Joel said. "We've had our people put on trial before, Premier. It has never ended well. *We* will deal with them."

"This is our planet," William said. He suspected he understood the true problem, regardless of what they were saying. *Could* Joel and Konrad hand the bastards over? If they couldn't, trying would merely undermine their position. No politician worth a damn would issue orders he *knew* would cost him everything. "We cannot allow…"

"We have already punished them," Joel said. There was an edge in his voice that made it impossible to doubt him. "They were flogged, only thirty minutes ago. I assure you they will not repeat the offense."

William shuddered. "They were flogged?"

"Publicly," Joel assured him. "Their crimes were read out, then they were flogged. They have paid for their crimes."

Konrad cleared his throat. "They were judged by the Elders," he said. The look he gave his son was unreadable. "And they were found guilty. They chose to take their floggings rather than leave the commune."

William took a breath. "I'm afraid that isn't acceptable to us," he said. "We need *all* of them handed over to us."

"Oh," Joel said. "And what are you prepared to offer in exchange?"

We have to bargain, William told himself. In truth, even if they *could* storm the spaceport, they didn't even know who to arrest. The Chief Constable had made that very clear. *And we have something to bargain with.*

"Your people cannot stay here," he said, quietly. "The conditions are disgraceful."

He paused. "My government was not expecting to have to deal with you," he added. "That said, we have managed to secure an estate to serve as temporary housing. It isn't perfect, but it will suffice until we disperse your population throughout the countryside."

"We insist on a place we can remain together," Joel said.

"The estate will be yours," William said. "In the long-term, you will eventually be able to set up farms of your own."

And that will change them, he added, silently. *Their farming methods won't let them raise a proper crop, not here. They'll have to embrace modern technology to survive.*

Konrad and Joel exchanged a long glance. "That would be suitable," Konrad said, finally. "I will insist on inspecting the estate first, of course."

William held up a hand. "Once the prisoners are handed over," he said, firmly. "We need to try them ourselves."

Joel smirked. "I thought it was a principle of interstellar law that a man can't be tried and punished for the same crime twice?"

"Your Elders are not an accredited court," William pointed out. "And you didn't follow interstellar procedure."

"We'll try and do better next time," Joel said. His voice suggested that he thought he'd won a point. "But they *were* punished for their crimes."

"I'm glad to hear it," William said. "However, we *must* insist on having the former prisoners and their rescuers handed over."

Konrad started. "Out of the question," he snapped. "You would not give the rescuers a fair trial."

"They assaulted police officers," William said. "And a female officer was nearly raped."

Konrad's face twisted. "A *female* police officer?"

Joel snorted. "The would-be rapists were flogged, hard," he said. "I can have their bare backs paraded in front of you, if you wish."

William felt sick. Attempted rape would get a man five to ten years on a chain gang, if his victim pressed charges. A flogging...that was cruel and unusual punishment. And, in all honesty, it wasn't enough.

And yet, he could see their point. Their experience on Tarsus had taught them that their people couldn't expect a fair trial...and they might lose their positions if they tried to hand the rescuers over. They'd be seen as heroes by the rest of the commune, heroes who had been callously betrayed by their leaders. And whoever replaced Konrad and Joel would know better than to compromise.

"Hand over the would-be rapists and the original prisoners," he said. Troutman was going to turn it into a political nightmare, but at least he would have got *something* from the deal. "If you do, you can have the estate. You'll have a chance to relax and fit into our society."

He sighed, inwardly, as Konrad and Joel chatted rapidly in a language he didn't recognise. It was a bad deal, perhaps the worst since...since the Kinsman Estate had been built and abandoned. Troutman wasn't going to be the only outraged MP, no matter how they tried to spin it. But it would have to do, if only to buy time. Crushing the commune and slaughtering its members was not an option. And nor was penning them up.

Diplomacy is the art of saying 'nice doggy' while you find a big stick, he reminded himself, firmly. *And more exposure to our culture - and life on Arthur's Seat - will wear them down.*

"We accept," Konrad said, finally. "The former prisoners - and the flogged fools - will be handed over to you, once we see the estate. And then...when can we move in?"

"As soon as possible," William said. "We have to get the rest of the refugees down to the ground."

"We also need our supplies," Joel said. "They're still on the ships."

"I'll have them sent directly to the estate," William said. He rose. "I'll have a car and driver assigned to you. He'll take you to see the estate."

Joel smiled. He thought he'd won, William suspected. And he seemed to think that he'd won more than William thought. There was a glint in the younger man's eye that bothered William more than he cared to admit. But the more contact the commune had with the mainstream culture, the more its society would change. They, like their distant cousins, would blend into the rest of the world.

Sure, his thoughts mocked him. *And what if you're wrong?*

But to that, he had to admit, he had no answer.

CHAPTER
TWENTY-SEVEN

> Accordingly, the problems facing the colonials simply didn't register to them. They were unreal. How could a man born and raised in the high towers of Imperial City understand the life of a dirt-poor farmer on the edge of explored space?
> - Professor Leo Caesius. *Ethnic Streaming and the End of Empire.*

It would have been undignified, Joel thought as he clambered into the government car, to shout and jump for joy. He was a Steward, after all, and Stewards had a reputation to maintain. But he couldn't help a colossal wave of exultation as John, Hannah and his father followed him into the car. He'd won! And he'd solved two problems at a stroke.

The car rumbled to life, cruising past the checkpoints and onto the road. Konrad had wanted to surrender, had wanted to hand over the prisoners without hesitation…it had been Joel who'd encouraged him to take a hard line, Joel who had sworn that the local government didn't have the nerve to pick a fight. The simple failure to storm the spaceport within hours of the riot - or even to reinforce the policemen on duty - suggested that the government was more interested in calming tensions than bringing matters to a speedy conclusion. And he'd been right!

And Jack will be on his way to jail, he added, in the privacy of his own mind. Losing Adam was a pain - Adam had been loyal - but Jack? Getting rid of Jack, after Jack had proved himself dangerously unreliable, was an unexpected bonus. *And maybe I can even convince him that he's still working for us.*

He shrugged, trying to meet Hannah's eyes. She looked away, staring pointedly out the window. Bringing her along might have been a mistake, Joel considered, but there were no other candidates. *Someone* had to check the female quarters, after all. *And* he wanted to show off, just a little. Hannah couldn't question his suitability as a husband after *this*. It meant bringing John too, just to ensure that no one could question their conduct, but *that* didn't matter. John wasn't brave enough to oppose him, even if John didn't want to *join* him.

The car turned, heading down a long - and almost deserted - motorway. Joel hastily recalled the maps he'd studied, weeks ago. They were on the ring road, cruising around the edge of Lothian. The locals seemed to have more cars per person than Tarsus, he thought, even though they *were* oddly primitive. But then, Arthur's Seat didn't produce anything like enough HE3 for a modern economy, let alone the raw materials they needed for an advanced industrial base. It was why the first settlers had been so keen to settle the world, so many years ago. They'd never anticipated a more modern bunch of settlers arriving.

He glanced up as the intercom hissed. "If you'll look to your left," the driver said, "you'll see a rather interesting tourist attraction."

Joel frowned, then did as he was told. The motorway was lined with trees, but they parted as the car drove past, revealing a small wooden and stone cottage in the middle of a field. There was something strikingly rustic about the sight, calling to him. And yet, there were holes in the roof and decay marks on the walls...

Hannah spoke into the silence. "What *is* it?"

"The sole surviving building from the first landings," the driver said. "They built hundreds of such buildings in the first two years, but almost all of them fell apart before the second landings began. This one was preserved, after the original settlers moved into better homes; the remainder were just allowed to decay into dust. Even now...if it wasn't for a team of custodians, it would be gone too."

John elbowed Hannah, making her yelp in pain. Joel nodded in approval. It was good that John was *finally* taking his brotherly duties seriously. Hannah shouldn't have spoken to the driver at all. Maybe he was finally growing up...John had a brain, when he chose to use it, even if he *did* lack nerve. Joel made a mental note to spend more time with him, then opened his mouth. He wanted an answer.

"What happened to them?"

The driver snorted. "Lots of little things, all adding up to disaster," he said. "This planet's biosphere is unusually tough. Much of the vegetation is inedible. The seeds the original settlers brought didn't stand a chance. They lost hundreds of people trying to figure out what could and couldn't be eaten, forcing them to struggle to clear enough fields to grow their own crops. Then the weather got a great deal colder throughout the third year…it killed too many of them as well as blighting the crops. They would have died out if the second wave of settlers hadn't arrived."

Joel shuddered. He'd heard several versions of the story, but they all boiled down to the same thing. Outsiders were *not* to be trusted. The original reports on Arthur's Seat had made it out to be paradise, a Garden of Eden where the Forsakers could finally live the way they chose. But they had been conned and the settlement had almost died…

The car turned off the motorway, passing a line of trees as it headed towards a large wire fence. Beyond the fence, Joel could see dozens of dark buildings, ranging from giant warehouses and industrial complexes to apartment blocks and stone cottages. Someone had attempted to lay out grassy fields and flower gardens, he noted, but they were so badly overgrown that they looked like small jungles. No one had tended to them in years. The driver stopped the car and waited. A policeman appeared from nowhere and opened the gate, beckoning for them to drive into the complex.

"Welcome to the Kinsman Estate," the driver said. He parked the car and yawned, loudly. "I'll be here when you want to go back."

Joel exchanged a long glance with his father, then opened the door and scrambled out of the car. The smell hit him at once, a faint scent of pollen and flowers, mingled with something he couldn't identify. He looked towards the nearest flowerbed and spotted a number of weird-looking plants, mixed with flowers and greenery he vaguely recognised. The planet's own native plant life had invaded the estate.

Or maybe it was there all along, he thought, as John and Hannah emerged from the car. *The second wave of settlers didn't find it to be quite as dangerous.*

His father followed them out, clutching a map in one hand. The estate was huge, easily large enough to hold twenty thousand or so settlers... although Joel was sure they would still be cramped. There were a number of fields at the outer edge of the estate, all seemingly empty...they'd have to be used for tents, at least until they managed to set up more buildings or started to drift out to the farms. And Joel was sure there *would* be farms, eventually. The government was weak, unwilling to seek or accept confrontation. They'd give the Forsakers whatever they wanted, as long as it looked like they were coming out ahead.

They have to make excuses, Joel thought, as he picked a building at random. *And as long as they can make excuses, they won't try to change us.*

He led the way towards the giant grey building, pushing his way through the towering grass and overgrown flowerbeds. It felt almost as if he'd shrunk, as if the world was suddenly a much larger place...he'd seen fields and farmland, but even the cornfields had been smaller to him. Small insects buzzed around, some spinning around his head curiously before flying off into the undergrowth. They weren't threatening, he thought, but it was hard to be sure.

John broke the silence. "How many of those insects are native to Arthur's Seat?"

Joel shrugged. He didn't know. And, in all honesty, he didn't care.

The door was open, allowing him to step into the building. There were no lights, but bright sunlight was streaming through the windows. It was huge, utterly immense...and utterly barren. There was nothing within the building, no industrial machinery or living space. Dust lay everywhere, a great carpet that shimmered under the light. He couldn't help feeling as though he was walking through snow.

Hannah choked, then turned and hurried back outside. Joel turned, just in time to see John follow her. He'd help her, Joel was sure. He looked around the giant chamber, silently assessing what they'd need to do to make it habitable. The dust would have to be swept up, of course, and supplies brought down from orbit...it would be a pain, he knew, but it was doable. The women would handle the cleaning while the men pruned back the undergrowth and readied their defences.

There was no sign of John and Hannah when they emerged from the building, but he could see dusty footprints leading towards a smaller apartment block. Joel shrugged, then led Konrad towards another cottage. It had probably been designed for one of the owners, he guessed. *He would make sure that his family got one of them, of course.* The cottage was not only defensible, it would be easy to seal off if necessary.

"It's suitable," he said, finally. "Don't you think?"

His father shrugged, his hands toying with his worry beads. "As long as we can live here safely," he said, finally. "But it came at a cost."

Joel turned away, hoping his father wouldn't see the contempt on his face. The Elders, the doddering old men…they clung to their powers when they were unchallenged, but they rolled over whenever anyone put up a fight. He'd listened to his father for too long, back on Tarsus. They needed to stand up for themselves, if only to get the local government to leave them alone. And their new home…

He peered west, towards Lothian. They were close enough to be visible, close enough to put pressure on the government…it wasn't perfect, but it would have to do.

Keep your eye on the prize, he told himself, firmly. Once their tools arrived, they could start planning their farms. It wasn't as if Arthur's Seat didn't have plenty of unclaimed land for farms. *And remember to play for the long game.*

"Premier," Sally said. "Steven Troutman requests an immediate audience."

William nodded, sourly. He'd expected as much. Technically, if Troutman wanted to push for a vote of no-confidence, he had to do it in Parliament, but there was nothing stopping him from delivering the message in person. Besides, Parliament wasn't due to meet again for another week. Troutman *could* have requested an emergency session, yet that would have given the game away ahead of time.

"Show him in," he ordered, looking up from his desk. He didn't feel particularly welcoming, but the formalities had to be observed. "And have tea sent in, too."

Sally nodded and headed out of the room. Five minutes later, she showed Troutman into the chamber. The Leader of the Opposition looked grim, William noted, but he didn't look determined enough to demand an immediate vote of no-confidence. That, at least, was a relief.

Of course not, William thought, as he rose to greet his rival. *If he loses, he has to surrender his own position; if he wins, he has to cope with the crisis himself.*

"Steven," he said, flatly.

"William," Troutman said. He sat down, his eyes never leaving William's face. "A rumour reached my ears, suggesting that you signed the Kinsman Estate over to the refugees. Is that true?"

William briefly considered denying it, just to waste Troutman's time, but it would be nothing more than pointless spite. A rumour…by now, Troutman would probably have people *en route* to the estate, if they weren't already there. They'd see the refugees as they planned the move into their new homes. And besides, enough policemen knew about the arrangement to make a leak inevitable, sooner or later. The Chief Constable had made it clear that parts of his force were on the verge of mutiny.

We've already had a number of resignations, William recalled. *They're starting to think they won't be backed up if necessary.*

"It's true," he said, flatly.

"Tell me," Troutman said. "Are you out of your mind? Or have you decided to pull a Phelps?"

William winced. Grand Senator Phelps had cleared the way for the Tyrant Emperor, the last Galactic Emperor with any real power. No one knew precisely *what* Phelps had had in mind, but he'd stripped away all the long-established safeguards and allowed the Tyrant a completely free hand. Phelps himself had died in the aftermath of the Tyrant's assassination as the Grand Senate regained control. His name had become a byword for traitor in the waning years of empire.

"No," he said, stiffly.

Troutman snorted, rudely. "You are rewarding bad behaviour," he said, sharply. "Do you really feel that giving them an estate will solve the problem?"

"It's a start," William said.

He felt a sudden surge of hatred for the man in front of him, a surge shocking in its intensity. Troutman wasn't the man in the hot seat. He wasn't the one who had to make the final call, any more than he was the man who'd take the blame if something went wrong. Troutman was free to carp and criticize like an upper-class housewife because *he* wasn't the one in charge. No *wonder* he hadn't moved to unseat William! The crisis offered plenty of opportunity to strengthen his hand without actually taking power.

Bastard, William thought.

"It is another surrender," Troutman said.

"We will have the prisoners handed over to us," William said. "We *compromised...*"

"One does not *compromise* when there is no *reason* to compromise," Troutman snapped, sharply. "Either we are in control of our territory or we are not! Either we are the sole source of power and legitimacy on this world or we are not. Either..."

"We're not in Parliament now," William said, tiredly. "You can save the bullshit rhetoric for your supporters."

Troutman shrugged. "Here's an interesting question for you," he said. "The Forsakers believe in the virtues of large families, do they not?"

"So do farmers like you," William countered. "I believe the average number of children per couple in rural areas is five."

"It is," Troutman confirmed. "I've been going through the data collected by the registers, up at the spaceport. As of yesterday, there were roughly thirty-five thousand Forsakers on the ground, two-fifths of them women of childbearing age. There's actually a very definite imbalance between males and females, something that ought to worry us."

He went on before William could say a word. "The average Forsaker family, based on the data we collected, has around four to six children," he added. "There's actually a number who have as many as *ten* children. And there is *nothing*, absolutely nothing, to suggest that the birthrate will decline over the next century. We could wind up being heavily outnumbered within the next few decades."

"You're exaggerating the case," William said, sharply. "How will they *feed* so many children?"

"You know as well as I do that algae can be used to feed millions of people," Troutman pointed out. "Earth had a high birthrate even though the population was, pardon me, trapped in tiny apartments in hellish CityBlocks. And we have far more room for expansion than a family on Earth."

"You're being paranoid," William said.

Troutman looked back at him. "And you're not being paranoid enough."

"These people have been through hell," William said.

"Our duty is to *our* population," Troutman snapped. "You know, the men and women who voted you into office? The refugees could have the worst sob story in history and I would *still* put our voters first!"

"They were kicked off their homeworld," William said.

"Tell me," Troutman said. "Is there anything, over the last few weeks, that suggests Tarsus was wrong in wanting to get rid of them?"

William felt another surge of sheer hatred. "Is there a *point* to this meeting?"

"Just one," Troutman said. "Do you think I missed your deal with the Unionists?"

"No," William said. Too many people were involved for *that* to stay buried for long, no matter how hard he tried. "I don't."

"You will *not* get that bill through Parliament," Troutman hissed. "And even if you do, do you think it will be *accepted*?"

"Parliament is the highest authority on the planet," William said. "I…"

"And yet there are strict limits on its power," Troutman snapped. "Here you are, turning against your own people…and for what? What the hell are you getting out of it?"

"I am trying to cope with a crisis," William snapped back. He waved a hand around the office. "If you want this job, if you want this office, organise a vote and kick me to the backbenches. Until then, shut the hell up!"

They stared at each other in mutual hatred. "Your attempts to cover everything up are failing," Troutman said, finally. "And the next time you surrender to the refugees, *Premier*, I'll call for a vote of no-confidence. Do I make myself clear?"

"Perfectly," William said.

Troutman glared at him for a long moment, then turned and marched out of the room. Sally entered a moment later, carrying a tea tray. William shook his head in grim amusement - he'd forgotten about the tea - and motioned for her to put it down on the desk. He'd just have to drink both cups himself.

"Call Sondra," he said. She was in conference with Director Melbourne, if he recalled correctly. "Tell her to get back here as soon as she can. We may have a problem."

"Yes, sir," Sally said.

CHAPTER TWENTY-EIGHT

Their grasp of reality, therefore, was poor. It was easier for them to think in soundbites and simplistic answers than understand the underlying issues facing the galaxy.
- Professor Leo Caesius. *Ethnic Streaming and the End of Empire.*

She was being made to wait.

Judith sat in an uncomfortable chair outside Director Melbourne's office, feeling unpleasantly as though she'd been sent to see the principal. The message had been terse, ordering her to report to the office by 0900 or there would be certain unspecified consequences. Judith had been tempted not to show up - she'd been in a foul mood, thanks to a nasty argument with Gayle and her own worries over Hannah - but she suspected that not showing up would merely be used against her.

She leaned back in the chair, reminding herself - sternly - that she was a grown woman and no longer in school. Director Melbourne might be in charge of coping with the refugees, but she had very limited powers over Judith. Hell, the more she looked at the legal position, the more she thought she could make a case that Director Melbourne had illegally imprisoned her after the riot. She'd been tempted to file charges, even though she knew it would probably go nowhere. The exact legal status of anyone during a state of emergency was *very* ill-defined.

And she thinks she can make me sweat, just by forcing me to wait, Judith thought, reaching into her bag. She'd put a couple of books in, along with her e-reader and a small selection of ration bars. *And yet, she's nowhere near as intimidating as Principal Seymour.*

She pulled out a book and started to read. Her father had been a firm believer in reading fiction, but Judith preferred factual books. She'd taken a couple of books on the Forsakers out of the library, trying to understand them better. It wasn't easy - most of the books had been written by the second or third generation on Arthur's Seat and were strongly critical of the Forsakers - but she thought she was making progress. And yet, it was becoming increasingly clear that neither Gayle nor Hannah had lived in a *true* Forsaker community...

Someone cleared her throat, loudly. Judith looked up to see a grim-faced older woman, looking down on her.

"The director will see you now," the woman said.

Judith nodded, returned the book to the bag and rose. The woman made no move to stop her carrying the bag into the office, even though she could have hidden something dangerous within its folds. But then, Arthur's Seat didn't have a tradition of political assassination or even random violence. That might change, she reflected morbidly, but for the moment it was a relief. She met Director Melbourne's eyes - the woman was sitting behind a desk, reading a datapad - then marched over to stand in front of the desk. There were no chairs for visitors.

She almost giggled. *It really does feel like going to see the principal...*

"Miss Parkston," Director Melbourne said. "Explain why you saw fit to defy my instructions *not* to talk about your experiences."

Judith looked back at her, evenly. "You never ordered me not to talk," she said. "And if you had, it would have been of questionable legality."

Director Melbourne's face darkened. "I am in charge of handling and resettling the refugees," she said. "My orders are legal."

"Actually, there are certain orders that *cannot* be issued," Judith said, silently relieved she'd taken the time to look them up. "You cannot, for example, forbid me from filing charges concerning criminal acts, regardless of whether they are aimed against me personally or I was merely unlucky enough to witness them. Nor can you forbid me from whistle-blowing if I see criminal acts, including sins of omission, carried out by my superiors..."

"No such acts were carried out," Director Melbourne snarled.

"Declining to rescue a young girl in danger is a sin of omission," Judith countered. "Holding me prisoner without proper care and feeding is a criminal act. And retroactively insisting that I keep my mouth shut, without any signed agreement, is legally unenforceable."

Director Melbourne gave her a baleful look. "Are you sure you're not studying law at the university?"

Judith kept her face blank with an effort. She'd thrown so many arguments at Director Melbourne because she wasn't sure which of them - if any - would actually stick, but it was clear that *one* of them definitely had. Perhaps more…any halfway competent lawyer could easily make a case for all of them. But she had no idea how well they would hold up in court.

"Being aware of one's rights is as important as being aware of one's responsibilities," she said. It was something her father had said, although he'd gone on to remark that rights must be *balanced* with responsibilities. "I would not have signed up to serve as an emergency volunteer, director, had I not read the paperwork very carefully first."

Director Melbourne looked as though she'd bitten into something sour. Judith rather suspected she'd been summoned to be browbeaten, then perhaps forced to recant her online statements in front of the media. Instead…she wondered, absently, just what the director considered a suitable fallback position. She could kick Judith off the emergency roster and no one, not even Judith herself, would complain. But apart from that, her ability to make Judith suffer were limited.

"You could be expelled from the university," Director Melbourne said, finally. "You have *not* comported yourself with the dignity expected of a lady and a scholar."

"The university would need a very good reason to expel me," Judith countered. She hadn't considered the possibility of being expelled, although in hindsight it was obvious. She'd used the university's datanet to broadcast her article, after all. "And it would be debated in court."

Dragging the university's reputation through the mud, she added, silently. *And now, when they are desperate for funds, would be a particularly bad time.*

Director Melbourne snorted, rudely. "Can we rely on you to refrain from making inflammatory statements in future?"

"The truth is an absolute defence in such matters," Judith said. There were literally millions of rumours flowing through the datanet, half of them completely unbelievable. "And what I said can be backed up in court."

"You might be wrong," Director Melbourne said.

"I might be right, too," Judith countered.

Director Melbourne stared at her for a long moment, then scowled. "The refugees are going to be moving out of the spaceport over the next few days," she said. "You can report to the spaceport tomorrow morning - at 1000 - to assist in the move, then in cleaning up the mess before the *next* set of refugees arrives."

She smiled, rather nastily. "And as you were not removed from the roster," she added, "I should warn you that failing to show up will be considered desertion."

Ouch, Judith thought. There was no point in arguing. Director Melbourne had managed to score a zinger after all. *A truly terrible detention.*

"Understood, director," she said, tartly.

Director Melbourne smirked. "See you tomorrow," she said, sweetly. "And I really would advise you not to be late."

Judith nodded, then turned and walked out of the room. She had a day, a whole day, before she had to report back to the spaceport. Maybe she could find Gayle…and then? And then what? Gayle had never forgiven her for writing that post, for revealing what she - and Hannah - had endured. And Judith found it impossible to forgive Gayle, too, for making light of Hannah's sufferings.

She stepped out of the building and walked back towards the university. The streets were surprisingly quiet, the handful of people within view glancing around nervously as they hurried to their destinations. A number of shops were closed, a number of stalls were missing…she winced, inwardly, as she noticed that one of her favourite roadside cafes was closed and shuttered. The owner had done such wonderful burgers…

And he's decided he can't stay open, she thought. What did that mean? Had he just decided to remain in the country until the whole crisis blew over? Or had the insurance company refused to pay for the damage, if there had *been* damage? Rumours insisted that insurance premiums were going up all over the city. *What does that mean for everyone?*

Deep inside, she had no answer.

"As you are aware," Captain Stewart said, "matters are now approaching a resolution."

Mike had his doubts and he knew, judging by the way the other constables shifted uncomfortably, that he wasn't the only one. It had been two days since the riot, two days since the police had been humiliated by a gaggle of refugees…two days since Bobbie had been put on administrative leave, the first step to gently dismissing her from the force. The mood in the room was grim. No one expected the matter to be resolved quickly.

And Stewart isn't helping, Mike thought morbidly. *He's not even trying to convince us of anything.*

"It has been decided," Stewart continued, "that the vast majority of the refugees will be transported to the Kinsman Estate. There is enough space there to house a large number of people in relative comfort and…"

A low rumble of anger ran through the room. The police force was a tightly-knit organisation. Everyone present knew someone who'd been attacked in the riot, even if they hadn't been there themselves. The idea of just letting the bastards get away with it was horrific, particularly as a number of locals were in jail, awaiting sentencing. And to think that they'd acted in *defence* of local women…

They won't find a jury willing to convict them, Mike told himself. *But it still makes us look like bad guys.*

"Quiet," Sergeant Cox bellowed.

Silence fell, sharply. "I know this is not an ideal situation," Stewart said. "But it is the best solution we have."

"Send them back to Tarsus," someone called.

Mike concealed his amusement as Sergeant Cox looked around sharply, but didn't seem to notice who'd spoken. The police force was on the verge of outright mutiny - and while its officers understood, their political superiors did not. They existed to protect and serve the public and now...and now, they were being told that the greatest *threat* to the public was being *rewarded* for its crimes. It was intolerable. Mike rather suspected that a considerable number of policemen would be handing in their resignations over the whole affair.

And if I didn't need the job, he thought, *I might be joining them.*

"The good news is that the people we arrested will be handed over to us, along with the two refugees who attempted to rape Constable Parkhurst," Stewart continued. "They will be put on trial within the week, then sentenced accordingly."

Mike coughed. "What about the wankers who *rescued* them?"

Stewart looked annoyed. "It has been decided," he said, "that the rescuers believed that the prisoners were in severe danger. Accordingly, they will not be prosecuted."

"Fuck that," someone snapped.

"Silence," Sergeant Cox said.

"I will not be silent," the speaker said. Constable Robertson pushed his way through the throng. "Attacking us is bad enough, Sergeant; trying to *rape* one of us is worse!"

"They're handing over the rapists," Stewart said. "Constable..."

"They should *all* be handed over to us," Robertson insisted. There was a low rumble of agreement. "Attacking us is a crime! There's no dispute about that!"

"And if they'd been arrested on Tarsus," Stewart said bitterly, "they would have gone into the cells and never been seen again."

Mike stared at him in shock. Stewart...he'd never doubted that Stewart had the best interests of his men at heart. The man had been a good constable, then a lieutenant...his promotion and assignment to the station had been warmly welcomed by his subordinates. And now...he was *defending* murderous scum who'd attacked a group of policemen and nearly raped one of them? It was unthinkable.

"Tarsus does not have a very nice government," Stewart added. "The Forsakers got the blame for most of their problems. They *knew* they would lose anyone who happened to be arrested…"

"So what?" Robertson demanded. "They came *here*! They committed crimes *here*! And we are to…to do what? *Tolerate* it? How long will it be before one of us dies? Will you still be making excuses then?"

"*Enough*," Stewart snapped.

He was ashamed, Mike realised suddenly. The Captain Stewart he'd known - he'd *thought* he'd known - would not have let such a challenge to his authority pass. But now…Stewart would have exploded at Robertson, if he hadn't believed - at some level - that Robertson was right. Someone a great deal higher up the food chain had to have leaned on him. It was the only explanation that made sense.

"It isn't our job to judge them," Stewart said. "It's our job to protect the people…"

"And we're not doing that," Robertson said. "What next? Are we to protect the refugees from a howling mob that wants them dead? Because if we can't protect the people, they'll take matters into their own hands."

Mike swallowed. There was no strong tradition of self-defence in the city, but the rural population *had* to take care of their own problems. It was easy to imagine posses already forming - perhaps called by the District Halls, perhaps not - to deal with the crisis. And if a posse *did* march on the estate, would the police get in the way? It might turn into a full-scale civil war.

Impossible, he told himself. *How did we fall so far so fast?*

"The government believes that the refugees can be slowly broken down into more manageable units," Stewart said. "And that exposure to our population will show them a better way to live."

Mike snorted. He wasn't the only one.

"Now, those of you who are assigned to the spaceport will be responsible for escorting the refugees as they make their way down to the estate," Stewart continued. "The remainder will continue to police the city…"

Afterwards, he asked Mike to remain. "The PCA has requested that the case be held open," he said, grimly. "Judge Silver granted them a stay of execution. I wasn't able to convince him to close it."

Mike cursed. After everything that had happened, he'd almost forgotten about the PCA and their absurd attempt to find him guilty of…something. Indeed, he'd decided the case would probably be quietly closed before it became a matter of public interest. But instead…

"They have *no* case," he said, numbly. "Why have they kept it open?"

"I don't know," Stewart said. "It's possible Coombs thinks he *needs* a scalp, even yours. I don't think the PCA have claimed *any* heads recently. But it's also possible that it's political, that someone behind Coombs has a *reason* to keep the case open. Watch your back."

"Judge Silver has political ambitions," Mike muttered. The judge had run for office during the last election…a Unionist, if he recalled correctly. He'd lost, but his party might just have decided to run him again. "This is political, isn't it?"

"I would keep those speculations to yourself," Stewart said.

He took a long breath. "This is a dangerous situation," he added, softly. "Bobbie's experience has not, so far, gone public. We have been given strict orders to keep that absolutely confidential."

"A woman is broken," Mike said, shortly. He hadn't seen Bobbie since their talk, but she wouldn't have been placed on administrative leave unless there was no hope of a speedy recovery. "And we choose to ignore it?"

"No," Stewart said. "*As I said*, they're handing over the people who assaulted her."

"It isn't their choice to hand them over or not," Mike said. "We wouldn't tolerate that from our own people, would we?"

"This is political, Mike," Stewart said. "And don't you forget it."

He shrugged. "Grab a cup of coffee, then report to the vans," he added. "You're going back to the spaceport."

Mike saluted, then turned and left the room. Cold anger, mixed with a bitter sickness, raged within his heart. He'd been a constable for ten years - he'd never sought promotion - and yet he'd never felt so *betrayed*. The charges against him were spurious, utterly unable to stand up to the merest scrutiny, but Judge Silver had decided the PCA could continue to try to make them stick! It was absurd. If they couldn't prove it within a week, let alone the time they'd had, they'd never be able to prove them...

...And they'd betrayed Bobbie too.

And the rest of us, he thought, as he stepped into the changing room. Her story should be all over the planet, but instead it had been covered up. Who knew what *else* had been covered up? *And how long will it be before one of us dies?*

He looked down at the terminal for a long moment. It would be easy enough to send a message to one of the datanet newsgroups, outlining what had happened and why. Who knew what would happen once *that* little datum was in the public sphere? And yet, sending it from a terminal inside the police station would be traced back to him. He'd need to be more careful. A whistle-blower was supposed to be protected from retaliation, but only a fool would count on it. Old certainties were falling everywhere.

It wasn't until he removed a portable com from the evidence locker and stuck it in his pocket that he realised he'd already made up his mind to blow the whistle, consequences be damned...

...And he knew *precisely* who to message.

CHAPTER TWENTY-NINE

> It was easier for them to believe that dirt-poor hick farmers were refusing more immigrants because they were bigots, rather than because the immigrants were simply useless and demanding.
> - Professor Leo Caesius. *Ethnic Streaming and the End of Empire.*

"Make sure you've got everything," Joel ordered, as he peered into the room. "We won't be coming back here."

John resisted the urge to say something sharp, then nodded to Hannah. His sister had packed up the clothes, such as they were; his mother, behind her, was either picking up stuff they wanted to take or shoving anything they didn't into a corner. There wasn't much, he noted, feeling an odd twinge of pain. The clothes they wore had either been donated by the locals or washed repeatedly, until they were on the verge of falling apart.

It'll be different once they land our supplies, he told himself, firmly. *The women will start sewing again.*

He pushed the thought aside as they made one last sweep of the room, then walked outside into the bright sunlight. The Stewards were running around, sorting out the people who would be heading directly to the estate from those who would be remaining behind, at least for the moment. Joel had picked most of the former personally, John knew, trying to make sure that the first settlers were ready to turn the estate into somewhere to live. It wasn't going to be easy, John was sure, but it should be doable. And anywhere, even a soulless estate, had to be better than the spaceport.

"There's Beth, over there," Hannah whispered. John turned his head, catching sight of a white cap covering an untidy mop of black hair. "I think she likes you."

John shrugged. "Her father wouldn't," he said. The words cost him a pang. If his father had lived...but he hadn't. "What prospects do *I* have?"

Hannah shrugged. John wondered, darkly, if she was teasing him. He hadn't met Beth, save for a couple of closely-chaperoned ceremonies. She was pretty, he supposed, and she came from a good family, but he knew almost nothing about her. Who knew what married life with her would be like? Joel was unusual in being so close to Hannah before they were formally married.

And even he doesn't spend time with her alone, John thought. *He can't.*

They joined the long line of people - men on the outside, women on the inside - and made their way slowly down to the gates. Dozens of policemen stood outside, watching warily as the Forsakers walked past. Behind them, there were hundreds of people, some carrying banners that welcomed the refugees and others that told them to go back where they came from. John winced as the crowd started to shout, despite the police presence. It looked as though the two groups of protesters were on the verge of going to war with one another, with the police and the refugees caught in the middle.

He forced himself to walk onwards, catching sight of Beth and her younger sister ahead of them. She *would* be a good wife, he was sure. He hadn't heard anything bad about her, not like Hannah - or another girl he'd known, who'd chosen to leave the commune long before they'd been thrown off Tarsus. She'd been caught in a compromising position, John recalled; she'd left, rather than accept punishment for her sins. What had happened to her? John knew he'd never know.

And Konrad will not speak for me until Joel is married, he thought. He felt a stab of hatred so intense that it surprised him. *By then, Beth will be married too.*

The shouts grew louder, the policemen running backwards and forwards to keep the crowd in line. John felt his heartbeat starting to pound, again, as the mass of refugees reached the motorway and turned west. Someone had helpfully marked out the route, he noted. They'd also added signs pointing to the first cottage, now surrounded by men and women in traditional dress. He stared, unable to believe his eyes. It was something out of a dream - or a nightmare. The men and women might be dressed traditionally, but they were standing far too close together.

"The Forsakers here have forsaken us," Hannah whispered, her lips very close to his ear. "I don't think they're *real* Forsakers."

John shrugged. Joel and his ilk might rant and rave about who qualified as a Forsaker and who didn't, but he found it hard to care. There were no strict rules, only guidelines covering everything from dress code to acceptable levels of technology. He'd even heard that, back on their original homeworld, there had been dozens of different communes, all with different ideas. Young men and women had moved between them until they found one that suited them.

But that won't happen here, he thought, morbidly. *Joel and his friends will see to that, won't they?*

Another group of protesters - two groups of protesters - were waiting for them by the estate, shouting and screaming at one another as the refugees approached. There was something *primal* in the air, a sense of burning anger mixed with resentment…one group wanted to welcome the refugees, the other wanted to throw them out - or worse. John shuddered, hoping desperately that the second group didn't win the debate. He honestly didn't know if the commune could survive being evicted a second time. Going back to space…the thought was horrific.

Hannah touched his hand. "She" - Judith, John realised - "told me that her partner was a Forsaker, descended from Forsakers," she said. "And they were fighting over welcoming us."

John shrugged. He didn't care what Judith's boyfriend thought. If he was willing to engage in a relationship outside marriage, he was no Forsaker. And Judith…he'd been brought up to believe that girls who surrendered themselves too quickly were sluts, but she wasn't slutty…not really. She was a decent person, even if she *did* wear skimpy clothes.

"He should be with her," he muttered, as they passed through the gates. "Or her brother…"

Hannah elbowed him. "Interested?"

John shook his head, quickly. Judith was likable, he had to admit. She had a way of presenting herself that somehow undermined all the horror stories he'd heard about Outsider girls. But she wouldn't make a comfortable wife. He wanted someone traditional, someone who would embrace the role of a wife and mother. Hell, he didn't think *Hannah* would make a comfortable wife for Joel. But Joel...

He looked up at his sister, feeling bitter helplessness. Joel wouldn't take defiance lightly, not from his wife. He'd force her to submit to him, whatever it took...

...And John, charged to defend her, knew he couldn't protect her from her future husband.

"Hey," Mike shouted, pushing as much authority as he could into his voice. "Stop that!"

The two youths, on the verge of throwing stones into the mass of refugees, turned and ran into the welcoming arms of their fellow protesters. Mike gritted his teeth in frustration, knowing that arresting the entire group would be impossible. Hundreds of protesters had turned up, some welcoming the Forsaker refugees and others demanding they be sent back to Tarsus. The police were badly outnumbered.

He turned away, cursing under his breath. The noise was deafening - shouts, screams, chants - and there was nothing he could do. There were only two hundred policemen on duty, only a handful of them carrying anything more intimidating than their truncheons. He had a nasty feeling, judging by what the police had already seized, that the protesters were armed with everything from baseball bats to pistols and hunting rifles. The gunshop nearest his home had been restocked with guns and ammunition, only to be cleared out by the end of the day. *Everyone* was arming themselves.

And this mess is partly your fault, he told himself. He'd dropped the portable com in the trash compactor, once he'd used it, but he was still surprised he hadn't been caught. *You told them about Bobbie.*

He felt a sinking sensation in his heart as he took in a new line of protesters, denouncing the refugees as rapists and demanding their immediate removal. Beyond them, other protesters loudly announced their willingness to do what the police would not - or could not. Others demanded that the police be armed, or that the estate be broken up, or that the refugees be scattered over the planet in chain gangs. And they denounced their opponents as traitors…

"A right fucking mess," Constable Harris said. He looked as grim as Mike felt. There just weren't enough policemen to do more than protect themselves if the two groups of protesters went to war. "An absolute fucking mess."

Mike nodded, turning to gaze at the other group of protesters. Many of them were descended from Forsakers, intent on welcoming their cousins. Others…he recognised some of them from previous busts, students who seemed to delight in drinking themselves senseless and then starting fights. The cynical side of him wondered how many of them were dating the protest leaders. *He'd* done plenty of stupid things back when he'd been a young man trying to impress a pretty girl.

His eyes opened wide as he caught sight of one *very* well-endowed woman. She wore a traditional Forsaker dress, but she'd cut it open, allowing her breasts to spill out. The display was so blatant that Mike found himself torn between the desire to stare and a flare of genuine disgust. And pity too, perhaps. He doubted the girl would be very popular amongst *real* Forsakers.

Or yes, she will be popular, his own thoughts mocked him. The gender imbalance amongst the Forsakers had been discussed endlessly in the police station. Everyone agreed it portended trouble. *Just not in the right way.*

The first wave of marching refugees came to an end, the police swinging the spaceport doors shut with an audible sense of relief. Mike watched them go, the protesters quieting as the Forsakers vanished into the distance. Some turned to follow, despite police warnings; others, less inclined to walk all the way to the estate, were already heading back to the bus stop. It made him roll his eyes. Walking back to Lothian wouldn't take *that* long.

His radio crackled. "The next group of refugees will be out in two hours," Captain Stewart said. "Sergeant Hamlin, I want you and your squad to move the prisoners back to the station."

"Aye, sir," Hamlin said.

"Everyone else, report back to the guardhouse," Stewart added. "We all need tea, I think."

Mike nodded. The protesters were definitely leaving, as if they hadn't realised a *second* group of refugees was going to be moved. He silently thanked God for small mercies as he surveyed the mess they'd left behind; empty bottles, countless placards, flyers either advertising the benefits or decrying the costs of mass immigration. They'd have to get a chain gang or two up to the spaceport, he thought. Picking up the litter alone was going to take *weeks*.

He stumbled over a banner and glared down at it. Someone had drawn a cartoon - a naked woman being chased by a gang of over-muscled men - and waved it in the air. He would have been darkly amused if the woman hadn't been wearing a police badge, pinned to her right breast. It didn't look anything like Bobbie, he noted, but it was still going to tar her reputation. And if he hadn't blown the whistle, he told himself, no one would have known about her ordeal.

"Mike," Captain Stewart said, when he reached the guardhouse. "Get yourself a cuppa, then sit down."

Mike nodded. Stewart didn't know he'd leaked information to the datanet. Whoever had gotten to him, they couldn't have kept him from tearing Mike a new asshole if he'd known the truth. But it didn't take a genius to narrow down the list of potential suspects to a manageable number. The only people who knew the story *and* had a decent motive to tell it were Bobbie's comrades.

Former comrades, Mike thought, grimly. *She will never return to us.*

He poured himself a cup of tea and sat down, suddenly feeling very tired. Several familiar faces were missing, either through resignation or outright desertion. A message had come down from HQ last night, stating that no further resignations were being accepted for the duration. For the duration of *what*, Mike had wondered. Arthur's Seat would never be the same again. He had to admit, if only in the privacy of his own mind, that he'd seriously considered deserting too. If he hadn't had a wife...

I could go out to the country, he thought. *And as long as I worked hard, no one would give a damn about where I came from.*

He sighed. Life had been so much easier before the refugees had arrived.

Judith was mildly surprised she hadn't been arrested, the moment she'd turned up at the spaceport. She had, after all, decided to rebroadcast an email she'd received about a female police officer being assaulted - and nearly raped - during the riot in Lothian. And how the refugees had rescued some of their own who'd been arrested by the police. The news had spread rapidly, fuelling the protest movements for and against the refugees. Judith had half-expected to be marched straight to prison.

But instead, she'd merely been given overalls and told to get to work.

The director chose a more subtle revenge, she thought, as they marched into the spaceport complex. *She put me on litter duty.*

"Pick up the rubbish," the supervisor ordered. "Put anything that can be recycled in one set of bags, everything else in the other."

Judith gritted her teeth as they went to work. The refugees might have been reluctant, once upon a time, to go into the spaceport itself, but their reluctance had faded as more and more refugees arrived. There were *piles* of litter everywhere, ranging from ration packaging to damaged clothes and destroyed books. Someone had clearly ransacked the spaceport library, removing a number of books and shredding them. It was petty and pointless and she knew the people responsible would never be caught...

Putting the thought aside, she and her team worked their way through the spaceport, picking up hundreds of pieces of litter. Some of the rooms smelt dreadful, so dreadful that she suspected the refugees had been taking shits on the floor. There was no way they could be cleaned without gas masks. The toilets were, if anything, in a worse condition. Both male and female toilets were utterly ghastly, as if the Forsakers hadn't known how to go to the toilet. She didn't want to know *what* they'd been doing.

"We're going to need medical treatment when we emerge," David said. He was a year older than her, the fourth son of a farmer. She would have been interested in him, she had to admit, if she hadn't been more interested in girls. "And probably disinfectant."

Judith nodded as she scooped up a bunch of clothes and dumped them in the bin. They'd need to have at least three showers and a bath before any of them felt clean again, after spending so long in the spaceport. She'd been in pigpens that were cleaner, even though pigs were disgusting animals. Her father had told her that cleaning out the pigpen built character, but all it had *really* done was convince her that she didn't want pigs of her own.

"We're going to have to scrub ourselves clean," she agreed. The spaceport showers were clogged and useless, so badly jammed up that she suspected the refugees had used them as makeshift toilets. She had a feeling that plumbers would have to be called to unblock the pipes. Perhaps they could just designate the spaceport a new waste disposal centre and save time. "Do you think they thought to bring portable showers?"

"Probably not," David said.

Judith sighed. She didn't understand it. The Forsakers might prefer to avoid modern technology, but they weren't barbarians. *Hannah* wasn't a barbarian. And yet, the evidence around her suggested that the refugees no longer cared. They'd fouled their own nest so badly that disease would spread rapidly.

She felt a sudden surge of anger as she picked up a set of bloodstained garments. The bastards didn't even let their daughters use contraceptive implants! Judith had gone to the doctor, the day she bled for the first time, and been given an implant. She hadn't bled since, not once. But Hannah and her sisters would have bled regularly…she clenched her fist in rage, dumping the garments in the bin. Their parents preferred to allow their children to suffer rather than use medicine to save themselves some discomfort…

Bastards, she thought. *Gayle* had an implant too. *They don't even let them know the possibilities.*

That would change, she was sure. The newcomers would learn the potentials of modern technology, even as they learned how hard it was to survive without it. And then…who knew what would happen? Hannah was already sneaking out of the commune, whenever she could get away with it. If rumour was to be believed, she wasn't the only one.

Judith smiled at the thought, then turned back to her work. There were more refugees in orbit, but everyone seemed to agree the flow was finally coming to an end. And then…there would be some breathing space, unless more arrived. The Forsakers hadn't been making themselves very popular…

And I can see why, she thought, grimly. Hannah was nice - she'd make an exception for Hannah - yet too many of her fellows were monsters. *They want to live here, but they're not prepared to do what they need to do to fit in.*

CHAPTER THIRTY

Therefore, the settlers, as far as the Grand Senate was concerned, were always in the wrong. A conflict between old and new, between long-standing settlers and corporations, could be framed as a dispute between the righteous and the evil. And they were convinced that they were on the side of right.
- Professor Leo Caesius. *Ethnic Streaming and the End of Empire.*

"Put them all in the warehouse," Joel directed, as the cargo handlers went to work. "We'll sort them all ourselves."

He allowed himself a cold smile. It had taken four days to prepare the shuttlepad - the men clearing away the foliage, the women dusting the warehouses - but it had been done, just in time to keep the Imperial Navy from becoming impatient. They'd started to land cargo shuttles in the estate almost as soon as Joel had given the word, moving countless crates into the warehouses without giving the local authorities time to inspect them. It had been nerve-wracking - Joel simply didn't have enough money to *bribe* the spacers - but it had worked.

And if they'd insisted on inspecting all the crates, he thought, *they would have found the guns.*

The cargo handlers moved with remarkable speed. They were using technology to make their job easier, Joel noted. He would have preferred to keep the rest of his people away, just to make sure they didn't pick up any bad ideas, but it couldn't be helped. There was simply too much demand for the supplies in the crates. God alone knew what the Elders would say - or do - if they found out about the weapons. Their willingness to surrender was disheartening.

"That's the task complete," the Imperial Navy officer said, finally. He held out a shiny datapad. "Sign here."

Joel signed, then watched as the officer and his crew piled back into the shuttles. He hadn't wanted them around any longer than strictly necessary, but it was still a relief to see them go without problems. Too many things could have gone wrong - could *still* go wrong. He turned on his heel, as soon as the last of the shuttles had taken off, and strode into the warehouse. The cavernous space was crammed with crates.

And yet, this is tiny, Joel thought. He couldn't help wondering just how much had been stolen back on Tarsus, or somewhere in the interstellar void. *We should have a great many more supplies.*

There was no manifest either, beyond a handful of vague notes. The weapons crates were marked - they were all listed as carrying seeds - but there was no way to know what was in the others, save by opening them up. Joel summoned some of his men and barked orders, telling them to transfer the weapons crates to the Steward Hall - a warehouse at the edge of the estate - and open the others. Their contents would have to be sorted out, then either put back in storage or distributed around the estate.

He didn't relax until the last of the weapons crates was transferred to their final destination. The Elders weren't the only ones he didn't want to know about them. If one of his rivals had seen them, or someone sympathetic to the local government…he didn't want to *think* about what might have happened. But no one had seen them. He opened a couple of crates, checking that the weapons and ammunition were still in place, then sealed them up again. They'd need to find a place to test-fire the weapons, he knew. There hadn't been a shooting range on the starship.

He strode back outside, taking a long breath and tasting the cool autumn air. The air smelt faintly of dust, unsurprisingly. A number of women were still dusting the apartment blocks, making sure they were fit for human habitation. Others were cooking for the first time in months, the smell reaching his nose and making his mouth water. He'd spent too long eating ration bars that tasted of cardboard and did unpleasant things to his digestion. Surely, it wouldn't be *too* hard to make them taste better.

Steward Jeff fell into step beside him as they walked towards the cottage. "We've piled up most of the cleared plants for compost," he said, bluntly. "We can use them next year."

Joel shrugged. It would probably be better to sell the dead plants to local farmers, just to build up some funds. He'd practically bankrupted himself over the last few weeks, first on the starship and then buying some much-needed supplies in Lothian. But it was a subject that would have to be approached carefully. The traditionalists in the commune, staunch believers in the circle of life, would want to use the compost to fertilise their crops.

But we can't turn the estate into a farm, he thought, sourly. *Half the ground is covered in concrete and the remainder...the remainder is too small to support us.*

"We'll see," he said. "It all depends on getting some farms."

He sighed as he bid farewell to Jeff and headed into the small cottage. The local government wouldn't give them land, not unless they demanded it. Tarsus certainly hadn't, even though feeding the Forsakers had to be a burden on their economy. God knew they'd certainly bitched about it enough. The farmers on Arthur's Seat might not welcome the competition, even though they had a whole second continent just *waiting* to be settled. There weren't many settlements on Minoa and none of them were particularly large.

His stepmother and Hannah were bent over the stove as he entered, his stepmother teaching her how to cook. Joel had no idea *what* they were cooking, but it smelt nice. He studied Hannah's back for a long moment, feeling an odd surge of affection. Hannah might be rebellious, she might have a poor reputation...and yet, there was something about her he liked. She would make a good wife, once he'd taught her the importance of obeying her husband. And their children would be wonderful.

And no one will ever dare question her reputation again, Joel thought, as he closed the door loudly. *And if they do, they'll answer to me.*

Hannah half-turned to look at him, then turned back hastily. Neither John nor her stepfather were around. Ideally, the women would be completely separate from the men, but the cottage was simply too small. Joel smiled at her back before hurrying into the next room. Konrad was sitting on a mattress, his fingers moving over a string of worry beads. He mouthed words as he prayed silently.

"Joel," Konrad said, as Joel closed the door. "I trust the prisoners were handed over?"

Joel nodded, shortly. Adam had believed what Joel had told him - that it was his duty to infiltrate the prisons - but Jack had gone absolutely mad with rage when he realised he'd been betrayed. He'd offered his back for a whipping, after all. He had thought - as he should have done - that the whipping was his sole punishment, that the matter had been closed. The Stewards had had to knock him down before handing him over to the local authorities.

"It was done," he said. He'd been careful to make it clear that the Elders were the ones who'd issued the orders. Let *them* take the blame. "The local authorities will punish them as they see fit."

And get rid of Jack into the bargain, he added, silently. It was unfortunate, but he couldn't lose. *And we managed to preserve some of our autonomy.*

"We must isolate ourselves," Konrad added, firmly. "I will be consulting with local allies to find the best way to isolate ourselves."

"Of course, father," Joel said. He didn't hold out much hope - the Forsakers on Arthur's Seat were Fallen - but it would keep his father busy. "Until then, I trust all is well?"

"Well enough," Konrad said.

He cleared his throat as he rose. "Soon, you will be married," he added. "You do recall the duties of a husband?"

Joel nodded. "Yes, father."

It was hard to keep the delight off his face. He would soon be married! His father would be his patriarch until he died, but a married man had freedoms denied to an unmarried man. It was true, he supposed, that he had more freedoms than most young men anyway, yet…he was going to be married! And to a true Forsaker!

"We shall discuss them anyway," his father said, sternly. "I will not have my son go into an unhappy marriage."

"Yes, father," Joel said.

"And then we shall make the preparations," his father added. "And then you will be married."

―――――

Judith couldn't get the smell out of her nostrils, even though she'd showered repeatedly in the four days since leaving the spaceport. She *knew* she had washed thoroughly, she *knew* she'd changed her clothes, she *knew* she was clean...and yet, the smell kept tormenting her. Cold logic told her she was imagining it, but cold logic was powerless against raw emotion, against the sense she would be smelly for the rest of her life. She just *knew* people were turning their heads to stare at her in disgust as she walked past.

At least the director didn't make us stay there for long, she thought. The boys who'd gone through the tents reported they were, if anything, worse. *But she'd probably have wound up with a mutiny if she had.*

She pushed the thought down as she skimmed through her blog. The torrent of emails hadn't abated, even though she'd made it clear she wouldn't be answering questions. She didn't *know* who'd sent her the original post, after all. And yet, online investigators had discovered more than enough proof - including a pair of witness testimonials - that the whole affair had happened, precisely as the original post said. It hadn't stopped her receiving a whole series of assorted death threats from all over the world.

Gritting her teeth, she deleted a whole string of badly-spelled emails and refreshed her inbox, hoping for a message from Hannah. She'd heard *nothing* from Hannah, not since the riot...Judith had hoped to see her at the spaceport, but there had been no sign of her. Judith hoped - prayed - she was alive and well, yet there was no way to be sure. Someone - she suspected Director Melbourne - had sealed all of the refugee files.

She glanced up as she heard a key turning in the lock. Gayle? It couldn't be anyone else, could it? The landlord had a key, but he couldn't enter without a very good reason or advance notice. She rose, walking into the hallway as the door opened. Gayle stepped into the apartment, looking tired. A large placard - welcoming refugees - dangled under her arm.

"Gayle," Judith said, carefully. What *were* they now? Girlfriends…or just roommates? Her skin tingled as she remembered the last time they'd made love, her body reminding her suddenly of just how long it had been. She wasn't sure where Gayle had *slept* over the last few days. "How have you been?"

"Welcoming people," Gayle said, flatly. "Where have *you* been?"

"Cleaning up the mess," Judith said. Gayle hadn't said anything about the stink, but Judith was sure it was just a matter of time. "The spaceport was filthy. I've been in male locker rooms that were cleaner."

Gayle's nose wrinkled in disgust. "What do you expect?"

Judith stared at her. "What do you mean?"

"You pen umpteen thousand people into a place that isn't designed for anything like that many," Gayle said. "What do you expect from people penned up like animals?"

"I've been in cleaner pigpens," Judith snapped. She turned and walked into the kitchen to put the kettle on. A cup of tea might calm them both down. "There's no excuse for shitting in the shower."

"There is if there are no toilets," Gayle pointed out.

Judith bit down the remark that came to mind. Instead, she picked up a couple of mugs and dropped teabags into them. It was enough to calm her down, although simmering anger - mixed with the grim awareness that it was over between them - hovered at the back of her mind. She'd *loved* Gayle. They'd talked about spending the rest of their lives together, about going to farm or set up home in the countryside. But now…she cursed the refugees under her breath. Whoever could have predicted that their mere presence would destroy her love life?

She splashed water into the mugs, then carried them into the living room. Gayle was seated on one of the armchairs, her body held so stiffly that Judith *knew* there was no point in trying to cuddle her. The days when they'd cuddled together on the sofa were over. Instead, she passed Gayle her tea and sat down facing her, cradling her mug in her fingers. The warmth had soothed her, once upon a time. It didn't now.

"I read your post," Gayle said. "Did it occur to you that it might have been made up?"

Judith looked back at her. "Did it occur to you that it might not have been made up?"

"True Forsakers would not have tried to rape a woman," Gayle said.

"True Forsakers tried to drag me into the spaceport," Judith snapped. She'd never felt threatened by any of Gayle's kin, but Gayle and her cousins in the spaceport - and the estate - had very little in common. "God alone knows what they would have done to me, if I hadn't been rescued."

She leaned forward. "And what might they do to you?"

Gayle coloured. "Nothing," she said. "I'm trying to help them!"

Judith wondered, absently, just what that meant. There had been plenty of calls for people to open their homes to refugees or donate supplies, everything from clothes and bedding to food and drink. Gayle and her fellows were probably doing everything they could to help. A nasty thought crossed her mind, but she pushed it aside. She didn't need to make things worse.

"I hope you do," she said, instead. "But they're not like you."

"And *you* are attacking them rather than trying to understand them," Gayle snapped back, sharply.

"They attacked me," Judith said. "One of them brutalised his daughter merely for daring to *talk* to me!"

It crossed her mind, a second too late, that it might be dangerous to tell Gayle anything about Hannah. Gayle might think she was being replaced, if she hadn't already given up on their relationship. Or that Hannah was betraying her own people by trying to move between communities, rather than choosing one and sticking to it.

"I never thought you'd turn into this," Gayle said. "These people are my kin!"

"They're not," Judith said. "They're nothing like you."

She took a breath. "Johan never treated me badly," she said. Johan - like Gayle - had come from a Forsaker family. They'd been rivals for class valedictorian, but he'd never tried to molest her, let alone do anything worse. He'd certainly never suggested she should go back to the kitchen and leave the *real* work to the men. "Nor did Hans. Or Klaus. Or Gil."

"Of course not," Gayle said. She'd had a crush on Hans, once upon a time. "They were decent boys."

"But the men in the spaceport *did* treat me badly," Judith continued. "And I wasn't the only one. Female workers were stared at, disrespected, whistled at...this isn't one bad apple, Gayle. This is a whole community that thinks women, people like us" - she pulled up her shirt to reveal her breasts - "are second-class citizens at best, servants at worst. You have *never* lived in one of their communities..."

Gayle stared back at her, icily, as she covered her breasts again. "And if I choose to do so?"

"Then do so," Judith snapped back. It wasn't as if there weren't a dozen other alternate lifestyles on Arthur's Seat. Her people were very good at minding their own business, as long as it was done between consenting adults in private. "But don't drag the rest of us down with you."

"I'm going to bring a family here," Gayle said. She waved a hand around the apartment. "I think we have enough room..."

"You are *not*," Judith said.

"You don't *own* this place," Gayle protested.

"Neither do you," Judith said. "The landlord might have a few things to say about permanent guests. You're not talking about a boyfriend or girlfriend! And even if he didn't, the lease gives us *both* a say in who stays with us. I say *no*."

"They need somewhere to live," Gayle said.

Judith wondered, suddenly, if *Hannah* would like to move in. Gayle might learn a few things from her. But Hannah seemed reluctant to take that final step.

"Not here," Judith said.

Gayle met her eyes. "You are condemning an entire group because of a few bad apples."

"And you are dismissing the *existence* of the bad apples," Judith countered.

"I can go to the landlord," Gayle snapped.

"I doubt it," Judith said. "You'd have to buy out my share of the lease."

Gayle stared at her. "You'd refuse me this...?"

"I can't stop you making stupid choices that hurt only you," Judith said. "But I can refuse to put myself in danger too."

"This is important," Gayle said. "Judith..."

"No," Judith said.

Gayle rose. "Then we are no longer together," she said, sharply. "You've changed."

"So have you," Judith said. But she wasn't sure if that was actually true. Part of her wanted to reach for Gayle, to pull her back, to say whatever she had to say to keep her. But she knew it would be disastrous. "Good luck."

"Thank you," Gayle said, stiffly. "I'll email you about the lease."

She stormed out of the apartment, slamming the door behind her. Judith stared after her, then fell back into the chair. It was over. Their relationship was over...

And all because of the refugees, she thought, bitterly. *What next?*

CHAPTER
THIRTY-ONE

It isn't a coincidence that this suited the more controlling aspects of the Grand Senate right down to the ground. A nice little conflict on a planetary surface could serve as an excuse to walk in, take over, install a planetary governor and then spend the next few decades milking the planet dry.
- Professor Leo Caesius. *Ethnic Streaming and the End of Empire.*

Courtroom One - Lothian District Court - was a strikingly fancy room, designed by someone who wanted to make it very clear that it was a court of justice. The judge sat behind a heavy wooden desk, flanked by the clerk of the court and the witness box; the jury box sat to the left, while both the prosecutor and defender sat to the right. The prisoners stood in a wooden box, flanked by four policemen; behind them, there were seats for a small audience. Mike couldn't help noticing, as he strode into the courtroom, that the audience seats were packed to bursting. Hundreds of others had been turned away when they reached the court, too late to get a seat.

"Constable Mike Whitehead," the usher said, as Mike took his place in the witness box. "Do you understand the oath?"

"I do," Mike said.

"Then swear," the usher said.

Mike cleared his throat. "I swear that the evidence I shall give will be the truth, the whole truth, and nothing but the truth," he said. "So help me God."

He kept his expression under tight control as the prosecutor rose to his feet. Cecil Vinewood had a reputation for being a stern, utterly uncompromising prosecutor, a man who had served on several government investigations as well as civilian court cases. The short wig and black garb he wore didn't disguise his intelligent eyes, let alone his icy determination to win. Mike hoped - prayed - that the defence counsel wasn't up to the task. He wanted the men in the box to *burn*.

"Constable Mike Whitehead," Vinewood said. "Would you please tell the court, in your own words, what happened when you were attacked by the accused."

"Yes, sir," Mike said. He took a moment to organise his thoughts. Vinewood would know, as well as any policeman, that personal testimony was often the least reliable of all. Any mistakes would be used against him. "A small squad of policemen, including myself, were charged with marching the prisoners back to the police station. The crowds were growing angry and the Incident Coordinator believed it would be better to get them into the cells before they were lynched. We searched the prisoners to make sure they weren't carrying any weapons, then marched them down the street."

He paused. "Midway to our destination, we were attacked by a swarm of refugees," he added, grimly. "The prisoner closest to me crashed *into* me, sending me sprawling as the refugees attacked our lines. I curled up to protect myself, then stood as soon as the attackers vanished, intending to assist those who needed it. At that point, I discovered that Constable Parkhurst had been attacked and molested by two of the refugees."

Vinewood nodded. "Do you believe her attackers were the men in the courtroom today?"

"Yes, sir," Mike said.

The prosecutor nodded. "Mr. Oscar?"

Mike gritted his teeth as the defence counsel rose. He'd never *met* Bill Oscar, but he'd heard stories about him. *Someone* was clearly determined to give the refugees the best possible chance at getting away with their crimes. It was bad enough that *most* of the attackers weren't going to be prosecuted...

"Constable Mike Whitehead," Oscar said. He had a plumy voice that annoyed Mike more than he cared to admit. "By your own account, you were knocked to the ground fairly quickly. Is that true?"

"Yes, sir," Mike said, hiding his irritation.

"Which means that you were in no position to observe the remainder of the episode," Oscar continued. "And yet you believe that the *accused* were the ones who assaulted Parkhurst. A *slight* discrepancy?"

"No, sir," Mike said.

"Explain."

Mike met his eyes. "During the immediate aftermath of the attack, sir, I assisted in collecting both video recordings of the incident *and* witness statements," he said. "I viewed the whole incident repeatedly. There is no doubt in my mind that the accused are guilty."

Oscar studied him for a long moment. "But you did not see the attack with your own eyes?"

"No, sir," Mike said. "However, I *did* see the recordings."

Vinewood rose. "My Lord," he said. "The recordings in question have been admitted as evidence."

"That is correct," the judge said.

Oscar nodded. "One final question, Constable," he said. "Do you believe that the police force brought the attack on itself?"

Mike had to fight to keep down the hot flash of anger. "No, sir," he managed. "We were just doing our duty. The prisoners we were escorting had been arrested in the aftermath of the riot and on their way to be processed. They might have been released later for lack of evidence, but they were legitimately prisoners. We were doing our duty."

"Thank you, Constable," Oscar said. He looked at the judge. "I have no further questions, My Lord."

"Thank you, Constable," the judge said. "Please wait in the antechamber until you are either recalled to the stand or dismissed."

Mike nodded and turned to leave, his gaze sweeping the room. Most of the audience appeared to be locals, but a couple were very definitely Forsakers. Relatives of the accused, come to watch and pray? Or merely witnesses? He wondered, not for the first time, just what sort of bargain had been struck between the government and their unwanted guests, after the riot. The government had shown that it wasn't willing to fight...

And if this trial ends badly, he thought, *it may bring down the government.*

Joel had decided, not without a slight pang, to discard his traditional clothing and wear a shirt and jeans combination when he strode into the courtroom. His claim to be representing the Elders might have gotten him passed through the guards, but he was grimly aware that the ordinary citizens were turning against the refugees. He'd heard stories about clashes between rival groups of protestors, clashes that could easily lead to attacks on the Kinsman Estate...

If the bad guys win, he reminded himself, as he watched Constable Mike Whitehead leave the stand. He vaguely recalled seeing the constable before, one of the men who'd snatched the Outsider girl out of their arms. *We have to be ready before the balloon goes up.*

A low murmur ran through the audience as the next witness - Constable Bobbie Parkhurst - was escorted to the stand. Constable Whitehead had worn his uniform, Joel noted, but his partner was wearing a civilian dress that wouldn't have been too far out of place in the commune. It definitely didn't disguise the shape of her body, unlike the uniform she'd worn earlier. And there was something about it that suggested she shouldn't be allowed outside without an escort.

"Constable Parkhurst," the prosecutor said, once Bobbie had sworn the oath. "Please would you describe, in your own words, just what happened when you were attacked."

Bobbie...looked unsure of herself. Joel couldn't help feeling a flicker of sympathy, mingled with contempt for both the poor girl and her society. What sort of monsters expected a young woman to do a man's job? She shouldn't have been allowed to wear that uniform, let alone put herself in harm's way. Didn't the men on Arthur's Seat know it was their duty to protect women from the outside world?

"We were marching the prisoners along the street when we were attacked by a mob of refugees," Bobbie said. Her voice was shaky. Forcing her to relive her experiences was cruel. "The attack happened so fast that we couldn't do anything to stop it. Two men slammed into me and knocked me down. I felt a hand groping my breast, then two hands holding my arms. Another man was struggling to pull down my pants."

She paused, tears glimmering in her eyes. "He got my pants around my ankles, then forced my legs apart," she added. "At that point, someone punched him in the stomach, shoving him away from me. I fell back to the ground as the first man let me go. Everything after that is a little hazy until I was back at the station."

The prosecutor nodded. "Do you recognise the assailants in the courtroom today?"

Bobbie pointed at Jack. "That's the man who pulled down my pants and forced my legs apart," she said. "I can't swear to the other one."

There was a long pause. "No further questions, My Lord," the prosecutor said. "Mr. Oscar?"

The defence counsel rose. Joel leaned forward, interested. He'd been told that Bill Oscar was the best public defender on the planet, the only man who might be able to mitigate the charges levelled against Adam and Jack. Hiring him was worth every last penny, he had been told. And yet, there was something slimy about him, slimy enough to make Joel shudder in disgust. Maybe, just maybe, something could be done...afterwards. The man had no place in civilised society.

"Constable Parkhurst," Oscar said. "Did you, in any way, suggest to the two accused that you were, in some way, sexually available."

A low series of gasps ran around the courtroom, followed by angry muttering. Joel winced, silently grateful he hadn't worn traditional clothes. The crowd didn't sound pleased. And the judge, behind his desk, looked furious.

"No, sir," Bobbie said. Her voice was shaking, despite her best efforts. She kept her hands firmly clasped behind her back. "I did not."

"And yet the accused, in their recorded statements, both agree that you came on to them," Oscar continued. "How do you account for that?"

Bobbie made a visible effort to stand straighter. "They're lying?"

"Both accounts agree," Oscar said.

He looked at the jury. "The accused are from a society where, pardon me, women are expected to wear loose-fitting clothes and refrain from contact with men," he said. That, Joel admitted, was true enough. "Their lusts were inflamed by the sight of a woman in pants!"

Joel blinked in shock. He'd heard that before, from both Adam and Jack before they'd been lashed, but he'd never expected *Oscar* to say it. The crowd didn't seem pleased either, judging by the angry mutterings. And the prosecutor…

"It is of no concern *how* lusty they were," he stated, flatly. "Such lustfulness does not count as an excuse for anything."

"I must remind you of the case of *Regina V. Hemlock*," Oscar said. "It was clearly determined that a person unwillingly under the influence could not be held accountable for his actions. We have a clear precedent."

"Which covered a lone case," the prosecutor said. He made a show of consulting his datapad, although Joel had no difficulty in recognising someone arguing from memory. "It was clearly established that Mr. Hemlock was drugged, against his will. His acts while under the influence were appalling, but not his responsibility. This case, however, is different. There is no suggestion that either of the accused were drugged, drunk or in any way suffering from impaired reasoning."

"But they were," Oscar countered.

The judge cleared his throat. "Might it be too much to ask that the defence counsel comes to the point?"

"Certainly, My Lord," Oscar said. "The defendants were not raised in a society where tight-fitting clothes were the norm. They were unprepared for the surge of lust they experienced when they discovered that Constable Parkhurst was a woman. As such, they cannot be held wholly responsible for their actions. I might refer you to the case of *Imperial V. Sakkara* and *Imperial V. Wesley*, both of which recognise the problems caused by cultural differences."

Joel couldn't follow the argument. Judging by the mumbles running through the audience, the spectators either couldn't follow it themselves or thought it was absolute nonsense. Oscar seemed to be gambling, but gambling on what? Joel honestly wasn't sure he wanted to know.

"There is a further issue, My Lord," Oscar added. "Both of the accused were tried and punished by their own people. I would direct the court's attention to the medical report, based on an examination conducted as soon as they were in custody. Both men were soundly whipped by their peers. Double jeopardy..."

"Has no meaning here," the prosecutor snapped. "My Lord, this is an inappropriate line of questioning - and, frankly, is rather more like making a speech!"

"Agreed," the judge said. "The defence will drop this line of questioning."

Oscar nodded. "As your lordship pleases," he said. "I have no further questions."

Joel kept his face impassive as Constable Parkhurst was escorted off the witness stand, despite a churning mixture of emotions he couldn't even *begin* to name. The idea of handing his people over for trial...it was horrific. He knew, all too well, just how badly it had gone for the commune, in the past. And, even without *that* consideration, watching Oscar at work had left him with an uneasy mix of guilt and shame. The man was completely without morals.

And if we win, he mused, *it will not please the crowd.*

"Gentlemen and ladies of the jury," the usher said, after the jury had filed back into the courtroom and the doors had been closed. "Have you reached a verdict?"

Mike leaned forward. Witnesses weren't allowed to re-enter the courtroom, but they could - if they wished - watch the final proceedings on the monitor. Bobbie sat next to him, saying nothing. They'd been forbidden to talk about the case, even though they'd both been told they wouldn't be recalled, but she hadn't wanted to talk at all. There was something brittle about her now, something broken.

"Yes, we have," the jury foreman said.

The judge inclined his head. "And is it the verdict of you all?"

"Nine to four, My Lord," the foreman said.

"Shit," Bobbie said. "That's…"

She put her head in her hands and began to cry. Mike reached out to give her a hug, then pulled back as he remembered what even a platonic touch could do to her. Nine to four…they needed a unanimous vote for the death penalty. He wondered, sourly, just which members of the jury had *not* found the defendants guilty. The bastards deserved to hang!

"Nine to four," the judge repeated. He looked as if he wanted to demand answers, but legally he couldn't. The jury had the right to keep its reasoning to itself. "Thank you."

He turned to face the prisoners. "Adam of No Family," he said. "Jack of No Family. You have been found guilty of sexually assaulting a policewoman with the obvious intention of going further, had you not been stopped in time. You will be taken from this place to a detention centre, where you will have the choice between spending five years on a chain gang or immediate exile from civilised society. Should you refuse to decide, you will be exiled from this planet."

Mike gritted his teeth. Five years on a chain gang wasn't *pleasant* - years spent breaking rock, clearing fields or even picking up litter couldn't be said to be *fun* - but it was far less than what the bastards deserved. Hanging was far too good for them. And as for exile…he wasn't even sure if they *could* be kicked off Arthur's Seat. The Imperial Navy might not take them back, while Mike hadn't heard of any other ships visiting the system. They might just have to stay in jail, at the taxpayer's expense, until they served their term.

Bobbie let out a little gasp. "I'm sorry."

"It wasn't your fault," Mike told her.

"Yes, it was," Bobbie said. She looked up, tearfully. "If I hadn't been so weak…"

"I got knocked down too," Mike said. He wished - not for the first time - that they had some powered combat armour. But there was none on the planet, as far as he knew. "You weren't the only one to be hurt."

But the only one to be molested, his own thoughts added. *The kicks he'd taken didn't compare to nearly being raped. She was subjected to a very sexualised assault, stripped of her dignity in front of her fellows as well as her self-worth.*

He rose, pacing the room as he struggled to contain his anger. The original set of prisoners had already been judged, but their rescuers... they'd been allowed to get away with it. Sure, the would-be rapists had been whipped and then handed over for judgement, yet they hadn't been alone. A gaggle of refugees had been allowed to assault the police and get away with it, convincing half the population that they could no longer rely on the police to protect them.

There was a knock at the door. It opened to reveal a pair of proctors, looking grim. "The protests outside have grown," the leader said. "Both sides are summoning reinforcements through the datanet. You are advised to remain here until further notice."

Mike nodded, wishing he had his uniform and truncheon. The urge to go out and crack heads was uncivilised - and unworthy of a police officer - but he had it anyway. If he marched out and started clobbering people...he'd probably get arrested and thrown into the same cell as Adam and Jack. If it gave him a shot at them...

Don't be stupid, he told himself, sharply. Jane wouldn't thank him for getting himself thrown in jail. A police officer who went off the rails would be lucky if he wasn't exiled. *Just be glad they're off the streets.*

He shook his head, bitterly. He knew it was just the beginning.

CHAPTER THIRTY-TWO

But such conflicts often failed to stop on command. A show of force could dull the flames of war, if only for a few years, but none of the underlying problems were actually addressed. The war might start up again as soon as the occupation forces were withdrawn.
- Professor Leo Caesius. *Ethnic Streaming and the End of Empire.*

"I'm afraid the message from Lanark hasn't changed," Sondra said. She sounded quietly furious. "They're flatly refusing to take any refugees."

William scowled. Lanark was a large town, population 10'000. There was no reason they couldn't take a few hundred refugees, save for the simple fact that their council was facing re-election and their opponents wouldn't hesitate to make political capital out of it, if they agreed to accept the refugees. And besides, rumours were still spreading wildly, growing more and more out of control. By the time one rumour was countered, a thousand more were already percolating over the datanet.

"It gets worse," Sondra added. "New Glasgow has called out a posse. Their District Hall states that it is ready to resist any attempt to send refugees in their direction, by force if necessary."

William shook his head, striding over to the window to peer down at the streets below. Two crowds of protesters, kept apart by a thin blue line of policemen, were hooting and hollering, shouting accusations that were lost in the din. One group supported the refugees; the other wanted to kick them off the planet…from so high, it was impossible to tell which group was which.

Sally cleared her throat. "With all due respect, Premier, there may be a more serious problem."

William turned. "Troutman?"

"No, sir," Sally said. "Economics."

She held out a datapad. "The refugees are putting a major strain on our economy, directly and indirectly," she said. "On one hand, we have to provide enough food, drink, bedding and shelter to keep them alive. That's a major drain on our finances. On the other, large numbers of people are leaving Lothian and heading out to the countryside. That's hit local companies quite hard. Our tax revenue for the rest of the year will be down."

"Making it harder to fund the resettlement efforts," William muttered.

"Yes, sir," Sally said. She crossed her long legs and leaned forward. "For political reasons, it will be difficult to set up new farms on Maxima. Large swathes of the continent have not been claimed, but it was always envisaged that the land would go to our descendants. There would be opposition even if there *weren't* claims that the refugees would eventually set up a country of their own. However, establishing new farms and settlements on Minoa will be extremely costly. We are in no position to afford it."

"Then raise taxes," Sondra said. "We have the authority to propose emergency taxation, don't we?"

"Parliament would probably not approve it," Sally said, flatly. "And even if we did, the levels of taxation we'd require would ruin our economy. My most optimistic projection is that seventy percent of our businesses would collapse within the year."

"Our economy is not that brittle," Sondra snapped.

"These are not normal times," Sally countered. "Every business that depended on the interstellar market is already on the brink of collapse. We simply don't have the money to shore them up when there's no guarantee of restoring our access to interstellar markets. It's impossible to do more than soften the blow as much as possible."

She shrugged. "And we can't even take out a loan," she added. "There's no one who could offer it to us, even if they *wanted* to."

William groaned as he turned back to the window. God *damn* the Imperial Navy. If there had been a few weeks - or months - of warning, the entire crisis could have been handled relatively easily. Or if they'd had the nerve to insist that the Forsakers be dumped on Minoa…but he'd allowed himself to be talked into providing humanitarian aid. He couldn't have just left them to die, could he?

But it had caused a crisis. His government was shaky, the only thing keeping him in power was Troutman's reluctance to risk a vote of no-confidence. And yet, the odds were steadily swinging in Troutman's direction. The alliance with the Unionists - and the price they'd demanded for their support - would cost him dearly, in the next set of elections. If, of course, he remained in office long enough to *face* the next set of elections. One more crisis would be enough to ruin him.

"The immediate crisis has been solved," Sondra said. "We have a working understanding now…"

"That's disputable," Sally said. William turned back to face her. "The polls are clear. A large percentage of our population now hates and fears the refugees - hatred which is blurring over to the descendants of Forsakers across the continent. The attack on the police, the near-rape of a police officer, the deal we made…"

She shook her head. "People are fearful," she warned. "And fearful people do stupid things."

"Like attacking their fellow citizens," Sondra said.

Sally leaned forward. "Our planet has - had - a relatively homogeneous culture," she said, flatly. "Sure, we have people who are descended from the original settlers and others who are descended from later immigrants, but there really aren't that many differences between them and the rest of us. The former had a crisis of cultural confidence; the latter *intended* to integrate from the start. There was no serious conflict when they arrived."

"They would have lost," William said.

Sally shrugged. "The point, sir, is that the vast majority of people on our world operate from the same set of assumptions about how the universe works, about what is acceptable behaviour in society. There really isn't *that* great a difference, whatever the Freeholders may claim, between a farmer and a city-slicker. They may have different upbringings, but they agree far more than they disagree. And the differences are comparatively minor."

"True," Sondra said. "And your point is…?"

"The refugees do not *share* that set of assumptions," Sally said. "To us, attacking a group of policemen is unforgivable; to them, it was the only way to save their people from an automatic death sentence. To us, a woman's clothing is of no concern; to them, a woman wearing skimpy clothes is signalling her availability. To us, individuality is of paramount concern; to them, the good of the commune is more important than any individual. To us, a person may marry whoever he or she wants; to them, marriage is a union between families, rather than two people…"

"So they're different," Sondra snapped. "So what?"

"So their behaviour appears unpredictable," Sally said. "What is intolerable to us might be tolerable to them. Their behaviour therefore seems horrific to us. Worse, our government seems to accept their explanations and excuses - putting them ahead of its own people. And so social trust is worn down to a nub."

She sighed. "Right now, people are preparing for trouble," she added. "And the *reason* they are preparing for trouble is because they have lost faith in our ability to handle the crisis."

Sondra scowled. "The problem will solve itself within a couple of generations," she insisted, sharply.

"That may be true," Sally said. "It is also irrelevant."

William turned back from the window. "How so?"

"We have compromised ourselves in the eyes of the population," Sally said, bluntly. "We attempted to cover up the…*incidents*…at the spaceport, then the full details of the riot in Lothian. Our cover-ups failed, making us look both evil and incompetent. They no longer have faith in us."

"We did what was necessary to prevent a greater crisis," Sondra snapped.

"The public doesn't see it that way," Sally pointed out. "They see it as a betrayal."

William eyed Sondra thoughtfully as the two women argued. Sondra *had* taken over principal responsibility for the crisis, after all. It would be easy enough to blame her for the problems. But even now, Sondra had allies in the party. If she refused to resign, he would have to sack her…and that would cause a civil war within the party. And if enough MPs refused to back him, he might find himself being openly challenged for his post.

And it might be too late to force her to take the blame, he thought, grimly. *There's enough of it to go around.*

"Then we work to mitigate the scale of the problem," he said. "And do what we can to feed refugees into the job market."

"That will be problematic, of course," Sally said. "The job market has been shrinking for the last few months."

She paused. "And there is another problem," she added. "What happens if we get lumbered with *more* refugees?"

William blinked. "More?"

"Tarsus wasn't the only world with large Forsaker communities," Sally said. "Durian, Paradise Rock and Calandos have nearly a *million* Forsakers between them. What's to stop them transporting their unwanted populations here and dumping them on us?"

"They wouldn't," Sondra said.

Sally smiled, humourlessly. "Why not? Sending them here is quicker and cleaner than committing genocide. And…why, *look*! We have a population that includes a large number of Forsakers! Why *not* send their distant cousins here? I believe that was the logic Tarsus used."

"It was," William said.

"We need to worry about the future," Sally warned. "Even if there's no prospect of more refugees, Troutman and his ilk won't hesitate to use it against you."

William nodded. But there was nothing he could say.

"I feel like a rookie again," Constable Paul Smith muttered as they marched through the gates. "I haven't been here since I was told that the streets would be safer with me on them."

"The trainers must have been drunk," Mike muttered back. "Or maybe they thought everyone would be rendered helpless by laughter when they saw you."

He took a breath as he glanced around, feeling oddly out of place. Lestrade Training Centre - the origins of the name lost in the mists of time - was where every police officer on Arthur's Seat had been trained, six months of everything from memorising the law to practicing unarmed combat and studying detective techniques. He'd lost a great many of his illusions about humanity during his basic training, even though Arthur's Seat lacked the giant crime rings and mass incivility of Earth. And yet, the day he'd first walked the beat in uniform, he'd still felt as though he knew nothing. Training was good, but nothing could beat experience.

A handful of rookies were running around the field, their progress monitored by a grim-faced officer in a green uniform. Another group were bending over a mock crime scene in the distance, being tested on their conduct. The five low buildings in the centre of the complex, he recalled, held everything from classrooms to a small library of law-related materials from across the universe. He'd been required to read case studies from a dozen different worlds before being allowed to pass his written exams.

"Over here," a voice called. An older man, wearing another green uniform, was waving to them. Mike didn't recognise him. "Get your asses over here!"

Mike did as he was told, joining a small group of experienced policemen. There were no women in the group, he noted; indeed, the orders to report to Lestrade hadn't been too clear on what they'd actually be doing. He recognised a couple of faces from Lothian, but the remainder were strangers. It looked as though someone had been selecting officers from all over the continent.

"I am Instructor Javier," the man said, once they were assembled. "For those of you who graduated more than three years ago, I am the Firearms Training Officer for Lestrade."

He turned. "Follow me."

Mike glanced at Smith, then fell into a jog as Javier led them down a path, round a building and past the unarmed combat training field. A female rookie was trying desperately to take down a man easily twice her size, but she didn't seem to be having much luck. Mike caught a glimpse of her instructor's face and smiled, knowing the poor rookie was going to be told off in no uncertain terms. There was no room for doubt or hesitation when one's target was so much bigger.

Javier stopped outside another long, low building, pressing his hand against a fingerprint sensor. Mike lifted his eyebrows in surprise - he hadn't seen such technology in mainstream use, not even in Lothian - as the door clicked open, revealing a firing range. Javier counted them in, then closed the door with an ominous click. Mike felt himself shuffling nervously as Javier stalked past them, then swung around to face the group. His face suggested, very strongly, that he was not a man to be taken lightly.

"Your records confirm that you all passed the basic firearms course with flying colours," Javier said, without preamble. "How many of you, since then, have used a firearm on duty?"

Mike glanced from side to side. No one seemed inclined to speak.

"You gentlemen have been chosen to be the first full-sized firearms squad for the past three hundred years," Javier continued. "You'll be charged with carrying firearms on duty and, if necessary, using them to protect the public. Some of you will find this morally objectionable, as we pride ourselves in not using lethal force. Others will be concerned about the possibility of being blamed for mistakes, mistakes that result in serious injuries or deaths."

He paused. "If any of you want to withdraw now, you may do so," he added. "It will not be held against you. However, if you stick with the course, you are committed."

Mike swallowed, hard. He'd taken the firearms course, just like everyone else. But he'd never carried a weapon on duty. He knew, all too well, that the PCA was just *waiting* for a chance to nail him. And yet...he *wanted* to do his duty. If he had to carry a loaded gun to do his duty, he'd carry a loaded gun.

Two constables turned and left, heading out the door. Javier spoke briefly to them, then closed the door again. "Last chance to back out," he warned. "Anyone who chooses to leave after this will be classed as a deserter."

There were no takers. Javier studied them all for a long moment, then nodded curtly. "These are MAG-47 military assault rifles," he said, removing a case from the shelves and putting it on a table. Mike and the others gathered round and watched as Javier opened the case, revealing a dark metal gun. "Unlike hunting rifles, they can be switched to fire bursts as well as single shots...depending, of course, on the exact situation. You can shoot yourselves dry very quickly if you don't know what you're doing."

Mike nodded, feeling sweat trickle down his spine. He'd used police rifles - and civilian pistols - back when he'd taken the course, but the military weapons looked...*nastier*, somehow. There was something about them, as Javier talked about the different features and settings, that worried him. And yet, there was something about the weapons that drew him to them too. Firearms were *the* great equaliser. An angry mob could be scythed down in a moment.

Which is the great temptation, he thought, grimly. He knew enough about guns to know that most shooting flicks were utter nonsense. *Guns don't make you superman.*

"You'll be able to quote the manual automatically when you're finished," Javier said. He smiled, rather coldly. "And believe me, you'll be firing these weapons in your sleep."

"I hope not," a constable said. "My wife will never forgive me."

Javier shrugged. "Once you have completed the course, you'll be bound by the guidelines on armed police officers," he added. "I imagine you won't have bothered to review them since you graduated, so you'll be given a copy to study at the end of the day. For the moment, all you really need to know is that any horseplay, particularly in front of impressionable civilians, will have the most dire consequences. Do you have any questions?"

Mike hesitated. He *hadn't* reviewed the guidelines in years. He'd never *needed* to review the guidelines. Now...what if he panicked and opened fire on innocent civilians? Or what if he accidentally lost the weapon? Or...

"Yes, sir," Smith said. "Where did the weapons actually *come* from?"

"A small stash of military-grade weapons was amassed by the Orbital Guard, a few decades ago," Javier said. He didn't seem surprised by the question. "Only a handful of guardsmen - and police officers - were told they existed. Ideally, they would never have been brought out of storage."

Mike nodded. No one had seriously expected trouble on Arthur's Seat, certainly nothing the police or a posse armed with hunting rifles couldn't handle. The idea of forming a standing army had been ludicrous, once upon a time. There was no threat, nothing to justify the existence of an army...and even if they did, any interstellar invader would have no trouble at all destroying the army from orbit. But now...

He shivered as he looked down at the rifle. It didn't *look* hard to use - all the military flicks he'd seen had suggested that soldiers were idiots - yet...he couldn't help thinking that his people had lost some of their innocence. Armed police on the streets, a genuine internal threat...what next? Interstellar war? Or a rogue government? Or what? He didn't want to know.

You have no choice, he told himself, sternly. *None of us have a choice.*

"No more questions?" Javier asked. He sounded pleased. "Good."

He took the rifle and held it up. "It is time to begin."

Chapter
Thirty-Three

> The refusal to recognise the existence of the underlying problems practically ensured it. It was unthinkable, politically speaking, to remove one of the ethnic groups or force it to assimilate. All the Empire succeeded in doing was removing any incentive for moderation on both sides.
> - Professor Leo Caesius. *Ethnic Streaming and the End of Empire.*

"Where *is* she?"

Joel paced the room, feeling oddly out of sorts. Hannah had been *told* to meet him - and her mother and stepfather - at 1300, but it was now 1323 and she was still not present. She'd gone out with her brother, he'd been told. It was something he'd put a stop to, once she was his wife. Even with John's company, a young girl shouldn't be wandering out of the home, let alone going into town. But he'd been too busy with his other projects to do anything about it.

"Women are always late," his father said. He sounded amused. "Don't be so impatient."

"Yes, father," Joel said, turning away so his father wouldn't see his reddening face. It was all right for Konrad, wasn't it? He was old and settled, his only son already a man. He'd never known a time when he hadn't been able to marry, when there might not have been a young woman of good stock suitable for him. "I am sorry."

He bowed his head, his mind elsewhere. The estate had changed in three weeks, becoming more and more habitable as the crates were unpacked and their contents distributed amongst the commune. There were still dozens of tents going up all over the place, but most of the population had a solid roof over their heads. *And* there were dozens of semi-Forsakers from Lothian coming in to help, bringing food and supplies to their brethren...

And protesters on the far side of the fence, he thought, sourly. He'd made sure to prepare the compound for an assault, if the protesters ever worked up the nerve to charge. The policemen outside the wire wouldn't do anything to stop them. *We'll have to fight sooner or later.*

"Do not worry about it," his father said. "You have an entire life ahead of you."

Joel shrugged. He knew he should be grateful. His father had married again, just to ensure that Joel had a Forsaker bride when the time came. The Elders might be doddering old fools - they'd wasted *days* arguing over just how much they should accept from their cousins - but his father was still doing the best he could for his son. Joel *knew* he should be grateful...

...And yet, he knew his contributions were being ignored.

Let them think they're in charge, he told himself, grimly. *He* ruled the Stewards now, not the Elders. *He* controlled the guns; he controlled the men trained to use them. *And one day, they can be pushed aside.*

He looked up, grimly, as the door opened. Hannah stepped into the living room, followed by her brother. Joel's lips curved in utter contempt as he wondered what sort of man would let the woman take the lead. But then, it wasn't as if they were walking into a stranger's house, was it? He leaned forward, wondering just what was in the bag Hannah had slung over her shoulder. Perhaps he should demand that her mother inspect it...

"Hannah," Konrad said. "Please, sit down."

Hannah's face flickered as her gaze moved from Konrad to Joel and back again. Joel had no difficulty in reading her expression. She thought she was in trouble, again. Did she have a *reason* to think she was in trouble? Going beyond the wire would expose her to all sorts of influences, none of them good. If a couple of young men could be shunned for spending too much time with Outsider women, what would it be like for a young woman?

But you're not in trouble, Joel thought, as Hannah sat. *This is the best thing that could happen to you.*

He felt a sudden surge of affection, mingled with droll amusement. Hannah looked very...typical, for an unmarried girl. She wore a long grey shapeless dress and a white cap, the latter indicating that she was a virgin. A widow would wear a black cap. And yet, there was something about her that called to him, something that marked her out as special. A little work to restore her reputation and she'd be the perfect wife for him.

And once I am in control, Joel thought, *no one will dare speak against her.*

John sat next to Hannah, eyeing Joel warily. Joel barely looked at him, unwilling to risk showing his disgust. Hannah had practically emasculated her brother, if only because John was unable to stand up to her. Joel would make it clear, right from the start, that *he* was in charge, that *she* would be expected to confine herself to the female sphere. He liked her, he cared for her...but he wouldn't allow her to dominate him. How could John have gone so badly wrong?

Their father died too soon, he told himself. *And neither of them developed properly.*

"This is our home for the next year," Konrad said, waving at the stone walls. They were now covered in handmade tapestries, all removed from the crates. A curtain hung in front of the female quarters, ensuring that men knew not to enter. "We will not get a farm until later."

Joel scowled, although he tried to keep the expression from showing. The local government might have given them the estate, but it hadn't been very clear on when the Forsakers could move to the farms. Joel had ordered some of his people to apply for positions on local farms - it seemed to be the usual way for a local townsman to become a countryman - yet only two of them had been accepted. The rural dwellers seemed even less inclined to tolerate the Forsakers than their cousins.

"But we are settled for the moment," Konrad said. "I have therefore decided that the time has come for you and Joel to be joined in holy matrimony."

Hannah started. "I..."

"You are really too old to remain unmarried," Konrad told her, severely. "And you have few other prospects."

That was true, Joel knew. Most young men his age wouldn't want to marry her - and if they did, their families would forbid it. Hannah simply wasn't very reputable. Her only other prospects were older widowers looking for a second wife, something that was largely frowned upon in the commune. An old man had no business marrying a girl twenty or more years younger than him. The thought was appalling. A man old enough to be his father marrying Hannah…

"I cannot get married," Hannah said, finally. Her eyes were flickering from side to side, as if she was unwilling to look at any of them. "I…"

"You are more than old enough to marry," Konrad said. "My son has good prospects. As his wife, as the mother of his children, you will have good prospects too."

Hannah looked at her mother. "I can't…"

"You can," her mother said, firmly. "I have done my best to organise a good match for you, Hannah. It was not easy. You will take it and be glad."

"The marriage will be held in four days," Konrad continued, remorselessly. "Once you are married, any stain on your reputation will be removed. I will be able to find your brother a match of his own."

"No," Hannah said.

Joel stared at her. She was saying no?

"Yes," Konrad said. "Your selfishness has cost the family dearly. You are lucky you have not been shunned. The time has come to put aside childish matters, take a husband and raise a brood of children. It is your duty."

He rose. "You and Joel may discuss the wedding plans now," he said, motioning for John to rise too. "The formal engagement will be announced tonight, after prayers. And I suggest you remember, young lady, that your actions significantly reduced your choices. No one came to pay court to you, not ever. You have no other suitors."

Hannah stared at him, her mouth moving soundlessly as her mother and her brother followed her stepfather out of the room, leaving her alone with Joel. Joel was surprised, more than he cared to admit. Konrad hadn't *told* him that Hannah didn't have any other suitors, but he'd always assumed there would be *some*. They just wouldn't come from good families. Or they'd have dark intentions.

"Hannah," he said, quietly. "We need to talk."

Hannah hunched up in her chair. "Go away."

"I can't do that," Joel said. A hot flash of anger burned through him. She was *rejecting* him, after all he'd done for her and her family? "We have to talk."

"No," Hannah said.

"We do," Joel said. He reached out and touched her chin, pushing it up until she was looking at him. "We have to get married."

"No, we don't," Hannah said.

Joel gritted his teeth, calming himself by sheer force of will. "Why not?"

Hannah looked at him for a long moment, then looked down at the floor. "I don't want to marry you."

The rejection stung, more than Joel cared to admit. "Why not?"

"Because…because I want to be something more," Hannah said. Her voice cracked as she spoke. "I want to be more than just a housewife!"

Joel regarded her with honest bemusement. "But it is your role!"

"I could be a doctor," Hannah said. "Or a *proper* midwife. Or…"

"Or what?" Joel asked. A thought struck him and he leaned forward. "Who's been putting these ideas into your head?"

Hannah looked up at him. "Does it matter?"

"Yes," Joel snapped. Hannah had been talking to an Outsider girl, hadn't she? The girl had clearly had an effect on her. "You're not an Outsider."

He reached for her bag. She clutched it, but he pulled it free, tearing it open to reveal a set of pamphlets. The first one talked about medical courses at the university; the second talked about possible careers, if someone had a medical degree. He tossed the remainder aside without bothering to look at them, feeling a flare of pure rage. How *dare* she?

"You stayed with us," he snapped, fighting to control his anger. "Why did you stay?"

Hannah glared at him, her face twisting with anger and bitter rage. "Because I thought my mother needed me," she snapped back. "I could have stayed on Tarsus!"

"You don't get to move between two worlds," Joel said. He clenched his fists, struggling to keep himself from striking her. "You are either a Forsaker or you are Fallen. There's no middle ground!"

"Why not?" Hannah asked. "Why do I have to be a housewife or leave? Why?"

"We made a decision to leave the sins and corruptions of the modern world behind," Joel reminded her. He'd answered the question before, he recalled, but never from Hannah. He couldn't help wondering if she'd ever discussed it with her mother. Girls rarely talked to the Stewards about their personal feelings. "We seek out a simple life."

He took a firm grip on his temper, shoving it into the very back of his mind. Women were flighty creatures, his father had said. Their emotions were strong, almost overpowering. And so they could not be trusted. Women needed men to show them the way, to guide, protect and discipline them. Hannah had had a chance to leave, months ago. She hadn't taken it.

Gritting his teeth, he went down on his knees beside her, taking her hand in his. She tensed, but made no attempt to pull back. Joel told himself, firmly, that that was a good sign. She was willing to listen to him, no matter what she said. All he had to do was find the right words.

"Your reputation is tainted," he said. "Marriage to me will solve that problem. No one will dare question you again. I will be a good husband, a good father…"

"How *noble* of you," Hannah said, bitterly. "You don't have to change, do you?"

"You cannot go on like this," Joel told her. "Your place in the commune is at risk…"

Hannah shook her head, her cap falling to the side. "Who cares?"

"I care," Joel said. "Your mother cares! My father - your stepfather - cares…"

"Your father married a widow just so he could ensure his son married her daughter," Hannah snapped. She jerked her hand back, hard. "He doesn't care about me!"

Joel nearly hit her. If she'd been a man, he *would* have hit her. How *dare* she? Woman or not, emotional or not, there were limits. His father had put his own reputation on the line when he'd married again, knowing he would have to tame a rebellious daughter and teach a young boy to be a man. Joel *knew* what his father had sacrificed. How *dare* Hannah treat it so lightly?

"Marry me," he said, harshly. He'd make damn sure she knew her place, afterwards. "You and I will…"

"No," Hannah said.

"Why not?"

"Because I don't *want* to marry you," Hannah said. "I don't *like* you, I don't…"

Joel hit her, his fist slamming into her chest. Hannah screamed, her entire body jerking forward. She swung her arm at him wildly, but Joel had no difficulty catching hold of it and yanking it forward, throwing her face-down over the chair. Hannah kicked out at him, then screamed again as he slammed his fist into her back. He stepped to one side, holding her down with one hand as he unbuckled his belt with the other. She was still fighting, despite the pain, still trying to get away from him. And then she kicked him in the knee…

Rage - red rage - overpowered him. He brought the belt down time and time again, lashing her back, her buttocks and the backs of her legs until she was sobbing helplessly, all resistance gone. Dark stains were visible on her back, suggesting he'd broken the skin…he found himself staring down at her as the rage drained away, torn between guilt and a desperate need to believe he'd done the right thing. She'd deserved it, he told himself. He hadn't had a choice. And yet, her rasping sobs tore at him. He'd lashed her harder than he'd lashed Adam or Jack.

"I have to join the boys for football," he said, carefully buckling his belt back into place. "I will be back tonight. We'll discuss the wedding then."

Hannah said something incoherent. Joel hesitated, then picked up her papers and headed for the door. She'd deserved the beating, he told himself firmly. No one could steer a course between two worlds. She was either a Forsaker, in which case she should accept the judgement of her parents, or a Fallen, someone who had no place in the community. And she'd insulted his father and stepmother. It was his duty to punish her, to keep her in line…

He turned to take one last look at her as he reached the door. She hadn't moved, her entire body shaking so badly that he couldn't help wondering if he'd inflicted permanent harm. He wondered if he should call a doctor, even though he knew she would probably prefer to be left alone to recover. A doctor...the entire community would know what had happened within the hour, if they didn't already. The cottage was surprisingly soundproofed, but Hannah's screams had probably been heard all over the estate.

"I'm sorry," he said, finally. "But you deserved it."

Hannah said something else. It didn't sound pleasant. Joel hesitated, then turned and walked out of the door, closing it firmly behind him. She knew, now, that he was not to be taken lightly, not to be dominated by a wily woman. And she would be happier for it, he told himself firmly. She had to know that she could no longer act in a disreputable manner. The lesson would sink in, now it had been administered.

We will be married, he promised himself, silently. *And then we will be happy.*

John had been surprised when Konrad had ordered him to leave Hannah and Joel alone, even though they were - technically - stepsiblings. It wasn't right, not when they were also betrothed. John couldn't help thinking that it portended trouble. Konrad seemed to think they would all be going to prayers, but John managed to get away from him and then run back to the cottage. He was just in time to see Joel leave, heading towards the edge of the field. It didn't look good.

He braced himself as he opened the door, then froze. Hannah was kneeling on the chair, her face blotchy with tears. He could see marks on her face and dark stains on her dress...she was whimpering, whimpering helplessly. John could barely move as he took in the horrific scene. What had Joel *done* to her?

"Help me," Hannah said. Even her voice was different. She sounded as though she was on the verge of collapse. "John..."

John stumbled forward and caught her, a moment before she fell off the chair. She seemed to be having difficulty walking, her entire body stiff and unresponsive. John was struck, suddenly, by just how light she was. Droplets of blood were falling to the ground. It was an utter nightmare. And Joel...Joel had done this to her?

"We have to get out of here," Hannah breathed. She seemed to be recovering, although it was hard to tell. "John..."

John stared at her, then nodded in grim agreement. If Joel was willing to beat her so badly when they were merely betrothed, what would he do when they were married? He had no idea where they could go, but it didn't matter. All that mattered was getting out of the estate before Joel came home.

"Let's go," he said.

CHAPTER THIRTY-FOUR

And, collectively, the wars sapped the Empire's strength. Vast amounts of blood and treasure were wasted on wars that the Grand Senate chose not to bring to an end. (Indeed, some factions didn't want the wars to end.) The sheer level of ethnic hatred the Empire had stirred up wanted, demanded, release.

- Professor Leo Caesius. *Ethnic Streaming and the End of Empire.*

Judith had been sitting at her terminal, writing an updated account of the spaceport situation, when she heard a faint tapping at her door. A horn hooted downstairs, surprising her. She picked up her pistol - her father had insisted she carry, if she wasn't prepared to return to the farm - and peered carefully through the peephole. John was standing in front of her door, looking terrified. Judith opened the door, careful to keep the pistol at the ready...

...And almost fainted when she saw Hannah, sitting on the floor.

"My God," she said. Hannah looked...*battered*. "What happened?"

"We told the driver you'd pay the cab," John said. "Do you have any money?"

Judith stared at him. *What* cab? Where had they come from? She hastily passed him a fifty-pound note, then helped Hannah stumble into the apartment. Prices had been going up lately and cabbies always overcharged the tourists, but fifty should be enough to cover it. She wasn't sure what she'd do if John needed more. The local ATM had been out of money for the last two days.

"Hurts," Hannah managed, as John hurried back into the apartment and closed the door. She sounded as though she was having trouble breathing. "I hurt!"

"Let me help," Judith said. She carefully positioned Hannah on the sofa, then started to carefully remove her clothes. John started to say something before stopping himself, his face pale. "I…"

She froze as she saw the marks. Hannah's back was covered in bloody scars, some still bleeding. She pulled Hannah's underclothes down and saw similar marks covering her buttocks and the back of her legs. Judith had seen horror - she still had nightmares, sometimes, about the man who'd been caught in a thresher machine - but this was unthinkable. Someone had systematically beaten Hannah to within an inch of her life, tearing her skin so badly that there was a very good chance she'd become infected. And her immune system was weak. This could *kill* her!

"I'm calling the hospital," she said. "And the police."

"No," John said. "They'll…"

Judith stared at him. "She needs help," she said. "And the person who did this needs to be arrested."

Hannah made a sound. It might have been a giggle. "You can't arrest him."

"Yes, we can," Judith said. In truth, she wasn't so sure. "This is…this is assault. He could have killed you."

John looked up at her. "But…"

"I can't even *begin* to tend to this," Judith said. Her medical training was nowhere near sufficient. Hannah needed proper treatment or she'd be carrying the scars for life, if they didn't get infected. Who could *do* this to a young woman? "What happened?"

"We argued," Hannah rasped. She shifted, uncomfortably. Being exposed in front of her brother had to be a nightmare in itself. "I told him I didn't want to marry him. We fought. He…"

Her voice trailed off. "I'm calling the doctor," Judith said, firmly. "And the police."

She reached for her personal com and tapped the emergency code. Services had been slow over the past few days - apparently, the extra demand caused by the refugees was overloading the system - but no one would risk interfering with an emergency call. She outlined what had happened, quickly, then put the phone down. The hospital staff would inform the police too, when they arrived. They had an obligation to alert the police if someone showed signs of abuse.

They'll do something, Judith told herself, grimly. She couldn't tear her eyes off Hannah's back, even though she knew it would embarrass her friend. *Won't they?*

"I'm staying," Hannah said. She sounded a little stronger, although Judith knew her ministrations had been largely cosmetic. "I won't go back."

John opened his mouth, then closed it. Instead, he reached out and took his sister's hand, holding it gently. Judith felt a sudden rush of affection that surprised her. Her brother was too old to be a real friend and playmate, although he had played with her when she'd been a little girl. There was just too great a gulf between them. But Hannah and John were friends as well as siblings, comrades in adversity...

"My family farm will have room for you," she said, quietly. Outside, she heard the sound of sirens. "You'll be welcome."

"We'll see," John said. "I doubt I'll be welcome anywhere."

The football match had not been a success, despite Joel's best efforts. He'd hoped to organise a series of games against Outsider teams - it would keep some of the young boys and men occupied - but his teams had refused to play against mixed or female-only teams, leading to a series of bitter arguments. The Outsiders had counterattacked by refusing to play unless the Forsakers accepted female players...

He scowled as he made his way back to the cottage. It was just another piece of proof that Forsakers and Outsiders couldn't co-exist. They were too different. Women were to be protected, not allowed to risk themselves on the playing fields. He shuddered to think of what would happen if a woman were hurt while playing...

The door was ajar when he approached. A shiver ran down his spine as he peered through the door, then pushed it wide open. Hannah was gone...a faint trail of bloodstains pointed towards the door, suggesting that she'd picked herself up and walked out of the cottage. He turned, peering down at the path, but saw nothing. Somehow, she'd made it out of the cottage and...and what?

He searched the rest of the cottage, just in case. There was no sign of her. Her room - he thought he could look inside, as they *were* betrothed - was empty. There wasn't any sign that she'd changed her dress or anything, yet...she couldn't make her way through the estate with a bloodstained dress, could she? Surely *someone* would have seen her? Unless...a nasty thought struck him. *John* could have helped her. No one would have questioned a brother helping a sister.

Someone cleared his throat, behind him. Joel spun around, fists raised. His father stood there, eying him quizzically. Joel hastily lowered his clenched fists, cursing himself for his mistake. A son who turned against his father...it was not to be borne.

"Father," he said. "Have you seen Hannah?"

"Director Melbourne has arrived," Konrad said. He didn't seem inclined to answer the question. "She has requested an immediate meeting."

Joel was tempted to refuse. He had a major problem on his hands. Who knew *what* Hannah was doing? And yet, he didn't dare let anyone else handle the negotiations. Who knew what *they* would do? What did the Outsider bitch actually *want*?

"I'm coming," he said. He took one last look around the room, then followed his father out the door. Night was gradually falling, plunging the estate into darkness. There were no streetlights, not entirely to his surprise. "What does she want?"

"She didn't say," Konrad said. "But she did say it was urgent."

Joel thought about it as they walked towards the guardhouse. He had no idea if whoever had designed the estate had intended the guardhouse to serve as a reception area as well as a security checkpoint, but it suited him just fine. There was no way he wanted *official* government officials making their way through the estate. Director Melbourne was particularly stupid - Joel didn't pretend to understand how her mind worked - but even she might notice something amiss if she looked carefully.

He cleared his throat as he stepped into the room. Director Melbourne was sitting at the table, her face grim. Her eyes flickered over him, an unreadable expression crossing her face for a long second before going blank. Joel met her eyes and *knew*, with a certainty that surprised him, where Hannah had gone. The treacherous bitch had betrayed them to the Outsiders!

Just like a woman, his own thoughts mocked. *You should have tied her up when you left.*

"This is not a social call," Director Melbourne said. The arrogance in her voice made his blood boil. "It relates to a very serious matter."

"That is understood," Konrad said. "And what *is* this serious matter?"

"Two hours ago, a young girl was admitted into hospital," Director Melbourne said, her voice very cold. "The doctors confirmed that she had been beaten savagely, beaten so badly that her life was in genuine danger. It was a genuine miracle that she even managed to reach the hospital before it was too late."

"I see," Konrad said, finally. "And this concerns us…how?"

"The girl is your stepdaughter," Director Melbourne said. "And her assailant was your son."

Joel forced his face into grim immobility. His father hadn't hesitated to give *him* a taste of the lash when he misbehaved. He might not object to Joel teaching Hannah a lesson, after they were married, but they weren't married *yet*. Perhaps they'd never be married. Hannah had betrayed the entire community. She would be shunned for the rest of her life if she ever returned.

"Such conduct is unacceptable," Director Melbourne continued. She looked at Joel, her cold eyes staring down at him. "We must insist that your son be handed over for judgement."

"It is an internal affair," Joel managed. The rage was back, bubbling below the surface. How *dare* she? "It is none of your concern."

"It *is* our concern," Director Melbourne said. She looked straight at Konrad. "And as you can see, the beating was serious."

She reached into her handbag and produced a datapad, holding it out so Konrad could see the images. Joel recoiled in shock. Someone had stripped Hannah of her dignity, not even allowing her an undergarment to cover her most private parts. Who could *take* such photographs? And the marks...Konrad grunted, his face expressionless. Joel knew him well enough to understand that he was in trouble.

Director Melbourne kept her eyes on Konrad's face, even as she returned the terminal to her handbag. "Your son has to come with me."

Joel closed his eyes for a long moment, gathering his thoughts. His father would fold, of course. He'd never shown any enthusiasm for defending the community against outside pressure. Joel could walk into their arms or be handed over...unless he took matters into his own hands. The commune wasn't ready to stand up for itself, not yet, but he dared not allow the precedent to stand. They couldn't make such a compromise, not without losing everything. Their *future* was at stake.

"I must talk to my son, alone," Konrad said.

"If you wish," Director Melbourne said. "But I must warn you that time is short."

Joel followed his father into the antechamber, his mind already racing. It was time. It *had* to be time. They couldn't delay any longer.

"Joel," Konrad said. "What were you thinking?"

"She insulted you, father," Joel said. "I thought to punish her."

"By beating her so hard she was on the verge of death?" Konrad said. "Joel..."

"This is an internal affair," Joel said. It was one last gamble, one last chance for his father to join them. "They have no right..."

Konrad slapped him. "No right? By God, *Joel*. What were you thinking?"

Joel touched his cheek, shocked. "Father..."

"You could have killed her," his father said. "You had no right!"

"I had every right," Joel said. The rage bubbled up again. This time, he let it flow. "You and the rest of the doddering old fools will betray us, like you did before. I won't let it happen again, not here. We will reach out and *take* our destiny! Do you understand me?"

His father stared at him. "Joel..."

Joel looked back. His father seemed diminished, somehow. He truly *was* a doddering old man - and a hypocrite too. He'd beaten Hannah - and John, and Joel himself - for far lesser offences than insulting the family patriarch. And perhaps he'd even beaten his wife - *both* of his wives. Now... Joel knew, deep inside, that he would never respect his father again.

"It's time to retire," he said, quietly. He reached into his pocket and produced the pistol. His father's eyes went wide when he saw the weapon. "Your day is done."

His father said nothing as Joel opened a closet and shoved him inside, carefully bolting the door afterwards. An Elder...Forsakers were raised to *listen* to the Elders. Konrad wouldn't have an opportunity to subvert Joel's followers, not now. He shouted for the guards to attend to him, then issued orders. The rest of the Elders would be under lock and key before they knew all hell was breaking loose.

Smirking, he turned and walked back into the meeting room. Director Melbourne was still sitting there, playing with her terminal. She looked up as Joel entered, her mouth dropping open as she saw the pistol in his hand. No doubt she'd believed that the Forsakers were unarmed. Didn't she know better than to trust a manifest?

"What...?"

"I have a message for your government," Joel said. "We are going to claim what is ours."

Director Melbourne stared at him. Joel wrinkled his nose as he smelt urine. She'd wet herself. The stupid bitch had *wet* herself! He felt a rush of power at the fear and shame in her eyes, the awareness - too late - that she'd been on the wrong path all along. She lifted her hands when he jerked the pistol, his eyes automatically looking for a wedding ring. Of *course* there wasn't one. What sort of man would marry such a woman?

Her mouth opened, again. "What message?"

"This message," Joel said.

He pointed the pistol at her forehead and fired.

John had never been in a hospital before. Indeed, he'd never been in a medical centre before, unless one counted the nurse's office at school. He'd always hated going there, knowing that the nurse disliked Forsakers almost as much as they disliked her. But now...

The hospital felt wrong. It was too bright, too loud...too many men and women running around. He sat next to Hannah's bed, holding her hand as she slept. Someone had sedated her, after using a piece of modern technology to heal her wounds. John knew he should have said something, that he should have objected to her treatment, but he knew his sister had come far too close to death. He couldn't bear the thought of losing her.

And what, he asked himself, *does that make me.*

He looked over at Judith, sitting on the far side of the bed. She'd had to argue to be allowed to stay, pointing out that Hannah needed a female companion. The doctors had looked too hassled to argue, although they had cleared it with John first. John hadn't objected. He was too busy fretting over his own life. If he wasn't a Forsaker - and he couldn't be, not any longer - what *was* he? Where did he belong?

The door to the ward opened. A pair of police officers stepped through. John felt a flicker of the old fear, backed by grim resignation, as they walked towards him. They looked...wary, their stances suggesting they expected to be attacked at any moment. It was not reassuring.

"John, Son of John?"

"Yes," John said, tiredly. There was no point in denying it. "That's me."

"We need to take your statement," the policeman said. "Will you come with us?"

John glanced at Hannah. "Don't worry," Judith said. "I'll take care of her."

"I'll be back," John promised.

He followed the policemen down a corridor and into a side room. It was utterly bare, save for a handful of plastic chairs and a medical device he didn't recognise. He couldn't help thinking that the room *belonged* in a police station. There was something about it that fitted, somehow.

The policeman motioned for John to sit down, then sat facing him. "Start at the beginning," he said. "What happened?"

John hesitated. It had been drilled into him time and time again, ever since he was old enough to understand. Outsider police were *not* to be trusted. They were enemies, just watching and waiting for a chance to attack the commune. He had been told to say nothing, to play dumb... whatever he knew, he needed to keep it locked in his skull. And yet...

Joel had battered Hannah so badly that he would have killed her, if she hadn't been taken to a modern hospital. And Konrad - and Hannah's mother - had let him do it. Joel had nearly killed his stepsister, his betrothed. What loyalty did John owe him? What loyalty did he owe the commune?

No one cared, John realised.

It was a chilling thought. Hannah *had* to have screamed. She couldn't have kept her mouth shut, not during such a savage beating. But no one had come to save her. Guilt stabbed through him, tearing at his heart. He was her brother, her ordained protector. What had *he* done to save her?

Nothing, he thought, dully. *I did nothing.*

"They were telling her that she would be married soon," he said, finally. He owed Joel and Konrad *nothing*. Let them burn. "She didn't want to marry him. I guess Joel didn't take that too kindly."

Of course, his thoughts mocked. *And what will he do when he finds out she's escaped?*

CHAPTER THIRTY-FIVE

Unsurprisingly, the steady withdrawal of the Empire's forces prior to the Fall of Earth unleashed a nightmare. Terrorists, insurgents and various militia forces came out of hiding and struck at their enemies. There was no desire for a peaceful end to any of the conflicts, merely a desire to bring them to their end.
- Professor Leo Caesius. *Ethnic Streaming and the End of Empire.*

Constable Alastair Gaffney gritted his teeth as the shouting, from both sides of the street, grew louder. Two groups of protesters, both probably armed to the teeth…which idiot had thought allowing them to protest together was a good idea? The council should never have given them a protest permit…although, with so many people angry as hell, they would not have waited for the permit before they began.

He rubbed his forehead, feeling trapped. The police were caught in the middle, watching the protesters warily. They were under strict orders to intervene if the two groups started fighting, but Alastair was honestly wondering if it would be better just to let them scrap it out and get the aggression out of their system. He'd been a policeman for ten years, ever since he'd graduated, and he'd never seen so much rage on the streets. The whole situation had just spiralled out of control.

Should just arrest both groups, he thought, sourly. The right to peaceful protest was enshrined in the constitution, but this wasn't *peaceful. Let them spend their energy in the work gangs instead.*

He paced up and down, his eyes passing over the protesters and the wire separating them from the estate. Some of the more violent protesters had talked about breaking down the wire and lynching the refugees personally, even though there was no way *anyone* could turn a blind eye to that. Others had talked about taking refugees into their homes, even billeting them on nearby residents. Alastair had no doubt that even *trying* to billet refugees on unwilling citizens would spark off a major upheaval. The vast majority of people in nearby apartments were locking their doors, stocking up on weapons and readying themselves for a fight. They no longer trusted the government or the police to handle the situation.

God help us if more refugees arrive, Alastair told himself. *We'll be overwhelmed within weeks.*

He glanced up, sharply, as he saw a gang of refugee men at the gatehouse. It was hard to keep his distaste off his face. The refugee males all seemed to delight in challenging the police, as if they saw the police as the natural enemy. They had no respect for the uniform, apparently. Alastair had been told that the refugees had been tormented by the police on Tarsus, but he didn't see it as an excuse. The police on Arthur's Seat were very different…

"Get down," someone shouted.

Alastair threw himself down automatically, one hand scrabbling for his truncheon as he rolled over and over. The refugees were carrying weapons…military weapons? He hadn't seen anything like them outside bad entertainment flicks. How the hell had they got them? And then the refugees opened fire…bullets ripped through the air, slamming into the anti-refugee protesters. Alastair crawled forward, watching in horror as bodies fell like ninepins. The refugees were firing on the protesters…

He hit the panic button, cursing the government under his breath. Someone had failed, he thought, as he crawled backwards. Someone had allowed the refugees to bring in weapons…there was no other way they could have obtained the weapons. Even if they'd looted a gunshop, which was unlikely, they wouldn't have found anything nastier than hunting rifles or sporting pistols. He gripped his truncheon tighter as he kept moving, wishing he had a rifle or pistol of his own. There was no way he could fight back with just the glorified club.

The noise - gunshots, screams, shouts - was growing louder, deafening him. It had to be audible all over the city. Gunshots weren't exactly uncommon, but military assault rifles...everyone would hear the racket. And then...and then what? There was a firearms team on duty in the capital, he thought, but they'd probably be outmatched. They'd certainly be outgunned. The Orbital Guard wasn't trained or equipped to fight an insurgency...

They're mad, he thought, numbly. He crawled around a couple of bodies, two young women wearing long dresses. Forsakers? Or protesters mocking the Forsakers? It was clear, from the bullet wounds, that there was no point in trying to help them. They were already beyond help. *How many people have they killed?*

He reached a patrol car and took cover. It wasn't a tank - he would have preferred an armoured car - yet it would give him *some* protection. He grabbed for his radio, intending to call for help, but the frequencies were jammed. The system was overloaded...it was impossible. Nothing like it had ever happened before. But then, the system wasn't designed to receive and prioritise thousands of calls at the same time. Half the city was probably trying to call the nearest police station, reporting gunshots and wounded. The thought almost made him smile, despite the situation. He had no doubt that his superiors already knew that all hell had broken loose.

The gunshots were trailing away now, only a handful of scattered shots ringing out as the attackers found more targets. Alastair braced himself, then peered around the car, ready to yank his head back at the slightest *hint* of trouble. The scene before him looked like a scene from hell. Bodies lay everywhere, the two protest groups slaughtered without mercy. The Forsakers had fired on *both* groups...he felt numb, even as he struggled to comprehend what he was seeing. Cars were burning brightly, the flames casting wavering shadows through the air...a handful of wounded were screaming, wordlessly begging for help Alastair knew would never arrive. The hospitals wouldn't send ambulances into a war zone...

And it is a war zone, he thought. He'd heard stories about terrorist attacks, but there had never been any terrorists on Arthur's Seat. There had been nothing to fight over. Hell, the government had happily purchased starship tickets for anyone who wanted to leave the planet, if they wanted to live somewhere else. *We are at war...*

He heard a sound behind him and turned. A young man was standing there, pointing a gun at him. He wore a mask covering the lower half of his face, his eyes flickering with hatred as he squeezed the trigger. Alastair reached for his truncheon, trying to bring it up desperately, but it was already too late...

Gayle Gambeson fought her way back to awareness, honestly unsure if *something* had happened or if she'd just had a very unpleasant nightmare. God knew there had been times, particularly after eating too much cheese for supper, when her dreams had been utterly horrific. But none of those dreams had ended with her waking up surrounded by bodies, all bleeding to death...

She took a breath, then almost choked. The stench of death was all around her. She shuddered, pushing at bodies that had suddenly become too heavy to move. Her awareness spun as she fought her way clear, her aches and pains suggesting that she was battered and bruised. And her memory seemed confused, almost damaged. She'd been in a protest group, hadn't she...

The memories surfaced, one by one. She'd worked with the refugees, bringing them clothes and food; she'd joined her fellow descendants, protesting the cramped and unpleasant conditions in the estate. She'd helped collect names for a petition, names of people who might provide temporary housing for refugees...she'd even started to talk people into donating money to the refugees. Surely, once the refugees had money, they could rent homes of their own. Gayle could even buy out Judith's share of the lease, then take a handful of refugees into her apartment. It wouldn't be hard. Judith - she felt a pang of bitter grief at the thought - couldn't rent the apartment herself. Neither of them could...

And if we can't stand each other any longer, she thought, *it might be for the best.*

Awareness crashed down on her as she finished pulling herself free and sat upright. Bodies lay everywhere, bleeding to death. She felt her gorge rise as she saw a headless corpse lying on the ground, her entire body shuddering as she saw mutilated bodies…all blurring together into a horrific mass. Hundreds of people, perhaps thousands, were dead…cars were burning, windows were smashed, buildings were pocked and charred…what the hell had happened?

She turned as she saw movement. A number of young men were advancing out of the estate, carrying guns. *Intimidating* guns. Gayle had never seen anything like them, let alone handled them. Hell, her parents had even refused to sign permission slips for firearms safety training in school. And the men were coming towards her…what had they done? Who were they? Their clothes marked them out as Forsakers…

Gayle couldn't move, her head spinning. It was hard, so hard, to think clearly. She wanted to believe that the anti-refugee protesters were responsible for the disaster, but why would they wear Forsaker clothes? The refugees…could the refugees have fired on the police and protesters? It was unthinkable. They'd gunned down people who were on their side! And yet, she couldn't avoid the truth…

A strong arm grabbed her, yanking her upright. Gayle's legs buckled and she staggered, almost falling against her captor. Merciless eyes stared down at her, running over her body in a manner that chilled her to the bone. Her blouse was soaked with blood, clinging to her skin…she tried to pull away, only to be slapped across the face. She would have fallen if she hadn't been held firmly upright.

"March," her captor growled.

The pain helped her to focus as she stumbled towards the gatehouse. Armed men were everywhere, watching her carefully. She hadn't felt so exposed since the day she'd realised she was more interested in girls than boys. The changing room had been an utter nightmare…she pushed the thought aside, desperately, as she saw other prisoners being herded forward, into the nightmare. Their faces were slack with horror. Nothing like it, absolutely nothing, had ever happened on Arthur's Seat, not until now.

Gayle gritted her teeth as she was shoved into a small building. God alone knew what it had been intended for, once upon a time, but now it seemed to be a prison. She flinched as her captor patted her bottom as he let her go, his touch sending unwelcome shivers down her spine. A dozen other women were pushed in behind her, looking as shocked and helpless as Gayle felt. It was hard, so hard, to wrap her head around what was happening. They had been taken prisoner…and then, what? Hostages? Or were they going to be married to the highest bidder? All of a sudden, the horror stories she'd spent so long debunking on the datanet seemed terrifyingly plausible. Judith had been right…

She sank down, sitting against the concrete wall. Judith had been right. Nothing Gayle had ever experienced - from her parents, from her grandparents, even from her weird uncle who refused to touch anything remotely unnatural - came close. The refugees had killed hundreds of people, perhaps thousands…there had been so much blood on the ground that she couldn't avoid wondering if millions of people had been killed. Perhaps the entire *city* was dead. It didn't seem likely, but nothing seemed likely any longer.

Judith was right, she thought. *I was a fool.*

One of the women was battering on the door, demanding to be released. Gayle ignored her as best as she could, trying to look around to find a way out. But the walls were concrete, the windows were too high and too small for a baby to crawl through and the door itself was solid metal. Escape was impossible. All they could do was wait and pray they were rescued before it was too late. But perhaps there would be no rescue…

She rested her head in her hands as she struggled not to cry. She'd been an utter fool. The refugees had *nothing* in common with her. And yet, she'd allowed herself to drive her girlfriend away because she'd thought more about the ideal than the reality. And now she was a prisoner, a hostage… they could do anything to her, anything at all, and there was nothing she could do to stop them. If some of the horror stories were actually true…

I'm sorry, she thought, although she wasn't sure who she was apologising too. Judith…or herself. *I'm truly sorry.*

But she knew, deep inside, that it no longer mattered. She'd lost control of her own destiny, the moment she'd been taken prisoner. And now her fate rested in someone else's hands.

"The Elders are locked up," Steward Yale reported. "They made a bit of a fuss."

"As long as they can't talk to anyone, they should be fine," Joel said. Everything had gone as planned, thankfully. His people were now in control of the estate, holding the entire complex under firm control. All the time he'd spent picking out the ones most likely to follow him and grooming them had not been wasted. "How's the ammunition?"

"We fired off a fourth of our entire supply," Yale told him. "And there's no hope of getting more."

Joel nodded. Arthur's Seat didn't seem to produce military-grade ammunition. The manuals insisted that civilian ammunition could be configured for military weapons, but they didn't actually go into details. Joel rather doubted any of his people could do the work, even if they somehow got their hands on the factories. They were located quite some distance from Lothian, after all.

We'll just have to hold position, he thought. The local government was weak. It wouldn't attempt to challenge them, now they'd staked out their territory. *They'll give us what we want rather than put up a fight.*

"Make sure you put the teams on the outskirts," he said. There was no way they could take and hold the entire city, but he didn't want to remain penned up in the estate either. "I want any policemen killed or driven out, along with any civilians who are unwilling to join us."

"Yes," Yale said. "The civilians are already fleeing."

Joel nodded. All had happened as he'd foreseen. The locals had crumbled, the moment he'd shown his might. And the Elders, the cowardly old men…by the time they were released, they'd see that there was no point in opposing him. The doddering old fools would bend the knee to youth and determination. They would serve him or else.

He allowed his smile to grow wider as Yale turned and hurried away. There was no point in delaying matters, not now. The unmarried girls would be matched up with his strongest supporters, no matter what their parents said. Given time, the female hostages would eventually be turned into brides too. His men would be *very* loyal once they realised what he'd done for them. There would be no more nonsense about settling in, about finding a farm, about satisfying the girl's parents...

They'll marry because I arranged their marriages, he thought. *And I will reclaim Hannah too.*

He clenched his fists at the thought. There were plenty of unmarried girls who would be honoured to marry him - and their parents would not object, not now that Joel was the uncontested leader of the commune. But he wanted Hannah. He was damned if he was allowing her to beat him. Making the local government return her would set the final seal on their craven surrender.

And if they don't return her, he promised himself silently, *I'll take her myself.*

He turned as Steward Gary walked up to him. "Nine men are dead," he said. "Five more are wounded."

Joel frowned. "How did they die?"

"Two were shot by armed protesters - or perhaps the police," Gary told him. "Another was killed when his Molotov Cocktail exploded. The remainder were killed by their own weapons. They didn't know what they were doing."

Joel shrugged. There hadn't been any time to practice - and even if they could, it would have been far too revealing. Nine dead...it wasn't bad, not really. He suspected that far more than nine policemen were dead. And while the planet's population had them badly outnumbered, they weren't concentrated in one place. Nine dead...they'd be hailed as heroes.

"Make sure the wounded get good treatment," he ordered. "Will they recover?"

"They may need modern treatment," Gary said. "The Elders..."

"The Elders have no say in the matter," Joel snapped.

He considered it. Allowing the use of modern technology would set an uncomfortable precedent. The Elders rarely allowed it unless there was no other choice. If people were shown proof that technology could make their lives better, they might not look past the benefits to see the downsides…

"Do what you can for them," he said, finally. "We don't have access to a modern hospital."

Gary nodded, then walked away.

Joel smiled to himself as he turned to peer out over the city. He'd won. He controlled the estate, he controlled the guns…he controlled everything he needed to make the local government bow the knee to him. And then…

His smile grew wider. The future looked bright and full of promise.

CHAPTER THIRTY-SIX

And why not? The Empire had destroyed any hope of a moderate solution. The old settlers had been forced to take the newcomers; the newcomers had been forced to move from their homes and land on new and unwelcoming worlds. (And, by this time, there were generations who were native-born.) Both sides saw themselves as fighting for the right.
 - Professor Leo Caesius. *Ethnic Streaming and the End of Empire.*

William gritted his teeth as he strode into the Parliament chamber, Sondra following at his heels like a kicked puppy. Troutman had moved with terrifying speed, as soon as the first verified reports had hit the datanet. He'd contacted the Speaker and demanded an immediate vote of no-confidence. William had barely had time to get an updated report from the Chief Constable before the summons arrived, ordering him to present himself before the Members of Parliament. In hindsight, it really shouldn't have been a surprise.

The anger in the chamber was terrifying. William had hoped, desperately, that the first reports would prove to be exaggerated, but - if anything - they were understated. Boos and hisses followed him - and Sondra - as they made their way to the front benches and sat down, the catcalls coming from all sides of the chamber. *Nothing* could make it clearer, now, that he'd lost the confidence of his backbenchers. The MPs were struggling to distance themselves from him before it was too late.

He caught sight of Troutman, sitting on the other side of the chamber and gritted his teeth in anger. Troutman had timed his move perfectly, capitalising on a disaster that would make it impossible for most of William's MPs to support him. Their positions were at stake. The datanet was already overflowing with rumours about recall elections, about MPs who wouldn't be backed by their local parties unless they turned on their leader. Hell, the entire *party* was at risk. It was quite possible that vast swathes of voters would simply change sides.

"Order, order," the Speaker shouted. Silence fell over the chamber. "The Leader of the Opposition has the floor."

"Honourable members," Troutman said. His voice was under tight control, but William could hear hints of anger in his tone. "Mr. Speaker. I come before you to demand a vote of no-confidence in the current government."

There was a long chilling pause. "My honourable friend" - he nodded towards William - "has repeatedly failed to come to grips with the challenge posed by fifty thousand unwanted immigrants. He has allowed them to flout our laws, he has allowed them to drain our resources, he has failed to bring them to heel. And what do we have now? Violence on the streets and hundreds dead, including fifteen policemen and a government official! This is a disaster!"

William kept his face expressionless with an effort. Valetta Melbourne was dead. He'd never liked the woman - he knew she had always been Sondra's puppet - but her death was a nasty blow. What good was the government if it couldn't even protect its own people? And, from a cold-blooded point of view, her death meant she couldn't be blamed for the disaster, even though she'd played a role in starting it. What had she said to the Forsakers anyway?

"The situation is out of control," Troutman snapped. "You have all seen, have you not, the list of demands? For a state of their own, for a constant supply of food, drink and power, for the eventual transfer of farmland and farming equipment…they have gone mad! We cannot allow ourselves to be dictated to by…by ungrateful bastards!"

No one challenged his words. That, for William, was clear proof that it was over.

"This situation is beyond partisan politics," Troutman said. "We must put the good of our own people first. The current government has not only lost its grip on the situation, it has lost the confidence of the *people*! I think I speak for the entire population of our homeworld when I say the current government must go."

He paused, dramatically. "Warnings were issued. They were not heeded. Signs of impending trouble were clearly visible. They were not heeded. One mistake might be forgivable, but our current government has shown a willingness to ignore trouble, to suppress bad news, to do everything in its power to hide its incompetence. It cannot be tolerated. I call for an immediate vote of no confidence and the formation of a government of planetary unity."

William forced himself to think as Troutman sat down. Troutman would become the new Premier, assuming he won the vote of no confidence. He'd have to assemble a new cabinet quickly - William rather suspected he already had a list of potential candidates. His shadow cabinet would make up the majority, but he'd need to invite representatives from the other three political parties too…

The Speaker cleared his throat. "I call upon the Premier to respond."

William rose, hastily considering his options. There hadn't been time to sit down with anyone, even Sondra, and plan a response. But then, he rather suspected the game was definitely up. He'd acted, as he saw it, in the best interests of his homeworld, but hardly anyone would agree with him. The remainder of the cabinet ministers were already considering their options, hoping to position themselves for a leadership bid. William's fall - and Sondra's - would open up plenty of opportunities for ambitious men. And yet, something in him refused to simply give up.

"There is no point in trying to disguise the scale of the crisis," he said, flatly. "My honourable friend is quite right to call this a disaster. There is nothing like it in our entire history. It is shocking and horrific and utterly unacceptable. We certainly cannot allow this crime to go unpunished.

"But we must also look to the future, beyond the immediate problems…"

He broke off as loud boos echoed through the chamber. William cursed under his breath as the Speaker gavelled for silence, knowing that at least half the boos came from his own side of the chamber. He'd lost them. They'd heard too many promises about the future to put much faith in them, not now there was blood on the streets. There was no way he could shove Sondra under the bus, either. The whole failure rested on his shoulders.

"The crisis can be handled," he said, finally. "I ask you all - I beg you all - to look beyond rhetoric and consider the future. How hopeless would the challenge of integration have seemed, to our ancestors? And how much did they achieve?"

He sat back, knowing that it would be futile. MP after MP rose to denounce him, hardly any daring to speak in favour. Those who had supported him earlier were now amongst the most vitriolic. They needed to burnish their credentials quickly before their enemies took advantage of the situation to recall them. And hammering a Premier who was on the way out was an easy - and safe - way to do just that. William wouldn't be in any position to take revenge.

I could always write my memoirs, he thought, as the Speaker called for the vote. *I'd have my revenge in print.*

By long tradition, anyone facing a vote of no confidence wasn't allowed to cast a vote in their own defence. William was tempted to defy tradition, but as the MPs filed through the doors it was clear that it would be utterly pointless. Only thirty MPs supported him, seventeen more remaining in the chamber and abstaining. He'd lost. He'd lost so badly he *knew* there was no way he could hope to retain his seat in the next election...

And yet, *technically*, he still had a seat on the cabinet. He *was* the Leader of the Opposition now.

He stumbled through a concession speech, torn between anger and an insane urge to giggle at the situation. The Empire Loyalists would need to choose a new leader - and that would take time, time they didn't have. *William* would still be their nominal leader until someone was voted into his place, which might be a poisoned chalice with the election on its way. *He* would still have a seat on the cabinet...

And he can't kick me out, he thought, hysterically. *Any more than I could get rid of him.*

"The situation is fluid," the Chief Constable said. There was something bombastic about his attitude now, something William found depressingly predictable. The Chief Constable needed to prove himself useful - and loyal - before the new government started a long-planned housecleaning. "As you can see, we have established barricades" - he stabbed a finger at the map - "in position to intercept any enemy force leaving the Kinsman Estate."

Enemy force, William thought. *Have we really fallen so far so fast?*

Troutman cleared his throat. "Can the police hold the line?"

"We've moved our armed response teams into position," the Chief Constable said. "I have also taken the liberty of ordering the remainder of the police to be armed. However, very few officers outside the new armed response teams have experience using their weapons on the job. We never planned for large-scale insurrection."

"A terrible oversight," Troutman said, dryly. He shot William an annoyed look. "This crisis was predictable."

William resisted - barely - the temptation to point out that the only people who might have started an insurrection, until recently, were the Freeholders. God knew there had been a lot of angry muttering about the Unionist scheme to rationalise the government. That was probably a dead letter now, along with the Unionists. They were already on the verge of a leadership struggle of their own.

The Chief Constable leaned forward. "Right now, we assume that they can defend the estate against us, at least until they run out of ammunition. We have no idea just how much they have left, but they have no way of getting more. In the long-term, they will begin to starve very quickly. We have already turned off both the water and power; there will be no food deliveries. Again, however, we have no idea how much food and water they have on hand."

William cleared his throat. "And as they start to starve," he said, "they will do something desperate."

"It's very likely," the Chief Constable said.

Troutman smiled, coldly. "The Orbital Guard could solve this problem with a single KEW strike."

Commodore Charles Van Houlton looked back at him, evenly. "Quite apart from the morality of condemning fifty thousand people to death for the crimes of a few, dropping KEWs on the estate will do immense damage to Lothian. Assuming that all the KEWs land in the right place, there will still be a considerable amount of damage. And, naturally, the hostages will be killed too."

William tensed. "Hostages?"

"They claim to have over a hundred hostages," the Chief Constable said. "There's over two thousand people unaccounted for, but we have no way to know if they're hostages, dead, lying low or simply weren't in the area when all hell broke loose."

"They may also have terrorists loose in the rest of the city," Troutman said. "There's already been a shooting incident on Main Street."

He looked at the Chief Constable. "Can your men rescue the hostages?"

"We don't have a dedicated hostage rescue team," the Chief Constable said. "Even if we did, getting the team to the estate would be problematic. My staff have been looking at options, but they've come up with nothing they think has a reasonable chance of success. There is no way to storm the estate without massive casualties on both sides."

William winced. Arthur's Seat had just lost more policemen in a day than it had lost over the last three hundred years put together. Policemen just *didn't* die in the line of duty, not on Arthur's Seat. If they had to storm the estate, hundreds would die…along with thousands of refugees. He hated to think about the interstellar reaction to the chaos. It was possible that no one would care, but it was equally possible that the whole affair had been engineered to provide an excuse for intervention.

But what do we have, he asked himself, *that would be worth the effort?*

"Then we starve them out," Troutman said. "A number of posses are already assembling. I can call them here to reinforce the police and provide security. Once they start to starve, they can surrender or die."

"The posses are not trained to patrol the streets," William pointed out.

"There's no choice," Troutman said. "Training up new policemen is going to take months."

William cursed under his breath. The posses had always been a two-edged sword. They worked to protect their freeholds - and their neighbours - but they weren't trained soldiers, let alone policemen. There was a good chance that they would be outmatched by the refugees, as long as the ammunition held out. And there was *also* a good chance that they would lynch refugees, if - when - they caught them. The posses weren't trained to gather evidence so their captives could be prosecuted, either. They were more concerned with ending the threat by any means necessary.

"They'll come out fighting," he warned. "They'll try to *take* the food they need."

"Then we will meet them in a place where *we* have the advantage," Troutman said. He met William's eyes. "Do you have a better idea?"

William shook his head. Negotiation wasn't a possibility any longer, not after so many people had been killed. The public wasn't in any mood to accept anything, apart from unconditional surrender. William had lost power because he'd failed; Troutman, damn him, wouldn't make the same mistake. He'd grasped power because he'd pledged to deal with the crisis. Now, he had no choice. He *had* to deal with the crisis.

And the quicker the better, William thought. *But how?*

"They'll see reason as they start to starve," Troutman said. He sounded confident. William had to admit he might be right. "They can be marched out of the estate, once they surrender. We'll move them to detention camps until we figure out a more permanent solution…"

"That might be what they want," William said, without thinking.

Troutman blinked. "Explain."

"Shipping the refugees here would have cost a considerable amount of money," William said, slowly. He knew very little about interstellar economics, but the principles had to be largely akin to planetary economics. "Tarsus could have isolated the Forsakers - or simply exterminated them. Their government is certainly unpleasant enough to do just that. Instead, they put them on freighters and sent them here."

"It was the Imperial Navy that brought them here," Troutman said, tartly.

"But Tarsus would have needed to press for it," William said. He'd dismissed the idea. But maybe Troutman would take it seriously. "Maybe the whole idea is to provide an excuse for intervention. For *invasion*."

"Maybe," Troutman said, finally. He sounded as though he was taking William seriously, although it was hard to be sure. "But what alternative do you propose?"

The new Premier waved a hand at the map. "A chunk of our capital city is no longer under our control," he said. "We have them sealed in, but our lines are brittle. They might be able to do a great deal of damage if they smash their way out and start rampaging through the city. It will take days to get the posses here..."

"We have to find a way to deal with the situation," he added. "Or we might as well drop KEWs and spend the next few years cleaning up the mess."

The hell of it, William knew, was that Troutman had a point. Holding the lines might prove futile until the posses arrived - and even then, it would be chancy. God alone knew how much ammunition the refugees had. William had seen estimates ranging from confident claims they were running out of ammunition to hysterical suggestions that the refugees had enough ammunition to take on the entire planet and win. Even the more restrained - but still pessimistic - suggestions were alarming. If half the crates the Imperial Navy had landed were crammed with ammunition, the war could go on for weeks.

We could lose the entire city, he thought. *And then...and then what?*

"My people are considering other options," the Chief Constable said. "Once we have the posses in place, we should be able to hold the line."

"And yet, more people will die," Troutman said. "A battle for Lothian will leave a great many people dead and the city devastated."

"And the economy will go belly-up," Gavin Stuart added. He didn't sound unhappy. Like most Freeholders, he viewed the interstellar-based economy with a sceptical eye. "Hundreds of people will be put out of work."

"Putting yet more strain on our society," Troutman said. He traced out a line on the map, thoughtfully. "We need a silver bullet."

He sighed. "And if we can't find one, we may have to go for the direct solution."

William shuddered. Tens of thousands of people died on Earth every day - or had died, before the entire planet collapsed - but nothing like it had ever been seen on Arthur's Seat. They'd considered themselves immune to the chaos gripping the galaxy, the waves of civil unrest and interstellar conflict as the galactic order fell apart. But now…it was hard, so hard, to speak. It felt like the betrayal of every one of their civilised principles.

He found his voice, somehow. "You'd kill fifty thousand people and… what? Over a hundred hostages?"

"It might come down to them or us," Troutman said. He met William's eyes. "And if it *is* a choice between them and us, I'll vote for us."

CHAPTER THIRTY-SEVEN

Bigger worlds, ones with police and military forces, often rounded up the unwelcome newcomers and deported them, either to unsettled territories or other planets. Ironically, in doing so, they perpetrated the crimes that had been committed against them.
- Professor Leo Caesius. *Ethnic Streaming and the End of Empire.*

"Joel did that for me?"

Judith looked down at Hannah, then back up at the television. The scenes on the display were horrific, snapshots and videos taken by personal coms and uploaded onto the datanet, then stolen by the television studios as reporters and cameramen were chivvied away from the Kinsman Estate. Dead bodies, burning cars…it looked like a nightmare out of a bad flick, not real life. And yet, she could hear gunshots in the distance, echoing over the city.

"I don't know," she said, finally. "Joel was the one who beat you?"

Hannah nodded. "He's always been a little unstable," she said. "Being a Steward just made it easier for him to push people around."

Judith winced. "What's *wrong* with him?"

"He's unstable," Hannah said. She shuddered. "And if he's doing that" - she waved a hand at the screen, which was now showing a pillar of smoke rising over the estate - "he's certainly taken control. The Elders might be dead."

"Why?" Judith asked. "Why does he even want you?"

Hannah laughed, bitterly. "My father died when I was twelve," she said. "I…I earned a reputation for being…for not being pure. People were talking. My stepfather married my mother, on the condition I married his son when I came of age. I *told* you that."

"I remember," Judith said.

"Joel is unstable," Hannah said. "I think…I think he truly believes that I have to marry him - more, that he has to marry me. That it is his *duty* to marry me. Normally…he wouldn't have been given much more of a choice. My stepfather would have told him his choices…he may even have thought that he was sacrificing himself for his father."

Judith snorted. "Sacrificing *himself*?"

"I have a poor reputation," Hannah reminded her. "Joel might be a Steward, with every prospect of becoming an Elder, but people would still talk. Joel would be giving up his chance to find an unquestionable wife…"

She shook her head, slowly. "And he's always been a strict bastard," she added. "He was always ranting and raving about the need to fight back…I think it broke his mind."

"And so he beat you," Judith said. Nothing justified that sort of treatment, nothing at all. "I don't blame you for not wanting to marry him."

"Everyone thought it would be a good match," Hannah said. "Everyone except me. They kept asking when we were going to marry, when we were going to start churning out children…"

She sighed. "But it wasn't possible," she added. "I *couldn't* have married him."

Judith frowned. She wouldn't have wanted to marry anyone, male or female, who exhibited the petulant and violent behaviour Hannah had described. And yet, there was something in Hannah's voice that suggested there was something else at stake.

"Why…?"

Hannah looked down at the bed. "I went to school on Tarsus," she said. "John hated it - so did Joel. I loved it. Being there…it was a chance to be someone else. And there was a boy there, a boy I liked. John never knew, I think. We were kissing and cuddling one day and then it went further."

"You had sex with him," Judith said, flatly.

"Yes," Hannah said. "It wasn't that good. He just…he just went in and out…I didn't feel much of anything. If there hadn't been a little blood afterwards…"

She shook her head. "I let him do it," she added. "But now...I am not a virgin. Joel would have been furious, if he'd discovered that after the wedding."

"What a dickhead," Judith said. She honestly couldn't say that her first time had been any good - young men had absolutely no technique - but it had got better. And while she preferred women, she had to admit there was *something* to passionate sex with a man who knew what he was doing. "Why didn't you tell your mother...?"

Hannah gave her a look that suggested, very clearly, that Judith had said something utterly stupid. "My mother would have killed me," she said. "And my stepfather...he would have been furious. He would have kicked us all out of the commune."

"That doesn't sound so bad," Judith said.

"My mother wouldn't have been able to live outside," Hannah said. "And now..."

She nodded towards the television. "I don't know what's happening to her," she added. "Or anyone."

Judith looked up as the door opened. A grim-faced man wearing a police uniform peered into the room. Hannah flinched, then relaxed - slightly. The police had talked to her before, when she'd been admitted, but Judith suspected she hadn't found it a very pleasant experience. She'd betrayed her commune, after all.

"Miss Hannah," the policeman said. "We need to talk to you."

Hannah nodded. "Can Judith stay here?"

The policeman looked at Judith for a moment, then nodded. "I need to ask you about the commune," he said. "And I need complete answers."

Hannah sighed. "I'll do my best," she promised.

"Joel was plotting trouble, right from the start," John said. The two policemen were taking careful notes. "He purchased weapons from a crewman on the ship and taught us how to use them."

Captain Sidney looked thoughtful. "Who taught *him* how to use them?"

"The crewman, I assume," John said. "None of us had any experience with weapons on Tarsus."

"But Joel might have obtained training from someone else," Sidney said. "Is that possible?"

John shrugged. "I don't think anyone had any firearms on Tarsus," he said. "Joel *might* have obtained a few from somewhere, but I don't think his father would have let him. None of the Elders were interested in resistance."

Sidney nodded. "And now?"

"I think Joel is in control," John said. "He had several dozen men under his direct control, sir, and dozens more who could be relied upon. I don't think the Elders ever knew about it."

"I see," Sidney said. "How is that possible?"

Joel struggled to explain. "The Elders are the ones who issue orders, after careful contemplation," he said. "The Stewards are the ones who actually carry out those orders, sir; there's a working assumption that a Steward will become an Elder when a serving Elder dies in office. Joel was in a very good position to issue orders, orders he could claim came from the Elders, without being questioned. Very few people would refuse."

"So the Elders have effectively been removed from power," Sidney mused. "Joel might have killed them."

"Joel wouldn't kill his father," John said. He disliked - even hated - Joel, but he had to admit that the bastard loved his father. "Killing the Elders…if he did and his followers found out, he would be lynched. We are raised to *listen* to the Elders."

"Joel obviously thinks otherwise," Sidney said.

He cleared his throat. "And the way he treated your sister…"

"Joel had never had an easy life," John admitted. "He was penned up with the rest of us, forced to endure public schools…he knew it was his destiny to marry Hannah…"

Sidney tapped the table. "Why are you making excuses for him?"

John shook his head, slowly. Sidney was right. There were any number of excuses for Joel's behaviour, but none of them justified what he'd done. Maybe he'd had a point, once upon a time; maybe he'd been right to insist that the Forsakers should stand up for themselves. But now the entire commune was on the brink of obliteration. Sidney hadn't pulled any punches when he'd pointed out that the commune was short on ammunition, short on manpower, short on any real understanding of the world around them. Joel could get a lot of people killed, if the fighting went on, but it could only have one ending.

He overplayed his hand, he thought.

"He has to be stopped," he said, flatly.

"True," Sidney agreed. "How would *you* stop him?"

John shuddered. He knew he didn't have the nerve to stand up to Joel. Even if he did...Joel would beat hell out of him, then shoot whatever was left for desertion. Or betrayal. Or whatever charges made sense to his addled mind. Releasing the Elders might work, but Joel would have made damn sure they couldn't be rescued. Konrad and his fellows were trapped, somewhere within the giant estate. John didn't even know where to *begin* looking.

"Joel is the problem," he said. Joel hadn't encouraged anyone else to strive for the leadership role, as far as he knew. "If Joel is removed...the others might lose their nerve and release the Elders."

"Smart," Sidney said. His voice was so flat that John suspected he was being sarcastic. "And how do you propose removing him?"

John hesitated. Sidney had already told him that the situation had stalemated, for the moment. The police couldn't storm the estate and Joel's men couldn't come out. But that would change as everyone started to starve. Forsakers were used to going without food - Tarsus had sometimes cut off food deliveries, just to remind everyone who was boss - but water shortages would start to bite very quickly. And once women and children started to suffer...

Joel would try to keep them going, he thought. *No one else would try.*

"You have to kill him," he said.

"Yes," Sidney said. "How?"

John considered a number of possible options. He could borrow a gun, walk back into the commune and shoot Joel in the head. But Joel would have him searched before facing him, surely. Or he could try to kill Joel with a knife.... no, that wouldn't work. Joel was stronger and nastier than him. He'd been quite happy to push John around when he'd had something Joel wanted.

He wants Hannah, John thought. Joel would *need* Hannah. He'd demanded her return as part of his list of impossible demands. Her return would prove he was in control of the situation. *And if she is used as bait.*

He swallowed, hard. The idea might just work...

...But if it failed, he was dead.

And the entire commune dies too, he thought. There was no way to avoid it. Joel was leading them to destruction. *My life...or thousands of lives.*

He took a breath. "I've had an idea..."

"Shit," Constable Smith muttered.

Mike nodded in agreement as he parked the patrol car, then swung out of it, weapon at the ready. The emergency call hadn't lied. A body was lying on the ground, a pistol lying next to the dead man's hand. Mike inched forward, wishing they'd had more time to practice combat tactics before the balloon had gone up, but no other threat materialised. The killers had been and gone a long time ago.

He keyed his radio. "I confirm a single dead man," he said. He looked up and down the body, searching for clues. "Cause of death appears to be a blow to the back of the head, inflicting major trauma on the skull. Clothing marks the man out as a Forsaker, probably a native rather than a refugee..."

The radio buzzed. "Are you sure?"

Mike scowled. Night was falling and it was getting hard to see, but he still had no trouble in making out the fine clothes. It wasn't a real Forsaker outfit, not something that would be worn day in and day out. There was certainly no wear and tear. They looked more like traditional clothes that would normally be worn two or three days a year, then put back in the closet. And the wearer...

"I'm fairly sure," he said, studying the pistol. Murders were rare in Lothian. Normally, a forensic team would be dispatched at once to sweep the area for clues. But now, the city was on edge. Half the population was either preparing for a fight or trying to get the hell out before it was too late. "He had a weapon" - he slipped his gloves on and picked it up, looking for the serial number - "number #4377SIW."

"It's not listed in the database," the dispatcher said. "Can you ID the victim?"

Mike scowled, then hunted for the deceased's wallet. "Adam Alanson," he said, after a moment. "He apparently worked at the local bank."

"I'll put a call out to them," the dispatcher said. There was a pause. "Stay with the body until help arrives."

"Understood," Mike said.

He shook his head. Normally, a murder would be terribly exciting. Half the city's police force would descend on the scene, hundreds of reporters on their heels. It would be the talk of the town. Now, with dozens of police and civilians dead, it was almost unremarkable. He wondered, absently, who had killed Adam Alanson and why.

A banker, he thought. Bankers weren't very popular, but most people considered them a necessary evil. *A banker with a handgun.*

He puzzled it over as another patrol car appeared. Adam Alanson was dressed in traditional clothes…maybe someone had seen him as a refugee and attacked him. But why had he been carrying the firearm? If it was on the ground, had he been holding it when he'd been attacked? It wasn't as if he was in a legitimate businessmen's social club or somewhere he might have reason to fear attack. Maybe he'd gone to meet a prostitute and everything had gone horribly wrong.

"We have orders to take the body to hospital," Constable Mathews said. Mike remembered he'd retired, two years after Mike had graduated from Lestrade. The government had called up retired policeman to help cope with the crisis, along with anyone with any form of military experience. "His killers may never be found."

Mike gritted his teeth. Murder was rare on Arthur's Seat…had *been* rare on Arthur's Seat, before the refugees had arrived. Now…he shuddered, feeling the firearm on his belt. They had definitely lost some of their innocence, whatever the outcome of the insurrection. Their homeworld would never be the same.

"Good," he grunted.

He took one last look at the body, feeling almost as if he'd failed, then turned and strode back to the car. Adam Alanson...his wife, if he had a wife, would mourn him, but she'd never have the satisfaction of watching his killer be sentenced to a lifetime of servitude. The mystery might never be solved. He opened the door and clambered in, shutting the door as Smith started the engine. Thankfully, the roads were clear as the patrol car headed down the streets.

"Got a phone call from my brother," Smith said. "His husband - one of his husbands - was at the protest. He didn't come home."

Mike winced. "Dead, perhaps," he said. He'd never seen the value of a group marriage, but he knew some people liked them. "Or one of the hostages. They haven't released a list, have they?"

"No," Smith said. "Stan was hoping I knew."

"Poor bastard," Mike said.

The car moved down the road, the radio crackling with brief updates. Lothian seemed quiet, but Mike spotted a handful of people staring out windows, watching the police car as if they feared it was a Trojan Horse. Perhaps they thought it was. There *had* been some police cars near the protest, hadn't there? Mike had no idea what had happened to any of them.

His portable com bleeped. Technically, it was against regulations to answer when he was on duty - even when it was his wife - but Smith wouldn't say a word. "Jane?"

"Mike," Jane said. She sounded relieved. "Are you all right?"

"Yeah," Mike said. He hadn't told her about the firearms training. She wouldn't have been very pleased to hear that he might be putting himself in - more - danger. "How about you?"

"Nervous," Jane said. "Should I be heading out to Uncle Joe's?"

"There's a curfew," Mike said, although he knew the police force was in no state to actually *enforce* it. "You shouldn't go out of the house unless it's urgent."

"But it is urgent," Jane said. He could just imagine her face. "What happens if the rioting comes my way?"

"Then get out when it does," Mike said. "Jane..."

His radio bleeped. "Hang on," he said. "I need to dash."

Smith shot him a droll look as he tapped the radio. "Car Seven, sir. Over."

"This is dispatch," a new voice said. Mike and Smith exchanged glances. The voice was utterly unfamiliar. "This is a priority call, code Sierra-Hotel-India-Tango. Report to 45 Longstreet. I say again, report to 45 Longstreet. Do *not* use lights and sirens. Report ETA once *en route*. Over."

"Shit," Smith muttered. He swung the car around, then barrelled down the road. "We should be there in fifteen."

Mike keyed the radio. "Dispatch, this is Car Seven," he said. He was no stranger to dangerous driving, but normally they had flashing lights and sirens to warn the civilians they were coming. If the streets hadn't been clear, he would have been worried. "We should be there in fifteen minutes. What's this about, over?"

"Report to the Incident Coordinator," the dispatcher said. "Over and out."

"That's us told," Smith said. He frowned as he yanked them around a tight corner. "You think this is a trap?"

"That was a valid emergency code," Mike said. If there was an Incident Coordinator already on the scene…something had happened, definitely. But what? "Let's go find out."

CHAPTER THIRTY-EIGHT

> Less savoury regimes reached for other solutions. Unable or unwilling to find a peaceful solution - or even deport the unwanted - they killed them. And there was no longer anyone left who could stop them.
> - Professor Leo Caesius. *Ethnic Streaming and the End of Empire.*

"Sunrise," Steward Yale said. "There's no movement out there."

Joel nodded. The surrounding blocks had been cleared, their occupants had either fled or surrendered. They'd be taught the proper way to live soon enough. The police were out there too, but he didn't know where. They certainly hadn't attempted to mount a counterattack during the night.

Weak, he thought. The police were practically unarmed. They were probably fleeing for their lives. *And we can take the entire city if we want it.*

"Good," he said. "I think…"

"The Elders need to prepare the bodies for burial," Steward Yale said. "I…"

"The Elders are currently preparing our diplomatic note," Joel lied, feeling a flicker of pure frustration. Why couldn't people just accept that he was in charge? He didn't have enough loyalists - yet - to risk letting the Elders out of confinement. "They cannot be disturbed."

"But the bodies have to be buried," Yale protested. "Joel…"

"The Stewards can prepare them for burial," Joel said, crossly. Maybe he'd expanded too far, too fast to ensure his people were loyal. But he'd had no choice. The Elders would have betrayed him - and the entire community - if they'd been given a chance. "Until then, place the bodies in storage."

Yale frowned. "*What* storage? There's no power…"

"Wrap the bodies up, then put them somewhere cold," Joel snapped. Honestly! Couldn't anyone think for themselves? The government had cut off the power, along with the water and food. Thankfully, he'd stockpiled enough ration bars over the last few weeks to keep the commune going for some time. "And dig a grave at the rear of the estate."

He gritted his teeth in annoyance as Yale turned and hurried away. His head was starting to pound, reminding him that he hadn't slept for nearly two days. He needed rest, but he didn't dare leave the estate without supervision. No one could be trusted completely, not even his loyalists. Betrayers were everywhere. And did *everyone* have to come to him with their pettifogging complaints?

You wanted to be in charge, his own thoughts mocked him. *And now you are.*

He strode along the edge of the fence, watching as hundreds of young men set up barricades and dug trenches. Most of them seemed to be working with a will, but he could see several of them casting dark glances at Joel's armed men. They doubted the wisdom of arming themselves, Joel knew. They feared the consequences of all-out war. And yet, the only way they would get any autonomy was by standing up for themselves. They had to make it clear, to all the bullies out there, that anyone who tried to pick on the Forsakers would get a bloody nose.

A dozen other men were picking up the bodies from outside the fence and carting them away from the estate. They might not be Forsakers, Joel knew, but *something* would have to be done about them soon. The weather was getting colder, unfortunately, yet it wasn't cold enough to keep the bodies from decaying. And he had no idea when they could be returned to the local government…

He shivered, fighting down the urge to yawn. His body was reminding him, once again, that he hadn't slept a wink. Gritting his teeth, he reached into his pocket and removed the injector tab, pressing it against his upper arm. Stimulant drugs were technically forbidden, he reminded himself as a rush of energy shot through his veins, but *he* was in charge now. *He could make the rules.*

There's nothing wrong with embracing modern technology, he told himself, *as long as it is done in a goodly manner, for the good of the community.*

"Joel," a voice called. He turned to see Olaf, heading towards him. "The fire teams are in position."

"Very good," Joel said. Olaf was loyal, if only because he was too stupid to be disloyal. "Do they have their orders?"

"They are to fire warning shots if anyone enters our territory," Olaf said. "And if the invaders refuse to turn back, they are to kill them."

"Very good," Joel said. He found himself grinning, widely, as another surge of energy ran through him. He'd taken too many stimulants, without having eaten anything like enough to support them. He felt as though he was on the verge of jumping out of his own skin. "Make sure they know who to obey."

Olaf nodded. "What about the girls?"

Joel blinked. "What *about* the girls?"

"We captured seventeen unmarried girls," Olaf said. "When are we going to marry them?"

Joel stared at him, his thoughts confused. Who had put *that* idea into Olaf's head? He had the awful feeling it might have been him, once upon a time. God knew he *had* promised to arrange wives for his supporters, the young men with no prospects, with no hope of finding a wife and raising a family. Olaf and the others like him had leapt at the chance. And now...

"They have to be taught their place first," he said, finally. It had been rare, over the last two decades, for newcomers to enter the commune. Very few remained long enough to marry and have children. "It isn't going to be easy."

Olaf giggled. "They can just lie back and open their legs," he said. He reached out and clapped Joel on the shoulder. "We're in charge now, aren't we?"

I'm in charge, Joel thought.

He found it hard to think straight. Olaf...Olaf was acting in a manner Joel would have considered impossible, only a few days ago. But now, all the old certainties were gone. The Elders were locked up and they were at war. Why bother with courtship, with appealing to the girl's patriarch, if *he* was the supreme leader? *He* could order the girls to marry his men, if he wished. And Olaf - and the others like him - certainly expected that he would do just that.

And the only reason they follow me, he told himself, *is because they think I can give them what they want.*

"You can marry them tonight," he said, finally. It wasn't as if the hostages were *true* Forsakers, even the ones *descended* from Forsakers. No one would *really* care what happened to them, would they? It wasn't as if he was ordering young girls from the commune to marry his men. "But we have to…"

"Joel," Yale called. He was running forward, waving his gun in the air. "We have a prisoner!"

Joel blinked, oddly relieved to see him. "A prisoner?"

Yale smirked. "Guess who?"

John knew, all too well, that he wasn't particularly brave. A brave man would have claimed the patriarchy for himself, a brave man would have stood up to Joel well before the commune had been dumped on Arthur's Seat. His legs felt shaky as he strode down the street, feeling utterly exposed. The buildings surrounding him were supposed to be empty, their inhabitants having fled the chaos, but it was quite possible that Joel had started to move his people into them. They'd make good defensive positions for the commune.

A cold wind blew down the street as he kept walking. The surroundings were eerily silent, so quiet he thought he could hear his own heartbeat. There weren't even any birds singing in the cool morning air. He walked past a handful of smashed cars, wincing as he caught sight of a body that had been battered into a shapeless mass. There was no way to tell if it had been male or female, let alone anything else. He muttered a quiet prayer for the dead as he walked onwards, feeling the back of his neck prickling with fear. Someone was watching him…

Joel isn't a real soldier, he told himself. The policemen had asked him if Joel had spent time watching violent movies, but John rather doubted it. It was forbidden to bring entertainment terminals into the commune, let alone use them. The policemen seemed to think that gave Joel an advantage, but John preferred to think otherwise. *He doesn't know what he's doing.*

He shuddered as he spotted a shop, one of the many small greengrocers dotted throughout the city. It had been looted, its shelves stripped bare...he winced, again, as he saw a body lying on the counter, utterly unmoving. A young woman, judging from the long hair...although he'd seen enough long-haired men on Arthur's Seat to know that long hair didn't necessarily prove anything. Someone had carved a sign into her forehead, but he couldn't read it without going closer. He hesitated, then walked up to the broken window and peered inside. The girl's trousers and underclothes had been torn away, revealing bare flesh...John recoiled, fighting down the urge to be sick. It was clear the girl hadn't died kindly.

It is forbidden to touch the dead, he thought, recalling one of the more interesting sermons he'd had to endure, back when the world had made sense. *They are to be buried as soon as possible...*

He flinched as he heard someone moving up ahead, but kept going, careful to keep his hands in front of him. The police had warned him that the Forsakers would be jumpy, ready to fire at once if they thought he was a threat. John half-wished he had a weapon of his own, even though he knew it would be worse than useless. And then he stopped, dead, as a trio of armed men appeared out of the alleyway. Their guns, their hellishly intimidating guns, were pointed at him.

"John," a familiar voice said. John fought - hard - to keep his face impassive. Colin was a worse bully than Joel, a young man who delighted in humiliating others. He would have been kicked out of the commune years ago, if there had been anywhere that would have taken him. "Well. *What* a surprise."

"I have to speak to Joel," John said. It was impossible to keep his voice from shaking, but Colin would probably be pleased. He *enjoyed* making other people fear. "My stepbrother needs to hear what I have to say."

Colin stared at him for a long moment, his piggy eyes twitching as he reasoned it out. John could practically see the thoughts flowing through his ugly head. Joel *was* in charge, wasn't he? And John was Joel's stepbrother...maybe, just maybe, antagonising him would be unwise. John wondered, absently, just what Joel had told his allies about Hannah. He wouldn't want to admit that Hannah had fled him after a beating, would he? He'd be a laughing-stock.

"We will take you to him," Colin grunted. He reached forward and caught John by the shoulder, shoving him down the road. John wanted to resist, but he knew Colin was just itching for a chance to use his fists. "March."

John didn't offer any resistance as Colin half-pushed him onwards. Instead, he looked around, silently assessing the scene before him. Dozens of buildings had been converted into strongpoints, armed men marching up and down as though they ruled the world. The unarmed Forsakers - it didn't *look* as though Joel had enough weapons to arm the entire commune - seemed torn between delight and fear. A number of them glanced nervously at John as he was walked past. None of the Elders were in sight.

Joel will want to keep them locked away, John thought. He couldn't see any women either - but then, Joel would have locked them up too. The women had to be protected - and kept away from their husbands and sons, lest they inspire divided loyalties. *What has he done to mother?*

The thought cost him a pang. He loved his mother, but he understood - now - that his mother had made a whole series of bad choices. She should never have married again, not at such a steep price. And she hadn't even paid the price herself! Hannah had paid - and would spend the rest of her life paying, if Joel dragged her back. John had no illusions about how her married life would go.

And if Joel isn't stopped, John told himself, *the local government might surrender to him.*

Joel was standing by the fence, Olaf and Yale standing next to him. John wasn't surprised to see Olaf - he was one of Joel's loyalists, after all - but Yale was a disappointment. He'd always been a nit-picking humourless nag, yet he'd never been *evil*. But then, times of crisis - he'd been told

- brought out the best and worst in people. God knew the crisis had certainly done that to Joel.

John met his eyes...and froze. Just for a second, he wondered if it actually *was* Joel. The face was identical, but the eyes were too bright and his entire body was twitching, his fingers flexing backwards and forwards. His face looked *off*, somehow; his eyes flickered from side to side, his tongue licking his lips nervously...John would have advised him to get some sleep, if he didn't think it was already too late.

"John," Joel said. He took a step forward. John had to fight the urge to step back. "What a *pleasant* surprise."

He swung his arm. John had no time to dodge before Joel slapped him across the face, sending him staggering backwards. He would have fallen if Colin hadn't been holding on to his arm. A chill ran down his spine as he realised that Joel could do *anything* to him, if Joel wished. There was nothing holding him in check, not any longer. He could kill John if he wanted...

"So tell me," Joel said. Even his voice was different. John couldn't help thinking of the teenagers, back on Tarsus, who had experimented with narcotic drugs. They'd acted all funny too. "Why have you come crawling back?"

"Hannah," John said. It was easy to push bitterness - and fear - into his voice. "She's going to marry a local."

He'd thought long and hard over what to actually *tell* Joel. Hannah was the only bait they had, the only thing that might bring Joel out of the estate, but...but who knew what would actually set him off? Technically, Hannah could leave the commune at any moment...yet Joel would never let her go. The idea of her marrying a local would be utterly maddening.

"I took her to hospital," he admitted. Let Joel think he didn't care about the beating he'd given Hannah, if he wished. Hannah would hardly be the first person to be beaten so badly she'd risked permanent harm. "She met someone there. She's going to marry him."

Joel leaned forward, his voice dangerous. "And you didn't think to stop it?"

"I can't forbid her," John said. "I...she has to be stopped before she leaves hospital..."

"Of course you couldn't stop her," Joel said. He reached out and shoved John in the chest, hard. This time, Colin let him fall to the ground. "You have always been weak. And now you have come crawling back to beg for help."

John flushed. Joel was right. He *had* been weak, very weak. And he'd cost his mother and sister dearly. Joel loomed over him, his face twisted between rage and a certain bitter amusement. If Joel killed him…it would be just, if it saved Hannah from a fate worse than death.

"You will take us to the hospital," Joel said. He bent down, caught hold of John's shirt and yanked him to his feet. "And we will bring her home."

"The police are there," John said, desperately. Joel had bought it! Against all the odds, Joel had bought it. "They'll…"

"Be crushed," Joel hissed. "And when I bring her home, we will finally be married."

John shuddered.

"This is not wise," Yale said. "Joel…"

"Shut up," Joel hissed. "Olaf, assemble a team!"

His temper overflowed. This was the very last straw! Hannah was not going to escape him again, let alone marry a local. She would pay, of course, for her betrayal, but after she'd been punished they would be man and wife. He would love her and care for her and protect her from the outside world. And her milksop brother…Joel glanced at John, then smirked to himself. John would die during the attack on the hospital, his death blamed on the policemen. Konrad's stepson would make an excellent martyr to the cause.

"She's just a girl," Yale said. He didn't understand. Of *course* he didn't understand. "There are countless girls who would be happy to marry you…"

Joel hit him. "I promised my father that I would marry her," he snapped. Why did Yale have to keep questioning his every word? Couldn't he see that Joel was struggling to protect the commune? "And I will not disobey my father."

"Your father is the patriarch," Yale reminded him. He rubbed his cheek, his eyes hard. "I think you should check with him…"

"Shut up," Joel snapped. He turned to see Olaf and a group of his most loyal followers, all carrying weapons and plenty of ammunition. They wouldn't question his orders - and he'd make sure they married the hostages, once the day was over. A mass wedding ceremony would cement the new order for all to see. "Let's go."

He caught John by the arm and pushed him towards the gate. "Take us straight to the hospital," he ordered. "And don't even *think* about taking us anywhere else."

Chapter Thirty-Nine

> But the weaker worlds were torn apart by ethnic conflict. They rarely survived in any recognisable form.
> - Professor Leo Caesius. *Ethnic Streaming and the End of Empire.*

"What we need," Smith muttered, "is one of those drones the marines use."

Mike shrugged as he checked and rechecked his rifle. It would be nice to have a UAV, peering down on the estate from so high that it couldn't be seen with the naked eye; it would also be nice to have stunners, powered combat armour and - while he was wishing for things he couldn't have - a patriotic scriptwriter. He'd certainly watched enough awful flicks where the enemy fired millions of bullets at the heroes, but - somehow - none of the heroes were actually *hit*. Real life was very different.

"There's a spotter team on the rooftop," he reminded Smith. Their firing position wasn't perfect, but it would have to do. "We'll have some advance warning."

Assuming everything goes to plan, he added, silently. The briefing had made it clear that the Forsakers, if they took the bait, would be walking straight down the road towards the hospital. Several barricades had been hastily removed, just to give the bastards a false sense of security. *If it doesn't, we might be in some trouble.*

He rubbed his forehead tiredly, wishing he'd had a chance to call Jane. But the Incident Coordinator had ordered him to get some sleep instead, warning that they'd need to be fresh when the shit hit the fan. Mike couldn't help feeling a strange mixture of frustrated, irritated and scared. He hadn't signed up to be a soldier, or a soldier-wannabe; he'd signed up to be a policeman, to protect and serve the people. And, in all honesty, he wasn't sure he wanted to *stay* a policeman. The job had changed radically in the last two months.

His radio buzzed. "This is Giles," a voice said. "They're on the way. I make fourteen men, thirteen armed."

Mike tensed. The enemy was coming right towards them, as planned. He checked his weapon again, wishing - desperately - that there had been more time to practice. They simply hadn't been able to go through all the reasonable scenarios, let alone come up with new ones that might otherwise have been missed. He had no idea how long it took to train a soldier, but he was fairly sure it was longer than two weeks.

He keyed his radio. "This is Fire Team One," he said. "We're ready."

The streets were as cold and silent as the grave.

John walked in front, Joel holding his arm in a vice-like grip. He wasn't sure *precisely* when they were going to walk into a trap, but he knew it would be somewhere along the way to the hospital. It was all he could do to keep himself from shaking, even though he suspected Joel would have taken a perverse pleasure in watching him cower in fear. Joel certainly didn't see any reason to pretend to like John any longer.

"You say she's in Ward Four," Joel said. "Is she with other men?"

"The doctors are men," John said. He knew it would anger his stepbrother. "And some of the nurses are men too."

Colin snorted, rudely. Nursing was a feminine profession, as far as the Forsakers were concerned, although few men would willingly allow their wives and daughters to serve as nurses. Why…it might bring them into contact with strange men! Even midwives were in short supply in the commune. John had a feeling that Hannah would have won a great many friends and allies if she'd become a midwife, if only because there weren't enough to go around. Even Konrad would have had to bow to pressure if half the commune wanted Hannah to remain unattached.

"The patients are mixed too," he added. "We have to get her out of there!"

Joel's grip tightened. He was angry. John knew that was a good thing, but perhaps not when Joel might turn on him at any moment. And the police were out there somewhere…they turned the corner, heading down a long road lined with trees. Someone had gone out of their way to make the stone buildings attractive, rather than merely functional. He hadn't seen anything like it on Tarsus.

"We will," Joel said. "And then we will be married."

Mike braced himself as the Forsakers came into view. They were striding down the middle of the road as if they didn't have a care in the world, as if they thought their guns make them invincible. He'd seen that sort of mindset before, normally in city-slickers who never handled guns until they visited the countryside. Normally, that sort of attitude was battered out of them before it was too late, but no one seemed to have tried to warn the Forsakers…

"They'll be lucky if they don't blow their own heads off," Smith muttered.

"Yeah," Mike agreed.

He rolled his eyes. There were four rules on firearms safety that had been hammered into his head, years ago. He'd been forced to memorise them before he'd been allowed to touch a firearm. The Forsakers had either never heard of the rules or had chosen to ignore them, even though they were for their own safety. Several of the insurgents were pointing their weapons at their fellows, while at least two had their fingers on the triggers. It was mildly surprising they hadn't had a negligent discharge.

We should be grateful, he thought, as he took aim. The orders were clear. They were to fire the first bursts over their heads, hopefully convincing them to surrender. If the insurgents returned fire, they were to be wiped out. *They don't really know what they're doing.*

"Fire when they are within the kill-zone," the Incident Coordinator ordered.

Mike nodded, silently cursing their sheer lack of experience under his breath. The plan had seemed perfect, on paper. But now, with the enemy walking forward, there was a growing likelihood that they'd spot the ambush and open fire. The entire area had been evacuated, but the last thing anyone wanted was bullets going everywhere. And giving the bastards a chance to surrender…

He sighed. As a policeman, he wanted to capture criminals instead of killing them; as a…whatever he was now, he wanted to kill his targets as quickly as possible.

"Here they come," Smith said. "Ready?"

"Ready," Mike confirmed. The enemy were walking forward, right into the kill-zone. "I am…"

"Fire," the incident coordinator snapped.

Joel had been fuming for the entire walk, silently promising Hannah a lesson she would never forget when he finally dragged her back home. She *had* to learn to comport herself properly, if she was going to be his wife. Going to the hospital was tolerable - marginally - but staying in a ward with male doctors and patients? It was impossible! And the mere thought of her marrying another man, an Outsider…he heard John grunt in pain as he squeezed his arm tighter. The idiot should have asserted his rights over his sister from the start…

…And then a hail of gunshots echoed out, bullets snapping through the air over their heads and pinging off nearby buildings. John threw himself forward, yanking Joel down as the remainder of the Forsakers opened fire, spraying bullets in all directions. Joel hit the ground hard enough to hurt, the pain clearing his mind just long enough to realise that he'd been led right into a trap. He'd wanted Hannah so badly that his mind had been addled.

A boot kicked him in the face. He looked up and saw John, drawing back his leg for another kick. John had betrayed him! He'd betrayed them all! His followers were falling to the ground, their bodies ripped and torn by countless bullets…he'd led them all into a trap! And there was no way he could escape. Growling, he crawled forward, intent on killing John before it was too late. He would have his revenge before they both died.

John was screaming something at him, but it was impossible to make out the words over the gunshots. Joel fixed his eyes on his target, pushing himself forward even as a slash of pain lanced across his back. John glared back at him, then kicked again. This time, Joel caught his foot and yanked it forward. John screamed in pain as Joel twisted his leg, then lunged forward, his hands reaching for John's neck. He'd crush the bastard before he died.

"Die," he said. "You…"

Someone slammed into him. Joel rolled over and over, barely aware of what had happened before *something* crashed into his arm. He felt it break, the pain so great that he couldn't help screaming. A man loomed over him, one fist drawn back…

…And then there was nothing.

John rubbed his ears as the shooting finally came to an end. They hurt, hurt so badly that he honestly wondered if he'd ever hear normally again. Modern medical technology could work miracles, he'd been told, but could it repair his ears? His leg hurt too, making him wonder if Joel had dislocated or broken it before he'd been pushed away. But there were other wounded…

He forced himself to sit up. Most of Joel's supporters were dead, their bodies so badly damaged that they were beyond salvation. Two were alive, but wounded; the policemen were hastily moving them onto stretchers, clearly hoping they'd survive long enough to reach hospital. And Joel… he was lying on the ground, one arm clearly broken. A policeman was standing over him, holding a truncheon against his throat. John honestly couldn't tell if he was alive or dead.

"Stay still," a voice advised. He looked up. A policeman was standing over him, his face grim. "You've been through hell."

John ignored him and stumbled to his feet. His legs felt wobbly, so unstable that he couldn't help wondering if they were made of jelly…

but somehow, he managed to stand upright. Joel was alive, he realised numbly. Twelve of his most loyal followers were dead or wounded, so badly wounded that they might not survive long enough to reach hospital, yet Joel was alive?

"Kill him," he managed.

The policeman shook his head. "We'll put him on trial," he said, grimly. "And then he will be punished…"

"It won't be enough," John said. He tried to stumble towards the body, but his legs betrayed him. The policeman caught him before he hit the ground. "*Kill him.*"

He cursed savagely, using words he'd never dared use in the commune. They'd never be safe as long as Joel was alive. He had his loyalists, he had his friends, he had his admirers…even now, with twelve of his closest allies dead or wounded, he was still dangerous. He would *still* want to get his hands on Hannah, he would *still* want to kill John, he would still want to stamp his will on the entire commune…he had to die. And yet, the policeman wouldn't let John end it…

Really, his thoughts mocked him. They sounded like Joel. *And do you have the nerve to end it?*

"He won't harm anyone, ever again," the policeman said. "I promise."

John snorted. He knew how much that promise was worth.

"Ten dead, two badly wounded, one prisoner," the Chief Constable said. His voice sounded tinny over the radio. "We captured Joel."

"Very good," Troutman said. He sounded pleased. William hoped he had *reason* to be delighted. Joel was the head of the snake, but would capturing him be enough to end the conflict before it got any worse? "Hold him in secure detention, then push the barricades up against the estate. Keep them trapped."

"Yes, Premier," the Chief Constable said. "Over and out."

"Very good indeed," Troutman said. He looked at William. "Do you want to be the one who talks to them?"

William blinked. "Me?"

"They need someone to lay down the law," Troutman said. "Someone who can make it clear that they have a choice between unconditional surrender and complete annihilation. The commune either surrenders or dies. No middle ground."

"I see," William said. "And what do you intend to do with them after they surrender?"

"I'll think of something," Troutman said. "But - right now - they're leaderless, running out of everything from food to ammunition...there won't be a better chance to bring the refugees to heel *without* killing them in vast numbers. Or would you rather I sent someone more likely to take a *very* hard line to handle the negotiations?"

William didn't bother to hide his displeasure. Troutman was making a political point. If William helped him, for whatever reason, William wouldn't have *any* future in politics. But then, that was probably true already. His party's leaders had already announced a conference to choose his replacement. Hell, giving them - yet another - reason to remove him was probably the best thing he could do.

And besides, he thought. *Whoever Troutman sends if I refuse is likely to be a great deal worse,*

"I'll go," he said.

"I never doubted it," Troutman smiled.

Konrad, Son of Elijah, had never doubted his son's loyalty. He'd worried about his temper, he'd worried about his pride, but he'd never worried about his loyalty. And yet, Joel had knocked him out and imprisoned him, along with the rest of the Elders. Worse, he'd beaten Hannah so badly that the photographs he'd seen of the wounds had shocked Konrad to the core. He was no stranger to the need to discipline people, but there were limits...

He looked around the meeting room, feeling utterly out of place. Yale had freed him and the others, but they'd emerged into a very different world. Joel was dead, his people were starving for lack of food...and the police were drawing the noose tight. Tarsus had been bad, but this was worse. The locals had a *very* good reason to hate them now. And the Elders, the wise men, had been thoroughly discredited. The entire commune was on the verge of fragmenting.

"Speaker," the Premier - the *former* Premier - said. William, Konrad recalled. A good name for a good man. "I'm afraid this isn't a negotiation. I have orders, strict orders, to make it clear that this is an ultimatum. You can accept it or you can die. There will be no further discussions."

Konrad swallowed. He'd always feared that Tarsus would find an excuse to exterminate the Forsakers. The only thing *keeping* them from doing just that was their desperate need for scapegoats. But now…Arthur's Seat had an *excellent* reason to commit genocide, to slaughter the entire commune. Joel - whatever he'd been thinking - had started a conflict that could only have one end.

"First, we want your unconditional surrender," William said. "You will hand over all weapons, up to and including combat knives and non-lethal devices. The police will patrol the estate in force - they are not to be molested in any way. Any attempt to interfere with their duties will be met with harsh reprisals.

"Second, the hostages are to be returned at once, unharmed," he added. "Any members of your commune who wish to leave may also do so, if we see fit to accept them. You will not attempt to shun them, exclude them or in any other way punish them for their choice.

"Third, the members of your community who have committed atrocities against our population - or yours - are to be handed over without a fight. They will stand trial in our courts and be punished for their crimes."

He paused. "As you are aware, a more permanent solution is required," William concluded, grimly. "Accordingly, if you comply with our surrender demands, you and your people will be transported to Bellwether Island. It is a fairly large island with good climate - you should have no trouble eking out a living there. You have enough farming tools, according to the manifests, to survive. We will assist you, if necessary, and we will provide enough ration bars to keep your people alive until the farms start to produce crops."

"That sounds ideal," Konrad said.

"We will maintain an airport on the island," William added. "You may live as you see fit, with the sole condition that anyone who wishes to leave is to be permitted to do so. As long as they obey our laws, they will be welcome. Any of our people who wish to join you may do so, if you accept them."

Konrad sighed. The terms weren't going to go down well, particularly amongst the more hot-headed members of the community. Luckily, Joel had discredited their claims for the next few years, while the more level-headed ones knew they were on the brink of being exterminated. Going to a large island sounded ideal. If they actually managed to set up farms and start producing their own crops...

He nodded. "That would be acceptable," he said. "But I would have to consult with the other Elders..."

"Very good," William said. He paused. "A word of advice? *Don't* mistake forbearance for weakness. Premier Troutman got the job because he promised he'd solve the problem you and your people presented. He'll be happy to look for a more permanent solution if you refuse this one."

Konrad bowed his head. Joel...he'd kill his son, if he ever saw him again. What had he been *thinking*? Damn the fool.

"I understand," he said. "And we thank you. It's more than we deserve."

"That's what Troutman thinks," William said. "And really...he's being more generous than I expected. Don't let this chance for peace go."

CHAPTER FORTY

In the end, like so many other problems, immigration and ethnic conflict was a nail in the Empire's coffin. A mute testament to the simple disconnect between the rulers and the ruled, between the protected and the unprotected, between the idealism of the sheltered and the reality of the vulnerable. And, in the end, it helped bring down the mightiest civilisation mankind had ever known.

- Professor Leo Caesius. *Ethnic Streaming and the End of Empire.*

"Apparently, our *dear* friend Coombs is taking early retirement," Captain Stewart said. "But you'll be pleased to know that his replacement cleared you of all charges."

"Thank you, sir," Mike said. He pulled an envelope out of his pocket and placed it on the desk. "However, I'm afraid my mind is made up."

Captain Stewart gave him a long look. "You're resigning."

"Yes, sir."

"Why?"

Mike sighed. "Six months ago, I believed that my superiors would have my back, if I ran into trouble," he said. "*Five* months ago, I learned that that wasn't true. Coombs and the PCA started on the assumption I was guilty of a set of vague charges, charges that would have been dismissed in any other circumstances. They didn't even have the guts to admit they were wrong…"

"That was political," Captain Stewart said.

"It should not have been, sir," Mike told him, bluntly. "Politics should not have anything to do with policing. Whatever the previous government thought, it was a deadly mistake to make it clear that investigations would be driven by politics, rather than facts. I no longer have any faith in my superiors."

"Including me," Captain Stewart commented.

"Yes, sir."

Mike cocked his head. "I put on this uniform" - he gestured - "and go out on the streets, putting my life at risk every day. I don't need a second set of enemies amongst my superiors, ready to stick a knife in my back at the slightest excuse. The PCA…is more interested in looking good than actually *doing* good. And officers like you roll over for them rather than telling them to get fucked."

Captain Stewart's lips twitched. "It wasn't *that* dangerous a job."

"It is now," Mike pointed out. "Most of the refugees are on their way to Bellwether, but there's still a lot of trouble on the streets. People lost faith in the government, sir. The social compact was broken."

He sighed. "That's why I intend to run for Parliament," he added. "Someone has to try to talk sense into their heads."

"You might be my boss, one day," Captain Stewart said. He met Mike's eyes. "Do you really feel betrayed?"

"Yes, sir," Mike said.

He held up a hand. "I understand that there is - sometimes - a need to investigate what actually happened," he said. "But I feel that the PCA went too far. They preferred to put the blame on the police, on *me*, rather than the refugees. And that was a deadly mistake. I am not the only one resigning."

"I know," Captain Stewart said.

He rose, holding out a hand. "I wish you the very best in your future career, in or out of Parliament," he added. "And if you ever change your mind, feel free to reapply."

"It won't happen," Mike said. He shook Stewart's hand, gravely. "Like it or not, we lost much of our innocence over the past few months. Too many deadly precedents were set, sir. Nothing will ever be the same again."

"We shall see," Captain Stewart said. "And if you *do* become an MP, I look forward to licking your ass at some later date."

Mike laughed, then strode out of the office. By tradition, a retiring officer was supposed to take one last tour of the station, but he found it hard to turn away from the doors. He'd cleared a leave of absence first, just to make sure he could retire without a formal notice period...it wasn't entirely honest, yet he didn't want to stay another day. He thought, briefly, of his desk... where he'd worked hard, once upon a time...and then walked out of the doors, heading down the road. He'd promised Jane he'd be home for lunch.

Goodbye, he thought, as he passed a pair of officers on patrol. Both of them carried guns on their belts. The sight still bothered him, despite everything. *And good luck.*

He sighed as he walked down the road. He'd already started to lay the groundwork for his run for office. Being a hero helped, but so did the lack of uncompromised candidates from all four main parties. And if he won election...he promised himself, silently, that he would never allow such a crisis to get out of hand again.

"You seem happier now," her father said, as he poked his head into the stable. "Are you *feeling* happier?"

Judith shrugged, expressively. Mucking out the horses was great, if one wanted an excuse not to think. Her father had made it clear, years ago, that cleaning up after the animals built character, although Judith privately suspected it also concentrated one's mind on what was truly important. Very few of her fellow students at university had ever owned anything larger than a dog.

"It has its moments," she said, finally. "She hasn't called me."

Gayle had talked to her once, after she'd been released. She'd confessed that Judith had been right all along, then admitted they probably needed some time apart. Judith had agreed, even though part of her had just wanted to take Gayle back to her bed. Their relationship had been damaged, perhaps destroyed, simply because they had different opinions. They needed a break just to know where they stood.

"Not a keeper, then," her father said. He leaned against the wooden wall. "At least your friends are doing well."

Judith nodded. Hannah and John had moved out to the farm, the former studying medicine in the nearby town while the latter was working on the farm itself. John had a long way to go before he matched Judith's father or brother, but he *was* working on it. He'd lost his reluctance to use modern farming technology very quickly, after experiencing life with and without it. Judith wasn't surprised. Hardscrabble farming was a great deal of effort for very little return.

"Hannah thinks highly of you," her father added. "Perhaps you should chase her instead. Or John."

"Hannah isn't interested in women," Judith said. Hannah's reactions were a little odd, by local standards, but she seemed utterly unaware of homosexual relationships. And yet, she also seemed unaware of local men trying to court her. "She may be asexual."

"She's also been through very hard times," her father said, dryly. "I think it will be a long time before she trusts anyone enough to let them get close to her."

Judith nodded. Apart from John, who was her brother, and Judith herself, Hannah didn't seem interested in making friends. But then, she'd been betrayed by her mother, her stepfather and stepbrother. Maybe it wasn't so odd after all.

"John's a decent lad," her father said. "Hard worker, which is more than can be said for that last layabout you dated…"

"*Dad*," Judith protested. She'd been in a rebellious frame of mind, dating a young man she knew her father wouldn't like. It hadn't worked out, unsurprisingly. Her father rarely hesitated to remind her of it, whenever she dismissed his opinion. "I don't know, to be honest. He's a good man, but…"

She sighed. She'd been raised to believe that brothers were supposed to look after sisters, although she suspected the age difference between her and her elder brother had made that a little more prominent. He'd practically been a second father to her, after their mother had died. And John… John had failed to protect his sister. Whatever his reasons, whatever his culture, it wasn't something Judith could ever condone.

"I have time," she said, finally. "It isn't as if I have to get married tomorrow."

"No, it isn't," her father agreed.

And I am lucky to have you, Judith thought, as her father left her to finish the job. *A refugee father might have treated me quite differently.*

It wasn't entirely healthy - it wasn't *remotely* healthy - but John carried a small photograph in his wallet, taking it out to look at it whenever he felt insecure. Joel, dangling from a rope...the hangman watching as John's stepbrother breathed his last. It had been a public execution, the first in Arthur's Seat's history...Judith had said, afterwards, that it was a sign of trouble to come. Criminals were rarely executed when they could be exiled afterwards.

He strode down the woodland walk until he reached the small town, waving cheerfully at a pair of teenage boys playing football. He'd played with them and the other teenagers and, once he'd got used to the idea of women playing football, he'd found it surprisingly relaxing, even fun. There was none of the sheer violence that Joel had brought to the game, none of the sadistic amusement Colin and his ilk had taken in injuring their players. It was...it was fun.

The small medical centre was set within a garden, half-hidden behind a line of trees. It looked very much like the ideal Forsaker cottage, a house built from natural materials and woven into its surroundings rather than something imposed on them. He walked up the path and knocked on the door, waiting patiently. Hannah emerged a moment later, wearing a white shirt and black trousers. John had thought he'd never quite get used to seeing his sister in a shirt and trousers, but now - their fourth month in the countryside - it was almost unremarkable. Besides, there were a couple of girls in the town who wore them very well indeed.

"Time to go home," he said. He stopped, astonished. "It is home, isn't it?"

"Yes," Hannah said. "This is our home."

She said nothing as they walked back to the farm. John suspected she was remembering their mother, wherever the old woman was now. It still cost him a pang, sometimes, to remember her. She'd betrayed them both, but…but she was their mother. And she'd refused the chance to remain in Lothian when the majority of the Forsakers had gone to Bellwether.

"I'm going to be going to the city in two months," Hannah told him. "I'll have to complete my training there."

John swallowed, then looked at her. "Will you be all right?"

"I hope so," Hannah said. "I have hope."

And that, John knew, was all that mattered.

"What made you play it like that?"

Troutman cocked his head as the maid poured them both tea, then withdrew. "What do you mean?"

"I'm glad you didn't kill them," William said. "And…and I'm glad that something of their nature will be preserved. But…but why did you give them Bellwether?"

Troutman raised his cup in silent salute. "Did you have a claim to the island?"

"No," William said. Troutman was *good* at getting under his skin. "And you know it."

"Bellwether is large enough to support an expanding community," Troutman said, sipping his tea. "And isolated enough to make it difficult for that community to cause troubles elsewhere. Or have someone else cause problems on its behalf."

He smiled, rather coldly. "Was it actually suicide?"

William scowled. "The police report insists it was suicide," he said. He knew precisely what Troutman meant. "There's certainly no evidence to suggest otherwise."

He took a sip of his tea. In truth, he found it hard to believe that *anyone* could have murdered Sondra and convinced the police it was suicide, but he had to admit it was possible. And yet…Sondra's career had been destroyed and she was on the verge of facing a string of both criminal and civil charges. Her clients were either dead or turning on her. Suicide might have seemed the only way out.

"Of course not," Troutman agreed. "But that woman could turn a silk purse into a sow's ear, given time."

William snorted. "Thank you for reminding me you're an asshole," he said. It was undiplomatic, but he didn't care. He was just a private citizen now, paying his respects to the Premier. "Even if you did give them an island…"

His voice trailed off. "What is it?"

Troutman raised his eyebrows. "What's what?"

William stared back at him, evenly. "What's the sting in the tail?"

"There's enough land to support them - and a community several times their size," Troutman said. "And they have the tools to farm, to build their ideal community…if they wish."

"And the catch?"

Troutman shrugged. "Nothing *much*," he said. "Just a little… *precaution*."

"A *precaution*," William repeated. He should have known. Troutman wouldn't have hesitated to put the boot in when he had a chance. "What have you done?"

Troutman leaned back in his chair. "Do you know what killed Earth?"

He went on before William could even *begin* to formulate an answer. "The planet's carrying capacity, thanks to modern technology, was huge," he said. "Everyone had enough to eat, so they just kept churning out more and more kids. And those kids grew up and started churning out their own kids. The population just kept rising until the CityBlocks started to explode."

His face twisted. "Someone *did* come up with a solution," he added. "It was easy enough to add a mild contraceptive to ration bars. Men who ate a steady diet of ration bars - and nothing but ration bars - would find it a great deal harder to impregnate a woman. But the bureaucrats on Earth preferred to have a vast population they could administer…"

"You put the contraceptives in the ration bars you send to the island," William said, flatly.

Troutman nodded. "Correct."

William stared at him. "You…you utter *bastard*! You've doomed them!"

"Hardly," Troutman said. "They have everything they need to establish their own farms and grow food. If they move away from the ration bars, their fertility will rapidly return to normal. And then…"

"And then *what*?" William asked. "What *else* have you done?"

"They'll face limits on what they can grow," Troutman said. "They don't allow themselves anything more advanced than horse-drawn ploughs. No gene-modified seeds, no combine harvesters…not even modern medicine. If they choose to remain trapped at that level, and we won't be *keeping* them there, there will be limits on just how far their community can expand. Either way, they won't pose a threat…"

"I'll tell the media," William snapped. "This is…this is abominable!"

Troutman gave him a wintry smile. "Go right ahead," he said. "The vast majority of the population will cheer."

He rose, meeting William's eyes. "You made choices, bad choices," he said. "Taking the refugees was a mistake, allowing them to dictate to you was a mistake, trying to appease them was a mistake…we hovered on the brink of outright civil war because of you and your sentimental decisions. And now…and now, half the population thinks we were too damn merciful in exiling them to Bellwether.

"Go tell the people, if you wish," he added. "You'll just wind up looking like a fool."

"You're a bastard," William said, stunned.

"An *unsentimental* bastard," Troutman said. "I put the interests of my people, my world, ahead of anything else. And you know what? *That* is why I have the biggest majority in Parliament! Go tell the media, if you like. Go tell the people. They think *you* caused this problem."

He took a breath. "And you know what? They're right. And now everyone else is paying the price."

William stared at him. For once, he had nothing to say.

The End

The Series Will Continue In…
WOLF'S BANE

AFTERWORD

Today's Western elites, in the U.S. as much as in Europe, have never been so self-confident. Products of meritocratic selection who hold key positions in the social machine, the bien-pensant custodians of post-historical ideology—editorial writers at the NY Times, staffers in cultural and educational bureaucracies, Eurocratic functionaries, much of the professoriat, the human rights priesthood and so on—are utterly convinced that they see farther and deeper than the less credentialed, less educated, less tolerant and less sophisticated knuckle-dragging also-rans outside the magic circle of post historical groupthink.

And while the meritocratic priesthood isn't wrong about everything—and the knuckle-draggers aren't right about everything—there are a few big issues on which the priests are dead wrong and the knuckle-draggers know it.

- Walter Russell Mead

When I outlined *The Empire's Corps* for the first time, intending to split the books between mainline stories and side-stories covering modern-day issues, I knew I would eventually have to tackle the subject of immigration. My original plot for *Culture Shock*, which was first marked down for development back in 2010, was very different. This was after the shockwaves of 9/11 and 7/7, but before Cologne and assorted other *Jihadist* attacks across Europe. In a sense, my attitudes had hardened well before the current Migrant Crisis, yet the Crisis - and the lacklustre response of establishment politicians - brought the looming demographic disaster into sharp relief.

Immigration is not an easy subject to tackle. Like many issues today, it requires maturity, a cold grasp of the facts and a determination to put the interests of the West - and its population - ahead of everything else. There can be no room for sentiment, yet sentiment is what the extremists on both sides use to fuel their arguments. A rational analysis of the situation is very difficult precisely *because* it is so highly charged. And yet, a rational analysis of the situation is precisely what we need.

I know, in writing this, that I will be accused of:

A) Racism.
B) Hypocrisy.
C) Both.

This will not surprise me. People on both sides are resistant to any sort of measured analysis of the situation. Instead, they scream emotive words and accusations, trying to bury valid points - such as they are - by branding their speaker all sorts of horrible things. But this is not an attitude that can be allowed to stand. A jerk may be a jerk, but that doesn't necessarily mean he doesn't have a point. Truth - objective and subjective - doesn't change, even when the speaker is a complete monster.

The charge of racism can be easily dismissed. These days, 'racism' is a meaningless word. It is, at best, an irrational reaction to skin colour and general appearance, not to culture, behaviour or anything that can be helped. A murderer is a murderer if his skin is white or black, regardless of the excuses he uses to justify his behaviour. It is not racist to call out a murderer, whatever his skin colour.

The charge of hypocrisy is rather more likely to stick. I am married to an immigrant woman and father to a mixed-race child. Furthermore, I spent several years in Malaysia as a long-term guest, during which time I cannot be said to have integrated. In my defence, my wife is a practicing medical doctor and harmless. She poses no threat to the country. And I certainly never intended to spend the remainder of my life in Malaysia. I did not believe that I would never leave, save for short holidays. My *very* limited grasp of Malaysian was not helped by a form of dyslexia. My linguistic skills have always been pitiful.

But this is not about me. It never was.

If you disagree with any of the points in the novel, or this afterword, I welcome calm and reasonable debate. I have a blog, a Facebook page and a discussion forum. But if you merely want to send me a stream of insults, accusations or threats, I'll let you know in advance that I will simply ignore them. Life is too short to spend it engaging in pointless and petty flame wars.

One of the classic academic jokes centres around attempts to ban a chemical called 'dihydrogen monoxide.' The prankster will reel off a list of horrible (and completely accurate) facts about the liquid, then call on his listeners to sign a petition against it. At that point, he will reveal that 'dihydrogen monoxide' is actually a scientific term for water, without which we could not live.

And yet, water can be lethal. We can drown in water. We can die by drinking poisoned water. Ask any sailor just how harmless the ocean can be and you'll get plenty of horror stories about storms, strong currents and tidal waves. We need water to live, but - like oxygen - too much of it can kill us. The level of danger, of toxicity, in *anything* is directly proportional to the dose.

Our political masters have told us, time and time again, that 'diversity' is good for us. But is this actually true?

There is something to be said, and I concede this point without a fight, for a diverse selection of restaurants in any given city. A good city will have something to accommodate every taste, from steaming hot curries to sushi and ice cream. I can spend the next fortnight going to a different restaurant in Edinburgh every day, without ever repeating myself. This sort of diversity is not a bad thing. Indeed, there are quite a few restaurants in the UK that fuse different styles of cooking together to produce a truly unique experience.

But diversity can become dangerous when different cultures are forced to mingle.

It is a blunt fact, no matter how much progressives try to deny it, that people raised in different cultures think differently. People raised in the West tend to have a touching (and sometimes unjustified) faith in government and the police that is not shared by people raised elsewhere. The

West's legal system, about which more later, is largely free of the deadly corruption present in the Third World. One can make a honest attempt to seek justice in the West that would be fatal elsewhere.

These differences can lead to all sorts of problems. A person raised in a culture where women are treated as second-class citizens is going to have all sorts of problems dealing with a culture where women are treated as equals. (Even shaking a woman's hand can be tricky if you're raised to believe you shouldn't touch an unrelated woman.) Someone raised to believe that a woman is the property of her family (who will protect her from unrelated males) will regard unprotected women as an open invitation. And a person who is incapable of picking up a veiled threat will simply not *recognise* that threat.

Sex is not the only issue of concern. People raised in the Third World will think nothing of corruption, nepotism and tribalism. A civil servant in the Middle East is practically *expected* to use his position to enrich himself, find cushy jobs for his relatives and all sorts of other things that we in the West find abominable. A tribal leader - whatever position he holds on paper - will only stay in his position as long as he is in charge of distributing largesse to his followers.

'Diversity' forces us to believe that all cultures are equal. Yet this leads to the inevitable conclusion that different societies must be treated differently. Something that is unacceptable in one culture must be tolerated if it is acceptable in others. And this is lethal because the law must apply to all, equally. Murder is murder, regardless of why the victim was killed; rape is rape, regardless of the motive behind the atrocity.

Our society can only survive if the law applies equally to everyone, regardless of their colour, creed, gender, wealth, family connections or religion. And we must enforce this with neither fear nor favour.

―――――

The first waves of modern-day immigration (into Britain, France and Germany) came from the steady collapse of the European colonial empires. Britain felt an obligation to Indian and other East Asian populations that the British Empire had settled in various parts of the globe and, reluctantly, the doors were thrown open. France, likewise, felt a certain obligation to Algerians.

This was not warmly welcomed by the native population. Governments struggled to deal with the problems it caused, often choosing to discredit people who tried to speak out against it. Instead of breaking down the immigrant groups and spreading them out, successive governments allowed them to form ethnic minority enclaves. The more immigrants that arrived, the more these enclaves started to look and feel like the worlds they left behind.

I have no idea why this surprised anyone. Humans have a habit of clinging to the familiar and shunning the different. Immigrants naturally clung to their own kind - and there were enough of them to limit their contact with the outside community. (This is why we also have expat communities of Britons living overseas.) They had a strong incentive *not* to go native. Indeed, as more and more of the foreign culture was imported, there were *very* strong incentives not to go native. A young man or woman who started to move away from the enclave would find themselves completely excluded, if they weren't forcibly dragged back home.

Politicians believed that the mere fact of immigrants being *in* Britain would make them culturally British. (The 'magic dirt' theory of immigration.) This was obvious nonsense. Absent a strong incentive to adopt British ways - and with strong *disincentives* to do anything of the sort - the immigrants effectively ended up redeveloping the communities they had left behind, complete with all the flaws. They didn't become British any more than my stay in Malaysia made me Malaysian.

Right now, immigrant communities in Britain - and much of the West - can be described as onions. The outer layers are culturally very similar to the surrounding British society; the innermost layers have very little contact with society and no desire whatsoever to assimilate. Indeed, clinging to their culture is seen as a form of self-defence. And this tends to lead to a dismissive attitude towards law enforcement, a reluctance to accept the law when it conflicts with cultural norms. The police are seen as intruders in the community, even - perhaps especially - when they are fronted by minority officers. Such officers are either expected to put their ethnic groups first - thus making them part of the problem - or regarded as outright traitors.

In this sort of terrain, conflict is practically inevitable. There are two reasons for this. First, as a community expands, it will demand that the local surroundings change to suit them. (As more minority children move into schools, there will be pressure to add classes on cultural norms, segregate the sexes, etc.) Second, such communities are often breeding grounds for extremism. A strong group of radicals can dominate an entire community because the cost of opposing them is higher than accepting them. (Remember, these people cannot trust the police to help.)

Worse, perhaps, breaking down the community's barriers is almost impossible.

These people do not always want to assimilate. Indeed, even when some of them *do*, they face strong resistance from their own community. Why should they act British when they practically grew up in a non-British community?

And even though they often despise or fear the extremists, they find it hard to 'betray' their own people by taking sides against them.

The problem with western governments today is that they are more obsessed with appearance than reality. (A common issue.) Decades of 'spin doctoring' have made it more important to look good, in the short term, rather than to actually *be* good. Long-term thinking is beyond the political elite. Accordingly, governments do their best to avoid or ignore problems rather than admitting that something has gone wrong.

Worse, perhaps, the political elites are increasingly separated from the people they are supposed to rule. They have lost touch with the people on the ground. It's easy, given the gulf between them and their subjects, to fall into the habit of believing that their subjects are simply in the wrong, rather than admit that they might have *legitimate* concerns. A person who lives in a gated community, for example, may have a more tolerant view of criminals than people who have no such protection. The former is often incapable of understanding why the latter wants criminals off the streets.

When it comes to immigration, western governments have effectively been hoisted on their own petard. Their response to public opposition to the early waves of immigration was to brand all such opposition *racist*. They were quite successful. But this has made it impossible for them to muster an effective response to the challenges posed by successive waves of immigration and extremism. Taking steps - like removing violent preachers or banning charitable donations that go straight to extremist organisations - would rapidly lead to them being branded racists. Their political opponents, who are effectively in the same boat, prefer to use the issue to their own advantage rather than put the good of the country first.

Matters have been complicated, furthermore, by the simple fact that expanding migrant populations have the vote. Politicians who refuse to pander to them find those votes heading to their opponents instead. (An issue made more dangerous by communities being told how to vote by their leaders, a common problem in East Asia.) Politicians are therefore reluctant to subscribe to any form of immigration reform, let alone a defence of British (and European) values for fear of being branded racists. Instead, they promote 'multiculturalism' and move to accommodate the newcomers, rather than insist they learn to assimilate.

This has percolated down through society. The security services were reluctant to target extremists for fear of being accused of racism. Police were reluctant to take too close a look at child sex grooming rings for fear of being accused of racism. Social services are reluctant to challenge cultural traditions…likewise. And so matters have steadily moved out of control.

By refusing to grasp this nettle, politicians have effectively gained the worst of both worlds. On one hand, the extremists believe that the politicians are weak, unwilling or unable to assert control; on the other hand, politicians have convinced their own people that the politicians are effectively traitors, untrustworthy idiots who are happy to sell out their populations just to look good. It doesn't bode well for the future.

If you've had the misfortune of enduring public schools, you'll probably recall a classmate everyone called the 'crazy kid' or something along those lines. This kid was a loner, not always by choice. He wasn't the strongest kid or the smartest, but he was dangerously unpredictable. His classmates never knew when he was going to start screaming insults, throw poop around or attack the nearest victim. Everyone else, even the bullies and jerk jocks, tried to give him a wide berth. No one trusted him.

The adults in the school and wider community didn't understand *why* the crazy kid was so isolated. They weren't the ones who had to deal with his behaviour, day in and day out. It was easier to believe that the crazy kid was a victim, rather than a perpetrator. The adults sometimes even knew enough (they thought) about him to come up with excuses for his behaviour, rather than trying to change it. Accordingly, they would pressure their children to make room for the crazy kid, to invite him to play with them. It never seemed to occur to any of the adults that the children might have good reason to avoid the crazy kid.

And then the crazy kid gets invited to a birthday party, goes completely mad and ends up causing vast amounts of damage to a parent's house.

This is not a perfect example, I will admit. But I think it gets across just how people are starting to think of immigrants and ethnic communities.

Our society is based on trust. Indeed, our society evolved because we developed, slowly, a trust-based system, enforced by courts of law. I, a mature adult, can enter into a contract with anyone else - perhaps a book publishing contract - in the certain knowledge that I have legal recourse, if the deal goes badly wrong. If I promise to deliver a book at the end of the year, I must deliver it; if the publishers promise to pay me, they must pay me. The vast majority of contracts, spoken or unspoken, are honoured because enforcement mechanisms are in place.

The importance of this cannot be underestimated. Nepotism is so prevalent in the Third World because only a fool would trust someone outside his own family. It is extremely dangerous to go outside the family circle because there are no ways to enforce whatever agreements are made. The law is simply not applied equally.

Right now, the vast majority of people no longer trust the governments, the political elite…or the immigrant/ethnic communities.

It is difficult to say just how bad the problem actually is. People have been discouraged from talking about it for so long that there is no *true* idea of the scale of the problem. How many immigrants are in Britain? Or Europe? Or America? How many of them are potentially dangerous? How many of them are reluctant - or flatly unwilling - to assimilate? Just *asking* these questions is enough to get someone branded a racist.

But, because of this, a deep-seated sense of unease, of suspicion, of outright fear is spreading across Europe.

It has become clear in the last sixteen years that governments are unable or unwilling to recognise that there is a problem and do something about it. Governments, hampered by political correctness, prefer to try to cover up their mistakes. People who speak out, who demand answers, are harassed, threatened or arrested. It has become clear that governments are no longer on the side of their people.

Is it too much to ask that a government puts the interests of its own people first?

Apparently so.

The rise of nationalism and nationalistic political parties in Europe and America is a direct response to politicians abandoning their voters. Those voters no longer want to hear about the economic benefits of immigration (a questionable concept, particularly when immigrants are unwilling or unable to work) or the joys of multiculturalism and virtue-signalling; they want action, they want definite steps, *not* words. Political correctness has infiltrated western governments to the point where they can no longer recognise the threat, let alone take steps to counter it. Their voters are going elsewhere.

Sympathy has its limits. It's easy to feel sorry for someone fleeing a war zone. But it is a great deal harder to feel sorry for migrants when the crime rate shoots upwards after their arrival, when taxpayers' money is wasted on feeding and clothing them, when governments cover up sex crimes rather than admit that there might be a problem. I think it is fairly safe to say that there is no sympathy any longer, outside the ivory towers of the political elites. But even those towers are built on quicksand.

I wish I was sanguine about the future. I'm not.

In choosing to destroy the moderate middle ground, in choosing to try to cover up the problem rather than come to grips with it, politicians have destroyed the faith in government - the *trust* in government - that our society needs to function. The rise of Donald Trump in the US, BREXIT and the series of crushing electoral defeats suffered by Angela Merkel in Germany…all are symptoms of a growing rebellion against the political elites and their view of the world. And yet, because the middle ground has been destroyed, it is unlikely that there can be any measured response to the situation. Sales of weapons are also on the rise. So are attacks on migrants and other immigrants. We may be looking at outright civil war across Europe.

Some people will say I am being alarmist. That the problem is not that bad - that we will not lose our way as a society because of it. But I am not so sure. In times of crisis, populations swing to the right and demand action, not platitudes. And the demand for action may push our society over the brink.

I hope I'm wrong. I fear I'm not.

Christopher G. Nuttall
Edinburgh, 2016

APPENDIX: ARTHUR'S SEAT BACKGROUND

Arthur's Seat is the second planet orbiting King Arthur, a G2 star roughly comparable to Sol. The system holds five planets, all rocky; Kiln, Arthur's Seat, Len Lothian, Gilmanton and Hawarden. Unusually, there are no gas giants and only a handful of asteroids, effectively limiting the system's value. Worse, differences between the planet's biochemistry and the human genome rendered the planet's natural plant life poisonous. It was because of the limited value that Arthur's Seat was only settled 300 years prior to the Fall of Earth.

Geographically, Arthur's Seat consists of two major continents - Maxima and Minoa - and a handful of small islands. The vast majority of human settlement is on Maxima, although there are a number of very isolated settlements on Minoa. The capital city - Lothian - is located on the shores of Mary's Sea. There are seven major cities emplaced around the continent and thousands of smaller towns, villages and hamlets within the interior.

Arthur's Seat was originally settled by an offshoot of the Forsakers, a religious commune that wanted a return to the simple life. The settlement was not only illegal - the Forsakers were conned; the person who sold them the settlement rights have no claim to the world - but doomed from the start. They simply lacked the technological know-how to either engineer themselves to live on the planet or start replacing the planet's natural wildlife with Earth-compatible crops. By the time the planet's *real* settlers arrived, the Forsakers were in desperate straits and, while some of their leaders were furious at being supplemented, they were in no position to do more than sulk. The remaining Forsakers largely abandoned their tenants and embraced modern technology. Indeed, they integrated with a rapidity that astonished the settlement corporation, which had expected violent resistance.

Politically, Arthur's Seat is divided up into districts. Each district elects one MP to Parliament and twenty-one District Councillors to the local District Hall. Elections are held every five years, with the political party with the largest number of MPs being declared the winner and its leader becoming the Premier. The leader of the second-largest political party is declared the Leader of the Opposition.

The Premier has the right to name his Cabinet, the men and women who supervise the Civil Service (the Leader of the Opposition is also entitled to a seat, although not technically a voting one), and draft legislation. He does not, however, have unlimited power. By law, all legislation must be debated by Parliament before being passed (and MPs need time to consult with the electorate). Unpopular laws have rarely survived the first reading, when they have made it through the Cabinet. It is actually quite difficult to pass legislation in a hurry.

Politically, Arthur's Seat is actually fairly quiet. There is some tension between the city-folk and the countrymen (the countrymen charge that the city-folk demand more than they should from the country) but it tends to be fought out on the football field, rather than on the battlefield. The only major excitement comes during election season, when the parties indulge themselves in unbridled slander of their opponents.

The major political parties, as of 300PS (Post-Settlement), are the Empire Loyalists, the Freeholders, the Unionists and the Isolationists. The Empire Loyalists believe that Arthur's Seat should remain loyal to the Empire; the Unionists believe that the slow program of settlement should be expanded as fast as possible, the Isolationists believe that Arthur's Seat should have as little to do with the outside galaxy as possible and the Freeholders believe in very limited government.

As of 300PS, the Empire Loyalists hold the majority - partly because of the importance of trade with the outside galaxy - but the Freeholders are the opposition. There's an unspoken alliance between the Empire Loyalists and the Unionists, while the Isolationists remain on the sidelines.

Arthur's Seat has no aspirations to play a major role in the galaxy, as it lacks the industrial or economic base to be a major power. It's Orbital

Guard consists of nothing more than two outdated destroyers, enough to stand off pirates but nowhere near strong enough to deter a major power. There is no real ground-based military either, save for a small number of highly-trained police units (and a larger number of part-time policemen). If there was a need for more manpower, the police would recruit posses from the local community, although thankfully emergencies are very rare.

Industrially, the planet is capable of supplying most of its requirements and exports a sizable quantity of food, spare parts and other essentials to the sector. However, it actually has a negative trade balance, as it needs to import quite a few items from the sector too.

The planet's population (the Arthurian/Arthurians), as of 300PS, is roughly ten million. Approximately ten percent of the population is descended from the original Forsakers, although there's no real difference between them and the later settlers, save for the names. The vast majority of the population follows Reformed Luther Christianity, but it tends to be very low-key. Most Arthurians believe firmly in leaving people alone, as long as they're not causing a problem to others. It just isn't worth fighting over.

Those who do break the planet's relatively few laws are sentenced to work camps or expulsion - they are given a starship ticket and told never to come back.

Printed in Great Britain
by Amazon